THE FLAME BEFORE US

THE FLAME BEFORE US

RICHARD ABBOTT

ISBN: 978-0-9931684-1-3 (soft cover)
ISBN: 978-0-9931684-0-6 (ebook format)

Matteh Publications

Contact:
Web: http://mattehpublications.datascenesdev.com/
Email: matteh@datascenesdev.com

For Roselyn, for family

Contents

Maps   ix

Part 1 – Ikaret   1

Part 2 – Hatsor   67

Part 3 – Equinox   139

Part 4 – Hill Country   217

Part 5 – Shalem   283

Epilogue   321

Notes   337

Also by the Author

Novels:
    In a Milk and Honeyed Land
    Scenes from a Life

Short stories:
    The Lady of the Lions
    The Man in the Cistern

Cover information

Cover artwork © Copyright Ian Grainger
    http://www.iangrainger.co.uk

Original Matteh Publications logo drawn by Jackie Morgan.

Original photographs taken in Israel and elsewhere.

Cuneiform jointly produced by the author and Ian Grainger.
The tablet reads:
    If the strong attack your strongholds –
    warriors your walls –

MAPS

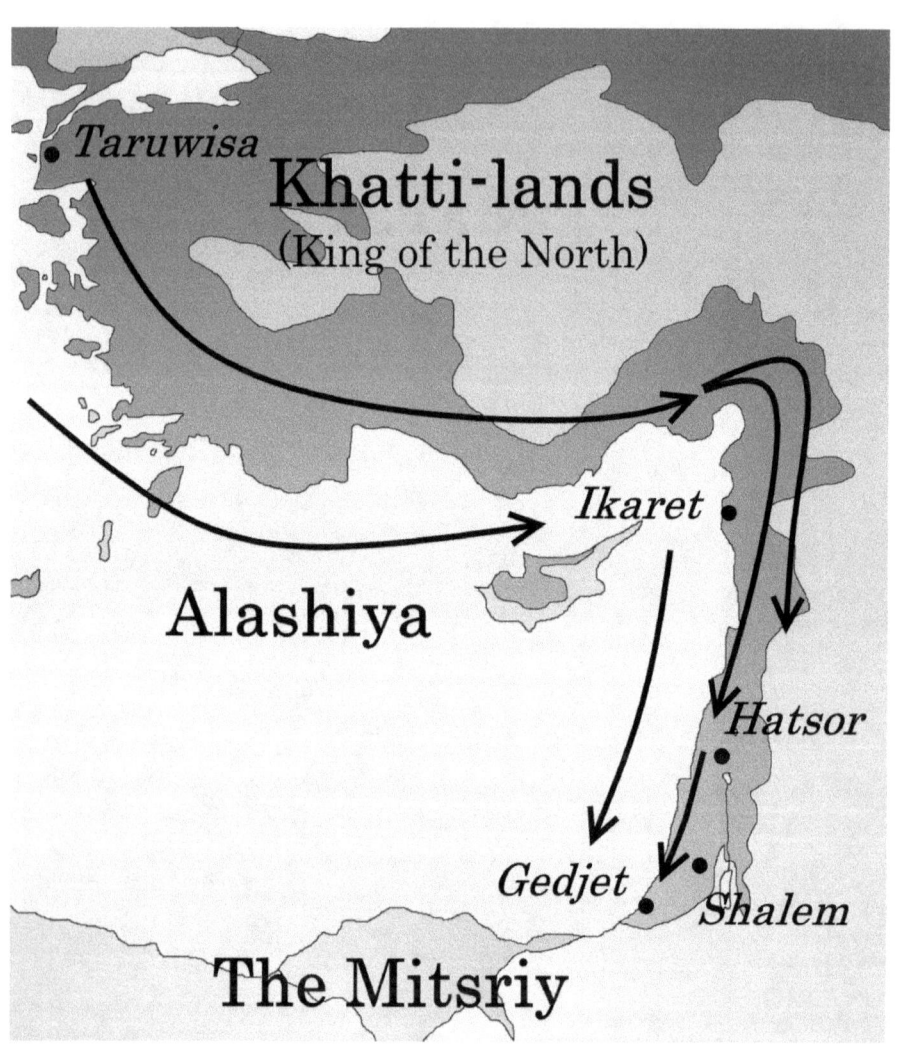

The Approach of the Newcomers

Bayth Ma'acath

Damaseq

Hatsor

Ramath-Galil

Yabesh

Sychem

The Four
Towns

Gedjet

Shalem

The Hill Country

Part 1 – Ikaret

~~~

IF THE STRONG ATTACK your strongholds –
   warriors your walls –
Go up to the sanctuary of Ba'al,
  Step to the holy place of Ba'al,
Then Ba'al, will listen to your prayer –
  drive the strong from the stronghold,
  the warrior from your wall.

~~~

꧁ ꧂

"BUT FATHER WILL BE BACK from the north before we have to leave?"

Anilat looked carefully at her mother, hoping to see some sign of the truth of the matter. But the old face, schooled in a great many years of diplomacy, was giving nothing away, and the old voice did not directly answer her.

"You will be leaving as he instructed, a half-month from now. I will wait for his return and follow on after. He has been called to attend to the wishes of the King of the North even now."

The last was, surely, a simple guess, perhaps even a needy wish. Anilat nodded slowly, wondering if, after all, her mother had no more information than she had already shared. All that she herself knew came from the brief report delivered by the weary rider as he passed by the envoy's house on his way to the royal palace of Ikaret.

Not long after his arrival, the city gates had been closed, and the priests were called out from the temple to bless and prepare the few city guardsmen who remained. Most of the army had already been sent north to join the collected forces of the great King of the North, assembling somewhere in the vassal territories along the coast. As well as force of numbers and weapons, they had taken wagon loads of supplies, honouring the requirements of the treaty.

The army had travelled by land, along the great Sea Road that ran all the way from the southern sedge lands of the Mitsriy up to the rugged hills in the north. But Ikaret had grown up facing the sea, and the sea still brought most of the wealth to the people. Although the hinterlands were fair, and the overland trade routes reliable, it was the port that gave life to the city. There were so few good harbours north or south along this coast.

For a time the royal family of Ikaret had offered allegiance to the Mitsriy, but no longer, not for many generations. Their loyalty had turned away when the ruler of the Khatti-lands, the great King of the North, had started to expand his sway. He was much closer to them in both distance and culture.

The Mitsriy protests were in vain; the city was simply too far north from their homeland to be retained. It was too far for an effective campaign of retaliation to be considered, even from the unruly collection of Kinahny vassal lands they controlled. Even the most warlike among the Mitsriy kings had never been able to secure their conquests this far along the coast. It suited Ikaret to have her ties of allegiance holding her to the north. The huge flocks of wading birds that feasted in the shallow waters around the bay, emblematic of Ikaret herself, had enjoyed prosperity and comparative peace for a very long time.

A little over two years ago, the first stories of raiding groups harrying the fringes of the settled lands had reached the city. A long way north and west of Ikaret, they mostly struck at island settlements, or very remote coastal towns which could not be easily reinforced. Rumours of troop losses had spread, and the great king had been swift to silence the more vocal of his critics. But the reports were still carried, by traders and officials more concerned about the immediate risk to their life and livelihood than the king's displeasure. Then there had been a lull for a while, and it seemed that peace had returned.

But as the weather turned colder, and winter drew close this year, forlorn and homeless groups had started to come down the Sea Road. The first few dozen of these were treated with kindness and a spirit of welcome. But dozens swelled to hundreds, and generosity could only stretch so far. Some of them stopped around the outskirts of the city, clustering in great tented pools around the streams and wells. Others moved on again, southwards, hoping to find better favour among the Fenku, or even the Mitsriy. They would have a long journey southward, along the Sea Road, but perhaps the effort would be worth while.

"Are the children ready to leave? Yours and your brother's?"

Anilat brought her thoughts back into the room and nodded firmly.

"Indeed yes, mother. Provisions are ready for all of us. My three little ones are with Auntie now and she is preparing them with tales of journeys."

She stopped, hesitant. How could she speak about her older brother and his refusal to leave the house? Her mother waited, her face shrouded by the hood she wore. She had never liked the climate here, and found the winter air far too cold for her southern body. Anilat had become used to it as she had grown up, and earlier today had relished the freshness of the sea breeze drifting in over the land.

"If User-Amun will not leave, you must be ready to take his children as well."

So she did know after all. If events took this turn, Anilat and her husband Tadugari would be taking five children when they left. But her brother's daughter and son were considerably older, and they should be able to help make the journey easier.

"Mother, when you leave here, where will you go? All the way back down to the Beloved Land?"

Her mother sighed.

"It is so many years since I was last there. So many years during which your father and I have moved from place to place at the bidding of the king. And my memories are clearer of Gedjet than of the Beloved Land. It is a great sorrow to me. It would ease my heart to see it one last time. But it is a long way, and I am already old. Listen now. You must take the children from here when the time is right. Your husband will wait too long: you must be ready."

"I will not leave him. If he stays, I stay, and the children with me."

"All of the fruit of my body is in this one city together. In times like these, that makes me afraid. Shall I see all of you taken together? The good of the family requires you to leave when the time is right. I will not hear argument about this."

The two women were silent together for a while. From the courtyard, they could hear the chatter of the servants arriving back from the fish market. Finally the mother spoke again.

"And what of your sister?"

"She says that she will follow whatever the great priestess decides. She says that for her, it is as though she was a chantress of the kind you used to talk about when we were young together."

"The more fool her to think so. The priestess is not so high, nor the temple so grand, that she should do that. And her with child as well. You see, Anilat? You must take the lead here and ensure that the children are safe."

"Why should she be anxious? She has confidence that even if some remnant of this enemy should escape destruction to the north, our own city guard will hold the walls and gates."

"Could the King of the North hold Taruwisa? Could his army hold his southern coastal towns? Do you think our soldiers have held the northern border?" There was a silence in the chamber. Her mother's breathing was rough, laboured in the damp air. "Well, how can I blame her? I sit here and wait for my own husband to come back from the north. Am I so different?"

"What about Taruwisa and the coastal towns? I had not heard anything of them?"

The old woman, eyes shrewd and bright in her lined face, made a little move of her hands. Anilat, understanding it as dismissal, gave a little bow and left the room.

⟨⌄⧨⌄⧨⌄⧨⌄⧨⟩

A FEW DAYS LATER, in the gloom of a cloudy morning, Anilat woke suddenly. A slave was kneeling beside her husband, whispering to him urgently. Tadugari looked grave, nodded, and then leaned back against the wall as the slave left the room. Anilat sat up, pulling the woollen bed drape against her shoulders in the cold air.

She looked about. It was too early to break the morning bread, but she could smell it baking in the kitchens behind the inner courtyard. The night slaves had left it to prove, and the day servants were arriving to finish it. She rubbed sleep from her eyes and stretched as Tadugari got to his feet.

"Was there news?"

He glanced at her, grimaced. A sudden anxiety clutched at her, and she leaned forward to see that the children were in the adjoining room still. They were all there, Haleyna and the younger twins Rishi and Ritsani, all asleep in a row. The Alashiyan woman Damatiria was with them. She had nursed all three of them in their infancy, and was always called Auntie by the whole family. Catching Anilat's movement through the arch that joined the two rooms, she scrambled to her feet. Anilat nodded to her and leaned back again.

"I must go up to the palace."

"So early? Has the king called for you?"

"For all of his retinue, from highest to lowest. Not particularly for me by name. I expect that my part will be to draft messages for the inland towns to ensure that they meet their obligations."

"Don't go. I do not feel good about today."

He laughed, kissed her, then called for a basin of water and his clothes for the day. She sat in the bed, pensive.

"Much as I would like to hear your voice instead of the king's, I think we cannot allow ourselves that pleasure." His voice was muffled for a moment by the thick cloth folds of a smock going over his head. "I will be back before long, to be sure. It will be another false report from one of the outlying farms."

She shook her head, discarded her blanket, and waved the slave away so that she could perfect his appearance. The air felt cold against her skin, but she would not let him go without the personal attention.

"King's envoy you may be, but I know when you are trying to lie, husband. Make sure you come back to us with time to spare if events take a turn for the worse. You go on: I shall offer incense for us both at the shrine of the household gods."

He nodded sombrely, ran his hands down her bare arms, kissed her again, then left with the slave. Auntie came up from the side room, bringing her own clothes over.

"This one, mistress?"

She shook her head. "Something darker, Auntie. Less cheerful." She pulled a face, realising just how much she had been affected by the look she had seen on Tadugari's face as she woke up. "Less conspicuous."

The day passed slowly. Every now and again the women and children would hear the noise of soldiers on the street, going in one direction or another, shouting orders or encouragement to one another. They sounded enthusiastic, eager, ready for anything.

𐤔𐤎𐤔𐤎𐤔𐤎𐤔

L ATE IN THE DAY Tadugari came back to the house. He looked weary. He sat at the table and was silent while one of the slaves washed his feet. The children came up, each in turn to give the evening greeting. He blessed them in his normal perfunctory way, then stopped himself, gathered them into a group beside his chair and offered up a much more substantial prayer. Anilat recognised parts of it from the annual ceremony at the gates of the city. Everything seemed very serious.

There was a silence afterwards. The slave was still kneeling at his feet, bowl and cloth beside her, waiting to resume her duties. Water dripped from her hands and puddled on the rough stones of the floor. He looked down at her, as though seeing her for the first time that day.

"No more for today, girl. It is sufficient."

She scrambled away towards the inner courtyard and the kitchen area. The door which led to the family quarters, on the opposite side of the room, creaked open. Tadugari rose to his feet and gave a little bow. Anilat hurried across to her mother, who was slowly making her entrance supported by her attendant.

"I shall eat with you tonight."

"Your presence honours us."

She settled herself with a sigh into her chair at the end of the table, her attendant standing behind her, and waited as the other family members arranged themselves in order along the sides.

"What was spoken in the king's house today?"

Tadugari looked at her, clearly torn between the twin needs to answer her question and keep the confidence of the palace. He looked down at the table.

"Well, the news will be filling the streets anyway by now. What point remaining silent? There has been no fresh news from the army to the north since last week, when there were reports that scouts had been captured and a full wing of chariots defeated. Nobody seems to know how the chariots were beaten: the enemy only have foot soldiers from all that I have heard. But as well as that, we lost the main part of the fleet today. Those that were in home waters, anyway."

There were little noises around the table, gasps of disbelief.

"How can this be?"

"Some ships were away. Some were only half-manned with most of their crew ashore still. Some were caught against a lee shore. A few tried to fight, but they were in no order. It was as though one of the palace guard ran alone against a pack of the mountain tribesmen. A proper formation of our ships should be more than a match for them, but we were caught unprepared, and divided so that we could not fight together."

"Who are they?"

He shook his head. "I do not know where they come from, but they move across the lands like a mountain lion at the sprint. We all thought that they were far to the north still. And at sea, ship to ship, they are fearsome."

"But what about the commander of the ships, father? How does he explain himself?"

Tadugari grimaced and closed his eyes.

"The chief of these waters surrendered after the first losses, believing that it was futile to fight. But he will not have to answer to the king for that; they tied his hands and feet together and threw him into the water just outside the harbour. We have other ships away from home, but they will not hear of this for some time. Weeks even. And if they come back one by one they will suffer the same. Better to make their way to another city and stay there for now."

Anilat looked at her mother, expecting to see the shock and anger she felt herself. Instead, there was a curious lack of any obvious feeling.

"You should all leave the city before the week is out. Better if it was tomorrow. All of you."

Tadugari shook his head. "The king has called us all back at daybreak. Anyone with military talent has had to stay there through the night. I was excused from that simply because my skills are not in fighting. Just now there is little need for a man whose ability lies in messages and treaties. So I have eaten with you here, but half of my friends are still there. I cannot simply arise and leave when I please."

She was unmoved.

"This man is only a local kinglet. It is not as though he is the great king who lives in prosperity and health beside the River. Not even like the King of the North who at least commands the allegiance of others. You should weigh his words and choose for yourself, not simply obey him."

He looked down at the table.

"My city has made no oath to your land for many generations now. We are at peace, and I honour your customs as though they were those of my own father and mother, but I cannot set aside the words of my king."

He looked around the table at the serious ring of faces and tried to smile.

"But see. The walls are in good repair. The gates are strong. The guard are confident. We have supplies in hand. The city has stood for hundreds of years and has weathered all that has been thrown at her. We are precious to the King of the North and he will not let us fall. This will surely pass."

Tadugari stood, followed by the whole family, as the old lady pushed her chair back and, leaning heavily on her attendant, got to her feet. She had hardly eaten anything. Two griddled sides of fish rested, cooling, in front of her in a bed of dark leaves.

"Hear me now. A time comes for every land when the gods turn their faces away. Even the Beloved Land has seen this before, when order turned back into chaos and the labourer in the fields lorded it over the noble. My heart tells me that a time like this is near for this city. It is not a time to be staying here amongst all of this."

She gestured up and around at the walls, with their cloth drapes and little statues of the gods. Tadugari straightened himself.

"Honoured mother of this house, tell me this. If you had been alive in your Beloved Land at such a time, would you have left your house? Or would you have stayed and shared the fortune of the whole land?"

They held each other's gaze for a long time. Finally she turned away, sighing.

"How truly you speak. I will go back to my rooms and prepare to meet my husband in my own way. The rest of you, stay and eat your fill without me. Daughter, bring the children tomorrow at noon for my blessing and to hear my word for you."

◆◈◆◈◆◈◆◈◆

ANILAT TAPPED AT THE DOOR of her mother's day chamber, stepping in once it opened. Her mother was sitting in the oldest chair in the room, a piece which she had taken with her every time she had moved. It came originally from the Beloved Land. Each of the four legs ended in a lion's foot, and the back rose up in a long support for the head.

She bowed until her mother's creaky voice released her, then moved across to sit at her feet. She stroked one of the lion paws idly, remembering again the years of her own girlhood. All that time ago, Anilat had sat for hours beside the chair, tracing out the shapes of Mitsriy gods and goddesses on each side. In the lazy afternoons she had listened to her mother's stories, felt both delight and fear, been moved to satisfaction or anger at the old tales.

That had not always been in this house, for they had moved from place to place as the king of Ikaret had commanded her father. But it had always been with this chair.

Her mother pushed back the Kinahny headscarf Anilat was wearing, and stroked her hair. The aged hand trembled a little. She looked up. Her mother was holding several things close to her body with her other hand.

"Daughter, I have called you here today in order to make our farewell to each other."

Anilat began to protest, but her mother's hand moved down from her hair to cover her lips.

"Listen now. My heart tells me that we shall not speak again. I have some things to give you, and my last instructions to tell you."

She shifted in the chair.

"Do you remember the story of my young life all those years ago in Gedjet? In the end I had two men seeking to marry me, both at the same time. Not that there was any real doubt in my heart, ever, but it felt good to be wanted like that. I was so young then."

She paused. Her attendant brought over a small juglet of beer, and she sipped a little of it. Anilat was curious. She had not heard of the other man.

"The second man was a village priest from some remote place in the hills. He could not speak our language very well, and I think he could not write the proper signs at all, but my father found him amusing. The man was quite wild. I remember thinking that perhaps he could be frightening. What would it be like to be with him alone? Of course I chose your father. It was the sensible thing to do."

There was another pause.

"But one regret I have is that you have never met your grandfather. He moved back to the Beloved Land soon after

I came into the house of your father. We used to write letters to each other, in those early days, but his were always very short. He was sent to serve as senior priest in Waset. I suppose he was kept busy with that. But I do feel he could have made more effort."

Anilat, realising that her mother was in a mood for revelation, was just framing a question when her mother continued.

"It cannot be very long since he passed through the Sea of Reeds. The last letter I received said that he had found a man who was fashioning his eternal house. But that was ten years ago." She halted and shook her head. "Ten years. How can that be? I have heard nothing since then, and cannot believe he lives on this side any longer. Even with that, he has had a longer life than I, and he has succeeded in being buried in the Beloved Land."

She held out the first item she held. It was a small wooden box, held shut with a leather thong.

"When you leave here, take this with you. Carry it with your most precious belongings until you can take it down to the Beloved Land and bury it for me there. It does not have to be in Waset: perhaps father would not want me there with him. But in some place that belongs to my people, a place that seems good to you. Find a priest who will perform the rites correctly."

Anilat looked at the box as she took it, wondering if she should open it.

"Keep the box closed shut. It has some of my hair, some nail clippings, and some of the fluids of my body. And some from your father as well."

She sighed.

"If we had a real priest here I could ask him where my husband's everlasting breath will live. Since he is not of our people I cannot be sure. But there is nobody I can ask. For now I will trust that if he is buried with me, we will be together again on the other side. So these fragments of our bodies must be together, even if our bones are scattered up and down this province."

"But he will be back soon?"

"In truth, I cannot say. What I hear from the north is very bad. We already knew that the army was in difficulty, but today I have received fearful news of the city of the great king himself. I think your father and I will only meet on the other side now, and that may well be very soon."

Anilat felt a surge of disbelief, and started to give it voice, but her mother touched her lips again to command silence. She passed over the second item. It was heavy for its size, and sounded of metal.

"This will keep you from want on the journey. You must go south from here. Make sure Tadugari gets a few soldiers to come with you. I have already sent him a message saying this. Quite apart from the weapons, those men will know the land. The coast road will not be safe, and you will need to follow the tracks inland."

"What is the third thing?"

Her mother gripped it tightly to herself. Through her fingers, Anilat could make out the shape of a black glazed vial with a tight stopper.

"This is for me, for when there is no other way out. I shall not be undertaking that particular journey with you."

There was a sudden rapping at the door. The attendant opened it, to find a messenger there. He bowed, and started to speak at once.

"Honoured ladies, the lord Tadugari, son of Anziniy, sends from the palace to say you must be make yourselves ready to leave by the end of the week. All of you, he said, from oldest to youngest. You must prepare yourselves for the journey. The enemy are on their way, and he cannot be sure that our army will protect us. The city may be surrounded before too much longer."

Anilat stood in consternation. Her mother scowled at the messenger.

"Too little, too late. The foreigners will be here tonight. By tomorrow morning the city will be under siege. You should all leave tonight."

"Forgive me, lady, but that was his word."

"Too little, too late, as I have said. Your people should know when it is time to leave."

The messenger shuffled his feet, looked around at the room, avoided her eyes.

"Forgive me, truly, but that was his word, lady. Will there be a message to take back to him?"

Anilat gripped her mother's hand.

"Tell him that we will be ready tomorrow."

He scurried away in relief.

"Can I help you pack some of your belongings, mother?"

"I shall not be leaving here with you. Bring the children to me now, and send word to your brother that he should do the same. After that, leave me alone to make my own peace."

◆彡◆彡◆彡◆彡◆

MUCH LATER, ANILAT LAY BACK in her bed, reflecting on the evening, enjoying the feel of the soft cloth of the sheet against her skin.

Her mother had prayed for and blessed each of the children with great thoroughness, which had alarmed her more than anything else which had been said that day. Anilat had avoided asking anything about what her mother had or had not heard through her own extensive network of scouts and informers.

On the other side of the arch, the twins were asleep already but she could hear Auntie talking with Haleyna. It sounded as though they were playing a word game full of rhymes and puns. Anilat tried to catch what they were saying, but the words were too quick and quiet for her.

Tadugari came in. Another messenger had come down from the palace, and Tadugari had taken him into one of the back rooms to hear him. She had no idea what had been said. Tadugari grinned at her, then went over to the children's pallets to offer prayer for them. Unusually, he included Auntie in the night blessing; as a rule he only did this at the head of year ceremony when he prayed a formal circuit around the entire household.

That done, he stripped off and settled beside her. It was several hours since he had been in the king's house, but the aroma of royal incense still clung slightly to him.

"All well, husband?"

He pursed his lips.

"Not really. There may be another summons in the middle of the night after all. Reports and rumours are mixed."

She looked away, and then back again.

"Mother feels that the future is very bleak for the city. That cannot be true, surely? The city has stood firm forever, back to what mother calls the time of the gods."

He was very slow to answer. In the pause she spoke again.

"Your message said we should pack and be ready at once, but also that we still had some days to spare. Which is it? And mother thinks that there is no more time left. I do not know what to think."

He shook his head.

"Neither do I, Anilat. I sent that message when one piece of very bad news came to us. But other news is better. I wish that we had not sent so many of the fighting men north. The city would be stronger if we had kept the bowmen, or a few wings of chariots."

"Why did we send so many? When they left, they spent all morning parading through the North Gate."

"We had to send a good number to honour the treaty. The king decided to dispatch almost the whole army. For one thing it shows him to be loyal in the eyes of the King of the North. And also some of the advisors told him it was better to halt the advance of the enemy far away. Better, they said, that they are held back near Mersin and never come down the coast towards us."

"That sounds wise."

"Perhaps it is. But it has also left us with little in defence. Only a handful of real soldiers, together with some old men and youths in training."

"But surely the advice is correct? The combined armies of the King of the North will fight them many days away from here. Our daughter towns will supply us with men for the walls."

"They already have. Most of them went north as well."

"Then some of the inland cities will send extra men to us. I know we would never expect help from the Kinahny kings, but we will get help from our trade allies, surely?"

"They are looking to their own walls just now. They say that bands of these newcomers have turned along the road that runs east of the mountains."

"So they have split their number. How ignorant they must be. When our army meets them, this will all be over."

He shook his head and paused again, deliberating whether to say something to her.

"What is it?"

"Anilat, you know what happened to our fleet outside the harbour the other day. Now, I do not know how many men can go inside their ships. But what if they simply carry them past the combined army and alight further down the coast? Nearer to us here?"

She stared at him.

"Why would they do that? They have to face the army at some point, and the city walls will hold them quite long enough. Did you say this to the king? Surely he will think it foolish counsel."

"If I were leading an invading army it is exactly what I would do. Wherever they have come from, they surely cannot face our army on the field of battle: they will lose to our might and discipline. So I would avoid open battle and dance about. Like a man with a knife fighting against one with a spear. But no, we did not say this to the king. Some of us talked about it between ourselves, but nobody raised it to him."

She looked up at the ceiling and shook her head. In the next room, Haleyna's responses in the riddle game were getting slower, sounding more sleepy.

"Look, Anilat, my sweetest fawn, there will be time to talk about all that another day."

He turned on his side towards her, reached out and ran his hand over her breasts.

"Just now, there may not be as much time as we hoped."

She smiled a little to cover her anxiety.

"And if there is not so much time?"

His hand drifted down her body to her waist. She touched his cheek gently.

"It is not the best day for this. If we have to make a journey, what if I was carrying another child?"

His hand stopped, resting on her stomach, his fingers still caressing the curves of her body. She waited to see what he would do, well aware that her body was already preparing itself to be joined with his. He looked into her eyes, full of desire. She counted back the time since she had finished bleeding last; difficult these days now she had become irregular. Then she relaxed a little, took a very long breath, let it out, and kissed him lightly.

"Perhaps I was wrong. It is a good day after all. And anyway, I am not so young as I was, and the life burns a little lower in me. And the days are not so important to keep in mind as they once were."

For a few heartbeats he still did not move.

"You are young enough for me. And just now every day is a gift. Listen, Anilat, if we should be separated by all this, I do not want us to have regrets that anything was undone. Forgive me any wrong I have caused you."

She hugged him, pressed herself against him. Little tears threatened her eyes.

"Nothing to forgive."

She pushed to the back of her mind a sudden image of squatting down to give birth in a windswept gully somewhere in the wilderness, and started instead to surrender to the ardour they shared. In any case, it would be many months before that might happen. "But if there is any way in which I have failed you, please forgive that in me."

He shook his head, kissed her with passion, and for a time they played their familiar game where he was a stag on the mountains, and she was a doe among the flowering forests. He came running down from the wild peaks to immerse himself in her gentle woodland glades, and left her again with some of his own wildness inside her. It was good: it was a time of reunion.

𒁹𒊹𒁹𒊹𒁹𒊹𒁹𒊹

IT WAS THE DARKEST HOUR of the night. Tadugari had gone to the palace and not returned, and Anilat had settled herself beside the children. The three of them were in a row, all asleep between her and Auntie. Neither of the women could sleep, though, and they exchanged wakeful glances for a time. Finally Anilat got up and pulled the drapes aside to see what was happening. Auntie came up beside her and wrapped a cloth over her shoulders.

"Don't let yourself be seen like that, lady. Not just now. You don't know who's outside tonight. It's not safe any more."

"Oh, Auntie, of course we're safe in the city. It hardly matters here in my own house."

"It surely does matter, lady. You don't know about these things, for which I'm very glad. I pray you'll never find out either. Nothing would ever be the same again. You don't know. And there's some of our own men that would take as they please these days, quite apart from that lot outside."

Anilat nodded absently, then gripped Auntie's hand.

"I went down to where the ancestors rest this afternoon. I took gifts and offerings to them. After what mother said last night I began to wonder if there would be another chance."

Auntie was silent. The moon at the window was still only a thin crescent, and she could only just make out the older woman's features. The dim light accentuated her foreignness. Since Auntie came from Alashiya, whose people traded the copper in the belly of their island with all the world, Anilat's ancestral devotions probably meant little to her. Where, she wondered, were Auntie's own ancestors? She abandoned the subject abruptly.

"Auntie, do you know who these people are? Where they came from?"

"Not for sure. But I heard one lad talking about them down at the market. Sounds to me like they're kin to the pirates and raiders we've endured back home for many years. Lukka, or Tursha, maybe. Or Peleset. Filthy ravagers. They band together in ships like locusts. There's a whole lot of different clans that join up from time to time for this sort of thing."

She leaned forward to try to catch sight of the harbour and the sea.

"Most likely my own people are facing the same lot. You won't get any help from there."

She stiffened suddenly, and her fingers seized hold of Anilat's shoulder. A sudden flame had come up from the docks. As Anilat watched, a second building caught light as the flames leapt from one roof to the next. Auntie was already moving across the room, pulling at a pile of clothes.

"You must dress yourself, lady. And not in fine stuff. In something more common, like we talked about in the evening."

Anilat stayed at the window, not understanding what was happening. The flames at the harbour were still spreading. Off to one side, in the direction of the lesser gate, another fire appeared. In the distance she started to hear noise from the fires. She shrank back a little as running footsteps sounded at the end of the alleyway. Auntie was pulling her away into the room.

"Put these clothes on, mistress, put them on now, there's no time to lose just standing looking at all this."

Anilat looked blankly at her.

"It's just a fire down at the docks, Auntie. Why do you want us to get dressed?"

Auntie handed her the bundle of her clothes and she started dressing without thinking. Then she stopped again, her outer smock loose in her hand. Auntie was shaking the children awake.

"Don't wake them, they've only just gone off properly." She stopped as Auntie turned on her, an unexpectedly fierce look on her features. There was more noise from outside, distant shouting. She went suddenly cold. "It is just a fire, surely?"

Her daughter was already awake, and the twins were stirring, grumpy and uncomprehending. Auntie was rapidly, efficiently pulling clothes onto them.

"They're in the city, mistress, that's what it is."

She saw the question starting to form on Anilat's face. "It doesn't matter how they did it, lady. We need to get ourselves along out of here. Mistress, please help me get the children ready now. You must think of the little ones here."

Finally stirred into action, Anilat pulled the smock over her head and began to help. Just as they were finishing, her mother's attendant came into the room.

"The eldest of the house has sent me with her words for you all. She has sent all the night slaves away to fend for themselves. She has chosen to meet her fate in the audience chamber, with me beside her. All of you, woman and child alike, are to go to the little room with the spy window and watch from there. Whatever happens you must not come out until everything is done. Do not let yourselves be found. After that make your way to the shepherds' huts beside the hill road and wait for your husband to meet you. And she says not to forget the things she gave you earlier."

She turned away again. Anilat stood with open mouth, trying to speak. She succeeded only after the woman had gone.

"What did she mean? Why does she want us to go to the spy room?"

Auntie finished tying the strings of a hat on to the younger twin, Ritsani.

"Seems to me it's the only room in the house that nobody will find who doesn't know where to look. Your honoured mother is expecting these invaders to get into the house soon. Mistress, can we do as she said now and get along there?"

Anilat nodded, and they went, urging the children ahead of them along the halls and corridors. They went round behind the household shrine, down into the cellar, pushed aside the little hidden door beneath the stairs and scrambled up again. They emerged into a tiny room, lined with benches down each side and a stool opposite them. At eye level there was a spy hole opening into the audience chamber.

Anilat had sat here often to watch Tadugari meet with others as an official duty – trade delegations, supplicants, spies, and foreign envoys. She had taken note of the words and signs they made to one another in their imagined secrecy, and shared it all later with her husband.

She moved across to the spy hole. From there, she could see her mother sitting at the chair with the lion paws. She was dressed in her finest clothes, and wore garlands of jewellery ostentatiously around her neck and pinned onto her embroidered tunic and shawl. The large room was full of dancing light and shadow from torches which burned at regular intervals around the walls.

Anilat knew that the spy hole was disguised as part of a stonework decoration, almost impossible to see from inside the room. Her mother's glance slipped over towards her every now and again. Beside her mother, sitting on a low stool, was the attendant: it was the first time Anilat had ever seen her not on her feet. On a little table beside them were two beakers of beer.

Close at hand in the tiny space, Auntie was quieting the children and settling them on the stone bench. The tiny room was full of breathing. Anilat realised that the noises from outside the building had greatly increased. She could not make out any words, but there was a confused sound of energetic passion.

They huddled in the confined space for what seemed a long time. At first, one or other of the children fidgeted, but before long they sank into sleep again. Anilat's mother and her attendant sat in silence. Her mother's hand rested gently on the other woman's shoulder.

Finally there came a banging at the outside door, slightly muffled by the stone walls. There was shouting, another bang, then a more systematic thumping sound. The wall trembled slightly under her hand, and in the shaft of light from the spy hole she could see specks of dust floating in little clouds where they had been dislodged.

Her mother moved at last, shifted her hand to briefly caress her attendant's head, and then poured two measures of fluid from the black vial she still held, one into each of the beakers of beer. Both women rose stiffly to their feet, held each other in a long embrace and then settled again. They looked at each other for a long moment, then drank together. The banging from the outer door continued steadily, mixed with creaks and the sound of splintering.

Anilat put her hand to her mouth, swallowing a sudden, sickening realisation. She reached out in the near darkness, and Auntie took her hand, held it firmly. The attendant put her head down in her mother's lap. The beaker she had been holding slipped out of her hand and rolled across the floor.

Her mother gave one last look towards the spy hole. Then a quick look of intense pain crossed her face, and the hand resting on her attendant's head clenched briefly. She sighed, snatched a sudden rasping breath, and leaned her head back against the chair. Her eyes stared without blinking across the room, reflecting the flames of the torches in their wall brackets.

The outer door gave way with a crash, and there was a shout of triumph, followed by the noise of many feet. Haleyna woke with a start at the noise, looking around wildly in the near darkness. Auntie held her, gathered her to herself, made little quietening noises. There was so much commotion in the building that the girl's upset could not be heard, but in the small room it sounded all too conspicuous.

A flood of men poured in to the audience chamber. There was a confusion of shouting as they saw the two seated women, then a stalking quietness as they came closer in a huddle around them.

One of them laughed, reached out and tugged at the largest of her mother's brooches. It pulled free of the fabric, and her mother slumped forward. The attendant's head slipped from its resting place, and her body collapsed to the floor, legs sprawling lifelessly one way and another.

The mood turned to frustration, and the inaccessibility of the women seemed to enrage the gang of men. Rough hands pulled at the gold and silver, the dangling jewels, the garments. With a tearing sound the fine clothing which had travelled all the way from the Beloved Land was divided up between half a dozen of the men.

Auntie's hand was tight on her own as Anilat watched from the spy hole, mute with horror. At the end, her mother and the attendant lay discarded on one side, stripped of valuables. The men were wearing the brooches and necklaces now, tied or draped around their leather outer wear. One of them, the leader she supposed, had tied her mother's shawl around his own neck. Most of the men had lost interest in the two bodies, and had started moving towards the other doors.

One of the gang turned the attendant over and pulled at her remaining clothes to see if the others had missed anything of value, laughing at her thin, aged legs as he exposed them. A second one spoke to him, in a language Anilat did not recognise, and pointed to her mother. Together they systematically pillaged her body, finding little pieces of precious things that had been missed at first.

There was more shouting outside, and the leader called to gather the others together. He briefly looked around the audience chamber. Anilat flinched back as his gaze swept across the spy hole, but the curls and prongs of the carved flowers kept it well hidden. He started towards the outer door. Most followed him, but the two men crouched beside her mother's body stayed where they were at her body, searching inside folds of fabric, pulling away the cloth until they found skin.

The leader stopped, called to them again, stood for a few heartbeats with hands on hips. He was standing beside a tall wooden stand with a torch tied to the top. He took it from its stand, pulled the torch from the top and threw it into one corner. He strode across the room, pushed the two men away from the body, then plunged the wooden stake through her belly. Anilat bent double and retched, feeling the shock of the thrust through her own innards. She moaned slightly, hands over her mouth, swaying to and fro on the spot.

Auntie shook her shoulder urgently, fiercely, although the shout of laughter from the room outside had easily drowned out her own anguish. When she made herself look out of the spy hole again the men had gone. The torch lying in one corner guttered and went out. The wooden pole that had impaled her mother still swayed to and fro. Torn shreds of clothing were scattered here and there. The lion chair, astonishingly, rested firmly in its place, untouched amongst the ransack.

There was silence except for the far away background noise in the city. The house was empty again. Anilat felt for one of the stone benches, slumped down onto it, and sobbed hopelessly. Auntie moved across to look out of the spy hole and winced, gripping Anilat's hand all the while.

They sat together in silence for a while, until Haleyna suddenly said, "How long must we stay in this place, mother?"

She shrugged, then realised that the gesture could not be seen. "It doesn't matter. None of it matters."

She felt Auntie stir restlessly. "Of course it matters, mistress. Your mother of blessed memory sat there with her finery on so that we would not be found. The way to repay her with honour and respect is to care for us all in the best way you know."

Anilat's eyes had adjusted again to the darkness. In the dim spear of light from the spy hole she saw Haleyna start to get up, move towards the light. "What has happened? I want to see."

Anilat reached out to stop her, but Auntie was quicker. "Not yet, little one. It's not good to look out there just now. Just wait here in the dark and help me see to the twins." There was a pause. "Well, mistress?"

Finally she looked up. "What do you mean, she sat there so we would not be found?"

"Well, mistress, with those thieves finding what they did on her, they didn't go searching through the house, did they? Who knows if they'd have found us if they started looking? Or seen signs that others lived here? She let them take all that gold and such so they wouldn't get what she treasured all the more. Mistress, you have to do all you can to keep these little ones safe. Or all that will have been for nothing."

She gestured towards the room. Anilat stayed silent for a long time. One of the twins stirred in his sleep, and without thinking she ran her hand over his shoulder until he relaxed again.

"Very well, Auntie. I can do that for her. But not yet, that crowd will still be nearby. We have to wait a while. But where do we go then?"

"Where she told us to. The shepherds' huts beside the hill road. That's where the master will meet us."

"I suppose so." She shivered, her breathing quickened, and her voice tightened. "If he can get away himself. What if the palace has been attacked? What if he cannot get free? What if... what if?"

She could not bring herself to finish. Auntie squeezed her hand.

"He's a good man, mistress. He'll meet us there, you'll see. Now, mistress, how long do you think we need to stay in this place?"

She stroked Haleyna's hair, wanting her to go back to sleep. If her daughter slept, perhaps all this would feel like a dark dream. If she listened carefully she could still hear riotous noises outside.

"We can't leave yet. Not while those beasts are on the streets. We have to wait until it quietens down."

"Best to get out while it's dark, though. Unless you want to stay here through the day until nightfall?"

"No. I can't stay here with all that just the other side of the wall. And they might come back to search again in the day. Or set fire against us." Her voice had started to rise, and her body was trembling. Anxiety roughened the movements of her hands, and Haleyna started to fidget. She forced herself to become calm again. Cool minded, as her mother might have said. She took several long breaths.

"We will wait here until there has been no noise outside for a while. Long enough that we think they have gone elsewhere in the city. Then we will make for the middle gate and the hill road. And after that?"

She paused. Her imagination failed her. Surely Tadugari would have joined them by then. Or perhaps the city guard would have rallied and driven the invaders out again. There were too many possibilities to think about.

"After that we will go to those huts and see what the day brings."

Auntie made approving noises in the gloom.

"So we'll let the twins sleep a bit longer, mistress?"

"Yes. But I don't know how they can sleep in all this."

"I suppose it's all too much for them, lady. They've found a way out of this room already."

"If only I could join them."

A SON ADDRESSES HIS FATHER.

Hekanefer, scribe appointed to carry messages for the military commander in Gedjet, in the Kinahny province, to Nesamenopeh, scribe of the great and noble city of the dead outside Min-Nefer, greetings and blessings to you. I write from the garrison building in Gedjet.

I pray daily that all the gods keep both you and the lady Hemesherit, the best of all mothers, in good health. Every day I am cast down in my heart because of being sent out here into the Kinahny province. Of course to be serving the Beloved Land is all one should wish for, but my body and breath yearns to be back in the land of my birth, and to be surrounded again with the loving arms of my family.

I have been garrisoned here at Gedjet these many weeks now. Gedjet is a large town, and our people have made it a worthy place to see. The great king User-ma'at-Re Mery-Imun, who lives in prosperity and health, has commanded the building of a great house of mysteries, sacred to all the gods. It will be magnificent. In his great wisdom, and to show the superiority of the divine lords and ladies of our own land, he has also ordered that ceremonies will be held in the name of the Kinahny goddess Anath on her sacred days.

But the work that I am doing here is also a mystery, and not in a sacred sense. The tasks I am given could be adequately carried out by a junior in training. I must be patient and humble and accept the instructions that I am given, but every day I long to hear that I have been transferred to another place of more importance.

Now, I am honoured that the military commander knows me and greets me by name each morning. They tell me that he is a man of skill and sound judgement on the field of battle, though I have yet to see this. He has trusted me with personal messages as well as orders and commands to his junior officers. I have been given a bodyguard of three runners and a fully-equipped chariot and its crew of two for the times that I am sent out of Gedjet to the outposts along the Sea Road. It is a generous allowance, and a recognition of the important place of the scribe in the army of the great king, who lives in prosperity and health.

But it is also a reminder that this land seethes with unrest. When we were last together, drifting downstream on the greatest of all rivers, on the little skiff which your father liked so much, we read together the advice that the advice that the scribe Hori gave to his friend. Do you remember? That wise man wrote of how perilous the roads and hill passes of this land can be.

Every word is true, and my bodyguard, stout warriors all, have assured me of it. I have not seen the Shasu robbers that Hori described, but that is surely because my guardsmen scatter them in fear before I come to the turn in the road. I would also like to say that I have not succumbed, in the way that Hori's foolish friend did, to the allure of the breasts of the women here. I have taken your sound advice into my heart, my father, and have reflected upon the prudent course of action on every occasion.

It is altogether disappointing, father, to witness first hand how the inhabitants of this region disrespect the Beloved Land these days. How short are their memories! All the benefits that we have given them are so easily forgotten, and they imagine that being their own rulers will bring so many advantages. We have given them the security of our overlordship for many generations, but it is all so quickly set aside. I read about the proud days of the past, when our authority was without question, and I long for them to return.

Another thing. Messengers have reached us here in Gedjet speaking of troubles in the Khatti-lands. They say that the King of the North has been at war with a lawless rabble who have come into the west of his land. That must mean they crossed the sea, for as you remember there is no land adjoining him on that side. There are tales that cities have been burned somewhere in the lands under his authority.

If this is true, then it proves beyond doubt what you have always said. The soldiers of other places are weak and without courage compared to those of our own Beloved Land. They are like a little puddle of water shrivelled up by the sun at noon in the depths of Kush. Had our own armies been there, this would not have happened. But the King of the North will not humble himself before our great king, the great sun of our land who lives in prosperity and health and sees all that happens in every land.

Now we have in former years sent great ships full of grain to the help of the King of the North's ancestors, on a day when his gods were angry and his crops failed. Perhaps on this day we will send ships full of chariots and riders to help him. But first he must learn to submit himself and fall seven times and seven times again at the feet of our great king who lives in prosperity and health. In the past the ancestors of the King of the North mistook the kindness of our generous hands for weakness. That will not happen again.

Another thing. Speak gentle words for me to the lady Ankhiriyt, chantress of the great god, and promise her that I have been faithful of intent in my betrothal to her daughter Nodjmet. Tell her that I have not looked idly on the body of another woman, nor entered a house where a woman is alone. I will not do this until that happy day comes when Nodjmet and I can be joined in marriage at the gates of the holy place.

Remind her that I am gaining a good name out here in this rough province, and that every day I long for the word of release. When that comes, I shall not hesitate, but will speed back to the Beloved Land.

Father, may the lord of all the gods look favourably on you. I speak of you every day to every god that I know.

A MAN ADDRESSES HIS BROTHER.

Hekanefer to his older brother Ramose, with happy memories of our last meeting at Tjaru. Every blessing to you.

Brother, how did you survive being here in this land? I remember that you spent five years in one part or another of this wretched province, travelling about at the whim of the governor. When father read your letters to us all, they were full of the good things that you had seen and heard. Only on that last night, when we met in Tjaru as I was myself on the journey here, did you tell me the truth of the matter.

How accurate are your words, and if only I had heard them before the day I said "yes, indeed, I am honoured" to this task. Of course I know that the calling of the scribe far exceeds every other job that men perform, but on some days I wish that I was not called so high! The soldiers here are idle with lack of action, passing the time in games of chance and wagers. Even the tanners and the washermen have an easy life here. Only the scribe works – and how he works, both day and night.

I have in my room the amulet you sent, and have felt no chill since the day it arrived. But the vessel of beer that came with it has long since gone, sadly. Every day I look into it, in case some god has performed a miracle on my behalf. O, how I missed the Beloved Land, and how I missed our mother's own beer as I drank it.

You will laugh to hear this. They gave me some uncouth men that trail around after me when the commander sends me here and there. I think they are supposed to protect me, but please speak to all the gods on my behalf that I will never need their help. Our little sister Mereriyt could defeat them all with her eyes covered and one hand still at work dyeing the cloth. But your brother has a bodyguard of five men now, so speak kindly to me when we meet!

Another thing. You were right to tell me about the house of the lady Taysenofret. This house was never mentioned in your letters to father, and I never speak of it to him either. I cannot go as often as I would like, through lack of silver, but the pleasures there draw me back like a moth to a candle in a darkened room. There is so little to do here in Gedjet. Since you were here, Taysenofret has acquired another house beside the first. She now calls the place "The Two Lands" and you decide as you approach whether to go to one or the other. Never both on the same evening.

One of the other scribes in the town told me that a girl from Kush has just been brought in to the houses. I think I would enjoy finding out more about the southern extent of the Beloved Land. The scribe of old wrote how the gods created different skin colours in every land between Kush and Khatti, and so it is. Truly Khnum the divine potter ensured that the glaze and the pattern of each delightful vessel differs from the next, and yet the balm within them is the same.

You asked about the news from the north. Look now, it is very muddled. Some say that the King of the Khatti-lands has lost a battle. Others say a city or two has been burned. Others deny all this and say that everything there is as it has always been. I have read each of the messages that reach the commander here from our spies in the north, and no two of them are in agreement.

So far as I can tell, our own king is waiting. I am sure that his scribes will write that he is being patient and still, like the lion before it strikes down its prey. But who can say? As it is, we have had no orders to move north. The troops are not exercised any more than they usually are.

The city rulers here are arrogant, and entirely provincial. Each one imagines himself some kind of potentate, when in truth they only lord it over little flocks of ignorant labourers. Small loss if some of them are burned within their pitiful homes. Anything which makes this unruly province easier to govern can only be a good thing.

Brother, I beg you to send me more beer with your next letter, so that I can taste the Beloved Land on my lips and in my stomach. I long for this duty to be over and done with, so that I can return to my true home. Write to me again soon: your news brightens my day and lifts my heart. Speak my name often to your children to remind them they have an uncle.

NIKLEOS WAS WALKING beside the lead ox. It had been slow work up and down the swell of the land in the afternoon sun, but his clan's aim was to get across into the rougher area ahead before halting for the night.

For part of the day there had been a track that they could follow, but that had turned east a while ago and they had abandoned it. He supposed that it led to one or other of the chain of cities off in that direction. The land there was arid and exposed: not at all to their taste.

The clan was spread out like a straggling flock, making no attempt to keep any kind of order, content simply to be in sight of each other. Elsewhere, other groups of wagons like their own were making their own progress, connected loosely by ties of kinship and covenant, but they were far away, out of direct contact. They had never felt an obligation to stay close to each other. Outside of the needs of war, not one of the clans thought to impose order on another.

It had been a long journey for them all, south and east after the great city of Wilios had fallen. That long siege, and the sack which followed, had been a moment of concerted initiative for them, a beginning of something new. They had gathered together for that in larger numbers than ever before, and come over the sea together in absurdly full boats. They had learned patience as they waged war outside the walls of Wilios, and finally secured victory by trickery and deceit.

Afterwards, a few of the smaller clans had returned across the sea to their former homes. Most of them, however, had carried on travelling, lured on by the thought of other rich prizes scattered up and down the land. The valleys of their former home seemed narrow, and the land meagre, compared to what lay on this side of the water. They had set off from Wilios with the grand intention of finding new homes.

That was a great many months ago, however. Nikleos' clan, and its leader Antos, had started to grow weary of the endless, relentless movement onward. Over the months they had lost friends and kinfolk: a few from sickness, but the larger part in war. It might well be a good way to die for those concerned, but for the ones who were still alive, every loss left the remaining families a little less able to manage. Before too long they would need to settle for a while and recover.

The heady unity of the original impetus was ebbing away. This land was so much vaster than any of the clan leaders had expected. When they turned from the flames they had set in Wilios, there was something grand about the sight of so many fighting men moving together, so many wagons and families all setting off as one. But the single coast road leading south from Wilios had branched many times, and each clan had followed its own inclination. The land was starting to swallow them up.

There were only a few young men with them now. Most of their lads were to the east, moving faster across the land with the raiding parties, making larger or smaller groups as the situation demanded. His own son Dekseus was with one of them, led by Tiripodikos. Other clans supplied young men to swell the gangs attacking the cities along the coast.

He dropped back to the wagon, letting the pair of oxen lead themselves for a while. Kastiandra, his wife, was busy with one of the sacks of supplies and did not notice him until his shadow fell across her arms. With the effort, her hair had escaped into wild straggles. She straightened, holding her hair up around her head as though it was properly braided before turning to see who had come near. Seeing it was him, she released it, and it fell loose around her face again. She leaned back.

"Thirsty again, husband?"

He shook his head.

"Not yet. I just wanted a change from seeing the face of that ugly beast beside me for one pace after another."

She laughed, and tilted her head to one side for him.

"Good enough?"

He grunted appreciatively. She stood up, balancing delicately on the swaying deck of the wagon, bundling her hair up into something more like a braid. The wagon was packed tightly in an excess of neatness, an outward reflection of Kastiandra herself. Only the sack she had been working with was out of its place. Before long, both the wagon and her own appearance would be neatly arranged again.

"Where are we?"

He shrugged. "I hardly know one name from another in this land. But one of the scouts told me that we were a little north and west of a city called Damaseq."

She shrugged, shook her head.

"No, I had never heard of the name when he told me, either. But our purpose for today is to get over that crest ahead. Beyond it the land is different, they say. Rougher, but we'll be following along the grain of the land instead of rubbing across it all the time. And in another couple of weeks we'll be skirting round the west side of a fair size mountain."

The wagon jolted across a sudden dip, and she kept her balance with one hand on his shoulder. He squeezed it, held it, feeling with his fingers the thinness of her skin over the bones.

"This same scout told me that Periphas will be here with the raiders in a few days. He is already heading this way from the coast road. There is a city that he wants to attack, a larger one, so he will be gathering more of the lads together."

"So we will see Dekseus again? For a night or so at least?"

"It seems so."

She nodded, pleased.

"So long as I do not have to welcome Periphas myself. He is a foul man, for all his skill in the fight."

She looked out towards the hills on the horizon, as though Dekseus might already be coming in sight.

"Also, you should know that Murtilis is over with Kastor's family again."

He glanced across to one of the other wagons, a few hundred paces away to his left.

"Arkelawos is not there, surely? You did not allow her to be with him?"

"No. Of course not. He is ahead scouting somewhere. I made sure of that before letting her go. Only the women there with Kastor."

She paused, took one last look around and then sat again on the wooden cross-bench.

"We should settle on an arrangement for her before the overflow of spring fills her heart like new buds opening. If it is to be Arkelawos then let us declare it, and let her move into Kastor's wagon and his household itself. Better we decide it now than she lets somebody else pick that particular flower."

He nodded but said nothing. She frowned at him.

"It has to be you that talks to Kastor. I cannot in all decency do that."

"I know. Do you think I don't know?"

A note of irritation had crept into his voice. He looked sideways at her, saw unguarded amusement on her face.

Before he could become angry, he also saw that the lead ox had started to drift away from a true line to where the slope was less pronounced. He waved his hand and shouted at it, to no effect. Kastiandra jumped lightly down to the ground.

"Go and see him now. Persuade him to plan something within the next few weeks. I'll keep these two going up the hill. And also, go to see Antos again when you have done that. He will name an out-of-family successor soon enough, now that he only has one son left alive. Make sure that it is you who he names."

"I am hopeful."

"Make it more than hope. Go and see him today. You have been the most loyal of his supporters throughout the journey. Make sure he names you, and Dekseus after you."

He nodded.

"He worries that we only have one son now ourselves."

Her face hardened.

"All of the families have lost sons. He himself has lost sons. It is not as if Moqsos was weaker than any of the others. It has been a difficult journey for all of us."

"I know. But he has to reckon all of these things when he chooses."

"I want to hear that we have done everything that we can do to persuade him. All that you can do."

A quick flash of anger came over his face.

"Don't you be telling me what I should be doing."

She refused to back down, and met his glare calmly.

"What I should be doing is looking after these oxen so you are free to go."

She ran forwards, whispered in the ox's ear, flicked the hazel switch a few times across its back, and tugged the traces across to one side. The wagon creaked and started to head back towards its proper path. Nikleos shrugged and branched off at an angle, aiming towards Kastor's wagon, its own pair of oxen straining at the slope.

⫦⫢𗀯𗀯𗀯𗀯𗀯𗀯⫢⫦

THE WINTER MORNING SUN had not yet warmed the dew from the thin grass, and the land felt damp beneath Kastiandra's feet. Nikleos was across on the other side of the rough circle of wagons, talking with Towanos. He would bring the oxen back with him when he returned. All being well, the clan would be on the move again before too much longer.

She finished grinding a few beakers of kernels of grain, poured the flour into a larger vessel, then climbed back into the wagon and stowed everything away in its proper place.

Hearing a call, she turned to see her daughter Murtilis coming back with some of the other unmarried girls from the nearby stream. They had been sent down there to wash garments made muddy in the rains of the last few days.

Murtilis handed the bundle of wet clothes up to her, then pulled herself onto the boards to help spread them here and there.

"I wish Dekseus could have stayed longer with us, mother."

"We were lucky enough to enjoy his company for a night, I suppose. There's no knowing when he and the others can come back to us and stay."

"No. I suppose not. But I always want him to be here longer with us."

They arranged the smaller items where they would not be dislodged by the irregular lurching of the day's travel. Finally they were done.

"Your father has been speaking with Kastor. They have not completed the arrangements yet, but it looks likely that Kastor will accept you as wife for Arkelawos. If that happens, you may not see Dekseus so much if he passes through here for just a night."

Murtilis looked rebellious. "But he will still be my brother. I need to see him."

"You will see him as much or as little as Arkelawos allows."

She held up a hand to still the words of protest which were forming.

"But I think Arkelawos is a reasonable man. He will not prevent you. Look at me: your father never forbade me from seeing Peritos or Etewoklewes when I came into his family's home. But you will not be here any more, and you must submit yourself to Kastor's family customs."

There was silence for a while.

"Will father and Kastor decide soon?"

"I think so. Perhaps a week or two."

Murtilis looked across at the other wagon, where Kastor was harnessing the first of his oxen.

"It will be strange to stay over there when the day's journey stops. To be helping Kastor's wife Aigla of an evening instead of you, I mean."

"You will get used to it. We both will, in time."

Kastiandra's voice caught a little with the last few words. Murtilis looked at her in surprise, but she stood up quickly, looking across the grass.

"Look, your father is coming back. Go and help him with the oxen. I'll make sure everything is secure."

There was a noise of preparation around the camp. Just before Nikleos was happy with the readiness of the wagon, Antos blew his horn for the start of the day, and his oxen lumbered into movement. One after another, the other families started forward.

They had been following a series of long valleys running generally north to south, with a westerly trend as well. From time to time, where the lie of the land had been favourable, they had crossed over a ridge to regain some eastward distance. Other clans were going down the coast, but their own preference was to stay well inland.

For a while, as the scouts had directed, they had gone in a broad curve around the base of a considerable mountain. Even this close to the coming of spring, it held a considerable cap of snow. They were well past the foothills now, and the valleys were giving way to more open terrain. Perhaps they would find a good place to settle.

Periphas had arrived with a very large group of the younger men two days ago. He had obviously been collecting together bands of raiders all the way across from his preferred route along the sea. Among them was the band Dekseus fought with. He had rejoined the wagon for a single night before Periphas led them away in the morning again. His target was a large town called Hatsor. The wagons would keep well away from the city, but the lads would pluck it in their stride, taking goods and spoils as they saw fit.

Dekseus had stayed up late into the night, talking animatedly with his father about his exploits. Murtilis had sat with him, enjoying the time and the strength of his arm around her in brotherly companionship. Finally they had settled for sleep, the children on the boards at the lower end of the wagon with their parents at the upper end, just as they had done since the journey began. It would not happen for much longer; within a short time Murtilis would become part of Kastor's family.

As the clan moved ahead, the wagons started to separate. It was not possible to keep any kind of regular formation or pattern on the uneven ground, and the pairs of oxen each chose one way or another as they saw fit. By the time they halted again for the evening, they would be spread in a wide straggle, only slowly coming together again as the group clustered around the place where Antos settled.

The pace each day was slow, frustratingly so for the scouts and the raiding parties who wanted to move at their own speed. It was a pace, however, which the oxen, the wagons, and the main part of the clan's members could manage without strain.

Part-way through the day, Nikleos was sitting between Kastiandra and Murtilis.

"Has Kastor agreed the terms for our Murtilis yet?"

"Almost. He is not quick to agree anything. I cannot decide if he likes the process of negotiating so much that he pulls it out like yarn from a skein, or if he is simply slow of decision. But we are making progress." Nikleos nodded to Murtilis. "I am hoping for good news for you before too much more time goes by."

Murtilis nodded, looked across at her mother, but said nothing in answer.

"It will be a useful match, I think. Kastor may be slow to choose, but he is honourable about keeping to a choice once it is made. And Aigla will teach you all you need to know about their household customs."

"She has already started, father, in the expectation that her husband will agree with you."

He looked at her in some surprise. Kastiandra laughed.

"Sometimes, husband, we women cannot wait for our menfolk to finish a conversation."

"Well, but the matter is not certain. Nothing must be said which would suggest that any of us was judging it before time."

"Of course not, father."

They rode in silence for a time, before Murtilis spoke again.

"Father, where is this place Hatsor which Dekseus talked about?"

He pointed ahead, and somewhat to their left.

"In that direction. If we were going there in the carts it would take several days. Dekseus and the lads with him will get there very much quicker, but Periphas will wait to attack until he has scouted out the town and its defences. Then he will wait for an auspicious day for the attack itself. It may be four or five days until they take the city."

"What will they bring us back from there?"

Kastiandra snorted.

"These days Periphas is in too much of a hurry to bring anything back. Time was that our people would take time over every city, scour it for everything of value. That's what the clans always used to do. It is what we did at Wilios. Now all he does is set fire and get away as quick as he can without waiting. He counts cities and towns by numbers today rather than for the wealth he can gain for us all."

Nikleos pursed his lips, nodded. Murtilis looked at them both, taken aback.

"Surely this is not true?"

"We'll not get anything new we can use for dowry, that's for sure. Your mother is right. All he wants now is the glory of leading boys into another town and setting it alight. We'll see little benefit. The lads in the attack will come home with empty hands."

"Why do they all follow him? I thought we did this for treasure?"

She paused, looked away from her parents in the direction Nikleos had indicated.

"I wouldn't follow him, to be sure."

"He's a difficult man to refuse. And people remember his exploits from the past, give him respect for that. The lads all think that he will turn them into great fighters, and they don't see clearly when they are with him. They just rush along after him. I'll be glad if we get all our boys back again. We don't need this fight at Hatsor, not really. Plenty for us to do on the way without looking for enemies."

Murtilis blinked. "Is there so much danger?"

Nikleos leaned forward and touched the hawk icon in front of him. Kastiandra looked across at her.

"Be glad that Arkelawos is not there, but that the lot that he drew sent him ahead with the scouts. He can earn glory and renown there, and when he needs to fight it will be to protect us here in the wagons, not just puff up another man's name."

⊧𐤉𐤉𐤉𐤉𐤉𐤉⊧

〜〜 ⚘ 𝇑 ⚘ 𝇑 ⚘ 𝇑 ⚘ 〜〜

A SON ADDRESSES HIS FATHER.

Hekanefer, scribe, to Nesamenopeh, greetings and blessings to my father. I write from the garrison building in Gedjet.

Today some grave news has come south to us. I must ask you to pay a special visit to the holy place and burn incense to whichever god has their festival day when you read this.

We have heard that armies of the King of the North have been defeated, not just once, as might happen by ill chance, but many times over. Ships came fleeing in haste down from the ports north of Alashiya carrying the news, and the reports of our spies have begun to say the same. We have written down the names of those spies who have given us true report before now, and those who have not.

Now if all the news were that the King of the North had lost soldiers, that would not be severe. He is a stiff-necked man who has turned away the offered hand of friendship before. Now he must accept the fate that has come to him. No. The burden of the news is that the cities which were lost all had defences of chariots, fully manned and supplied, and that they were defeated by men on foot only.

These city troops were not ill-trained Kinahny men, nor Khatti labourers, father. They were not seasonal levies eager to return to their crops and fields. They were riders and runners who were a full part of the army of the King of the North. It is beyond belief.

The commander is questioning men in the ships to find out how such a thing happened. It has never been heard of before, not since the day when our forefathers first learned to hold the reins and wield the bow for battle. The news has brought fear to the Kinahny city rulers; some of them are now starting to ask for help from the Beloved Land again, though others remain set in their stubborn ways. Danger is still a long way north of them, but they feel its nearness.

The soldiers here have spoken of this. The King of the North, they tell me, does not fill the hearts of his men with boldness in the way that our own great king does, who lives in prosperity and health and on whom every god smiles with favour. Our soldiers will admit that the chariotry of these northern kingdoms have skill and ability, but they also say that they lack heart. They have the temperament of neither the panther nor the bull. They have strength in numbers, but not of spirit.

If the day comes when the wicked enemies who have done this to cities in the north should try to pillage and loot along the Sea Road, they will sing a different song. It will be a song of defeat, and a song praising the name of the king of kings and sun of suns.

Another thing. In your letter you were angry about news some deceitful men had told you about me.

How can I persuade you that their words are untrue? I fully remember your words about not making wagers, and how it is better to throw silver into the sea.

How can you think that your son would forget the advice of his own father? Please tell me that these things have not been said to the lady Ankhiriyt or her daughter Nodjmet.

It is true that in this foreign city there are places where a man can lose wealth by gambling. At least, so I have been told, and so I believe, though my eyes would be closed as I walked beside such a place. I do not think I would even recognise such a den of thieves if I passed it in the street. You must cast away this untruth and think of me as your loyal son.

For my part, I think of you with respect every day, and not a single hour passes without me speaking your name in blessing to every one of the gods. And along with you, of course I praise my beloved mother, the lady Hemesherit, who is in every way an adornment to our Beloved Land.

Speak pleasant words to my sister Mereriyt and tell her that the shawl that she helped to weave has been a warm hand of kindness in the endless cold and damp of this province.

Another thing. I think it quite possible that the commander may move his men north along the Sea Road. We will be moving north, further into this province, to defend the lands of the great king who lives in prosperity and health against his enemies. Perhaps half the garrison of Gedjet will be sent on similar tasks, and we will work closely with the small detachments already scattered here and there in the cities and forts of the land.

If that happens then of course I will be at the commander's side every day. I will still write often, and there will be messengers to carry news to and fro along the road. But pray for your son when the day of danger comes, that I might uphold the family name in a way that you will find honourable.

A SON ADDRESSES HIS MOTHER.

Hekanefer, scribe, to the lady Hemesherit who lives near Min-Nefer, greetings and blessings to you. I write from an outpost along the Sea Road.

Most fruitful and tender of mothers, I pray to every god that you are in good health when you read this. My father said in his last letter that you were anxious for me, so here is a letter in my own writing so that you may know that all is well.

Your concern for my well-being is like seeing the rays of the sun at dawn or hearing the calling of the birds as they arrive from their migration. I know that the news I sent to father about my commander and his forces moving out of Gedjet, north along the Sea Road, must have alarmed you.

But do not be anxious, O best of mothers. I am in the midst of the strongest and most loyal soldiers in every land. Our charioteers are better trained, our runners faster and more fierce, and our scouts have keener senses than any others I know. I am as safe here as if I were in the house of the great king himself, who lives in prosperity and health.

Another thing. My father still writes as if those wicked tales about me might have some truth. Speak to him, most understanding of women, and assure him that your son would not be found in the house of a Kinahny gambler. My eyes are closed to such things; my thoughts attend completely to my duties. I have heard the soldiers speak in whispers of these things, but even they would hesitate to enter such a place.

Another thing. I know how very kind-hearted you are, and your inmost being would be consumed with pity and grief at many of the sights I have had to endure. We have learned that at least some of the tales that have reached us from the north are true. Great cities have fallen to some unknown enemy, and the King of the North has even lost battles in the open field as well.

If that king asks for help, of course the Beloved Land will answer. The treaty of brotherhood between that king and our own supreme lord who rules over all the world has stood firm for a hundred years, and we will not be counted as faithless. But he may not ask, for he is a stubborn man who is puffed up with his own importance.

I cannot say how these defeats have happened, and I am sure that our own soldiers and officers will acquit themselves better. But I was speaking of the dreadful sights we have seen.

We have started to come across groups of people who have left their homes and their land and fled south for their very lives.

You would weep to see mothers and children with nothing now to their name except for what they carry. The fortunate ones have a small cart which they drag by hand, since their pack beasts have been lost or eaten. Once or twice I have seen little trolleys pulled by a household dog, since no donkey or ox could be found.

They say that more of these refugees are still in the Fenku lands, further north in Djahy, but we have met a considerable number already. It seems that great throngs are coming south. How will this land receive so many more people? How will they find food or shelter?

Our commanding officer has made a wise order, that we are not to give out of our own rations. Our men will need their full strength to fight this enemy, if indeed he dares stand up against the armies of the sun of suns who rises in splendour over every land.

Some unscrupulous men in the ranks were making outrageous demands of these women in exchange for food and beer. I myself was involved in punishing one man, a scoundrel who was thinking to become rich out of their misfortune. He is from the Beloved Land: he should know better.

If you were here, my mother, I am sure that you would find a way to comfort these people. As for us, our duty is clear, though dreadful. We must continue to march north past them so that we can stand in their defence. The best way to help these people is to shut our suffering ears to them and hold firmly to the lands which are rightfully ours.

Once again, mother, I pray to all the gods that you are in good health and good fortune as you read this letter. Remember to speak to my father and assure him of the strength of my commitment to duty. Praise my name to Ankhiriyt mother of Nodjmet when you meet.

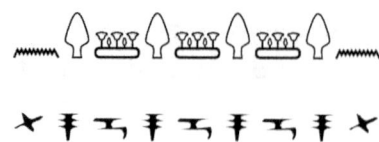

L ABAYU STEPPED FROM HIS DOOR into the early light. Now that the villagers of this clan had cleared the belt of trees just below the crest of the hill, he could see all the way south across the valley to the wooded ridge opposite. It was a magnificent view. Behind him and to his left, the houses swept in a arc either side of the track that led down towards the Sea of Kinreth. One day soon they would finish the circle and have a settlement that was more defensible.

The mist was hanging in thick swathes in the creases of the land, and the late winter sun was slow to warm it away. Normally at this time, he would be listening to the familiar sound of Ashtartiy starting the grindstone on its daily cycles. Around homes and behind doors, work was starting in Ramath-Galil, and he lifted his hand in acknowledgment as Shemiram went by the house to check his overnight snares for game. But Ashtartiy was no longer here.

He turned to go back in, when he was stopped by the sight of a youth running up the track. He was wearing the kef of the town of Merom, but tied around his arm just now so as not to restrict his movement.

He reached the open ground in the middle of the houses and stopped, catching his breath in great gulps of air. He looked round at the doors and windows, waiting for a response. There was a short pause, and then Pedayah, the village headman, walked over towards him, carrying the cup of welcome.

As Labayu joined the growing circle of curious people, the youth finished the cup and handed it back to Pedayah. He was breathing steadily now, and the flush of exertion was fading. He tied his kef properly and looked around the ring of faces, waiting for permission to speak. Pedayah nodded.

"A bright morning to you, lad."

"And a morning of light to you, sir, and to your people."

They exchanged formal greetings between Pedayah and the youth's own headman for a short time. Finally that was done.

"Look now, what brings you to us today, and in haste?"

The lad looked down at the cold ground briefly, the better to remember the words he had been told.

"Sir, I have been sent around with a word from the clan head Shillem. The word says that the king of Hatsor is sending men and chariots both. Large numbers of them, far more numerous than your whole village. He is demanding more tribute, and he will also take some more of your young men with him as runners. He will be here on the third day from now, or perhaps the day after. The clan head Shillem says that each settlement is to make its own choice how to act."

There was a ripple of discontent around the circle, but until the headman replied, nobody would speak aloud. Labayu waited along with the others. The news was not unexpected, and Pedayah had already sat with the elders to discuss their response. For a short time, only the breeze from the west stirred the hilltop village.

"I say that we will leave Ramath-Galil for the time being. We will move south for a time to be closer to the rest of our people. I will not give away our wealth or our sons to Hatsor."

A collective sigh came from the group. Pedayah rounded on them abruptly.

"You all knew this would happen. We will leave now, but we will come back to these houses that we have built before the year is out. This is nothing new for us. I remember wandering as a child, and to wander was the life of our fathers. It is nothing new."

He looked at Labayu.

"Is there any news from your scouts that would lead me to make a different choice?"

"Not yet, sir. I am waiting for Shimmigar to return from the north. There are odd stories we hear of new people arriving there. Some say they come peacefully in ox carts, others that they form great bands to attack cities. But it is as you say: we cannot wait longer."

Pedayah turned away. Labayu knew that he was disappointed by the response. There was nothing to be done – if there was no word from his scouts, he was not going to make one up just to make the headman feel comfortable. Pedayah turned back to the youth who had brought the message.

"Take refreshment before you go, lad, and then take the message on to the other villages. Tell them that we will be moving down to Sychem. We will leave today, immediately after noon. When you return home, take my respect back to clan head Shillem, and thank him for his thoughtfulness. We will return to our homes here as soon as we can."

The group started to disperse. Most families had already gathered their possessions together the previous night, ready to go. However, there were always a few things more to pack, and bulky items to be hidden away in the folds and creases of the land outside the sown patch. Two households had chosen to remain: the family who maintained the village shrine refused to abandon their calling, and their closest kin would stay with them.

Pedayah called Labayu over to him.

"If ever there was a time when your Sons of Anath plan was going to prove its worth, it is now. But you have brought me nothing. You give me no choice except to abandon the village."

"If there is no news, there is no news."

"No news is no use to me. I expected more. Abiy'el told me to expect great things from you."

Labayu shrugged.

"I have no interest in rumour. From what we know, leaving here is the best plan. We always knew that. Your choice is the best one now."

"So you have heard nothing at all?"

Labayu frowned, then decided against his better judgement that it was worth saying something.

"As I said, I am expecting Shimmigar in a day or so. He has been further north, past Hatsor on the west side, near Bayth Ma'acath, trying to find out more about these people I spoke about. He has been tracking a couple of groups here and there. See now, the groups in ox carts and those who plunder cities are the same people. The young men roam here and there in the land to raid: the women, the older men, and the children ride the carts behind them. If they have sacked cities then the king of Hatsor should fear them more than us."

"Will this Shimmigar be back here before my people leave?"

"Most likely not. I will wait for him and catch you up on the way south."

"So whatever news he brings, my decision is the same."

"It is."

"And can I know that these new people will be friends to us?"

"You cannot. But you should try to talk with them. They are the enemy of our enemy. There is hope here. They may become new allies; together we may be able to challenge the king of Hatsor."

"Unless they see us simply as vassals of the king, and fair game for their hunt. I cannot take that risk."

The headman turned away, then glanced over his shoulder.

"I suppose you don't care much for the northern families. You should keep yourself in the south, where you belong."

Labayu ignored his words and returned to his house. He had become used to frequent unpleasantness about his origins since moving up from his native town of Kephrath three years ago. He liked the region, which still had the wildness of a border territory. The hill country north of Kephrath was starting to fill with Ibriym settlements, and places that had been deserted for years now seemed crowded to him.

His people had been the first to cut a covenant with the Ibriym when they arrived. It was within Labayu's lifetime, but only just, and he did not remember the time before they came. In the south of the land there were feelings of affinity, of acceptance, but not here. Once you journeyed north past Sychem it was always the same. The family groups which had settled up here seemed unable to remember that not all Kinahny people were the same, and that some had been in alliance right from the start.

He went back in to his house. It was almost empty. He had collected what few items remained from the two side rooms into the larger main area. Even within this, he only really used the half with the cooking fire now. The rest was so much spare space. It was stark, and unlovely: a fitting mirror to his own feelings.

He had heard of the king of Hatsor's planned sweep around the edges of the Galil a half-month ago, and had sent his wife Ashtartiy, with their two children, back south to her mother's house in Giybon straight away. The king's soldiers would almost certainly seize him for their wars if they knew of his skill. He had wanted freedom to escape into the wilderness when they came, and sending Ashtartiy back to Kephrath was the simplest way to do that.

The children were more upset than either adult. Ashtartiy had never liked the north, and the marriage arranged by her parents had only ever reached mutual acceptance rather than fondness, still less love. She had only reluctantly agreed to come with him to Ramath-Galil when Abiy'el had asked him to go, and was more outspoken than he was about the regular hostility from the clan here, both men and women. It had always seemed like exile to her, and she had seized the chance to go south again with relish.

He wondered, again, whether his choice to bring her north was one cause of their estrangement. Not least among the differences between Kephrath and the settlements of the Ibriym was the place of a woman. Ashtartiy had grown up with the expectation that the household would be hers: a man would be invited in as husband, but the household passed from mother to daughter. The household stood or fell according to the woman's management, and she established its place in the wider community.

But this was not so among the Ibriym, where sonship was all-important. Whenever Labayu, through force of long habit, introduced himself through his mother's name, he met with looks of derision. It was worse for Ashtartiy, who was never acknowledged by others in her own house as anything other than Labayu's wife. She felt her dignity had been swept away, and resented it bitterly.

Labayu went into the empty house. Not for the first time, he wondered why he stayed in this northern region. There were other men like him, others who called themselves Sons of Anath, who plied the same trade east across the River, or south where the land became arid and inhospitable, or west down to the coastal plain where the soldiers of the Mitsriy still patrolled. Each of those had its own challenges, but at least they did not face disdain and rejection every day. The northern settlements were the least friendly towards his people.

When Abiy'el had asked him, the task had sounded exciting, challenging. The idea of leading a small band of skilled fighters around the northern marches of the land had seemed inspiring. They would watch over the scattered villages of the Galil and the Merom hills and try to push the boundaries outward. But the effort was wearing him down like the grain that

Ashtartiy used to grind every day. Perhaps he should simply tell Abiy'el he needed a change.

Labayu had wanted to talk the problem over with his father, but he had died three years before. He had worked his whole life as trapper and hunter, and had carried weapons in anger only a handful of times. Labayu had been inspired to defend the land against human prey, using those same skills to hunt and trap hostile enemies. But inspiration could only make so much headway against constant prejudice.

He looked around. Except for his pack of travelling supplies and weapons, there was nothing more he wanted to take with him. Ashtartiy had taken what she could, and he would simply leave the remaining pieces. The headman and his people would be expecting to return to fill the village again at some point, but he would not mind if he never saw the place again.

ᚷ ᚠ ᚱ ᚠ ᚱ ᚠ ᚱ ᚠ ᚷ

TWO DAYS LATER, LABAYU SAT ALONE in his doorway, in the almost-empty village. Only the family members of the shrine-tender, together with that of her brother, were still nearby. Even they had prepared a place to hide nearby for when Hatsor came. They would stay there while the king's soldiers came through the village, and then emerge later.

The rest of the population, a hundred or so adults and children, had left just as Pedayah had wanted. Noon had scarcely passed on the day the lad had come with Shillem's message when they were on their way. It was getting close to the time that Labayu expected the men of Hatsor to arrive. The morning had almost passed already, and he had become decidedly anxious.

Shimmigar was overdue. Labayu had no particular doubts about his ability to avoid the men of Hatsor, since he knew the land so well, but nevertheless he was worried about his friend. There was no shortage of danger in the lands north of Kinreth, and all of his squad were realistic about their future. He wondered again how long he should delay before following the rest of Ramath-Galil south towards Sychem.

He knew that he would be able to hide near the village as long as he wanted, but if he was to be of any use to Pedayah on the southward journey he needed to move soon. As it was, he would scarcely catch them before they reached Sychem. How long should he wait for Shimmigar?

At first there had been plenty to do to pass the time; most of the usual daily tasks still had to be done. Then he had busied himself by sharpening and finishing off some more arrowheads.

When he had tired of that, he had started scratching his name on each one as the seer and priest had taught him as he grew up. Then he had added, slowly at first, Anath's name to the other side. He snorted in amusement. All his life he had identified himself as Labayu son of Shaharti, and putting Labayu son of Anath was a real difficulty. But Shaharti's name was longer, and the blade was not large enough for it.

It had been Abiy'el's idea. He wanted to call together a group of independent fighters and name them after Anath. She was a goddess that inspired fear more than love: she stalked the land for retribution, quite unlike the renewal offered by her altogether gentler niece Taliy. So the Sons of Anath had been born.

Labayu had been chosen to lead the group here in the north, insofar as such a varied crew could be led. His people had for years conducted raids down into the coastal lowlands for petty gains of livestock, silver, or the occasional slave. Now he was responsible for more serious forays into the unsettled areas in the northern marches.

Most of these Sons of Anath were drawn from his own people, or from others who had also joined with the settlers in covenant. The Ibriym were still learning the ways of this land, and in truth were not yet very practiced in the skills needed for the work. To Abiy'el, it had seemed the ideal way to serve the interests of both his own people and their new allies.

Not all of Abiy'el's people shared this view, however, and resentment ran close to the surface. Even the name was becoming something of a controversy. Labayu's own people appreciated it, along with others who had grown up here in the land, but some of the Ibriym did not. There was a small but vocal faction who wanted no dealings with the gods of the land. Perhaps one day they would have to call themselves the Sons of Yahu instead. He looked at the name he had inscribed on the arrowheads: Yahu would fit there as easily as Anath.

A voice called out, and looking out northward he saw Shimmigar cutting across the open meadow between the scrub and the houses. Akiy was with him. They both looked uninjured, but weary, as though they had travelled a long way with little rest. The shrine-tender's husband looked out briefly from his door, and then slammed it again when he saw them.

Labayu stood up and raised his arm in welcome. Shimmigar and Akiy jogged over to him. Their breath was loud in the quiet air. He poured them some mixed wine and water and waited as they gathered themselves. They stood in the shade at the front of the house: the sun was bright, but not yet hot.

Shimmigar threw back the first beaker in a single swallow, held the empty vessel out for a second, and laid his pack nearby, along with a second bundle, long and thin. It clanked metallically, and Labayu glanced briefly at it as he poured more wine.

"You're later than we planned?"

"And lucky to get here this soon. We were going to rest another night up near Kedesh and get here at first light tomorrow, but we heard that Hatsor's men were coming and thought we should hurry."

"I think they'll be here today."

"Indeed they will. We saw them toiling up the track not far away. The first of them will be here very soon."

"I should tell the shrine-tender and her family. And we should be going. You can tell me the rest as we walk."

They left the house, and Labayu headed across to the remaining pair of occupied houses.

"Still just a shrine-tender? No priest and seer?"

"Too small yet. There's a man and his wife come up the track from Kinreth once a month, and for some of the festivals. The headman here has hopes of getting a priest here before long."

Akiy laughed.

"Good old Pedayah. It's not hope he has, but ambition."

The door opened, and the shrine-tender's husband looked out at them without friendship.

"I suppose you are leaving now?"

"We are. The king of Hatsor's men will be here shortly, and we will be well gone by then. Is there a word you want us to carry to Pedayah?"

The man shook his head. Shimmigar saw the shrine-tender behind him in the house and grinned at her.

"A fair day to you, lady."

The door slammed shut again. Shimmigar shrugged, and then laughed.

"A wonder you put up with this, day after day."

Labayu turned down the hill to head south, but Shimmigar pointed instead back the way he and Akiy had come from, along a short ridge and into the scrub.

"You need to see this for yourself, chief."

"I told Pedayah I would follow after him as soon as I left here."

"He can wait. You should see this first. But we'll be away from the village now, before Hatsor gets here."

Labayu looked south again, considering. In truth there was no real need for him to catch up with Pedayah and the others yet, and his curiosity had been aroused by the little that had been said. He nodded and turned back north.

"North it is, then. Enough distance from here that Hatsor will not look for us, then you must tell me what you have seen."

⋏ ╪ ⊼ ╪ ⊼ ╪ ⊼ ╪ ⋏

L ABAYU, SHIMMIGAR AND AKIY TROTTED for a while down the gentle slope amongst the budding trees, then up again along a steeper track. Once they had put the distance of a couple of ridges between them and Ramath-Galil they halted in amongst a group of boulders. Shimmigar unwrapped the long package he had been carrying.

"Take this one first."

He passed over what seemed at first to be a bronze leaf, attached to the end of a broken wooden shaft. Labayu took it and turned it in his hands. It was shaped like one of the arrowheads he had been working on earlier, but was considerably larger, and the shaft was thicker than anything he would normally use.

"Too big, isn't it? It's not going to come off the bow very well. Nor have the range. Why were you trying this out?"

Akiy laughed, and exchanged a knowing glance with Shimmigar.

"I said he wouldn't see it."

Labayu looked from one to the other.

"All right: what am I missing here?"

Shimmigar took it from him, held the broken-off shaft in his hand and made as if to throw it.

"What if you didn't use a bow?"

Labayu sat back and nodded with realisation.

"It's for throwing? A javelin? But still, you'd never get the range. Somebody with a bow would always have the advantage."

"Leave that a moment then, and look at this."

The second item in the bundle was a sword, perhaps half as long again as the one that Labayu used. He frowned, picked it up to gauge its quality.

"I haven't seen a blade like this before. Good at the slash, not so good at the thrust, I think. The balance is further out from the hilt. And it's heavy. I wouldn't want to use it for too long at a time."

He put it down on the ground and looked at it quizzically. Shimmigar got out his own sword and lined up the hilts to compare the two. Side by side, the extra length of the new weapon was striking.

"It makes your sword look like an ox goad."

"I can still kill my enemies with this ox goad."

Labayu picked the long sword up again. With the hilt, it was as long as his arm.

"You'd have the advantage of reach with this, if only you could finish the fight quickly enough." He looked at the other two. They had sobered from their earlier humour. "Look now, who is using weapons like this? I still don't understand the javelin, but I can see a use for a sword like this. But these must belong to outsiders?"

Shimmigar nodded.

"There are whole clans of them coming south. The fighting men are grouped together in packs, mostly down the Sea Road but some inland. The others, families and older men, they are coming this way in ox carts. I told you this before. The ox carts, the fighting men: the same people. From what we heard, some have settled along the way but the main groups are still coming."

"Where do they come from?"

"Hard to tell. They speak a different tongue. My guess is they are from out east somewhere, but it is only a guess. But it's not where they come from that is important. You need to hear about how they fight. Then these weapons will make sense to you."

He paused, and Akiy took up the story.

"This is why we were late, chief. We came on a small group of these people, up past Leshem. Mostly young lads, one or two older men leading them. They were careless: never saw us from start to end. We watched them closely, listened to their speech – not that that did us any good – and just before we were going to come away they encountered some chariots from the king of Leshem. We hid out of sight, thinking they would avoid the fight, but not at all. They lined up with those javelins that you've seen, and taunted them to attack. We watched these newcomers spread out in a narrow line, and the chariots did what they always do, coming up towards them and wheeling a short distance away so the bowman aboard could get in a couple of shots."

"So Akiy and I hid there. Now I won't say that these were the best charioteers I've ever seen, and they missed far too often with their bows. But these lads were fast on their feet, and when they threw their first javelins that was easily a third of the chariots gone."

Labayu looked from one to the other. "What do you mean, gone?"

"That's what I'm telling you. They didn't aim for the bowmen or the driver: they went for the horses. A two-horse chariot with one horse dead – or even lamed – well, it just stops in its tracks."

"So each of these lads had two javelins, a few had three, and when they were done there were hardly any chariots still on the move."

"They clashed each other, you see, chief, once the formation was spoiled."

"So then they ran forward with these long swords of theirs and finished it off – of course the runners and the fallen riders were no match at all by then. Not once they were down like that, not up against these swords."

Labayu picked up the javelin end again in one hand and the sword in the other.

"So a gang of youths on foot defeated chariots?"

Both men nodded.

"Look, it was only a small formation, not even a half wing, and these youths lost some to arrows, and a few in the fight afterwards. We picked these weapons up from one of the fallen who was off to one side, while the others were stripping the bodies. But most of them were untouched and ready to fight again. Of the chariots, I reckon just a couple got clean away, and some of the runners just ran for it when they saw what was happening. Who knows where they ended up: back at their home towns without ever going back to the king is my guess. Leshem lost that whole lot as a fighting force."

They fell silent, waiting for Labayu to make a decision. He stood up, looked around to make sure there was still nobody overlooking their position, and then turned to face south, where Pedayah had gone with the other villagers. Some way off, he caught a glimpse of a family of deer grazing amongst the thin vegetation. The spring growth had not yet started in earnest, and they would need to roam at some length to gather enough food.

"Well. Should the people of Ramath-Galil hear this first, or should I see these people with my own eyes before going to them?"

He turned again to the two men.

"If we had known how to fight like this we could have made better work about pushing down into the lowlands. It was chariots that stopped us doing that a few years ago, and we had no idea how to face them on foot. Hushim's men just had to abandon the attempt and come north. Maybe they'll have a chance to cut out some space here if Leshem has been defeated. But if we learn how to fight in this way, we can spread further. Do you think these new people would ally with us?"

Shimmigar shrugged. "We were not minded to talk with them, just to see what was happening and report back. And I do not think that there were any true leaders there to make covenant with, just young lads and a few older men directing the fighting. You would need to find their clan heads first."

Labayu thought about the problem, while the other two men waited for him. Before too long he had made up his mind.

"Look, Shimmigar, I need to make sure Pedayah knows about these people. Not that he will appreciate me taking the time to tell him, but I think it is my duty. And more important, I need to make sure that Abiy'el has heard. I need to take these weapons to show him as well."

Shimmigar wrapped them up again and passed the bundle to him.

"Take them. I have no use for them. And if I want more I know where to get them. Now, if we found an unbroken one of these javelins I would keep it and train myself how to use it. It's a handy thing."

"Do you want us to come with you, chief?"

"No. I want you two to find this band again, or another one like it, and trail them. You said they were careless, so I suppose you can do that without being seen?"

They nodded.

"And see if you can pick up some of the others on the way. Even two or three would make a difference. I shall be a day or two following Pedayah south, then a bit longer catching you up again. Where did you say you found them before?"

"Some way north of Merom, chief, inland from the Fenku lands."

"Then one of you meet me at the oak grove by Gath-Leshem on the sixth day from now. The other, and whoever else you find, keep following them. When we all meet I'll be able to see them for myself."

"What will you do?"

"I don't know yet. Let's follow this plan first before deciding what happens next."

The two men nodded, and then Labayu took the weapons and set off at a lope. He would need to swing wide around Ramath-Galil in order to avoid Hatsor's men, and then make very good time to fulfil his promise to Shimmigar and Akiy.

Richard Abbott

Part 2 – Hatsor

THE FOREIGNERS PLOT in their islands,
  scatter in war all the north-lands.
Khatti and Kode, Arzawa and Alashiya
  desolate as if they had never been.
They came towards The Beloved Land,
  the flame was before them,
  their hands and hearts raised,
  high and boastful –
but the heart of this god was ready.

Richard Abbott

A NILAT, AUNTIE AND THE CHILDREN sat in silence. At first shouting still resounded from the street outside, but it slowly moved away to other places. When the quiet had lasted without interruption for long enough, Anilat shook Haleyna awake again, while Auntie woke the twins. There was a short time of protest, then little whispers in the dark.

Auntie slid the bolt open on the trapdoor and lifted it slowly. Little motes of dust sparked in the shaft of light from the spy hole. A noise came from the outside door, men's voices pitched low and anxious. The two women exchanged looks, then Anilat forced herself back to look out into the room again. Auntie lowered the hatch even more slowly and carefully than she had opened it.

The voices came closer, moving between room and corridor as they searched the house. Anilat was trembling, and gripped the rough stonework to steady herself. She could not make out words, just a murmur of speech and footfalls.

The first man came into her view, cautiously peering round the edge of the doorway. Anilat found herself breathing again. The man, though dishevelled and ragged, wore the emblem of one of the city nobles on his shoulder. He looked around the room, winced at the sight of the two bodies, and called softly to the others.

There were three men in the little squad, all wearing tokens of one or other of the leading houses. The man who had first appeared glanced through both of the doors at the head of the room to check they were safe, then came back to the chair. Gathering some of the torn clothing, he covered Anilat's mother as best he could.

The last man to arrive had tied a band around the top of his arm. It was stained with blood, but showed her husband's colours and household mark alongside that of one of the other nobles. Overcome with relief, Anilat called out from her hiding place. The men jerked, looking around anxiously to see where the voice came from.

"Men, men, we're hidden over here in a secret room, wait there until we come out to you."

Auntie pulled the trapdoor open again, making no effort this time to be quiet. The women bundled the children down the steps, along underground, and back up again beside the household shrine. Auntie stopped with the children in the corridor.

"Mistress, I'll stop here with the little ones while you talk to those soldiers. I don't think the children should see your honoured mother like that."

Anilat nodded and, drawing herself in an attempt at pride, went into the audience chamber. The men were in a little group facing towards her. Close up, she could see that they had narrowly escaped from a fierce struggle. The leader, the one who was wearing her husband's colours on his arm, came over to her.

"The lady of the house? Lady Anilat? My name is Khuratsanitu. Your husband, the lord Tadugari son of Anziniy, charged me with the duty of seeing to your safety. At least, as best I can in all this ruin."

Anilat was staring with morbid fascination at her mother's body. It had been mostly covered over with cloths by the soldiers, but one leg was still exposed. Her face, oddly peaceful, looked up to and beyond the ceiling. The soldier followed Anilat's eyes.

"You knew this woman, lady?"

She nodded, nearly retained her self-control, but broke into a sudden wail.

"My mother. She stayed... she stayed in here while we were hiding."

The soldier nodded, stood beside her in a solemn, erect posture. Anilat realised that he meant it as a sign of respect.

"My officer did the same. It's the only reason I got away from the palace. He stopped in there at a door so me and the boys could get out." They stood there for a few heartbeats before he shuffled his feet. "But we can't be here any longer, lady. It's not safe, not any more."

Anilat nodded, knelt beside her mother's body, closed the eyes and kissed them. A bitter smell lingered around her lips, and Anilat realised that one hand was still clenched fiercely around the little black bottle. She rose slowly to her feet, accepting the help the soldier offered her. Then she turned away and walked towards Auntie and the waiting children.

They moved outside. The lead soldier turned to her.

"Where to next, lady? Your honoured husband told me to set towards the shepherds' huts on the hill road, but now you're here the choice is yours."

She nodded. "He said as much to me." She looked around vaguely. "Which way should we go?"

One of the three cursed vehemently, and spat into the road.

"I'm not going to any shepherd's hut. I should never have come this far with you. I'll take my chances somewhere else."

Before any of them could say anything he had run off down a side street. She looked at the two remaining soldiers.

"What now? Will you leave us too?"

"No, lady. I gave my word to your honoured husband and I'll see it through. Out to the huts at least, we'll see you safe out to there. He'll tell us what to do once we meet up, I've no doubt."

The younger man nodded as well. They went on a cautious way, winding to and fro through the maze of streets. Here and there in the distance they could hear and see the sounds of the city's rape. Anilat followed the lead without thinking, not recognising any of the paths or buildings. It was one of the poorer regions, emptied already of its occupants.

The streets and alleyways were twisted and narrow compared to the wide lanes near her own home, and the houses pressed close together. Roofs and doors were low, and the stones were raggedly fitted together. Refuse and waste lay thickly in the corners and ruts. There had been little enough here to attract the invaders, but even so the shadow of their passage lay heavily on it.

Bodies of men and women, old and young, were scattered in and out of the buildings. Anilat's children trotted past the corpses with blank eyes, and Anilat herself was soon beyond noticing the marks of violence. She knew nobody who came from this quarter of the town, and had long since stopped looking to see if she recognised faces.

Once, while they hurried across an open source near the top of a hill, they caught sight of a great mass of people pressed together along the main city artery, leading towards the great gates down from the palace and temple. There was a noise of confusion and inchoate pain, and the struggling crowd was illuminated only by the flames of burning buildings to either side. From time to time packs of men, like jackals, harried the edges of the crowd and snatched victims away.

Down by the docks the fires seemed to be settling into a steady blaze, while nearer buildings, more recently set alight, rushed up in sudden flurries of sparks. Anilat stopped to catch her breath at the highest point of the ridge and turned, trying to catch sight of her own house, but it was lost in the confusion. The second soldier urged her on; Anilat abruptly realised she did not know his name.

They reached the open space in front of the middle gate. Khuratsanitu eased his way slowly forwards to check that nobody was around, then waved the others on from where they had crouched behind some wreckage. The gate stood wide open, with its bolts and bars forced back. Two or three guards lay dead nearby, along with some other fighting men that none of them recognised.

The group slipped out through the gate. The stone arch rose high over them, impotent in its failure to protect the city.

Outside, there was a small crossroads. To left and right, roughly levelled tracks curled around the walls to join the Sea Road. Ahead of them, the path heading towards the ridge of hills to the east was clear and open. Apparently the city occupants were trying to escape away down the coast rather than inland.

They continued past a few bends in the track, keeping going until the city wall had slipped from sight and the way began to rise up from the coastal plain. The leading soldier looked at the women and children and called a halt. They turned to one side and settled among some stones, hidden by a screen of bushes from anyone moving along the road.

They shared out some food and passed around a skin of weak wine. Nobody spoke for a long time. Finally the younger soldier shook his head.

"I heard someone in the palace say that some of our own men opened the gates to them."

Anilat looked at him in disbelief, but he persevered.

"And they rushed the walls like animals. With most of the army away north serving with the great king there were just not enough of us."

The leader shook his head, took another swig of the wine.

"Seems to me they landed from those ships of theirs. The first fighting was down by the docks. Then some of them got through to the north gate and opened it up for the rest. When they defeated the few ships we had in home waters there was nothing to stop them."

Auntie nodded. "The first fires we saw were down that way. Then it spread wider."

Haleyna looked around as though she was only just realising where they were. "Where's father?"

The adults exchanged glances. "He will meet us at one of the huts along the road here, Haleyna. That was the word he sent to us."

The soldier nodded. "That's what he told me as well."

Anilat found herself breathing hard, and her hands were clenched tight. Who knew what might have happened in the city that night?

"You were right beside him then? What did he say? Where did he go?"

"I was right beside him, lady. He sent me away from the palace with a few of the lads to get to your house before anyone else. He said he would meet you all at the shepherds' huts up along the track."

"Are they far away?"

"Not far, child. The rest of the journey is easy now, but the road climbs a bit just round the next bend."

But Anilat was still thinking over the soldier's words.

"Why did he not come with you? Did he stay at the palace?"

"No indeed, lady. Look, a group of us was cut off from the main buildings. Out in one of the scribal houses. We just about got the inner door closed when that mob forced the main gate. That's when my officer stayed back so the rest of us could make it through."

He fell silent, his expression closed. Anilat persevered.

"But my husband?"

"Oh. Yes, lady. We could see it was no use being in the palace. He was the only one there who could give orders like this, the rest of us being just commoners, so we all looked to him. Though he's not a fighting man. No disrespect, lady, he said as much himself."

Anilat nodded impatiently. The other soldier nudged him.

"Get to the point, Khuratsanitu, the lady wants to know where he went. We'll be here all night the way you're doing it."

The first man shook his head. "Look, Tarmanni, I was telling it the way it happened. Now I've lost my way in the telling."

He took off the leather cap he was using as helmet, stared at it, and loosened a buckle slightly. The younger man looked at him, shook his head, and continued.

"Lady, we all slipped out of the slaves' entrance into the street. There were six of us then besides him. He wanted three of us to go with him and the other three to come for you. But a couple of the lads just ran for it as soon as we were out of there, none of us could stop them. So us three came this way and he took just one with him. Just before we split up he said to us he was going to your brother's house, lady."

She nodded. It made sense that Tadugari would try to rescue her brother's family as well. She tried to piece together memories of the night.

"I think you told me some of this before."

The young man nodded. She pursed her lips, trying to think what else she should know.

"Did he speak about my sister?"

The two soldiers looked at one other. The older man replied.

"Not a word, lady. Whereabouts in the city was she?"

"Up at the temple. She was in training there."

He was shaking his head.

"We were nowhere near there, lady. But it won't be good for her. Not from what I know of the way this rabble came through the city. I heard one of the other lads saying. . ."

The younger man jabbed his ribs and interrupted.

"We don't know about that either way, lady. But look now, your brother's house. Why will your honoured husband have gone there?"

Anilat was still caught up in the first man's words. The temple area was some distance from the way they had taken through the poorer quarter, so they could not have been near her. Her heart was overwhelmed, though, with the idea that one of the mistreated bodies that had passed had been that of Djoseret-Ibeti.

She stood up, hands trembling, and looked back down the hill. The walls, and the middle gate, were hidden by the land's swell, but a red glow flickered in the sky, reflecting off the low clouds. A pillar of smoke was drifting slowly south.

Auntie looked at her, took one of her shaking hands, and replied for her.

"There are two older children at his house. Well, there were. My lady's husband will have gone to fetch them."

The older man shook his head.

"Just what we need. More children."

Anilat did not hear him, lost still in the dark coils of her own imagination. Auntie gave him a sharp look. The other soldier interceded.

"There might be some household guards as well. Could be a regular party when we all meet up. Either way, we need to get moving again."

Anilat said nothing, but came over and started chivvying the children. The younger soldier, Tarmanni, had scrambled up on top of a ridge to one side and was looking back towards the city. She joined him, leaving Auntie to finish gathering the group together.

New fires were leaping up in parts of the city which had previously been untouched, but older ones were dying down into a steady glow of heat. At this distance from the city, the river of people flowing out of the southern gate could not be seen.

"I wonder why nobody else came this way?"

"Well, lady, everyone thinks this lot came down from the north. So they ran away south. This was a clever plan of your noble husband's. Nobody else thought of it."

She touched the pouch containing her mother's relics, hidden underneath her smock.

"But we will go south ourselves, will we not? In the end, I mean."

"Not for me to say, lady. But that's the only way that makes sense. I expect the lord Tadugari had in mind to follow the hill tracks inland and find a way down to Hatsor that goes nowhere near the Sea Road."

"Will we be safe at Hatsor?"

She had never been there, and knew it only from accounts brought back by travellers. Her mother had had spies in the king's palace there. Beside her, the soldier said nothing. After a short time she moved carefully back down the sandy slope and hugged each of the children in turn. At least they were still with her.

〱〺〱〺〱〺〱〺〱

ANILAT AND THE CHILDREN started to climb as the track started up the ridge. At first, until the place where they had halted, the way had been surfaced with stones and padded earth. Now it was just a rough path through the leafless bushes. In late spring it would be a glorious place, alive with flowers. Just now it was dismal.

They wound to and fro amongst the marks of sheep and donkeys, buffeted from their left by the north wind. As they approached the crest the soldiers halted again by some rocks at a sharp bend.

"Best wait here, lady, with the children, while we take a look."

The men branched off the path and moved as quietly as they could through the scrub. Anilat sat beside the track, her hand on Haleyna's shoulder. Auntie was still standing, an arm around each of the twins. There was a long pause while nobody spoke. Anilat found herself consumed by a despairing lassitude.

"They're coming back, mistress. With somebody else, too. I can't tell if it's the master, it's too dark. I think, I think there's more than just one more person with the lads."

Anilat looked, stood up very slowly, breathed slowly. Her innards shivered with the wait. Haleyna, with better eyes in the gloom, pulled away before she could stop her. She ran over to the group as it drew closer, calling out as she went.

"Dantiy, Yasib, you're here. I'm so glad."

The formless group became people, became her husband along with her brother's children. The shivering inside turned itself into sobs, and her cheeks were wet with tears. She stood, unable to move, as he came over to her and took her hand very carefully, as though she might all too easily break into pieces.

Haleyna finished embracing her cousins, and came back to stand beside Anilat. The twins were moving forward from beside Auntie. They all wanted to receive acknowledgement and blessing from Tadugari, but he stood irresolute, silent, disengaged from all of them after his one act of taking Anilat's hand.

Now that she could see him more clearly, she could see how haggard he looked. The fine clothes she had last seen him in were bloody and torn in places. She bit her lip and felt quickly for wounds on him. He avoided her eyes and looked at nothing, twisting his fingers continually around each other.

"Are you injured, my heart?"

He shook his head, closed his eyes and looked away from them all to where fire and smoke could still be seen against the horizon. He tried to speak, failed, and shook his head again.

The older of the two soldiers cleared his throat and took a step forward.

"Pardon the intrusion, my lord, but should we not get ourselves into the cover of the buildings?"

Tadugari stared blankly at him and then looked around, as though he had forgotten all about the huts nearby. There was an awkward pause. Auntie gathered all the children into a little flock and started shepherding them past the two soldiers towards the shelter.

"Now there's a good idea. Let's all do as the captain says."

Anilat gripped Tadugari's arm and pushed him slightly in the right direction. He started walking with her.

"Is everyone else inside already?"

The muscles of his arm jerked under her fingers.

"My brother, I mean, and Sanay-Sura. Maybe some household guards. Surely they came with you?"

They were at the door. The hut consisted of a single room, roughly divided into two unequal parts by a low stone partition reaching only to knee height. She supposed that in happier days it separated the animals from their keeper. The smaller part was lined with rough stones, while the rest had dung trodden into bare earth.

A stale smell of animals and lack of use hung in the air, and there was nobody in the hut. A fire had been set long before, ready for lighting, and a few part-used wax candles stood here and there, but the stone walls were cold and slightly damp. In some places, water puddled amongst the sheep and goat droppings. It had been empty for a considerable time.

She looked at Tadugari, perplexed.

"Why are the children here, but not my brother and his wife?"

Tadugari sat on the low stone wall and looked at the ground. She could only just hear his reply.

"I met User-Amun near his house. He had tried to get to the temple. To your sister. But there were too many of them. So he came back. I met him near the house. But that filth had been there first. A lot of them."

He stopped, swallowed, and seemed to be casting about for words. Anilat felt a chill across her skin and pulled her shawl closer around her. She flared up and turned on the two soldiers.

"Get that fire going, can't you?" Auntie was still near the door. "Keep the children over there. All of them. And get them doing something useful. I won't have them just standing around."

She sat beside Tadugari.

"Tell me."

He shook his head.

"I never saw anything like it. I cannot speak of it."

He glanced very quickly at her and then avoided her eyes again.

"So when User-Amun saw what they'd done to her he could not contain himself. He took a sword and just ran out into the night, swearing every oath he knew. I sent the bowman who had gone with me from the palace after him. I have no idea where they went after that."

"But you did not go yourself?"

He seemed to be searching for words.

"I went through the house to find Dantiy and Yasib. User-Amun told me to. And to see if there was anyone else left. But there was only the two of them alive. They were hidden in an alcove upstairs, at the back of the house beside the shrine room. You remember, our twins hid up there when they were playing a game last summer. I thought of the place as soon as I went up the stairs. Yasib came right at me when I found them there, with a long knife and all. He didn't know it was me, thought the worst had come. He only just stopped himself before stabbing me with it."

She started to speak again, but he held up his hand and took a long breath.

"Seems that Sanay-Sura put them there, told them not to come out unless they were sure who was nearby. They said they had no idea what happened downstairs. But I think they must have heard. Anilat, they must have heard it all. Everything. I don't want to talk about it."

He stood up abruptly, moved over to the newly lit fire and tried to warm his hands. Haleyna came over to him.

"Are we going to pray the sunset prayer, father?"

He ignored her. Anilat looked at him, then at Haleyna and shook her head.

"Not tonight, I think. It is too late now."

"So the three of us came the fastest way we could. Nobody stopped us, nobody got in our way. And at least you are here. When this place here was empty I thought you had not got away either. I thought it was just me and those two left of our whole family. I thought... I mean... " He stopped abruptly. "I wondered what the point was of escaping at all."

This time when he fell silent she could not bear to ask anything. Each alone, they tried to find sleep.

✣ ✣ ✣ ✣ ✣ ✣ ✣ ✣

THE NEXT MORNING DAWNED with a pale light above the hills. There was hardly any wind, but occasional gusts came from the sea, bringing a smell of smoke and a fine drift of ash. A heavy drift that looked like fog hung across the coastal plain.

Anilat left the hut and went over to Tadugari. The three men had drawn lots for who should stay on watch through the rest of the night, and he had picked the last session. He was staring down towards the coast, and did not notice her until she sat beside him.

She took his arm, kissed his fingers, brushed some loose dust and ash from his sleeve. He made no response, but simply sat there with unseeing eyes.

"What are we going to do now, my husband?"

He shrugged, said nothing. She tried again.

"Where does this track go now? Can we follow it?"

He glanced up the hill.

"Damaseq, Ebla, Emar. Or Qatna, I suppose. Gargamish or Hatsor if we pick up the right road a little further inland. Anywhere, really."

He turned back again to look downhill. Little eddies of on-shore breeze stirred the cloud bank, allowed glimpses of the sea beyond. At this distance it looked calm, placid. He wore a confused, haggard expression.

"It was to be the hunt tomorrow. One of the king's own sons wanted me to ride beside him on the chase, and sit beside him at the feast. I won't be able to do that now. How will I earn his favour again now that I ran away?"

She stared at him in disbelief, and her voice sharpened in anger.

"How can you be thinking of the hunt? My city is ruined. My mother died, and her body was treated vilely before my eyes. My brother and sister are gone, and I have to believe them dead. Out of all this I have my own three children, and my brother's two. And all you can talk about is missing the hunt?"

He hunched down under the torrent of words and said nothing. She looked around in exasperation. The hillsides around the hut were empty and desolate, and the west was shrouded and gloomy. It was a bitter place.

"Well?"

He groaned.

"I should not have left, Anilat."

"What do you mean?"

"I left my friends, my work, my king back there. I could not save your brother or his wife. It would have been more honourable to die inside the walls. Die with the city herself. Your mother was right."

She shook her head, then, realising that he was still not looking at her, shook his arm. Concern was pushing away her rush of anger.

"You came to be with me. With your children. You brought out Dantiy and Yasib. You even saved those soldiers. Even if the rest all die on the road, Ikaret still lives in us. We can go somewhere else. One of those places you mentioned."

"We have no food worth speaking of. No way to survive the journey. Better to stay here, go back into the city in a day or so when it has settled down."

"We have silver and precious things. Mother gave them to me last night. Before..." She stopped, knowing that he had not seen what had happened in the house, knowing also that she did not want to talk about it.

"Anyway, we have wealth that we can barter for supplies."

He looked briefly at her as though a spark of interest had rekindled, then turned away again.

"Well, that is something. Now we just have to decide where to go."

"South. Somewhere south. Is one of those places you mentioned south of here?"

"Damaseq is. And Hatsor. We can find the track that leads to Hatsor easily enough from here. But look, it is not a short journey."

"How long?"

He frowned. "A king's messenger dispatched in haste, able to change horses at will, would complete the journey in a week. If it was just you and I, and all went well, at least two weeks. With the children, and if the journey is hard, perhaps three weeks. But I think it would be better to go east. Away from all this."

"No. I want us to go south."

He looked surprised at her determination, but shrugged. Yasib came out of the little hut and joined them.

"South it is, then. But I am concerned about us all staying as a group. We should split up again. We would move quicker that way."

She shivered. "We have only just met up. And we have lost so much already. I don't know that I can bear the idea of separating. Is there no other way?"

Tadugari refused to meet her eyes. His gaze alternated between the western horizon and the ground at his feet.

"It makes no sense to stay together. We will delay each other. We look a more vulnerable target for anyone of evil intent. And we do not have enough soldiers to protect us. I should have gathered more men as I left. Everything I did yesterday came to a bad end."

"I won't be parted from my children."

There was silence between the three of them. Finally Yasib spoke up.

"Uncle, aunt, look, Dantiy and I will go separately. We can move quickly across the land, and the two of us can hide if we need to. I know the tracks and the waypoints just as well as you do. We can take care of ourselves. Let us decide a place to meet and whoever arrives there first can wait for the other."

Tadugari glanced at him, nodded briefly. Anilat frowned.

"I do not like the thought of the two of you alone like that. Take one of the soldiers with you."

"And leave you with just one guard?"

"I think so. One guard will protect us if need be from hostile villagers. But if we encounter the main pack of these invaders then two are no better than one. Let us not deceive ourselves about that. Husband, what do you think?"

Tadugari shrugged again, then realised that the other two were waiting for him to reply.

"Yes, take one of them. Makes no difference to us. No, in fact, take the younger one. Khuratsanitu has more personal loyalty to me, and I am not sure that he would agree to leave us at this point."

Anilat opened her mouth to protest again, but Yasib nodded calmly in acceptance.

"We should go soon. All of us, I mean. We have no idea how long this place will be safe."

Tadugari stood up, nodded wearily, and started back towards the hut. Yasib followed him, leaving Anilat still standing there.

"No, wait, look, I need to know where we are going. I cannot bear the thought that we will all just go our separate ways. Where are we going to meet up again?"

"Which way do you want to go?"

"South. I told you. I promised my mother I would go south. What about this place Hatsor you mentioned?"

The two men looked at each other.

"Hatsor, then?"

"Hatsor. At first, anyway. Further south than that if we need to. It will take the three of you less time than us, but we should be there within three weeks. If we do not arrive by the next new moon, then assume the worst and make a new life for yourselves."

They roused the others and ate a little food to break their fast. Before long Yasib, Dantiy, and the younger soldier were ready. Anilat stood back while her children said goodbye again to their cousins, then tried not to weep at the unexpected loss she was facing so soon. She watched as the three of them turned up the track and vanished from sight around a curve of the hillside.

Before long their own larger group was ready. Leaving the hut behind, they followed the earlier tracks up the hillside, branching right before long, onto a smaller track. Khuratsan-itu led them without hesitation.

Just before they went into a stand of trees, at the entrance to a small valley, he stopped and turned around.

"This is the last sight we will have of Ikaret, honoured ones."

Anilat turned and gazed for one last time at the dying city. The pall of smoke lay like a shroud over the bay and wreathed the headlands to north and south. The flocks of wading birds were hidden from sight.

Tadugari walked on without looking back, and after a short, uncertain pause, the others followed him. The path meandered into the trees, turning a little to their right as they went.

A MAN ADDRESSES HIS BROTHER.

Hekanefer to Ramose, from a remote and inhospitable spot along the Sea Road.

Well, brother, it seems that my father is forgetting about the stories of my wild and reckless antics which had somehow reached his ears. If it was your words which caused this change of heart, then I am in your debt. But perhaps it was our mother's voice, or even some of my own writing. Or perhaps his thoughts have simply moved on from one thing to another, like a hippopotamus grazing among the reeds.

But also both he and mother keep writing about Nodjmet. Brother, I find myself becoming low in spirit about her. Father is convinced that the match will favour our family. Perhaps it will, but I can raise no enthusiasm about her at all. I can only think of her as a mother of children, and not a feast of delights for me. Our times of coupling were enjoyable, to be sure, but exceedingly brief.

You will know by now that I have been moved north with the whole band of soldiers. Whatever else you might say about this commander, he is certainly determined to show obedience to his orders and to be a good example to his men. From the moment I read out to him the orders that came out from the Beloved Land no time was lost getting the men on the march.

He always steps out at the head of the column leading his men onwards. I had expected a last night of pleasure in "The Two Lands", and then a comfortable sleep in my own bed. But it was not to be. Long before the sun had set we were on the road.

Another thing. You may have heard that travellers are fleeing towards us from Djahy and beyond. I can tell you that this is true. We have passed many of these already. There is good profit to be made supplying them with this and that, for they are in desperate need of supplies, and are carrying a great deal of silver and such like.

The commander frowns upon anything too blatant, however. One of the men, a spearman from near Waset, was beaten with rods nearly to the point of death for being indiscreet about the trade he was making. The foolish man tried to buy a young girl from her own mother to serve his tent, and the family concerned was one of rank. They protested to the commander, and his punishment was swift. But so long as you are careful how you manage things, there is great opportunity.

Another thing, brother. I have lost the scrappy bit of cloth that our sister Mereriyt sent to me. It was far too small to be of any real use, and one night in the camp while I was using it to hold a hot pan it caught alight. I am telling her that I gave it to a homeless child; please uphold me in this if she asks.

This place where we are staying is appalling. There are no comforts here at all, and the commander lets nobody leave the camp and visit the towns nearby. But even if he did let us go, the places are contemptible. There is nothing out here for a man of culture. Their attitude is disrespectful, their houses are like hovels, and their writing is crude and unrefined.

Nothing about this land is worth writing down. Remember me before all the gods that this conflict will soon be over, so that this scribe can come back and live in the place of scribes, and not in some miserable tent pitched in the open field.

A SON ADDRESSES HIS FATHER.

Hekanefer to Nesamenopeh, my esteemed father, greetings and blessings to you. I write from our encampment near the town of Akka, in the region of Djahy.

I must write of shocking news to you, father, so that you hear it from me and not by rumour. Yesterday a whole group of chariots was lost in a skirmish. You can imagine that the hearts of the men have been shaken by this. Our commander is doing a magnificent job at rallying their courage and urging them to ready themselves for the next conflict.

It is like this. For many days we passed groups of people from different towns. One day we began to meet those who had fled Ikaret. Ikaret! Now the leaders of that town were seduced some generations ago by the words of the King of the North, and spurned the benefits of the pact they had enjoyed with us for such a very long time. So perhaps they deserved their fate. But truly it was a great city, and one which we had all thought would stand firm against this inundation.

But no. We have heard how the gates were lost, the king and all his palace put to death, and the city set on fire. The stories do not all agree, and perhaps only the gods will ever know the truth. But for certain that great city will be standing empty and desolate now. They say that many of the people were cut down in the streets and lie there still, unburied and without any kind of decent ceremony.

I will confess, father, that this unsettled me. I saw an older man and woman on the road one day. At a distance, they looked so like you and that best of mothers, the lady Hemesherit, that I almost cried out, left my place at the commander's side, and ran to them. My eyes saw not this unhappy couple but rather the two of you, and in my imagination the flame before them consumed not the towers of Ikaret but our own beautiful house near Min-Nefer.

How I miss that house, and my happy times there when the whole family would gather and be brought food and entertainment by the slaves. How I miss the kindness and nobility of my own parents, my brother, and my sister. How I miss the cool of the garden with its trees around the fish pond, and the paved way winding down to that best of all rivers.

But I must continue. So yesterday, one of our scouts came back with news for us, that a gang of these foreign rebels were advancing only a short distance north of us. They are scattered in small bands here and there in the land, you see, and do not gather themselves into an army. By this time we were some way north, perhaps due west of Damaseq but not far from the coast.

Of course the men were on fire with the desire to show strength, but the commander stayed cool in temperament. He sent a single company of chariots out to meet them, together with their runners, and he himself watched from a vantage point. I stood at his side so that there would be no delay sending his report back to Gedjet and the Beloved Land.

I fear to say that not one of the chariots returned to the camp from that attack, and only about half of the men. The wicked enemy fight like cowards, not arm to arm and eye to eye but at a distance, using javelins which they throw with considerable strength and accuracy. Many of our horses were struck down before the bowmen could truly show their skill. I realised suddenly that if a chariot loses just one horse from its pair, it cannot move. The arrows and, a little later, the sickle swords of our men had some effect, but it was not sufficient.

I was stricken in my inmost being, but took care to faithfully record every word of the commander as he spoke. Because of oaths I have taken, I must not repeat them, not even to you, my honoured father. However, he gave an accurate and detailed description of all that had happened, and a fast horseman set off at once to carry the news southward to the great king who lives in prosperity and health.

That night the commander spoke stirring words to his senior officers, and to me among them. He strengthened the limbs of the weak and rekindled the hearts of the faint. Without shame I count myself among those who had been cast down. For a time my heart had truly melted inside me. But as he spoke I remembered the greatness of our land and of my own ancestors, and was restored, as were we all. We had lost a skirmish, but our people are wise and attentive to lessons learned in times of peril.

At least now we can put a name to our enemies; they are drawn from a number of different tribes with names such as Sherden, Danuna, Peleset and Tjekker. Some I know from the standard lists, but others are new to me. Their homelands, as you will remember, are mostly on the islands in the Great Green Sea to the west of the Khatti-lands. Some have travelled even from the mainland which lies beyond that.

Like locusts, they have plagued the fringes of the Khatti-lands, Alashiya, and so many other places for many years. In the past, they even joined with that wicked enemy among the Rebu, Merey, who was so thoroughly defeated by the great king who has gone to the horizon to become a god, the mighty lord Ba-en-Re Mery-Imun. But never have they appeared before now in such numbers, or pushed so arrogantly along the coastlands.

A time will come very soon when we can meet these invaders on the field again, and on that day we shall not be struck down in this same manner. Instead we will rise up in the name of our great king who lives in prosperity and health, and carry on the tips of our weapons all of his fierce anger and his thirst for vengeance.

So, dear father, speak of me with all the gods, and trust that your son is doing all that he can to ensure that our family name is remembered with praise. Tell my mother that I am entirely unwounded and that, although my hands trembled with the nearness of battle, my heart remained steadfast and strong. Surely I will write again soon. Also I long to read words that you have written in your own hand, so that the refreshing pools of the Beloved Land might water my soul.

NIKLEOS' CLAN CAMPED FOR THE NIGHT in a valley bowl far enough beyond the crest of a ridge that their progress was clear. It had been a long drag upwards through the afternoon. The character of the land had changed again as they had worked their way south, and their pace had slowed considerably. Although the land was flatter, it was clothed with stands of low trees and scrub land. It was not like the great forests that stood further north and nearer the coast, but it was dense enough to seriously impede progress.

The sun was still quite high in the early spring sky when Antos blew his leader's horn to call a halt, but a considerable time passed before they made camp. Finally the wagons were arranged in their circle, the beasts were inside, and fires had been set. The boys who had been tasked with the day's hunting had all come back, prey in hand, and the smell of cooking drifted across the encampment.

He shook his head. With the young men constantly away with the raiding parties, the group was never properly mixed. Boys, older men, and women of all ages filled the camp and shared out the tasks that would normally fall to the lads. Perhaps in a few months they would settle again and life would return to its usual pattern.

Nikleos watched as the women of his family prepared the food. It crossed his mind that Kastiandra was too thin, but that would not change until they found a place to settle. All of them would stay too thin while the journey continued. When he thought back to their life on the other side of the sea, she had had a much more attractive roundness to her form which had been peeled away from her on the journey.

There, in their farmstead just outside the village where Antos had been arkon, there had been lamb and mutton whenever they wanted, plentiful butter and cheese, and honey always available from the bees who inhabited a nearby stand of trees. They had left that all behind when they set sail for Wilios. The men, himself included, had always boarded the quick ships to raid isolated towns or islands, but this was something new.

Families and clans from many different valleys and coastal bays had united that time, stirred up by Akamunas to seize the great prize of Wilios. It had been a fine sight, all those ships together crossing the water. The siege had been long and hard, and it had exposed violent disagreements among the clans themselves, but in the end they had done it. The enterprise had become too big, too prideful, to halt.

The final capture and plunder of the city had soon been turned into song, but it had left his people with a hard choice. Antos had led his people onwards, instead of returning over the sea. Many other village arkons had done the same, eager to find other cities with quick plunder, quite sure that any of them would be easier than Wilios. And so now here they were, heading south through this land of which they knew nothing, unsure where or when to settle.

He sighed. Kastiandra might have become too thin in his eyes, but he had grown fond of her and appreciative of her neatness in arranging the wagon. She had not been his parents' first choice for a wife. He himself had only been second in line for her, behind another man who had been killed in a raid. But it had worked out well enough for both of them. He trusted her with the wagon, and with his children.

In any case, family life continued, and the next generation had to be planned for. He had spent most of the afternoon with Kastor, and had finally come to an equitable arrangement about Murtilis and Arkelawos.

Arkelawos himself was somewhere in the thin screen of men out ahead, scouting to give warning if they came across riders or chariotry. It was important work, but most of them resented the drawing of lots which had placed them there. They would rather be with the raiding groups, working their way slowly along one of the main roads running north and south through the land, plucking the towns like ripe fruit as they went. By the time the several groups of wagons found their own settlements, the fighting men hoped to be all together again, wealthy and full of renown. But somehow, it seemed that the wealth always slipped away from them.

Periphas, together with the rest of his fighting group, had come back only briefly after taking Hatsor. He himself had immediately gone back towards the coast road with a large contingent. Tiripodikos and his lads, including Dekseus, had been sent instead along one of the inland trails.

Dekseus had spoken about Hatsor as he sat with them on the wagon for an afternoon before leaving again. The city had been a place of many houses and temples. It had been a good time to strike there, as the king had already dispatched many of his chariots elsewhere, and those that were left were quite ineffective. Their own losses had been small, but painful; Antos no longer had any sons alive.

Nikleos, out of curiosity, had ridden over to see what was left after his people had passed by. The fringes of the town were in ruins, still smouldering, with groups of people trying to recover something of their former life. But it had been only a quick foray; much of the town was scarcely touched.

The citadel of the town still looked down on what had been its thriving suburbs. As Nikleos had expected, the gain to his clan had been slight. Periphas had been in a hurry to rejoin the main groups of warriors, so had not taken the time to sack the city properly. Nikleos' eyes were not very experienced at such things, but it seemed clear that the place could recover, even if it would take a year or two.

As he had returned to the flock of wagons he had passed the open space where some part of the king's army had tried to make a stand. Unlimbered wheels and broken chariot bodies littered the field, along with the stripped bodies of their riders. A few broken javelins lay here and there, but most had been recovered for the next fight. He had wondered idly as he rode by which of the dead men had been killed by his own son.

Like everywhere else, the king of Hatsor's chariotry had failed in the fight. Even had the pick of the king's men been here, the result would have been the same. Like the rest, he had tried to have a show battle with his noblemen. It would have looked spectacular to see the horses pulling the lightly-framed two-wheeled chariots, wheeling and dancing across the open greenery. But with today's warfare it was futile.

Of course, it would only be a matter of time until some commanding officer would work out that the old way of fighting had been swept away by the new, and would find a way to stem the tide. Until that time Periphas and the other raiding groups who had pledged to take this journey would capture and pillage city after city.

Murtilis was handing him a bowl of stew and some flatbread. Looking around, he realised that she and Kastiandra were waiting for him, as indeed they should. He pulled his errant thoughts away from Hatsor, and spoke out a quick blessing to the divine lord Diweus so that they could eat with a clear conscience.

They ate for a while in a companionable silence. Before long the edge of their hunger had been taken away, and Murtilis had started to share the news from Kastor's wagon. Nikleos let her talk with Kastiandra for a while before taking advantage of a lull in the conversation.

"Kastor finally agreed today that you would be suitable as wife for Arkelawos."

She nodded, unsurprised, and said nothing.

"Kastor will want a proper viewing of you when we settle somewhere for more than a night at a time."

He grinned at her.

"Not as if he doesn't know what you look like already, but this has to be done correctly. And quickly, too. He said you could move into their wagon beside his wife herself as soon as both families have pledged the matter, even before Arkelawos and the scouts come back to us. Kastor already knows what wealth you will take into his family, though perhaps when the lads get back from the coastlands, everything that we have here will seem only a small handful."

He paused, looked across at Kastiandra and back again.

"You'll make a good wife, I think."

"I should hope so, father."

She began to say something else, when Nikleos suddenly stood up. There were footsteps from behind the wagon, several people approaching from out of the night. He drew his long dagger from its belt pouch and took a step in that direction. Kastiandra scrambled to her feet in front of Murtilis, one of the cooking cleavers in her hand. Murtilis put another bough of wood on the fire, but it would take time to catch.

"Who goes there? Show yourselves."

There was an answering call from the night, in another language. A foreigner, then, but making no attempt to hide himself. A longer sentence, equally incomprehensible. A man coming out of the gloom with two youths, one either side. All three were wearing headscarfs of different designs. The man's hands were out towards him, empty of weapons.

Nikleos relaxed a little, lowered the knife. Kastiandra was still on guard, wary of the strangers. The man spoke again, meaningless noises.

"I don't follow you. Use another tongue. Tell me who you are and why you are here."

The man shrugged, looked around, then made some more noises. But the lad to the right of the older man, who had been listening carefully, frowned in thought and then spoke up. He was not quick in his speech, and used some odd expressions, but at least he could be understood.

"He says, he says, we come not meaning you any hostility. Only three of us, ourselves."

Nikleos nodded. It was not right that the three of them had passed by those who were on lookout duty, even if they did mean no harm. But that was hardly the problem of these strangers, who had come right up to him without stealth and without weapons in their hands.

"So where have you come from?"

"From the north, good sir. From the city of Ikaret. Do you hear of that city? It is a few handfuls of days to walk."

Nikleos shook his head. Whether one city name or another, it was all the same to him. It was likely, however, that this Ikaret was a place that one of the clans had visited in their tour of plunder. The youth rushed on.

"It is a great port itself, sir. Many people, much trade."

His face fell. "That is, I mean, it was great. And for sure it will be great and full of magnificence again on a day soon."

Nikleos said nothing still; it meant nothing to him if the place vanished without trace.

The lad was about to speak again, when the older man shook his arm and said something in his own tongue. Nikleos had no idea what was said, but the tone was angry, and the man's posture proclaimed that he was unhappy with the turn of events. The third person, head shrouded in a plain white broad scarf, suddenly spoke, and Nikleos realised she was a young woman. He exchanged glances with Kastiandra, who lowered her own knife. There was another burst of conversation, and at its end the lad turned to him again.

"Honoured sir, we are truly grateful if you can help us with food. We can repay you with silver for the kindness." He paused, and then rushed on. "The soldier here wants that to be all I say, but my sister asks if you can grant shelter for the night as well."

Nikleos looked at Kastiandra again. She made a little vertical move of her head, small enough that only he would know, and not the others.

"This man; does he understand what you and I say?"

"Sir, indeed no, not one single word."

"Well, then, he has a look of a soldier, but you do not speak like one. Tell me more about him."

"He is our guard, made so by my father's sister's husband. But he does not know this land, and I do not think he has a plan for us. Not a reliable one, in any case. His directions have not always been good."

One of the dry branches that Murtilis had put on the fire suddenly flared up, and the faces of all three showed more clearly. The lad was not so very different from his own son in age; a little younger, perhaps. There was a wary, guarded look on the older man's face, but weariness and sorrow clothed the other two.

"Do you trust him?"

The lad looked down, pursed his lips. The older man shook him again, said something in a questioning tone. Nikleos spoke again in the little silence which followed.

"Tell him that we grant food and the protection of my roof and my right arm. To you and your sister I say that we grant shelter as well. For a night at least, according to our custom. Then tomorrow we will talk about the future."

He nodded at the guard. "Up to you how you explain this to him."

A look of enormous relief crossed the young man's features. He turned and spoke rapidly in their own tongue to the other two. The older man nodded at first, then argued, clearly loathe to accept the hospitality. To settle the matter Kastiandra took the arm of the young woman and placed her sitting between herself and Murtilis, then put a bowl of food in her hands. The guard stood irresolute for a moment, and in the silence the young woman spoke quickly to her brother, listened to his reply, and then turned to Kastiandra. Her words were halting, but clearly heartfelt.

"I thank you for this kindness itself, honoured lady. My brother and I are in your debt."

They sat in a circle together. The two youths had accepted the situation readily enough, but the guard was still wary. His eyes looked everywhere, and he looked ready to defend himself at the slightest provocation. Every time something was said in the language he could not understand he would stare at the speaker as though trying to divine the meaning of the words.

The brother was reasonably fluent, though clearly out of practice; Nikleos guessed that he had been tutored in childhood and had not had reason to use the tongue since then. His sister was less able, and sat for the most part in silence as she tried to follow the flow of words.

They were voracious eaters, and grateful ones, and Nikleos supposed they had lived on scant rations for a number of days. Even the guard seemed appreciative of the food that he received, and after each helping said something which sounded like gratitude. Watching them, he decided that the sister was the elder of the pair by a small margin. That would make her about the same age as Dekseus.

"So tell me about this city of yours, lad, this Ikaret."

"It is a great city, with our own king himself who walks in covenant with the great King of the North. We trade with the cities of the land, and over the sea to places in the islands. Everywhere. But ill times come upon us and enemies come. Our gates are torn down and our soldiers are killed and our houses are burned."

He was concentrating intently on getting the words correct as he spoke, and showed no sign of any feeling. But his sister's face fell into shadow, and she looked away from the firelight towards the north.

"How is it that you are with this soldier now?"

The young man swallowed. His sister suddenly spoke up.

"Don't talk about it, Yasib. Please don't talk about it."

Their guard, seeing the exchange between them, added a question in his own tongue. The lad nodded once, twice, then shook his head and turned back to Nikleos.

"I must ask your patience, good sir. The words are full of pain for us both."

There was silence for a time. It was not late, but the youngsters were flagging with fatigue; without the stimulation of speech the boy was starting to doze. Nikleos decided to delay questioning until the next day. He stood up. The soldier watched him narrowly.

"Your sister will sleep between my wife and daughter. You and your guardsman can settle on the ground, in the lee of my wagon itself. Tomorrow is a day when we will rest the beasts and not ride on. We will talk then, decide what we shall do with you."

⊨≡╫╫╫╫╫╫╫╫≡⊨

THE MORNING AROSE WITH MISTY FINGERS trailing round the folds of the land and drifting through the squat trees. Nikleos lifted a corner of the cover beside him and stepped out onto the ground. The dew was cold on his feet. Under the wagon the lad was stirring. The older man was already sitting upright on a nearby rock, whittling a piece of antler with his knife. He glanced briefly at Nikleos but made no attempt to talk.

Nikleos walked over to check the oxen, nodded to other clansmen doing the same, then went back to the wagon. Kastiandra looked out.

"The girl doesn't know how to braid her hair. Says she has never done it in her life, and that her headscarf is sufficient for modesty."

He shrugged. "Different customs, I suppose. Let her keep the headscarf for the time being. But be quick about getting ready. We will all need to break our fast before long."

The boy stood up and made a little bow to him. Nikleos could not remember ever receiving a bow before.

"Good sir, my sister Dantiy speaks truth to your lady wife. You see, in our people, although both men and women wear the kef, it is more important for the woman's dignity that her hair is covered."

He laughed, amused.

"For her dignity? Why so?"

"Because her hair is..." He stopped, searching for words. "Her hair is a sign only for a man she chooses. Now that Dantiy is not a girl these many years, it is not right to show her hair to just anybody."

It was intriguing, but not urgent. "Lad, tell me. You know our speech, you have been taught it quite well. Do you also know the lie of this land?"

"Both yes and no, sir. I have never walked on these hills before. But I have heard them explained, and I know the list of names to go from place to place without getting lost."

"If we climbed that hill there, could you tell me? And look now, tell me, your sister called you Yasib last night. Is that your own name or that of your family?"

The youth stood up beside the wagon, pulled his clothes into order and settled his own headscarf into place. He was obviously quite casual about the fact that his own head was not fully covered.

"My own name, good sir. As for the land, I can only try."

Nikleos pointed at the soldier, who had also stood up.

"Say to him that he must come as well. I will not have him stay here alone with the women."

There was a brief exchange in the other language, and then the three set off. The guard was trailing a little way behind. They went up the shallow slopes of the bowl, then more steeply up a crag to the east.

Near the top, they came fully out of the bank of mist into the sun. The remaining dew sparkled left and right. Some way ahead of them was a deep, broad valley, full to the brim with mist. It ran north and south. The young man looked up at the sun, then turned a circle to look around at peaks on the horizon. Then he pointed.

"They call that the Valley. As though there is no other valley anywhere else to speak of. It becomes deeper and deeper as you go south. There is an inland sea of bitter water a few days that way. Perhaps a week from here, I cannot be sure.

Nothing flows out of it. North, that way, there is a smaller lake, fresh water, very pure. Beyond that again the city of Hatsor. A small lake beyond that. A river connecting all three, flowing south."

"I know the name of Hatsor."

"We had wanted to stop at Hatsor to wait for other members of our family. But it had been attacked by the time we got there, so we left it and came on south."

Nikleos looked at him to see if he would continue, but although the lad had paused briefly, it was simply to turn towards the south-west.

"Now, over there the Mitsriy have cities and guard places all along the Sea Road. I can recite the correct order of the names when you need me to. Gedjet is the main one, but it must be a long way south from here, I think."

"And where is your city of Ikaret from here?"

The guard had been paying no attention, but at the familiar word frowned and took a step forward.

"North along the coast, good sir. Perhaps three weeks walk, longer in one of your ox carts. First you get to the coastlands of the Fenku. Then after that..."

The older man suddenly shouted at him. His hand was on the hilt of his weapon, and his face was contorted with rage. Nikleos stepped forward to be beside Yasib's shoulder.

"What is he saying? Why is he angry like this?"

Yasib's face was white, anxious, and his voice shook a little, but he remained facing towards the guard with his head up.

"He says that I betray my people when I tell you where one place or another can be found. He says that we do not know who you are or what you mean to do with us. He says..."

The other man spoke again, a long speech which sounded full of repetition and ire. Nikleos watched, curious to see how this would turn out. Eventually the youth held up a hand to break into the flow of words, spoke in what sounded a commanding manner. There was an arrogance about the boy, an assumption of authority, which intrigued Nikleos.

"He says that I am not thinking about what I am saying. But in fact, good sir, I find myself wanting to trust you more than him."

He paused, thinking.

"He has been a good guard, and a faithful one, since we separated from my father's sister and her family. But he is only a guard and I will not have him decide my future like this."

Nikleos waited, but the exchange between two stopped at that point. The older man was simmering, but contained himself, and the lad apparently felt it should not be necessary to continue.

"I think that we will go down again to the wagon. The women will have food prepared by now."

The mist was dispersing as they went back down the hill and skirted around the periphery of the encampment. The camp was stirring now, and several of the other men looked curiously at his companions. Back at the wagon the new girl, Dantiy, was helping Kastiandra and Murtilis set out food, learning new words and phrases as they worked together. Yasib started over towards them, but Nikleos took his arm and shook his head.

"Plenty of other work you can do to earn your place in the wagon. But first we must make choices. I have given you a night's hospitality according to the travellers' custom. If you want to stay longer we must come to an arrangement. But perhaps you want to move on again with the day. For sure your soldier will have an opinion."

The boy gave his arrogant lift of the head again.

"He may have an opinion, but he does not choose for me or my sister. It would be fair to let him choose for himself. Make your arrangement with me and I will explain to him what the choice may be."

There was a burst of female laughter from inside the covers of the wagon, and Dantiy could be heard repeating something and then laughing again. Yasib grinned.

"My sister sounds as though she is making family once again. She would laugh like that back at home." He suddenly stopped and looked very grim. "There's no more of that for her. Or me. Nothing left except our journey together to find a new place."

Nikleos watched him struggle with grief for a time. He was convinced that some branch of his own scattered people had passed through this Ikaret on their way south. The guard, he was sure, had guessed this already, but the lad was still uncertain. It would be better to separate them sooner rather than later.

"Yasib, lad, when the morning meal is over, I will take your guard to another man who may speak your language. Someone in this camp will do so, and I feel sure it is Towanos. It will spare you the need to retell the words all the time."

Yasib nodded.

"Very well. This man's name is Tarmanni."

The other man glanced up at the sound of his own name, but did not speak. Yasib rose to his feet as the three women appeared. Nikleos, still seated, looked at him curiously, wondering again what other customs the young man followed. No doubt time would tell.

As head of the household he bowed his head and prayed aloud to the lord Diweus to bless the food for their bodies, not in the least concerned how much the newcomers understood of his devotions. At very least they recognised that they were in the presence of the sacred, and remained silent until he had finished.

As they finally started to eat, Yasib turned to Tarmanni and spoke rapidly in their own language, pointing at Nikleos a few times and then gesturing around the camp. It was clearly not a palatable solution to the older man, and Yasib answered several objections with a rising impatience. The girl, Dantiy, joined in after a while, seemingly on an equal footing. Finally Yasib turned back to Nikleos.

"My thanks for your patience, sir. Tarmanni will go to talk with your friend after the meal."

He turned his attention back to the meal – flat bread with olives, hummus and a soft white cheese – with obvious relish. He turned to Kastiandra.

"My thanks for this, lady. This is as welcome as gentle rain in the summer heat."

Kastiandra raised her eyebrows, looked apologetically at Nikleos and made no reply. Yasib stopped himself, aware of a mistake, and glanced at Dantiy. She nodded and repeated what he had said, stumbling a little over the words in the compliment. This time Kastiandra smiled in acceptance.

"Surely this is no more than a mouthful along the wayside. You are very welcome."

Tarmanni ignored the exchange and continued to eat. Yasib turned to Nikleos.

"Did I cause offence, sir?"

"You are a stranger, and a man. Even as an overnight guest, among my people it is not right for you to address the women of this house directly. Your sister can do this: you should not. You would do well to remember this if you go to one of the other wagons. It will be different if you stay longer with us and we swear a pact with one another. Would you not do the same if we were in your house?"

Yasib shook his head, and his melancholy, never buried very deeply, returned to the surface.

"If I had a house and took you in to share food, you would be free to speak as you please. But I have no house, and here I shall be bound by your customs."

$$\Vdash \mathbb{W}\mathbb{W}\mathbb{W}\mathbb{W}\mathbb{W}\Vdash$$

AFTER THEY HAD FINISHED EATING, Nikleos rose and instructed Yasib and Tarmanni how to remove the wagon's cover and fold it for the day. They lashed the curved ribs that held it away from the floor against the wooden sides. That done, Nikleos gestured to Tarmanni to follow him. The soldier looked reluctantly at Yasib.

"I shall come with you. It fulfils my responsibility to him, and will reassure him that no harm is being considered. Besides, who is there to speak with if I stay here?"

Nikleos took them across the middle of the circle of wagons. The oxen were tethered in a group at one end, and in the empty space away from them some boys were practising throwing blunt javelins towards a large straw target. Eumedes, an older man, was tutoring them. Tarmanni stared at the group with dark eyes, and hissed between his teeth. He turned to Yasib and muttered something in their own tongue. Nikleos watched them closely. Yasib looked doubtful, said something in answer, shook his head.

Whatever Tarmanni might have said in reply was, happily, lost by their arrival at Towanos' wagon. Some brief conversation revealed that Towanos could indeed talk with Tarmanni, albeit in a rather halting manner, and Nikleos started back with Yasib. They stopped and watched the boys with their javelins for a while.

"In Ikaret, do you train your boys like this?"

"Not really with throwing weapons. Some learn the bow. Some learn to direct the chariot horses, and the best ones train to shoot arrows while riding at speed. Boys from the common families learn to use a spear or the stabbing sword. Now, when the city fell it was at night. They say that traitors opened the gates and set fires near the docks. If we had been able to meet the attackers with chariots the city would stand yet. But they were away from the city, serving the great King of the North along his borderlands."

Nikleos pulled a face. "That day has gone. I have seen battlefields littered with broken chariots and dead horses, where living men armed with javelins and the long sword mastered them. Against that, a chariot is no better than an ox cart, and is fit only to carry men to the place where they will fight hand to hand."

Yasib thought for a while, then turned away from the up and down curves of the missiles.

"I was in training to be a runner; a man who keeps close to the chariots in order to protect the fallen on our side and harass those of the enemy. I do not really have the speed for it, but my father wanted me to learn the runner's discipline before ever I took up the reins. Still less be the bowman on board. But perhaps now I will never be a rider."

"Why would you want to be?"

Yasib looked at him. "Why not? The rider has a place of honour among men of rank."

"Look at these boys, Yasib. They are learning the javelin. When they are older they will learn the longsword, but already these boys could defeat a chariot."

Yasib shook his head in disbelief.

"They have no skill with the bow."

"They do not need it. There are ten boys here. Think of them spread out so that your bowshots would not easily strike them. They dodge here and there with the speed of youth. They throw ten javelins, and even at their age one or two might hit a horse at the walk. Another few years, and most will hit a horse at the trot or the canter."

"You fight against horses?" He sounded shocked. "What harm have the horses ever done to you?"

Nikleos shrugged. "We fight to win battles. No horse: no chariot. No chariot: no kingdom. Better for you that you never become a rider, perhaps."

Yasib looked at him, a long measuring look, and then turned again to watch the boys. Most of the casts missed, but with every volley, one or two hit the large bundle of straw. After a while they stood up together and walked on in silence. Shortly before reaching the wagon, Yasib stopped again and took a deep breath.

"Sir, I need to ask you. What road have your people taken to get here?"

Nikleos nodded, having expected the question.

"We came over the sea from our homeland to sack Wilios itself. Ah, that was a great deed, which deserves its own story. One day, somebody will tell it properly. A few of us went home after that, but most liked this land and stayed on this side of the water. We want to settle somewhere, when we find the right place. My people came around the coast from Wilios, south and then east for a time. Do you know the place that I mean?"

"There is a group of towns near several river mouths all together, before the coast turns south again."

"Yes. Yes indeed. There was a division of the roads there. Some groups followed the coast down; mostly those who had clansmen in ships to prepare the way ahead. My people followed a road inland and turned south once we were east of a chain of mountains."

Yasib squatted down at a patch of bare ground, picked up a small stick and scratched out two lines, one going from side to side and the other joining at one end to run up and down. He pointed.

"This is the coast. This here is all sea, with some large islands in it. Up there is the land of the King of the North, who was our overlord. Wilios, which we also call Taruwisa, is right over beside the wagon wheel, beyond where I have drawn. Here and here. . . " he placed some little pebbles, "are the towns we talked about, at the river mouths."

Nikleos frowned at the sketch, took the stick and drew a wavy line.

"We travelled this way, east along the coast. Then about here we came away from the sea, to pass inland of a mountain range."

Yasib added some scratch marks in the soft soil to represent the higher land, then placed a large stone straddling the north-south line of the sea shore. As he spoke he added extra stones.

"Ikaret is here. Over this way are some other big towns – Gargamish, Damaseq, Hatsor."

"We went past Hatsor." Yasib looked at him. He shrugged. "I think the inhabitants will remember our passing for a while to come. You told me the other day that you had planned to stop there."

"Yes: we had arranged with my father's sister and his family to meet there. They will be several days behind us, I think. They had young children with them. Surely they cannot have got there ahead of us."

He stopped, shook his head. Nikleos remained silent to give space for his anguish.

"I pray that they were slower. When Dantiy and I saw what had happened there we continued south. What would be the purpose in stopping at Hatsor now? The next place we would all head for, this far from the Sea Road, is Shalem. Perhaps we will meet there."

He dropped another stone rather to the south of Hatsor. There was no hope in his voice. Nikleos looked at him, then gestured again at the map and stepped back in order to see it as a whole.

"You are good at this."

Yasib shrugged.

"It is what my father trained me for. I had thought to use this skill in the palace, not here in the Kinahny province."

"Kinahny?"

"It is the name of this region. You and I both crossed into it some way north from here. Ikaret is certainly not in its borders, Damaseq certainly is. The Mitsriy have ruled the land here for a long time. Now that you have visited Hatsor you will have come to their attention. They have withdrawn many of their soldiers, but they are still too powerful for you to meet in full battle."

Nikleos nodded slowly, lost in thought for a while.

"If you choose to stay with us, can you repeat all this to the other clansmen? And Antos, our arkon? Show them this plan?"

"I can."

Nikleos walked the last few paces to the wagon and rummaged underneath it with a clatter.

"This is the other weapon I was going to show you."

He pulled out a large sword. It was longer than Yasib had expected, and was edged on both sides. He took it from Nikleos when he offered it, and tried out a few lunges.

"It's heavy. Not so good at the thrust."

"It is not made for the thrust but for the slash. You're think-ing like a nobleman, Yasib. You're thinking of a single fight between champions."

He took it back, set the sword swinging in a great arc which lopped several limbs from the nearby bush.

"This is not a nobleman's weapon. But it wins battles for us. I have used it in the past, but my legs are not so good now and I have handed over the fighting to my son."

He replaced the sword in its place under the wagon. Nikleos went to climb up into it, but Yasib stopped him.

"Good sir, you spoke before of a pact that we must take if we wish to stay here. What are my choices? And Dantiy's?"

"You can move on today, and we will give you some supplies to send you on your way. There is no debt between us. Or you and I can swear an oath that we will bring no harm to the other. My oath will bind my family: yours will bind your sister as well. Then you may stay at the lower end of the wagon. We will agree what work you will do for your keep."

"We have silver."

"So you have said before. But work is more use to us than silver just now."

Yasib nodded. "Allow me a time to talk with Dantiy, and we will answer you before noon."

DANTIY HAD HELPED MURTILIS as she put away the last of the beakers they had used for breakfast. The plates were already stacked in a heap inside a great round pottery basin which she had not seen used yet. She looked around. Every piece of space in the wagon was packed with an excess of neatness, tucked in and protected, ready for when the pair of oxen would tug erratically at the harness on the onward journey. Outside, they could hear Kastiandra's voice as she spoke with a neighbour. Murtilis was looking at her.

"The men will be gone for some time yet. I could show you how to braid your hair in the way that we do, if you like?"

Dantiy laughed. "It is kindness itself, Murtilis, but I think I prefer to wear the kef as I have done since I was a girl."

Murtilis sat back, obviously at a loss what to say next. Dantiy took pity on the younger girl and sat beside her.

"But perhaps it would be good for me to know. Show me, if you will."

"Well, that's good then." She opened a wooden box and took out a polished metal mirror and a brush with stiff bristles and an ivory handle. "See this. My father took this from a city he burned when I was just a few weeks out of my mother's body. He gave it to me after he came back on the ship and it has been mine ever since."

Dantiy looked at the beautifully finished pieces with mixed feelings and dark thoughts. "What city?"

Murtilis shrugged. "I do not know. But we were still living across the sea somewhere, before ever we sacked Wilios and came on this journey. Father would remember. He used to tell me it was on an island on the middle of the great sea."

She held the brush dreamily, then looked suddenly at the bleakness of Dantiy's expression.

"What is it, Dantiy?"

"My own city was burned, and Yasib and I have had to flee for our lives with nothing to our names but the few items we carry. My father is gone. My mother was treated shockingly. I shall never see them again, nor stand in the home of my family."

Murtilis was silent, one hand to her mouth, watching Dantiy struggle with herself.

"It wasn't us, Dantiy. It wasn't us who did that to your home. I only mean kindness to you. It can't have been us. Please don't be upset so. It wasn't us."

Dantiy took several deep breaths, reached out to the other girl's hand and took it.

"I know you mean good to me, Murtilis. Ill chance guided your words, and they struck at a raw place inside me."

Murtilis looked across at the sacred hawk icon fixed to the timbers at the front of the wagon.

"Then may Hiraks Kirkos take away the darkness of the words. There now, see, that's done. Now let me show you how to braid your hair."

She paused, her hands hovering near Dantiy's head.

"Are you allowed to take off your headscarf for me?"

"My kef? Oh yes. But you know this; I did not wear it last night here in the wagon."

She untied the knot at her throat and folded the cloth onto her lap, letting her hair fall like a black wave below her shoulders. Murtilis sat behind her and started to brush, gently at first.

"You have nice hair. You should show it off more." Dantiy moved impatiently. "Stay still, please. I know, the kef is for modesty, you said so. But you are not wearing it now."

"We are women together. It is fine for us."

The hands paused. "But not for you and a man?"

Dantiy laughed. She was becoming more relaxed with the rhythmic brush strokes, forgetting where the brush had come from.

"No, not for me and a man. Well, I am not so careful around Yasib, since he is family. And I have taken my kef off for a man before, when the time was right, at one great festival or another."

"Oh. I see. That will be like me unbraiding my hair for Arkelawos when we are married. Father has arranged it all and as soon as Kastor has viewed me and agreed the transaction with oaths, then I shall move to his wagon. I won't see Arkelawos until he comes back with the other scouting men, but when he does then I shall unbraid my hair for him."

She made an awkward sound that could have been a laugh. "And the rest as well. So, you were married, back at Ikaret? What happened to your husband? Was he away from the city when you left?"

"No, I am not yet married. My family never made the arrangements. I suppose now it will fall to Yasib to do this. What a thing. However will he know what to do? If ever we meet my aunt and her husband again, they will have to instruct him."

Murtilis paused her brushing, and she stayed silent. Dantiy picked up her kef, unfolded it, and continued.

"If I was married, I would not have a plain kef any more. A sign of my marriage would be embroidered just here, so that everybody could see."

Murtilis leaned forward a little so that she was very close, and her voice became very quiet. Dantiy turned her head to see curiosity and anxiety mingled in her face.

"But you said you had unbraided yourself – taken off this kef – with a man. Aren't you still intact?"

She stopped, and her hand gestured below her waist and closed itself into a little ball. Dantiy looked her directly in the eyes, surprised but without shame.

"Do you think I am still a little girl?"

Murtilis put a finger against Dantiy's lips and whispered directly in her ear.

"Stay quiet about this. Mother would thrash me if she thought I was planning to do this with Arkelawos. She would slap me if she believed I was even considering it in my heart. And if anything happened, and Arkelawos put a child in me, father would kill us both to purge the shame from his household. You must not tell mother we have said this to each other."

Dantiy, moved by a sudden sisterly impulse, turned to caress the younger girl's cheek and forehead. Murtilis' face was long and thin, just like her mother's.

"You have my promise. But you should know that it is not something to be afraid of."

"I am not afraid. Not really. But mother must not hear that we have talked about this. Now, I have seen the goats many times in their season, and I have helped to hold a mare while the stallion covered her. Can it be so different for a man and a woman?"

Dantiy smiled a little. "It will not quite be the same, when you are face to face with Arkelawos. You will find out."

Murtilis ignored her at first and went back to her brushing. Suddenly she stopped again and put her arms around Dantiy.

"If the men think you are a virgin then they will value that, and one or other will take you as wife at some stage. But if they decide that you have been with men like a whore and a wicked woman, then they will pass you from one to another and use you as they please. Even if it is not true of you. I cannot bear to think of that for you. Now, if they think you are a widow and your man has died in battle then they will honour you and keep their hands away from you until you choose otherwise. Dantiy, it is the only way that is safe for you. Trust me in this."

Dantiy took a deep breath, nodded, and kissed Murtilis on both cheeks. Outside, Kastiandra's voice became a little louder as her conversation drew towards a close. Murtilis suddenly spoke again, still in a low voice.

"What would your kef look like if you were a widow?"

"For a time I would wear it with dark thread across the middle, and with a ragged edge as though I had torn it. The one I had worn in marriage would be torn in half and placed in my husband's memorial place. After a time I would unpick the dark thread so that it was plain again, but I would add the right colours in the fringe to show I had been in another family."

Murtilis made a noise of assent and whispered, "Think of a name."

Kastiandra climbed back into the wagon. She gave an approving nod when she saw what her daughter was doing.

"See mother, she has good hair, and long enough. Should she part it here or further up, would you say?"

"Higher, I think."

Dantiy sat patiently as mother and daughter arranged her hair, plaiting it either side and then gathering the plaits together on top of her head. Kastiandra fitted a silver clasp in place to hold the arrangement together while Murtilis held the mirror up in front of her. She nodded as she saw herself. The result was, in fact, quite pleasing. She turned her head from side to side.

"I don't think I could pass as one of you, but this is good. My thanks to you both. But I should still feel quite naked without my kef."

"Wear the scarf over that braid, so you are modest both by your customs and ours."

Dantiy nodded and gave the mirror back to Murtilis who started to pack it away again.

"And I shall show Yasib. No shame there."

Kastiandra looked around at the work the young women had done before and rearranged a couple of the pieces.

Murtilis took a deep breath and grinned at Dantiy behind her mother's back.

"Mother, could we give Dantiy some of the dark thread you have in the mending box?"

"For sure we can. I will get it now. But what do you need dark thread for?"

"I said she should have asked before, but she did not know if a guest could say this. But this kef she wears should have a sign of her lost husband, to show everyone that she is a widow."

Kastiandra turned and looked directly at Dantiy.

"Ah. I see. Yes, I can share some thread. What was your husband's name?"

There was no particular sorrow or surprise in her voice, simply a recognition of death and the common experience of women.

"Halmanu. Son of Abdony."

"I have been wondering why a woman of your age was travelling with her brother. Was your husband killed in the city?"

Dantiy thought briefly how to keep the story simple.

"In truth, lady, I have lost count of how many of my people were killed where. And I have not seen his body. But I know where Halmanu would have been serving in the king's palace, and I know for sure that he could not have survived the attack there. His honour would not let him leave his post."

Kastiandra nodded, said, "Ah," again, and rummaged in another box to find some dark thread and a bone needle. As she gave it to Dantiy she placed her hand on her shoulder.

"I lost the man I was first betrothed to, just a week before we were to be married. He was killed in a raid, trying to bring back treasure to please my eyes. But child, see how things can change. Nikleos has been fair as a husband to me, and is a good father to my children, though neither of us expected to be with the other."

There was still no real expression in her voice, and she sat and watched in silence as Dantiy stitched a criss-cross pattern in the plain white cloth of the kef and then tore the edges to make a ragged fringe. When she tied the scarf again, the dark was prominent over her forehead.

"How will your people know what this means? What sign would one of your own women wear to show this?"

Kastiandra shook her head.

"No sign. What need of signs? We are a small group, and everybody would know the truth of the matter. Leave it with me. I shall spread the word with the other women, and the whole camp will know before tomorrow is done."

There was a sudden clatter on the underside of the wagon, and Dantiy froze to the seat, startled. Murtilis took her hand.

"Don't be alarmed, it is just father come back again. It sounds as though he is getting his sword out. Perhaps your brother wants to look at it."

A MAN ADDRESSES HIS BROTHER.

Hekanefer to Ramose, from some place that the gods have abandoned.

Well, brother, we have been moved inland from the Sea Road and have followed some small tracks to reach our destination – wherever that is. The march here has been dreadful.

The commander received orders late in the afternoon yesterday, and we struck camp at once. You once told me about some officer you had known, who took every word as true in the grossest and most obvious manner, and lacked any sense of the delight to be found in word-play and subtlety. I think my officer must be his brother, perhaps even his twin. The orders say to march at once, and so he marches at once.

I had received permission from him to do some reconnaissance the next day in the town of Akka near to our former camp, looking out for additional supplies. With all the people fleeing south, the villages have little to give us. Or so they say; my guess is that they have hidden what they have in caves and cisterns for their own use. We do not have time to conduct a search, and their little village eyes know it. You would think that they would be glad of our protection, but no. You can see it in every face – they expect us to be gone again soon, and they expect to be welcoming new overlords.

But back to my trip to Akka. Of course I was hoping for some pleasant diversion from the deprivations of the campaign. One of the other soldiers, who had been this way several times before, told me of a place where a man may make wagers on all kinds of sports and games. It sounded intoxicating! I was all ready for this, but the chance was denied me. Orders came: orders must be obeyed. We struck camp at once and were on the road again. And here we are.

But I cannot tell you where we are, not because of some military oath of secrecy, but simply because I do not know. I can tell you that we are on top of a low ridge, and that on the hill opposite is a small town. Between it and us is a wide open stretch of grass, perfect for the deployment of chariots. But I do not know the name of this place, and we are so far out of order from the standard waylists that you and I both learned, that I cannot make a guess. All that I can say is that we are well inland from the Sea Road, but not yet near the Kings' Road.

Another thing. Along with the orders we received a new detachment of men. But they are not out of the Beloved Land. They keep themselves as a group together and have little to do with our own men. I have listened to their speech among themselves, and it is not like our own. More like that of the Khatti-lands, perhaps, though they do not come from there. I heard one of the junior officers say that they are paid soldiers from some island in the middle of the Great Green Sea.

Such men have served occasionally in our army before now, from time to time since the great campaigns by which we bestowed civilisation and stability on this province. Perhaps three hundred years before now, I suppose. But such men have also served our enemies: they wage war for profit, not out of commitment. Also. they carry long swords of a kind I do not know, and javelins of considerable sturdiness. These weapons are like those that were used by the enemy to defeat our company of chariots recently. The common soldiers keep these people at a distance, but treat them with respect.

What does it mean for us, that we need to rely on these people? There are spearmen of Kush who fight alongside us, but we have been allied with Kush since the time of the gods. They are like the left hand to our right. But these islanders are new to us – it is a mere handful of generations that we have known them. Is the world changing so much that we need such allies now?

Brother, often I write in jest to you, knowing that you will understand the sincerity of my heart. But I must use my ink and brush now to write more soberly. My soul is profoundly unsettled just now. I feel we are approaching a crisis of battle, and I fear for my life. The men feel it, the chariot-horses feel it: even the donkeys carrying the supplies feel it. Alliances are changing: battles are changing. What will happen to the peace that we have cultivated around us these many years?

If it should be that I never see the Beloved Land again, remember me daily before the gods so that they might lovingly lead my deathless spirit across the Sea of Reeds and into the lightland. In such a case the parts of my body might never be properly prepared by a priest, nor be returned to the homely soil of the Beloved Land. I must trust my eternal being to the prayers of those who love me, and the gracious and godly intervention of the Two Ladies and their helpers.

In truth, I wish now that I had made Nodjmet pregnant when last we lay together. As it is, if I should die tomorrow, no part will be left of me on this earth, but only the fading memories of those who love me. Ah, if only I had left my seed in her, and it had been an auspicious day for the act.

If she was pregnant now, then with my last breath I would know that something of me would be starting to stir in her body and would outlive me. I counted back the weeks, and if that had happened then she would be nearly half way towards the birth now. Her body would be starting to show the outward signs for all to see. Her mother Ankhiriyt would have been livid with anger, but I could have died content.

But enough of that: I should not give myself over to death just yet! I have found a man, a middle rank officer, who says that he can play Senet. Pray first that the gaming sticks fall well for me, and only then for the life of eternity.

A SON ADDRESSES HIS FATHER.

Hekanefer to his father Nesamenopeh, greetings and blessings to you. I write once again from our camp in Djahy.

I will be the first to say it – glorious news, my father! After the weariness of the marching, and the disappointment of the defeat which I related to you a little while ago, now at last comes the victory for which we longed. I might dare to hope that the worst hour has passed. It is like the day when the town mayor stands beside the waters and says "Look! The inundation is over and the waters recede."

I must write this in haste so that it travels with the messenger who even now is receiving detailed instructions from the commander. That brave officer will, I am sure, receive the gold of praise from the great king himself, who lives in prosperity and health. Surely he deserves it for the steadfast way in which he rallied his men, prepared his plan, and then carried it out in every detail.

The whole camp is full of celebration. It is like seeing the summer sun rise over the marshes when the flocks of Pewenet return from their migration.

I feel your impatience, father. What is this victory? We remained in our camp for several days, on the nub end of a long ridge across a valley from a small town. Some of the men grew restless, wanting to look here and there for our enemies.

But the scouts, that are our eyes and ears, were out in the land, bringing the commander all the news. Not even a wild animal moved in the undergrowth without his knowledge.

Now a day came when he knew that a band of this enemy was on the approach. He gave strict orders to his men, both those from the Beloved Land and those others who joined our camp quite recently. At first some of the men used to treat them with disdain, but now they are all brothers in arms, and they rejoice together.

That night the officer conducted a ceremony which I have never witnessed before. He ordered me to write on some old pots the tribe names which we had learned – Sherden, Peleset, Danuna, Tjekker and so on – and then he broke the pots in pieces with the rod of office he holds. All the men were cheering – myself as loud as any of them – to see these tokens of our enemy reduced to sherds.

The ceremony is from the time of the gods in the Beloved Land, and I felt truly joined in spirit to those gods, and our first fathers who served them. Why is it, my father, that we have ceased to do this great enactment of divine appointment?

We saw the enemy in the middle of the morning, advancing in open order from the east. My commander watched from a place with a clear view of the action, and had men near him with great horns and flags to make signals. And of course I myself was at his side, ready to record everything that he said.

So he sent out a half-wing of chariots, not this time to engage the enemy, but to make a great show of manoeuvring and wheeling in the valley. They looked splendid, as they always do, but today they were not even to attempt to fight.

Those wicked enemies did not know this, though, and when they saw the chariots circling, their hearts were deceived into seeing another quick victory. Their leader, a tall youth of considerable running speed, was the first to lead their charge. But the riders had their orders.

Before ever the enemy could get within range of their javelins, the commander ordered the blowing of horns and waving of flags, and so the chariotry unravelled their circle and sped away to safety. The paid soldiers arose from their hiding places in the long grass and among the low shrubs on either side, and unleashed their own missiles.

I hope you can imagine, father, the mood of shock and alarm that gripped the assailants when they were caught in this way. Our new helpers showered them with missiles, then ran at them with those long swords which I mentioned. They were fighting in the same way, but they were men rather than boys, and they had a weight of experience that this enemy could not hope to match.

The second officer, standing close at hand, said how their leader showed his youth when this happened. He should have changed his plan: he should have withdrawn his men at the first sign that we were handling the battle differently. But he did not, and a considerable number of his men will never be led again. He should not have run: in his shame he should have stayed to die on the field of battle.

Our own soldiers rushed down from the ridge when the battle turned, and they were as fierce as lions of the desert when hunger stirs them. The enemy leader indeed escaped, together with a portion of his men, but they were humiliated on this occasion. May it be the first of many.

My father, I must finish this now, for the messenger is getting ready to ride. The commander is about to go into the valley to speak with his men, and I must be at his side. Speak grateful words to all the gods for the wise plans of the commander, and for the safe preservation of your son. Speak words of reassurance to my mother, and tell her that I will write to her soon.

AS LABAYU CRESTED A RIDGE and paused between two of the fig trees which fringed it, he caught sight of the people of Ramath-Galil. They were almost all on foot, with a few donkeys or carts in the crowd, and to either side the village flocks spread out in noisy wings. Progress was very slow, partly to accommodate the elderly, the very young, the lame, and the pregnant, and partly because the herd animals would not survive a fast pace. They were still some way north of Sychem, and Labayu had reached them sooner than he had expected.

He increased his pace again and before long was passing amongst the slowest of the families. He spoke briefly with those who greeted him, ignored those who muttered against him, and made his way through to Pedayah. The headman was towards the front of the crowd, in the centre of a compact group of men.

To his relief and great pleasure, Abiy'el was there as well, together with some of his immediate followers. Pedayah had sent ahead with news of their progress, and the Ibriym war-leader had chosen to come in person up from Sychem. He had spent some time with each of the several other villages which were making similar journeys to avoid the king of Hatsor, and it was chance that he happened to be here, with Ramath-Galil instead of another village.

Pedayah greeted Labayu in his normal perfunctory manner, while Abiy'el embraced him warmly. Labayu was relieved on two counts; he would not have to search for the warleader somewhere in the hill country, and giving the news to Pedayah would be vastly easier now.

They continued walking at a slow pace as Labayu described what his men had reported from the north. As he had expected, Pedayah was not very interested in the news. The king of Hatsor was a much more pressing problem to him, and the arrival of a new group from the north seemed more threat than opportunity. So far as he was concerned, they were just another source of competition for the land.

Abiy'el was much more alive to the possibilities, and his men passed the foreign weapons amongst themselves eagerly. They were fascinated by the thought of a way to successfully confront chariots, and the memory of their defeats in the coastal plain was still raw. Since Labayu was only passing on the report of his men, he was unable to answer many of the questions which they asked him.

He was eager to start north again, but Abiy'el wanted to find out more. It was frustrating. His men were several days away, facing considerable risk if they were caught, and he was not yet able to join them. His thoughts were distant, and he only just caught what the warleader was saying.

"I cannot come with you myself: there are too many of my people out here in the wilderness. I need to make sure all of them reach the safety of the other clans. But I also need to know if we can ally with these newcomers."

"They are no friends of the kings in the cities. Not yet, at least. And from what Shimmigar told me, they do not intend friendship. But all he saw was a skirmish in the open country. If they are sending envoys to some of the kings to ally against others, he did not witness it."

"So you think they might be choosing sides among the kings of the land?"

Labayu spread his hands wide.

"Who can say?"

"If they are, I want them to choose us as allies. They are newcomers, as are we. Covenant might be good for both of us. As it has been in the alliance between your people and mine in the south towards Shalem."

"If only all of your people would remember that all of the time."

Abiy'el made a noncommittal noise, but before he could speak again Pedayah interrupted, bursting out with a flood of words.

"They are more likely to think that the kings rule us as well. We live in their territory, we pay them tribute when we must, they try to take our youth for their battles. Even the Mitsriy count us in with the kings when they come raising their own taxes. How will these people see us any different to the common Kinahny? If I had stayed at Ramath-Galil and waited, would these people have defended me? Or would they have ravaged the village thinking we were just part of Hatsor?"

Abiy'el frowned. "Look, Pedayah, this land had its own life before we came. The Mitsriy had ruled here without any real challenge for many generations. All that I have learned tells me that the hill country was once full of people, and that now they have gone away. Then we came, and we are filling the empty spaces again. From south of Shalem up to beside Hatsor, from the coastal plain to the other side of the River, our people are making homes. We are taking the land that the Mitsriy leave behind."

He held up a hand as Pedayah shook his head impatiently.

"Now we have made some allies, such as the people of the Four Towns. Kephrath and the others. We have agreements with some of the kings of the land not to interfere with one another. We have even defeated one or two of them. But there are parts of this land where the Kinahny kings are our enemy. They dominate us, and they say what we can and cannot do. If we can make covenant with some new ally, who will help us sweep away the kings who are against us, that has to be good."

They walked on without speaking for a while, as the noise of the village moving south washed around them. Abiy'el looked around and grinned.

"I like being on the move again. There's something grand about being a people moving all together."

Pedayah looked at him, anger creasing his forehead below his headman's kef.

"I'll do it because I must, and I will rally my people as best I can, but we have poured time and effort into Ramath-Galil these last few years. It grates me to just leave it all behind. This should be our land now, and we should not have to move here and there at somebody else's whim. In Yahusharar's day my father confronted his enemies. Now we just run away ahead of them."

"You were quick to want to go when you thought Hatsor was the worse enemy. When did you become a warrior?"

Pedayah ignored him and continued speaking to Abiy'el.

"I want to know when we will go back there. I want my people to live in the houses they have built, and eat from the fields they have planted. You are our warleader: when will you make war to get our homes back again?"

Abiy'el looked at him mildly. "When I know who I am fighting."

He stopped and turned to Labayu. Other people flowed around them like water around a rock.

"I need to know more about these people. Go back to your men, Labayu. Follow these newcomers here and there, see what they do. If it seems that they want to settle, I want to know. If they make peace with this king or that, or if they kill this king or that, I want to know at once. Send word to Sychem, or come yourself with the word. If I am not there, I will be out in the wilderness with my people, or else down at Shalem to negotiate with the king there."

"Shall I talk with them if the chance arises?"

Pedayah was shaking his head, and as Abiy'el hesitated he spoke up again.

"Like as not he'll ally with them against us. We don't need alliances, Abiy'el, we just need to stand firm ourselves against these newcomers. We never needed alliance before, not really, and we certainly don't need it now."

Labayu ignored him, repeated his own question.

"Shall I talk with them if the chance arises?"

Abiy'el spoke quickly to stop Pedayah interrupting.

"Perhaps. Certainly yes, if they look as though they might make terms with Hatsor or one of the fortified cities. But better if you track them without being seen yet, while we learn more. Look, if you can find out who their clan heads are, then try to bring them to Sychem to speak with me."

Labayu nodded slowly, aware that Pedayah disagreed with the decision. He suspected that after he left, the village headman would again try to undermine whatever he said, but at this point his first duty was to the warleader's instructions. He exchanged farewells, left the foreign weapons with Abiy'el, and turned again to the north to be with his men.

ㄨ ㆆ ㄱ ㆆ ㄱ ㆆ ㄱ ㆆ ㄨ

L ABAYU APPROACHED GATH-LESHEM from the south, alert for any signs that the small village had been attacked. There were none: life seemed to be continuing in the way it had since the site had been occupied by the Ibriym. He had no idea if this might mean that the invaders had not reached this far south yet, or whether small communities like Gath-Leshem simply had too little wealth to attract attention. He was missing information which would help him see a pattern in all this, and he intended to rectify the lack once he had met the others.

He rounded the settlement well to the west of its fields of vines, and the little groups of people working in them. He had no interest in speaking with the town elders. The oak grove where he had arranged to meet Shimmigar and Akiy was a little way out of the village, crowning the upper slopes of a shallow hill. It was visible at a considerable distance, and they had often used it as a meeting place. The oaks were still leafless yet, and the scattered pines showed up dark and sombre amongst the bare branches.

As he came into the grove, there was a whistle from up ahead. Akiy was sitting on a branch in one of the trees ahead, and lifted a hand casually as Labayu came towards him.

"Shimmigar is still out tracking this group?"

"Yes, chief. Not on his own, though, Ghazam is with him. And I picked up Uriel on my way here, he's over on the other side of the grove in case you passed that way." He stopped to give a longer, shriller whistle. "But I don't think that Shimmigar will be just quietly tracking. He's on the hunt now."

"Why is that? What happened?"

"Well, I tried to stop him, chief. I told him you wouldn't want this. But he wouldn't have it, said it was the duty of a Son of Anath and that you'd be all for it if only you knew. He wasn't going to stop on my word."

Labayu frowned, listening to Uriel approaching from the other side of the grove of trees.

"Just tell me, Akiy. What happened?"

Uriel came over, and Labayu embraced him while Akiy was scrambling down.

"It started when we were still trying to pick up the trail. There's a little piece of sown land up a good way past Leshem, the furthest north that any of the Ibriym ever settled. Almost up to Bayth Ma'acath."

"I know it. On their own in mostly Kinahny land. A single family, didn't have much to do with anyone else."

"Right. Well, they won't be having much to do with anything now."

They set off north and west together, Labayu following the lead the others set. Their pace was fast, but easy enough that they could speak as they moved. Akiy continued. Uriel was a handful of paces ahead.

"Shimmigar wanted to check on them, but we could see as soon as we came over the ridge that we were too late. The place had been set on fire, the flocks were scattered everywhere, and nobody was left alive."

"Nobody?"

Akiy shook his head.

"Now chief, this was strange because we thought that these newcomers only intended harm to the kings of the land and their cities. I don't know what happened here. The head of the family – a man, you know, not like you and I are used to down in the Four Towns – and they say that he was a hot-tempered man as well – maybe he said something to offend."

They fell silent to watch their footing on a stony section of the track which led them steeply up onto a crest, running sinuously above the damper ground either side. Labayu thought wryly to himself that he seemed to have been crossing the land at speed for days. At the top, they were able to talk again.

"So what did you find?"

"What you'd expect to find in a holding full of people which had been overrun by a warlike mob. Nobody living, for sure, except the youngest son, an infant who we found in a heap of cloth behind his mother's body. We took him to a nearby village, left him with a woman whose boy had died right after the birth. Well, Shimmigar took it badly."

"In what way?"

"Look now, he swore an oath that he would have revenge. These were people we had promised to protect, you see. They were Ibriym. Not just some Leshemite clan or a stranger. He took it personally."

Uriel dropped back to be beside them, and they paused at a spring to rest and drink a little of the water where it bubbled up from the earth.

"I have never seen Shimmigar like that. He would not wait for anything, just went right off with Ghazam on the trail and sent me back to meet you."

"How long ago was this?"

"A day and a half, near enough."

"Where was he going when you left him?"

"He told me to meet Uriel and then go to Gath-Leshem and wait for you. He was going to track down the group that did it. Him and Ghazam both. Most likely he'll have found them before the day was out. These raiders don't know how to hide themselves, chief, they leave a trail anybody could follow. It doesn't take any skill."

Labayu looked at Uriel, who nodded.

"I've not seen this lot, but I followed another group for a while further over towards the coast. They were just boys, really, out scouting ahead of a group of wagons. Not a serious warband. But anyway, they had no skill at covering their trail, and no idea I was there watching them. Shimmigar will have no difficulty following them. But you're right, as a rule they attack cities and leave the little places alone."

"That's what Abiy'el is hoping for. He wants us to talk with them, stop them making alliances with the cities up here, make our own covenant with them if we can. He thinks they might help us in our own struggles with the Kinahny kings."

"I think they're something new in the land, chief. They don't speak like anybody I know, they have different customs. They burn their dead instead of putting them in the ground. They're not like us."

"Well, but we're not like the Ibriym, yet we managed to join together when they came. We had reason for that: you remember the story about the former chief and his greed. The Ibriym were good for us, and we have been good for them. We need to calm Shimmigar down from his wrath, so we can talk with these people."

Akiy pulled a face. "Shimmigar is not in a mood to talk. You'll be wanting to get to him quickly, I think, before he does something that cannot be repaired. We'll need to pick up the trail ourselves first."

They took another mouthful of water, then Uriel pointed slightly north of the line they had been following, and they set off again.

ㅅㅕㅈㅕㅈㅕㅈㅕㅅ

IT TOOK LABAYU SEVERAL DAYS to find Shimmigar. Akiy, Uriel and he had crisscrossed the land several times where they thought they would find him, and never had the region seemed so large. Labayu was possessed by a sense of desperate urgency, and became increasingly frustrated at the succession of sunsets.

They finally moved further north, further even than Hatsor and Bayth Ma'acath. They first thought they had struck success when they followed a group of youths heading east from the coast, but a few hours convinced them otherwise. The group, many heavily injured, were limping back towards some home camp. Their leader was a tall lad, doing his best to get them all back to safety after some defeat.

Labayu could not work out what might have happened, but after spending some time spent circling around out of sight, he was convinced that Shimmigar was not there.

They moved on, and then for a day or so were busy avoiding groups of raiders all heading back towards the coast. They had clearly gathered together for a purpose that Labayu could not guess, and were now separating again. Each group was easy enough to evade, but once again the process took time.

Finally, after far too long a span of time, they came across Shimmigar, setting his camp late in the evening at one of the landmarks they all knew, beside a copse half-way up a hillside. There was a wild, ferocious aspect to him which Labayu had not seen before.

At first he would not say anything about the intervening days. Shimmigar had sent Ghazam away towards Hatsor at one point, and the two had only just come together again. He resented anybody's intrusion on his solitary pursuit. But then as the last light faded from the sky and the stars started to appear in the dome of the sky, he started to talk to them. He was cleaning his sword at the time; his ragged clothes and hair were silhouetted against the sky.

"So you kept your old sword? I thought you were going to get yourself one of those long ones the newcomers are using?"

Labayu scowled to himself at Akiy's bluntness. He himself had been thinking how to approach the subject less directly. Shimmigar laughed shortly.

"Wouldn't touch one of their blades just now. They're not handy like this one is. But I kept myself a couple of their javelins." He gave a last polish to one side of the blade and then sighted along it. "You called this an ox goad, chief, when you saw it alongside one of the others."

"And you said you could still kill with it."

"And so I can. And so I have been."

"And so tell me what happened, Shimmigar."

Shimmigar put the sword by his side and lay back against the slope, a dark shape in the lee of a scrubby tree. For a moment Labayu thought he was not going to answer, but then his voice drifted out of the shadows again.

"Has Akiy told you about the farm? Elishama and all his family?"

"He has."

"Well, I wasn't having that. They can't just come into our land and do as they please like that. So I tracked down one group and another, listening to them as they spoke around their camp fires – not that I could follow what they said, it's all strange to me – and seeing what they had with them. Then after some days I found a group who were carrying spoil from Elishama's house. I knew it by some silver cups they had."

He turned his head to look away down the slope.

"So then for the next few days I followed them, further away in the day and closer up at night. They set sentries but they don't know the ways of the land like we do. Those sentries were like rabbits in a pit, especially the first couple of nights when there was just one at a time."

"You killed them."

"And very easy it was, too. This little ox goad did very nicely, much neater than their great weapons."

He held the blade up against the sky, which had grown rich with stars. There was no moon.

"Sixteen I killed in that group, most of them in the night while they rested, a few in the day if they dropped behind. By the time I left they were terrified at every shadow along the track. They never saw who it was that picked them off one by one."

"Sixteen?"

"I wish it was sixty. Or six hundred. They should never have touched Elishama's household."

Labayu lay back, thinking. This was not at all what Abiy'el had wanted. Before he was ready to speak again, Akiy's voice came from the other side of Shimmigar.

"We tracked a group a few days back, with a lot of wounded. Tall lad leading them."

"That wasn't me. That was a different lot, just lads who'd got the worse of an encounter somewhere. Someone else did that to them, not me."

"I wish you hadn't sent me back to get the chief here. You shouldn't have had to do all that on your own."

Shimmigar laughed shortly. "Elishama was a friend to me, when so few of the Ibriym up here would have anything to do with us. You know what it's like. It was a personal matter."

"So why did you stop?"

"Oh, they were joined by another group. A big man leading them. Sported a red sash, which didn't flatter him but meant something. They were more afraid of him than of me. But he knew how to organise them, night and day, and I could see it was best to lay low for a while. I'll go back and finish the job another time."

Labayu shook his head. "And what do you think they'll do now, Shimmigar? Where do you think they will go?"

"I don't really care where they go or what they do, so long as it's away from our land. You've seen them; there are little groups going all over the place. I don't think they have a plan. If we push back hard, right from the start, we can turn them in a different direction. Make them some other land's problem."

Ghazam snorted.

"I saw as many of them as you did, Shim, and I don't think they'll just go away. That new leader you saw is likely taking his revenge on a settlement somewhere near here."

"What if he does? This is Hatsor's land, not ours. Let him do what he pleases up here. But not in our land, not to our people."

There was silence for a while. Eventually Labayu sat up.

"When I spoke with Abiy'el he wanted us to make covenant with them if we could. He wants to make sure they don't become close with the kings of the land."

"You can't make covenant with murderers like that. You could never trust them. And anyway, how are you going to talk to them? They have their own language. I can't follow it, and I don't think you will either."

"There must be someone among them who speaks Kinahny. Or Fenku at least."

Shimmigar laughed derisively. "A nice wish. But they've come from much further away. Don't know where exactly, but the walk to the Fenku ports is nothing compared to what this lot have done."

Labayu frowned, a useless gesture in the night.

"I have to try, Shimmigar. Abiy'el asked me to."

Shimmigar stood up abruptly and paced to and fro.

"I won't do that with you. I'm not even going to try to make peace with them until they abandon their killing ways. They struck first: we strike back, harder, until they yield. That is how it works. That is what Anath would do if she were here herself. We are called her sons: we do her work."

He stopped pacing, and turned to face them. His whole air was defiance.

"But this what Abiy'el wants, Shimmigar. He's our war-leader."

"Then let him lead us in war, not make little noises of weakness. I won't join you, Labayu. Tell me that you'll fight them, and I will be beside you every step. But tell me that you are going to try for peace, and we go separate ways.'

Labayu tried to sound conciliatory. "Look now, we'll talk more in the morning."

Shimmigar sat again, but with a little distance between him and the others. "I'll take the first watch. At least I still remember how to be at war."

After a pause, with only the ordinary night noises around, Akiy's voice broke the quiet.

"If you don't come with us, what will you do, Shim?"

"Go off with my ox goad again. See if I can bring my count up to sixty. Or six hundred."

Part 3 – Equinox

PRAISE NOW AKAMUNAS,
    who went with us against Wilios
Where sword and spear was stronger
    than the charge of chariots.
Gold was gathered,
    women wailed,
Their menfolk mastered,
    scattered in the smoking sky.
Praise now Akamunas,
    the slaughterer of cities.

Richard Abbott

⊨�⍾ symbols⊨

≠⍌⍊⍌⍊⍌⍊⍌⍊≠

ANILAT CHEWED AT THE TOUGH MEAT of the shaphan that
Khuratsanitu had snared. After the day's walk, while the
sun was still quite high, he had successfully caught it basking
among the rocky outcrops piled up to the east of the track.
Auntie had turned it into stew, and judging from the noises
the twins were making, their portions were good.

She looked again at the shallow bowl with her serving: it
was tasteless as well as tough. She glanced at Haleyna, and
caught the expression on her face. She was pushing the strips
of meat around her bowl, torn between hunger and dislike.
Clearly mother and daughter were sharing the same part of
the animal. She caught Haleyna's eye, deliberately speared
some of the meat and pretended to enjoy it. They grinned at
each other.

They were all sitting just outside a small hut, placed a
short distance up the hillside from the southward track. Part
of the roof had fallen in where it sloped down to meet the
ground, but the half facing downhill was still good. There was
plenty of dry wood nearby, and setting the fire to cook with
had been easy. If only the results had been better.

Khuratsanitu was sitting up on top of a taller rock, from
which he could see some distance up and down the valley.
Tadugari was near him, but his face was cast down and he
was, again, unresponsive. Anilat had no idea how to bridge
the gap that had opened up between them, and her attempts
had been repeatedly met with indifference or rejection. Meanwhile, as he had slipped further into inaction, Khuratsanitu
had rather exaggeratedly taken up the role of guardian.

Her bowl was almost empty, thankfully. She had thought
herself hungry enough to eat anything, but this meal had almost defeated her. Only a sense of duty had constrained her
to continue, and the sense of setting an example as mother of

the household that Haleyna could mimic one day. She leaned back against the rock and closed her eyes.

Every time she did that these days, images of bread filled her inner sight. Never fish, or fruit from the market, or figs from the trees that the slaves had trained along the walls of the inner courtyard, but only bread. The soft buttery flatbread they used to make at home was always the first one to fill the eyes of her heart, but then the longer, crisper wafers of the temples and palaces followed. Even the dark, coarse loaves the labourers made for themselves appeared to her.

So far on their journey they had scrupulously avoided making any contact with people. They had skirted widely around villages, and hidden off the track if there was any sound of other travellers. This had served them well while they still had the meagre supplies they had brought with them, but Anilat knew now that they could not carry on in this way.

"When we next come across a town, one of us must go in to it and bargain for food."

She saw Tadugari's face close off with rejection, and spoke again before he could say anything.

"We cannot go on day after day with so little food. And we will walk further every day if there is no need to stop and hunt so often. If you will not go in, I will do it myself. Mother gave me silver for the journey so that we would not be in want. I will use it, if nobody else will."

Khuratsanitu glanced down from his seat.

"The honoured lady is right. We lose time with having to hunt every day."

"I don't know that it's wise to show ourselves like that. We're still not that far south of Ikaret, not really. What if the place has been captured by this rabble? We should get further away first. We should have gone east as I said. We should never have come south."

"But I told mother I would go south. You go east on your own if you must. The rest of us will go south. Auntie will come with the children and I, and I am sure that the guardsman will come too."

Khuratsanitu looked uncomfortable at the prospect of being forced into a choice.

"Sir, lady, look now, I can go into a town when we find one. Neither of you need go. One soldier alone will not attract attention, and I will just say I am acquiring supplies for my commander. Which is true. Look, my lord, the rabble you speak of do not want to capture. Either they pass by, or they burn."

"One way or another, we must have food. Bread, for a start. And some grain and beans. I am not eating shaphan all the way to Hatsor."

Auntie nodded. "We can make the silver your honoured mother gave us go a long way. No need for any of us to do without."

Tadugari nodded reluctantly, and stood up to bring his bowl over to the others. Khuratsanitu suddenly stiffened, ducked down low, and turned his head to Auntie.

"Damatiria, smother the last of the fire. Now, do it now. And all of you hide among the rocks. Quick now."

Tadugari scrambled to the ground and Anilat gathered the three children in a group squatting around her. By the time they had done that, Auntie had beaten out the glowing sticks and patted down the strips of grass they had lifted earlier. They waited, silent, as Khuratsanitu carefully came down to them, keeping low to the ground. He looked left and right, then pointed to a gap between two of the larger rocks.

"Through that way, quickly now, if it please you. We can get further up the hill without being seen. We do not have much time: we need to get up to that little crag over there."

They scrambled diagonally up the slope to the rocky out-crop that he had pointed to. By the time they were safely be-hind it they could all hear a noise of men approaching. They peered cautiously through crevices and gaps in the rocks.

The head of a ragged column of about thirty soldiers was almost level with the hut where they had eaten. They had no particular order, and made no effort to walk in step. Most had leather jerkins, some had leggings, and one or two had hel-mets slung over their shoulder. Each one had two or three javelins and a long sword tied loosely to their pack. They formed a lively, if confusing, group. So far as Anilat could tell, most were not very different in age to Haleyna, with only a handful of older men scattered here and there.

Khuratsanitu grimaced, looked at Tadugari, who nodded. "If these were not at Ikaret, they are close kin. But there are too many of them to do anything. There are always too many of them."

Someone near the rear of the group called out, and they came to a halt, clustering in a circle. For a heartbeat Anilat thought that their earlier fire had been found, but the atten-tion was inward towards a tall man who was gesticulating, not up the valley sides. He wore a broad red sash, and carried himself as their leader. The circle spread out, and she realised that there were two prisoners among the youths.

They were both dressed as runners: they would have gone into battle alongside the chariotry on foot, not riding. Both had their hands tied, but the tall man cut the bonds of one of them. The prisoner looked around the circle and made no move. One of the youths stepped forward, sword in hand, and tossed a second sword over near the man. The crowd had gone silent, jostling one another to see what was happening.

The runner did not try to pick the sword up, until one of the others pushed him from behind. He walked over to the weapon, bent down and held it loosely, point down to the ground. The tall man called out to him. Khuratsanitu shook his head, and Anilat wriggled across to him and whispered.

"What are they saying?"

"I cannot follow most of it, but that big man just told him that he must defend himself. If he wins, he can go free."

The noise had started up again from the ring of spectators. The runner was now trying to defend himself, but even to Anilat's untrained eyes he seemed clumsy and ill-prepared. His adversary, on the other hand, was confident with the long sword he carried. Before long the runner had been disarmed again and had several large gashes across his upper body and arms. He stood there, looking around as though dazed.

The youth stepped back and looked across at the big man who had spoken before. He said something, gesticulated to the runner. There was a pause in which nothing happened, then the man strode over and shouted in the youth's face. Even from high up the hillside his fury could be heard. The young man took an uncertain step or two closer to his adversary, turned again to look around, and then suddenly ran towards him, making a series of wild chops with the sword. The unarmed man fell, writhing on the ground while the youth kept hacking away at him until he lay still.

The second runner was pushed forward, and a different youth came out of the circle. This time the runner snatched up the sword and ran straight at his enemy, shouting. The young man, caught unprepared, was forced back several paces in a desperate defence. The ring of onlookers moved with the pair, making no attempt to intervene. But the prisoner's impetus ran out after his first wild rush, and before long he was felled. The youth, blood running from his own wounds, thrust his sword firmly into the runner.

A great cheer went up, and the big man came over to embrace the youth. The crowd jostled around him and there was a buzz of congratulatory noise.

The first fighter was still standing on his own near the body of the man he had killed. He cleaned his sword on the grass, then picked up the second sword and cleaned that one as well. Finally one of the other lads noticed him and called him over. The big leader pointedly ignored him.

After a while the group moved over to the little stream, filled water skins and pouches, and set off south again, leaving the two bodies where they lay. Anilat rested her head on her hands and lay still for a time, trying to let the tightness in her body wash away. The valley was silent again, except for the sound of some crows calling to each other on the ridge opposite. Tadugari stirred and spoke, still in a whisper.

"We can't go south now. Not with those filth ahead of us."

"Your pardon for contradicting, lord, but it's the safest way of all just now. They're faster than us, and we will know right away if they have gone into a town or passed it by. Following them south is a better choice than ever."

"And I won't go in any other direction whatever you say."

Tadugari took a long breath and finally nodded.

"Tomorrow, though. We will go no further today, except to get away from this place and those bodies."

They lay still for a while longer and then, very cautiously, went back down to the hut and turned south along the valley. A short time later, when they settled in the shelter of a grove of trees, Anilat called Khuratsanitu over to be with her. He sat beside her on the dry grass. Auntie was nearby, among the trees, stretching out some bedding material. Haleyna was a little further away, unpacking something from her bag.

"Was that big man teaching the lads to fight?"

"No indeed, lady. They already knew how to fight." He stopped, and then at Anilat's questioning look, carried on. "He was teaching them to kill an enemy. Those boys will have fought against targets, or play-fought against each other. The youngest ones will never have known what it is to kill the man in front of them."

She nodded, unsurprised. "And you do this in the city guard?"

"Of course, lady. Some of the prisoners are good as slaves, some even as recruits. But others are fit only for practice. What else would we do with them?"

"And what of the women you capture?"

He hesitated, glanced briefly at Auntie, and then only said, "Well, we do not use them for killing practice."

"I want you to show me how I can kill my children if it seems they might be captured. I will not have them go through that."

"There are a few ways. But lady, surely it will not come to that?"

"You will show me. I gave the three of them life: I will take it away again myself rather than see them humiliated like those runners. Now show me."

She turned to face him and they both stood up.

"You might find it easier to do this from behind them."

"If I have to do this, I will face them so we can witness each other's anguish. Now show me."

He swallowed, glanced around uneasily, then looked back at her without raising his eyes to her face.

"You don't just stab at them without thinking. It won't work, and you will hurt them more. You count down their ribs."

His hand stopped, trembling slightly in mid-air. She looked at him impatiently.

"Well?"

"I cannot touch you, lady. It would not be proper."

She frowned, frustrated by the conventions that bound him.

"Auntie, come here a moment. I need to see what I have to do."

Auntie joined them, and Khuratsanitu looked relieved. He pressed Auntie's smock firmly against her body and started again.

"You count down ribs to here and find the gap between this one and the one below. Count them exactly so as not to make a mistake. Make sure you keep the blade exactly level and press in hard, just this side of their body, not in the centre. That will go straight into their heart."

He stopped, released Auntie and nodded to her.

"It's the easiest way I can teach you just quickly, lady. But I pray to all the gods it does not come to this."

"So do I. But at least now I am prepared for the worst."

She started to sit back down again, then turned back to them.

"My thanks to you both for that. I am most grateful for your kindness."

Khuratsanitu and Auntie looked at one another for a long moment. Then she smoothed her smock against her chest, turned away, and went back to laying out the bedding. The guardsman took a long breath, walked across to the edge of the grove, and looked up and down the valley before settling himself at a lookout position leaning against a rock.

╪⽊⼭⽊⼭⽊⼭⽊╪

KHURATSANITU WAS AGAIN IN THE LEAD as the group approached a crossroads, with a grove of carefully tended olives and a large standing stone to mark it. Just over half a month had passed since leaving the shepherds' huts and starting south. The coastal strip that they knew so well had been left behind long ago, and their path had skirted the western edge of the inland mountains before branching further away from the sea.

Anilat had a vague feeling that the coast, and the main road that ran close to it, was only a few days' journey from them, over to their right, but could not be sure. Their own route had been largely empty of travellers, and she presumed that those who had fled Ikaret, and perhaps other ports as well, were still hugging the Sea Road in the hope of finding shelter somewhere.

A substantial track wound away to their left up a long shallow ridge. Most of the animal and cart tracks followed in that direction. A smaller path turned back and right, leading eventually down to the Sea Road. The way ahead, curving around the olives, was middling in size, and clearly had seen only irregular use.

Tadugari and Khuratsanitu were pleased: they both knew this branching of the tracks. The left-hand way led to Damaseq. Hatsor was ahead of them, a little over a week away at their current pace.

Anilat had never travelled along these paths before, though she had in the past been along the Sea Road both north and south. Both of the men were familiar with the route, though, and although they had sometimes stopped for a while to consider at the occasional branches and divisions in the road, they had never been in serious doubt.

The party had settled into something of a routine after a day or so, only briefly disrupted by the events in the stony valley. They went at a pace which the children could manage, slow and steady. They were covering more ground each day now that they did not need to hunt so much. Every couple of days, if a village was near to their path, they could negotiate for bread and other supplies. Their store of silver, though shrinking, was still plentiful, and Anilat blessed her mother's name every night.

So far Khuratsanitu had been able to find somewhere to stay each night. Mostly they rested in huts on the edge of pasture areas. This early in the season they were unoccupied, but in the summer months they would be occupied as the flocks moved higher up the hillsides and further away from the villages and towns.

She was buoyed up by the thought that they were so near to Hatsor. When she had first chosen their destination it had just been a name, just one name among others in the list that Tadugari had recited. Only its southerly direction had given it any meaning. She had only known that Hatsor was a Kinahny town. That meant that they would be able to understand the speech with comparative ease, and their appearance would not be odd. Some of the customs would be strange, but the places of worship would be familiar.

At least in name, the entire Kinahny province was still under the rule of the Mitsriy king. Perhaps they would find some representative of her mother's Beloved Land here. For sure the Mitsriy had withdrawn their soldiers from some of the cities, in order to patrol the Sea Road and the garrisons strung like beads along it. The balance of power was changing, and she did not know what she might find. But perhaps there would be a Mitsriy priest there who could help her to bury the last bodily remains of her parents.

At very least, Hatsor was starting to gain the qualities of a real place in her mind. She had quizzed the men for details about it, and then entertained the children by making up stories about its people, and making little mounds of stones and twigs to represent its citadel for them. Auntie had joined in enthusiastically, and the evening camps had been cheerful times for Haleyna and the twins.

She felt that she had been successful in making the journey good for them. The cost to herself was considerable, however. The fall of the city and the death of her mother, followed so soon after by the separation from Yasib and Dantiy, weighed very heavily on her. She threw herself into the task of enlivening the children, but once they were asleep there was nothing to fill the hollow of her soul.

At first, her heart had turned over in anxiety at every place where the track divided. It seemed all too likely that Khuratsanitu might make a different choice. She had no idea how they would endure without him. He carefully deferred to Tadugari at every decision, but when it came to action, they all relied heavily on the guardsman. She had no idea how long he would stay with them.

After Anilat had insisted on the need for food, it was Khuratsanitu who cautiously entered little places to trade silver for supplies and news, Khuratsanitu who found and scouted out their overnight stops, and Khuratsanitu who had made sure they were well hidden on the two occasions that groups of strangers had been in the area. Whether these other parties had had anything to do with the enemies at Ikaret could not be said, but nobody wanted to find out.

Tadugari, on the other hand, remained withdrawn. Anilat no longer expected him to act the envoy, to lead them by entering towns with his head held high and his voice full of authority and command, so that the local elders would treat their party with respect. Indeed, he could only rarely be coaxed near villages of any size, and he did so hesitantly. As they left again, and the places had dwindled into the distance, relief contested with misery on his features.

He spoke irregularly with the children, and when he did, it was with impatience. He had ceased offering the sunrise and sunset prayers with any real fervour, and even the weekly offerings, which he had never skimped on before, were carried out in a brief, perfunctory manner. The gods had become remote for him. He was cold and unresponsive to her, at a time that she urgently needed affection and tenderness. Everything was loss.

As they left the crossroads behind, Anilat found herself once again beside Auntie. They were aiming to get another couple of hours walking behind them before finding somewhere to stop for the night. The three children kept shifting to one side and the other, left and right, left and right.

Ahead of them she could hear the two men talking. Tadugari was once again lamenting the hunt that he would not be able to join. Her thoughts filled briefly with a burning rage: was there nothing else to talk about?

To her surprise, though, it seemed that Khuratsanitu had also been a regular participant. The common soldiers apparently had their own part in it alongside the nobility, and all shared alike in the drinking afterwards, regardless of rank. The anxiety that had been building within her for several days suddenly burst out.

"Auntie, I'm frightened that Khuratsanitu will leave us at one of these branches in the road."

She was aware that the other woman was studying her, but she kept her own face forward.

"Why would he do that, mistress?"

"Well, perhaps he could do more for himself if he wasn't having to look after us."

They walked on for a few paces. Tadugari and Khuratsanitu were a little way ahead, pointing at a distant hill shaped like the back of a goat, and Anilat continued in a very quiet voice.

"My husband isn't himself just now. What if he says something to offend? We're not in the city any more, and we need Khuratsanitu. We have not yet called upon his skill with weapons, but every day we depend on his vitality and willingness to help. What if he thinks that there's better for him in one of these little places we go past? I can't bear the thought of us being alone. Me and the children."

"Will you talk with him about this?" Seeing Anilat shake her head, she continued. "Then is there something you want me to say to him on your behalf?"

"I don't know. I don't know what any of us might say. Nevertheless I am frightened. I don't know what I am saying. But I had to say it to somebody, and Tadugari won't listen to anything I say. Nothing at all."

"It's all right, mistress. There's no need to worry about this. Khuratsanitu is a loyal man. I don't think he would just leave you."

Anilat nodded, finally meeting Auntie's eyes, and they spoke no more about it. But that evening, around the fire as they were cooking, Auntie stayed close and attentive to Khuratsanitu.

╪╫╫╫╫╫╫╫╪

A FEW DAYS NEARER TO HATSOR, they came unexpectedly on the signs that there was a village nearby. The road abruptly became better kept, and in the distance they could see signs of cultivation. They were in the sown land and no longer in the wilderness. Judging from a nearby track which branched off, the town itself was a little to one side of the road, hidden from their view by some trees.

The group halted, uncertain as to how to proceed. Tadugari shook his head.

"I think we should go no closer. They might never know we had been here."

Khuratsanitu frowned and pointed to where a young figure was running away from them round the edge of the wood.

"Too late for that, sir. That one's seen us for sure. If we were wanting to just push on we should move quickly. Or we could go back north for a time and work a way around here?"

"Let's not go backwards. There's no harm this far into the Kinahny province, surely? The villages we have passed have been unharmed: only the great cities and towns are at risk, it seems. Could we stop with them for a night? We would do well to get some more food from them, husband."

Tadugari looked up and down the road, undecided. "Who can say? I don't know these people. None of us do. But I suppose it will be safe, this close to Hatsor. Whatever this place is called, it surely is under the protection of the king there."

They dithered for a little longer, before reaching a mutual consensus and turning off the main track towards the trees. As they rounded the last curve of brushwood, they realised that the village had suffered. The doors and shuttered windows of many of the houses had been broken down; the roofs of others had been burned. Gates which had once penned animals in place swung wide open. A few bodies lay haphazardly in the grass nearby. The damage was casual, however, rather than systematic.

Tadugari stopped short. "We should move on. There's nothing here for us. And for all we know the band who did this is still nearby. I don't want to come all the way safely from Ikaret, and be killed here. Why should this place have been attacked? What is different about it?"

Khuratsanitu took a few steps forward.

"I think it's safe now, sir."

"In any case, we still need food and other supplies. Even if the village is empty, there will be food."

"Not quite empty, mistress. There's a woman over there."

Auntie was pointing to a house on the right, where a face had appeared briefly and then hidden itself again. Khuratsanitu nodded.

"I'll go and see who it is."

He walked forward, then realised that Anilat had come with him. He looked at her, his face creased with concern. She carried on walking, moved ahead of him.

"We don't want to frighten her, do we? You stay back: near enough to help if something happens, I mean, but not so near as to look a threat."

He kept several paces behind her as they walked up to the house and stopped a short distance from the door. It stood slightly ajar. Anilat called out once, twice. At the third time the door shifted slightly, and a woman's voice came from the inside.

"You're Kinahny?"

Ikaret had never considered itself any part of the Kinahny province, but now was not the time to make that distinction.

"Near enough. We have come down from Ikaret."

"Then you should go back north again. The land has troubles here."

"We fled from Ikaret when it suffered its own troubles. Perhaps even the same enemy that came here."

The door crept open a little more, and they could see the shape of a figure in the shadows inside. "Look, we just want some food. We can give you silver for it. We are not thieves."

"Silver?" The woman in the house laughed, rather bitterly. "What would I do with silver? Look at this place around you now. Look at me now."

"It would be yours for a better day. It will not spoil, and we will not take anything that you cannot give."

There was a long pause, and then the door opened. The woman stepped out into the sunshine. Her face was heavily bruised, and she had tied a piece of rag around her head instead of a proper kef. Underneath that, her hair was matted with soil and ash. Her skirt was torn and filthy, ragged and bloodstained. She smelt of misuse and lack of care. She looked at Anilat proudly, defiantly, but pointedly ignored Khuratsan-itu.

"So where is this silver?"

Anilat held out a double handful of shapeless pieces she had taken from her pack earlier. They had originally been a part of an old pectoral ornament, which had been damaged beyond repair several years ago. Portions of it had been hacked off from time to time for occasions such as this one. The woman took it without comment, looked at it closely, and then led them to one of the less damaged outbuildings. There was a good supply of food in it, both perishable and longer lasting.

"Take what you want. There is too much for me here."

Anilat left the others picking out what they would need for the next few days, and followed the woman back to the original house.

She stopped in surprise as she went in. The house was organised in a fever of neatness. Every wooden utensil and clay pot in the cooking area was in place, the two chairs were placed directly opposite each other around the spotless table, the handful of stools formed a geometric pattern near the fireplace and the family grindstone, and the floor had been apparently swept only moments before. Where the woman's hair and clothing were tangled and torn, and the outside world was in turmoil, order reigned inside the threshold of her house.

"You were left here alone?"

"Yes."

Her gaze slid away from Anilat's questioning look.

"We thought we saw somebody else as we came down the road. Somebody younger."

The woman shrugged.

"Perhaps the others will come back some time. Those who were lucky enough to run away early. The women of my family have tended the shrine here for generations. I thought even beasts would honour that, but my place in the sacred stones meant nothing to them. I pleaded with the first one that the stones were holy, and he just laughed, saying that I should be pleased he was doing this in a holy place. Most of them were just boys, but he was too strong. He had a red sash. To prove he was their master, I suppose."

She moaned, an eerie sound in the empty room. "Mastering boys, and overpowering women. What could anybody do?"

Anilat opened her mouth to ask what had happened, but thought better of enquiring too much about the woman's experience. Outside, she could hear the voices of her three children arguing over something. The village woman wrapped her arms around her body and rocked to and fro, keeping her eyes down.

"Look now, we are wanting to go to Hatsor. We have planned to meet my sister's children there."

The woman was shaking her head jerkily.

"Don't go there. Keep away from there. Don't go there. The city's all gone."

Anilat shivered. "What do you mean, gone?"

"Like here. Like your Ikaret. That lot went to Hatsor first, then came back to here. We were just an afterthought."

"Wait. I must tell the others. Let me get them."

"Don't bring your men in here. I can't even look at them. You mustn't. Bring your woman helper if you want. But not your men."

As Anilat left the house, she saw the woman placing the stool back in its original place with great exactness. She ran over to the other building and told them about Hatsor.

Tadugari sat down on a nearby stool and put his head in his hands. A sudden memory of her mother's expression for grief, head on knee, slipped painfully into Anilat's heart.

"Look, I need to get back to that woman. You carry on getting supplies together here, but she won't have anything to do with you men."

"I should stay here and make sure these two choose the right things."

"Very well." She looked around the room. "Haleyna, you come back with me."

She turned to go. Khuratsanitu was standing in the open doorway, his short sword held loosely in one hand. "Be careful, lady. I am sure somebody is watching us."

She glanced at the houses, the overturned cart nearby, the line of trees to the north fringing the disorder. She could see nobody, but she trusted the soldier's instincts.

"Nevertheless. I need to find out more from her about what happened here. And at Hatsor."

The room was still perfectly laid out. The village woman had not moved. When she saw Haleyna she grimaced, then suddenly stood up and hugged her before sitting back in a heap again. At Anilat's nod, Haleyna drew up another stool, sat beside her and took her hand. She gripped it back with a fierce intensity. Haleyna looked disgusted by the woman's smell, but said nothing.

"This is my daughter, Haleyna."

The woman nodded, and kept hold of Haleyna. She said nothing, and Anilat tried again.

"We need to know what happened here. And when? How long since all this happened?" She gestured around in a circle.

"Perhaps a week since they came here. And we heard about Hatsor only a day or two before that. They're animals."

"And you have been alone since then? Where are all the others?"

She nodded, but with her eyes averted. "The others left to scatter into hiding places. We all agreed they would stay there two weeks. But I told you already: I was the shrine-tender for Bayth Ma'acath. My mother cared for the village shrine until her death, and I would not leave it."

"That is the name of this place? Bayth Ma'acath?"

The woman nodded again but said nothing.

"So you stayed? Who stayed with you? Why didn't your family stay?"

She shrugged. "My husband stayed. They killed him. Small loss. Maybe better for him than for me."

"Nobody else stayed?"

The woman suddenly wailed in the little room, a sound that sent shivers all up and down Anilat's back. Haleyna flinched, suddenly frightened at the sound, but stayed sitting where the woman held her.

"They killed my boy in front of me. What had he done to them? What had any of us done? The big man in charge, the one with the sash, he said as he took me that it was all for revenge, and we would think better another time, but what had we done? Surely their quarrel is with the kings of the land, not with us? What are they revenging for? We've lived in peace in the land all these years. We had never seen them before."

Anilat was convinced that the shrine-tender was not telling the entire truth, and was wondering how to find out more without straying too far into the woman's pain.

"They never found my secret, though, I kept that from them no matter what they did. They never found out. I beat them in that."

Abruptly she sat bolt upright, her head craning towards the door. Anilat listened. There was a new voice outside; a man, talking with Tadugari and Khuratsanitu.

"Come, quick, I'll show you where you can hide."

She had Haleyna by the hand and was pulling her towards the back of the house. Anilat stood up and hurried over to her daughter.

"What are you doing? They're just talking to someone outside. Most likely it's one of your own people come back again."

"Do you think I don't know what my own people sound like? It's all starting again. Let me put your daughter somewhere safe. They won't find her. We have to stay out, there's no room for more than two. But we won't say anything. At least they won't be found."

Anilat felt cold inside. Had they escaped Ikaret only to be caught at some little hamlet like this? She let the other woman take her out of a back door. Haleyna was struggling a little at the woman's grip, so she took her other hand and tried to quieten her. She touched the little knife she had carried at her belt since Ikaret, rehearsing to herself the instructions Khuratsanitu had given her. Haleyna saw the movement of her hand.

"Please don't kill me, mother. I know the soldier showed you how, but don't do it now. I won't let you. Let this woman hide me instead. I'll be safe there."

Anilat clenched her hands tight, and nodded once. As they hurried on she found the little hilt of her knife and touched it again for reassurance. They had not yet reached that extremity, but if it came she wanted to know her hand would not hold back.

They were hidden from the front of the house, crossing a little alleyway between buildings. Just on the right was a cistern. The woman heaved a stone from the wooden lid and lifted it. Inside another girl was standing on the internal ledge. She was a couple of years older than Haleyna, and was looking up at them with frightened eyes. The woman's reticence abruptly made more sense.

"Get in there, girl, get in there with my daughter and stay there until we come back."

She closed the cistern lid and pulled Anilat away in a different direction.

"We can see what they are doing from over there. But whatever happens to us, we say nothing about our girls."

Anilat followed her down a narrow alleyway, stepping over half-burned pieces of roof timber. The track made a turn at the corner of the house, but the woman, moving more slowly now, went across a vegetable patch to a low screen of fruit bushes. The vivid new leaves were speckled with ash.

From between the bushes they could see Tadugari talking with a stranger. Khuratsanitu was nearby, and the twins were with Auntie, looking in the nearest house. The stranger was dressed as a trader, and two well-armed young men stood at a distance holding several roped donkeys. The woman clutched Anilat's arm and hissed in her ear.

"Why did you not tell me you had other children?"

Anilat shook her head. There had been no time. And surely the woman could have listened for herself. They were too far away from the men to hear anything except fragments of what they were saying. Tadugari was mostly silent, asking only the occasional question, but the trader was very expansive in his answers.

After a while the trader pulled out a little pouch of liquid – wine, she presumed – took a short drink and passed it over to Tadugari. He glanced at it and shook his head. He asked something about Hatsor. The trader frowned, pointed away east, then again in a different direction, more nearly south.

Then he looked at the twins, said something in turn. Auntie stiffened and gathered the twins closer to her. Khuratsanitu took a step or two closer to them. The trader's guards let go of the donkey's ropes and had hands near their weapons.

Tadugari shrugged, shook his head, then pointed across to the house where Anilat and the village woman had been talking, where Haleyna had been. The woman's fingers dug into Anilat's arm again. The trader was silent for a moment, then laughed, letting the tension run out of the air. A little while later the trader, the two guards, and the little procession of donkeys moved off towards the west.

When they were out of sight, Anilat turned to the woman. "You go and get the girls out of that cistern. I'll find out what happened and meet you back in the same house."

She pushed through the bushes and crossed over to the others. The twins ran to her and she put an arm around each. Khuratsanitu was watching where the strangers had gone, shaking his head slightly.

"What happened? Who were those people?"

"Just a trader and his guards from out east. Gargamish originally, I think, but on a route past Hatsor across to the Fenku."

"I didn't like them, mistress. And I didn't like what he was saying about the twins."

Khuratsanitu came over to them, looking sombre. "I don't think you should have told them about your daughter, sir."

"What was he saying?"

Tadugari shrugged. "It was nothing serious. He did not mean it."

Anilat looked at Auntie, who took a deep breath.

"He was saying that people would pay a lot for child workers just now. That a pair of lads would fetch a good price if you knew the right contacts. And what he called a fresh girl was particularly valuable."

"And you didn't just send him away then and there? And you told him about Haleyna? What came over you?"

She was shouting, frantic with anger and fear. Tadugari looked away, shrugged again.

"Well, they're gone now. No harm done. And we are short of food anyway."

Anilat stared at him, furious, struggling for words at first. "How dare you say that? We have a whole village of supplies just here. And well over half of my mother's silver. How could you weigh up my children like that? How could you let that take root in your heart? What must that trader think of us all?"

Tadugari looked ashamed, bent his head as though in a fierce wind. Anilat stared at him, and when no response came she stormed away with the twins back to the house where Haleyna was waiting. Khuratsanitu and Auntie looked at each other and then carried on collecting things from nearby houses.

A MAN ADDRESSES HIS BROTHER.

Hekanefer to Ramose, on the morning after victory.

Well, brother, I have survived my first battle, largely by being nowhere near the point of danger. I have written to our father concerning the battle, and will not bore you with repetition. I am sure that he will pass the news on to you, and indeed anyone else who passes by. How happy was my heart that my place was to stand beside the chief officer and record all his words, and even more that his plan required him to observe from the vantage point of the craggy knoll rather than be down in the blood and confusion of the valley.

No, this letter concerns the time when the battle was done. We went down from our place of clear sight to walk among the men who had fought the battle. It was a sweaty, bloody place by then, with the ground all torn up by the wheels of the chariots and the feet of the soldiers.

Our men were still working their way around the field, dispatching any of the enemy who still lived, and stripping them of their possessions. There was little enough to be gleaned, for those enemies were obviously a poor and miserable lot with scarcely any items of real value among them.

And of course the soldiers were bringing trophies back so that each could receive their reward. I have heard that most officers now ask for the hands of the defeated enemy to be brought back; this one adheres to the old traditions and wants to see the proofs of manhood. All around the field lay dead young men who had been mutilated in this way. That was simply the reward for their folly, but I soon found it a most sickening sight.

As I walked beside the commander to the place where he would reward his men, we passed several of the slain who were no more than youths. One indeed looked to be the same age as our own brother would have been, had the sickness not taken him that winter. We had defeated not men, but boys. Twice shocking, then, that boys like these had defeated our own charioteers a few days ago, and have torn down great cities which have thrived for so many years.

As I looked on the heap of proofs of victory which the soldiers had gathered, it struck me that these boys had had their manhood cut away in every sense. A great rage kindled inside me, not against these miserable defeated enemies, but against the wicked leader who sent them against us.

After that we stood off to one side and the commander spoke to us all. He cannot use words like a scribe, or even a priest, but he can reach the hearts of his men well enough. Also, he does not continue beyond what is necessary. I could wish this happy trait was shared by more people.

Anyway, he mentioned by name every one of those who had acquitted themselves well in the fight, making no distinction between native born and stranger. His memory for the details of the battle was quite extraordinary. Clearly the soldiers thought that every word of his speech was worth cheering. I must keep remembering how recently it is that they knew defeat, and how much they need victory in order to feel truly alive.

He also announced rewards for the collection of the trophies. Naturally it was my duty to record all this. The sight of the private parts of men has never been of interest to me, and that was doubly true for this heap, which was all too obviously youthful rather than manly. I found the whole affair quite distasteful, and the business took much longer than decency required.

Another thing. One of the dead on our side was the man who said that he knew Senet. I played him a few times before the battle, and he was in fact of rather modest ability. I gave myself a handicap to even the play between us, but even so it was never really a challenge. Despite all that, I shall miss him now, and I do not believe that there is anybody else in the camp who can play the game.

Once it was all finished, Ramose, I made time for myself to contemplate. I walked away from that gruesome place, and hid myself for a while in one of the peaceful groves of trees nearby. I had a need to immerse myself in the things of the gods rather than the things of men.

It seemed to me that the whole thing – the fighting, the blood, the counting of body parts – all of today was like a tiny copy of all that has happened for our Beloved Land in this province.

We came out from our land wanting to meet true companions. We wanted brothers and sisters out here with whom we could share in the delight of the gods, the pleasure of wise conversation, and the furtherance of the way of truth.

What have we found? We have found ungrateful city rulers, men and boys who would rather die than join in fellowship, and women with whom one cannot form lasting ties. Never once have we found people from another land with whom we can talk as equals.

Somewhere in the lands of this world, somewhere within the circle of the sun's path, somewhere there must be such a people. I fear that we will never find them: they will be forever over the horizon in the place we do not find. Perhaps we will not once in all our lives find the land that could be our brother. So how happy I am that I have a brother of my own to speak with!

Enough of this for now. I am told that we will move on again tomorrow. The commander has not troubled to tell me where we will go, and in truth unless it is back to a city of some repute then I have no great desire for any particular direction. A part of me still craves some other diversion to soothe my spirit and relax my body, but the greater part is content to follow this commander.

Even now I can hear you laughing that I was in no great personal peril. You are right, of course, but every one of us on that field felt his nerves stretched tight and his blood racing, and every one of us was uplifted afterwards by his speech.

I was not born to be a soldier, and my deepest desire is to be back again amongst cultured men and women, but if I must be here then it is good to be beside him.

Remember me to your wife, who is like a true sister to me, and to your children, my beloved nephew and nieces. I hope to visit you all again before the next inundation, by which time this sorry business will surely be over and done with. When you go to the house of our parents, tell them again, and tell Mereriyt also, that I was safe at every moment of that battle. Remember me also to all the gods, that I shall remain just as safe when the fighting comes again.

A SON ADDRESSES HIS MOTHER.

Hekanefer to his mother the lady Hemesherit, greetings and blessings to you. I write from our camp somewhere west of the city of Hatsor.

Best of mothers, I felt that I should write to you in my own hand again. I am sure father has told you of the battle that was won, and that the fierce hearts of our men kept me fully safe from any harm. There will be other battles, I think, so please speak to every god so that the hand of their protection will be around me and in front of me.

I have told you about the squad of foreigners who joined our own men recently, and how their new way of fighting helped us to defeat the band of enemies recently. Well now, we received new orders sent out from the house of the great king User-ma'at-Re Mery-Imun himself, who lives in prosperity and health. And not just our contingent, so I understand, but each and every similar one engaged in the defence of the Beloved Land.

It is like this. Every soldier in the squad has been issued with two javelins, and two in twenty have new swords of the longer pattern used so effectively by these foreigners. One day I suppose every soldier will carry such a thing. You can believe that some of the men grumbled at the new equipment that they had to carry now.

"It has not been like this before in the days of our ancestors," they said. These words were heard by the commander, but instead of punishing them for rebellious thoughts, he stood up in front of them all. "Indeed the weapons are new, but this is because the enemy is new, and if we do not learn to fight in a new way the gods will leave our Beloved Land and go to dwell in another place."

And so every man must now practice with these javelins, and the few with the long swords must train with the foreigners who are our allies. This happens at first light and again before dusk. And as well as that we keep on the move, not staying in any one place more than a night. We are looking for another of the small bands of invaders, to defeat them with our new skills and our new weapons.

But I know that you will grow weary of news of war. Let me tell you instead something of this land. Now that spring is with us, it has become a place of considerable beauty. Of course nothing compares to the Beloved Land, in all her moods and seasons, but I can understand at last why the great kings of old were moved to come here not just once, but time after time.

The leaves and the flowers are fragrant and delicate, the animals are varied, the birds are full of song and bright feathers. I have read many accounts of this place written by scribes of old, but they do not tell the full truth; they are often gloomy, and forget to mention the splendour that is here.

We have not been near the main roads and tracks of the land for some time, and so have not had to witness the suffering of all those who fled the fighting in the north. Instead we chance upon some small village or town, a place that has so far been innocent of this conflict. Or at the end of a day of marching perhaps there is no town, but instead a grove of trees, or a sacred circle of stones, or a silent pool waiting like a mirror to be found.

O best of mothers, I wish that you could see these places, but I am sure if ever I brought you into this land, I would not be able to find them again. They are like hidden gifts in the old stories, which appear for a day and then vanish again.

Each morning as I start the day's march beside the commander, I feel that I am leaving behind some secret treasure of the land, an adornment fashioned by one of the gods for the delight of another.

Another thing. You said in your last letter that I have stopped talking about Nodjmet daughter of Ankhiriyt. I suppose that this is true, and indeed I cannot remember the last time that I wrote down the signs of her name. I have not forgotten her, not entirely, but she has grown faint beside the sights and sounds of this province.

I am convinced that this is simply because of the war we are fighting just now. When peace and stability is restored, and the world returns to its rightful order, then surely the memory of her face and voice will fill my heart again.

Remember me to all the gods, mother, and think of me as you sit under the shade of the sycomore figs, beside the little stream that runs through our own garden.

Perhaps in some mysterious way the waters of that stream are joined to the waters I pass beside, and as I dabble my hands in their coolness I can imagine your own voice as you read these my words.

INSIDE THE WAGON, YASIB SAW that Dantiy's kef had been altered, with a mourning pattern now woven into it. She spoke before he could.

"See, brother, the lady Kastiandra gave me a length of dark thread for my kef so that I could wear the sign of Halmanu's passing properly."

There was a trace of a smile in her eyes which he was sure nobody else would see.

"How kind an act that was. I trust you have expressed gratitude from us both. But look now, you and I must talk about our future here."

He turned to Nikleos.

"Might we have some time together alone? I will be nearby with my sister, in plain view of you all, but we will talk better in our own tongue."

They left the wagon and went to sit on some rocks in the shade of the scrubby trees.

"Congratulations on your marriage to Halmanu. Even if you are a widow now."

"Be quiet, brother. Turns out that being a widow is the safest thing for a young woman among these people. This way I can avoid being molested. Nobody here knows that father would never have accepted Halmanu as my husband. As for you, don't you start trying to lie with any of the clanswomen either; like as not you'll end up both being killed to cover the shame of it. The girl's own father would see to it himself."

"In truth?"

She nodded, and took his hand. "I think they mean well, but their customs are strange. You should restrain yourself until you can find a nice Kinahny girl."

"Are there any nice Kinahny girls? You know the men in Ikaret have a proverb about that."

She shrugged. "If we do not plan to live according to their rules then we should leave now. Where has our guard gone?"

Yasib pointed across the circle of wagons.

"Over there. I think he will not want to stay. He thinks these are the people who plundered Ikaret. His heart is full of hate."

"Other towns, perhaps, but not ours, I think. The daughter says that they did not pass that way."

"I agree. I listened to Nikleos, and am sure that he was speaking truth when he told me that they followed the roads inland, not along the coast. They may be distant kin to those who attacked Ikaret, but they are not the same. I think we need to stay with these people."

She sighed.

"My heart knows that you are right. But I swear this, brother, if I find that they were involved after all, I shall want blood."

He nodded soberly.

"I think we should share revenge together. I don't yet know what would satisfy me."

"Show me the man who violated our mother and I know only one thing that will satisfy me." She looked away, towards the north. "But I miss Ikaret, and I think I shall miss it forever now."

He waited, watching dappled light and shade play across her face. She continued.

"I miss the sun rising over the hills ahead of us, and setting into the open sea behind. I miss our house, and our garden. I miss our mother and father terribly. I miss the singing from the temples and the ceremony of the royal processions. I miss the ships coming in to the docks, and the endless flocks of wading birds around the bay to the north. I even miss the fish we used to eat four days out of five, and I never thought I would say that."

"We need to stay with Nikleos and his people. Everything I see here tells me that we need to get them to accept us."

"I agree. But how? Blood ties are important to them and we are strangers."

"Then we have to make ourselves useful to them. Get them to do whatever they do to adopt us into the clan." He touched the signs of widowhood on her kef. "How long did you tell them you would be in mourning?"

She laughed. "I was vague." She stopped and looked directly at him. "What exactly are you suggesting I should do?"

"Whatever we need to do to survive here. Up to you what that is and when you do it."

She raised her eyebrows.

"Well, indeed it is up to me. Mother taught me what to do to persuade a man, and when and how to do it. But you will leave the act itself to my own choice. And in the meantime, what will you be doing to allow us to survive?"

"Making myself an invaluable source of knowledge. They are very ignorant of life in this region, and they know they need a guide."

"So we are agreed that we stay? It is the best choice?"

"I believe it is. Just now these people are unstoppable. We need to remain with them and rise up with them while they carve their way through this land. Until they call a halt and settle somewhere for good. Then we choose again."

She took his hand, squeezed it, and waited until he looked her in the eye.

"Be careful, Yasib. We know very little about these people."

He shook his head very slowly. They got up together, and walked back arm in arm towards the wagon. As they did so, they saw Tarmanni coming back across the circle towards them. They waited until he came up close. He was tense with suppressed passion but waited for Yasib to speak.

"Did you learn what you needed from that man Towanos?"

"I did, sir, and my advice to you is that we move on right away. You've seen what goes on here. This lot are from the same stock as those who burned our city. I won't stay with them. None of us should."

"They're not the same people."

Tarmanni stared at them. "Near enough kin to persuade me. You're not saying you'll be staying?"

"I think we will."

"I'll have nothing to do with them. With respect, sir, but neither should you. Out of memory for the dead in the city. Your own family, even. You can't do this."

Yasib drew himself up.

"You'll not be telling me what to do and what not to do. If you don't want to stay, I release you from your service. You are free to go wherever you choose. But do not presume to tell me what to do."

There was a look of barely concealed contempt on the soldier's face.

"Oh well, sir, thank you for your kindness, sir. I'll just finish in your service now, sir, and be on my way without troubling you again, sir."

He turned away from them and started organising his pack, still resting where he had left it beside the wheel of the wagon. Yasib took a half-step towards him, but Dantiy took his arm again and shook her head. Instead, they turned away and climbed up on to the back-boards of the wagon beside Nikleos.

"Sir, my sister and I would be honoured to stay with you. Teach us what promise to make to you and your family."

"Will your guard be staying? He must make his own oath."

"He will not be staying."

"Then you come with me, and we will find two other men to witness the oath. Your sister will help the women get your place ready."

As they set off towards the nearest wagon, Tarmanni was finishing his own packing. Yasib turned round once to see him heading west, climbing out of the bowl of the land. He frowned and followed Nikleos. Another connection with Ikaret had been cut away; now there was only himself and his sister who could remind each other of the city.

$$\mathbin{\text{=╫╫╫╫╫╫╫=}}$$

T HE NEXT DAY WAS BRIGHT over Nikleos' camp, and once they had stirred into wakefulness it was time to move on. Oxen were harnessed to the wagons again, possessions were tied down and fastened safely for the journey.

After Yasib had returned from taking the oath of peace, Arkelawos' father Kastor had come over to view Murtilis. She had sat there obediently silent through the whole business, dressed in her best tunic and skirt, while Nikleos and Kastor had agreed the finer details of the transaction. Dantiy and Yasib had watched with fascination.

Finally, she and Kastiandra had embraced tearfully, and Murtilis had walked the short distance back with Kastor to his wagon. Nikleos had walked beside her, carrying a little chest with dowry and her spare clothing.

Then he had come back alone and empty handed. Murtilis was sitting now on the boards of Kastor's wagon beside Aigla. She had become part of Kastor's household, but would have to wait for Arkelawos to return before making the last stage of the journey from virgin to wife.

That evening, as Dantiy worked with Kastiandra in place of a daughter, Yasib went with Nikleos to the circle of elders and talked about the journey ahead. He sketched all over again the rough outline of the land, but this time spoke in considerable detail about the towns ahead, and the extent of Mitsriy power that they might expect to find.

To Nikleos' delight – since it would reflect well on his own standing on the community – the information was received well. As Yasib explained to Dantiy as they sat talking together before it was time to sleep, most of the families by now wanted to find a place where they could settle again as farmers. If his words could direct their path to such a place, he would earn their gratitude.

The wagons lumbered on through the morning, slow, noisy. Yasib had persuaded them to alter their direction. Their previous southward path would lead them further into Mitsriy territory, but with no obvious goal in view. Now they had turned back to retrace some of their steps.

The change had faced them towards Hatsor again, but Yasib did not intend to go that far. Instead, they would ford the River at an easy crossing place well away from any towns. The Mitsriy had no real interest in the lands on the far side of the River, but the occupants of the little towns and villages might well appreciate extra hands at seedtime and harvest.

Everything went well until around noon. Then Arion, from his wagon away on the west side, blew a horn without warning, and the whole group bunched together and slowed to a halt. Through the low trees and scrub they could see some figures approaching. There were a couple of horses, but these seemed to be carrying baggage, and the accompanying people were on foot.

Calling and shouting came from Arion's wagon, and Kastiandra suddenly gripped Nikleos' arm.

"They're calling us, husband. Why are they calling us?"

He shook his head.

"Hold the beasts here. I'll find out."

He climbed down to the ground and started walking across. Other men were making the same journey, drawn by the commotion. Part-way, as Dantiy and Yasib watched with Kastiandra, he started running. Kastiandra drew in her breath and worried at the leather reins with nervous fingers. Dantiy nudged her.

"You go across too, lady. We can keep the oxen here in their place while you find out what is happening."

They watched as she ran across the stretch of land. The stir among the people was growing, and then suddenly from the knot gathering off to one side a wail of anguish came up. Yasib stood up on the boards, trying to see.

"Not good news, I think."

Several more cries of losses and pain drifted across. Murtilis ran up from behind them.

"Do you know what it is, Murtilis?"

"Aigla says that it is the group that were raiding across toward the coast road. Dekseus was with them, but I can't see him there. I can't see him at all. He should be there."

At that point Nikleos and Kastiandra separated from the others and started back towards the wagon. Nikleos and another man were carrying something between them, and Kastiandra had a pack slung across one shoulder. Murtilis made a little mewing sound in her throat, but stayed clinging to the wagon.

Yasib jumped down, ran over and took the pack from Kastiandra. The two men had between them the body of a lad about Dantiy's age. He had suffered several wounds, his eyes were closed, and his face was distorted with pain, but he was alive.

They got Dekseus up on to the wagon boards, then the other man left for his own family. Kastiandra scrambled up beside her son and started to wipe his face. Murtilis was immobile, staring at him. Nikleos tapped her on the shoulder.

"Go on back to Kastor's wagon, girl. Aigla will be needing you there, I think. She will never see Otus again, so go and be a daughter to her now. We'll tell you soon enough if something happens."

Dantiy had drawn water from the great clay travelling container, wetted a cloth, and knelt beside Kastiandra to help her. Kastiandra looked up, her face raw and anxious.

"No need for that if you don't want. This is a family matter."

Dantiy shook her head and carried on.

"Seems to me we're not so far away from family to you now. Let me help here."

They worked together at cleaning and then binding up the injuries. Nikleos watched the whole process, silent and grim-faced, with Yasib beside him. Finally he heaved a great sigh when the women finished winding a long strip of cloth around his son's shoulder.

"He'll not be fighting much for a while now. But he lives."

Kastiandra looked briefly at him.

"He'll not be doing anything much at all. And husband, you need to know that he still might not live through this."

"Don't speak such things. He's strong. He's young. He'll be up in no time."

She put her hand on her son's forehead. "He has a fever, taken up after he was cut, while they brought him back here, I think. He could die tonight or tomorrow, and all we'll have gained is the chance to bid him farewell."

Nikleos swallowed and looked around at the other wagons. Most of them had a similar scene taking place.

"Always knew this could happen one day. But I thought we'd get longer than this."

"What happened, sir?"

"They were on a raid near a small town a day or two's travel towards the coast. I'll know the name soon enough. It all looked like it always does – chariots out there in a circle – so they all went out in the usual way with javelins. Like I showed you."

He stopped, shook his head.

"But this time the other leader was cunning. The chariots were a sham. They wheeled around and kept out of it. Instead behind them was a troop of javelin throwers just like us, but more of them. Along with another squad armed with spears off to the side. Tiripodikos, who was leading them, he should have backed off then, but he thought he could handle it. Half a dozen fell on the field before he saw sense, and nearly everyone got wounded. Several more died as they fell back, and a few more on the journey to find us. Took them several days to find us."

He looked around again at the cluster of families.

"Now look at us; almost every household grieving a loss. We're lucky, to get back a living son."

"Don't tempt the gods who are watching all this, husband. Some of them are fickle. We might well lose him by the morning. I don't know of anything else I can do except try to make him feel comfortable."

Dantiy leaned back and then took Kastiandra's hands. Both women's clothes were marked with Dekseus' blood.

"Lady, please listen to me. I think I can help him, if we can gather the right herbs. You do not know the qualities of the plants which grow in this land, but I do. We passed some of what your son needs a short time before we stopped. Others are quite common and we will find them nearby."

Kastiandra stared at her, then at the pale body of Dekseus. He was breathing raggedly, with long shallow gasps broken by occasional larger gulps.

"Lady, please, let me find the things I need. Yasib can help a little, but he only knows some of what is needful. Most of all I need a quick ride back along our track to find what I saw earlier."

Nikleos jumped up. "Look, if green things are what you need, why wait? Eumedes will loan us a horse. I'll ride back with you myself and watch out for danger."

Some time later the bitter smell of herbs being heated in water drifted around the wagon. Dantiy had found what she needed easily enough, but the place had been considerably further back than she remembered. Yasib had gathered what he could from near the camp, and Kastiandra had stayed at her son's side.

By common agreement the clan had halted. Another of the young men had died, and nobody had the will to move on. Yasib helped Nikleos set their part of the camp to rights while Kastiandra worked with Dantiy to apply new bandages soaked in the herb mixture. Little cries came from Dekseus as they did this, but then they had held his head up so that he could drink the steeped brew. After that he was exhausted, and sunk back into sleep.

"There, lady. What can be done, has been done. All that is left is prayer now."

"How soon will we know?"

Dantiy looked at Dekseus and shook her head.

"I would like to say tomorrow, but the fever grips him very tightly. I think we will need to do this all over again tomorrow, in the morning and the evening both. Then we must wait until the next day to know for sure."

She paused.

"You should both hear that I cannot say for sure that this will work. Your son may yet die of this."

She stood up too quickly, and wavered on her feet. Nikleos put out a hand to steady her.

"Is there anything we can do? For him, or for you?"

"We must stay with him in turns and watch night and day. Make sure he does not hurt himself without knowing. Also, he must have no food, but he may have water if he asks for it."

She looked wearily up at the sun, which had circled around and down to the horizon since she had last looked.

"As for me, I need to rest."

Dekseus had drifted in and out of awareness during the first night, with moans and half-formed words escaping his lips from time to time. None of them slept well. But by the end of the next day, it was clear that he was going to live.

All around the camp, other sons faced a similar struggle: most lived, and some did not. Tiripodikos, who had led the group, walked away from the camp after a while. Later in the day he was found dead on the ground, his own sword through his body where he had fallen on it.

Towards the end of the day somebody thought to call back the group of scouts who had been out ahead. Arkelawos was among them. Much later, after Dantiy had finished her turn to watch Dekseus and was settling down to sleep, she remembered seeing Murtilis stand nervously to greet her new husband, and wondered how the night was passing for her.

That evening Nikleos left Yasib and Dantiy with Kastiandra on the wagon. He said nothing as he set off. They watched him go out of the hollow of the camp, up the side of the nearby ridge, into the darkness.

It was Kastiandra's turn to be with Dekseus, and she was sitting at his head. Dantiy was working through a pile of minor mending and darning which had built up. Yasib was putting a decent edge back onto Nikleos' farming tools, long unused.

Finishing one, he stood up, stretched, and peered over to where Nikleos had gone. Kastiandra looked up at him.

"It is a clan ceremony. You have no place there."

Dantiy glanced across at her.

"If you need to be there, lady, we can look after Dekseus and the wagon."

"I would only be there if it was for a family member. Mothers will be there, and unmarried sisters. The wife of Kassanor. But not other women. I am grateful beyond measure that I need not be there."

Yasib nodded, still looking out into the gloom. A light mist was rising from the moist ground.

"It is to mark the passage of their death, then?"

She shrugged and said nothing. Some distance away a flame flickered, wavered uncertainly, and then strengthened into a fierce glow. He turned his head to her, curious.

"You burn your dead? In Ikaret we put them in the ground. Simple burial outside the walls for the poor. A stone chamber in the city for the wealthy, made holy by the priests. They rest with their ancestors, together in vaults. Sometimes even below our houses themselves. But you burn your dead. Why do you do this?"

Kastiandra looked acutely uncomfortable. Her hands worried one another, and she fiddled with the sheet covering Dekseus. Dantiy looked at Yasib impatiently and shook her head at him. She put the sewing down, moved to sit beside the older woman, and took her hands to still them.

"Lady, your people should be glad that this mist has risen to receive them. Taliy is our Lady of mist and dew, and she is gracious beyond measure to the stranger as well as the native-born. She is revered here among the Kinahny just as much as she was in Ikaret. It is a good omen for your people. The land itself is welcoming them."

Kastiandra said nothing, but her shoulders relaxed and her hands became still again. In the distance, where the flames were now steady, they could hear the sound of a low, solemn chant. Every now and again a woman's shrieking wail sounded out, high above the deeper notes.

There was silence in the wagon for a time, until Kastiandra suddenly spoke again, in a very low voice that the other two could hardly hear.

"We do not speak of the dead. Especially not while all that is happening."

She gestured up the hill.

"They must move on to their own place, and we do not want to hold them back. Let their bodies go to the fire, and their spirits move on. We respect the king of that other world, but we do not want to attract his attention."

She looked around quickly, stood up and held on to the hawk icon at the front of the wagon for a few moments, and then sat again. Turning to Dantiy, she spoke in a much louder voice.

"Tell me about how your people gather the fruit of the land. I want to imagine what we will find when the trees come to harvest."

THE NEXT DAY DANTIY WAS SITTING beside Dekseus, idly watching the oxen methodically grazing nearby, when a hand reached out.

"Who are you?"

She looked down at the young man. He was very pale and weak, but awake and clear-minded. She called out to Kastiandra, who came the few paces along the wagon as quickly as she could. She was crying suddenly, and gripped Dantiy's hand before embracing her son.

"Dekseus, Dekseus, I am so happy. I thought we had lost you." She looked across to where Nikleos was busy and called out, beckoning urgently as he turned. "Look, my son, this is Dantiy. She helped you. She knew how to find herbs to heal you."

Dekseus looked confused.

"What sort of name is that? Who is she? And how did I get here?"

Nikleos jumped up onto the boards with a great clatter and ran along to them. Dantiy slipped away unnoticed and went to join Yasib. They sat together under a nearby tree and watched the reunion. Yasib pointed across the clearing.

"Aktitas died just this morning. His foot went to rot from the injury and it spread up his leg. It stank fearfully for the last two days. But I think he will be the last to go. Dekseus was one of the weakest of them all, and now that he is mending, I think that death has left these people for a while."

She leaned against him.

"I don't even know why we did all this, Yasib. I haven't worked like that for anyone before. Once we started, we all just took it for granted. Us and them. I am so tired now."

He put an arm around her. "Once we stayed, we had to help. And at least nobody is wary of us now. That has to be good."

He paused, clearly unsure how to continue. She pulled away and looked at his solemn face.

"What? What is it?"

"The silver is all gone from my pack. I had just over half of what was left, and it is all gone. Your pack is fine: I checked."

"How can this be? Nikleos would not do that. I am sure he would not."

"I agree. I think it was Tarmanni. I never looked from the moment he left until yesterday evening. But the pack was too light when I picked it up, so I checked. Everything else was there, but not the silver."

She was silent for a while.

"The wicked, wicked man. How could he dare?"

"I think he hated us for staying here. It was a little revenge he could take. But we have no way to get it back again now, not after all this time. I kept silent last night, since even then there was no point in pursuit. All of us were busy. And maybe we should not tell Nikleos and the others. No point us looking weaker than we already are."

╪╪╫╫╫╫╫╪╪

AFTER A FEW DAYS DEKSEUS was able to walk unaided. He was slow, and he stumbled often, but it was hailed as a great sign. A few evenings after that, in the circle around the fire, talk turned to whether the clan should at last move on again. It was the time when day and night were equal, and after the shared meal there was to be a dance and celebration. One of the young men, who had been injured even more seriously than Dekseus, could still only just sit up, but all the rest who had survived were now on foot.

The debate drifted idly to and fro as the food was shared – green herbs, game birds, and deer acquired from the land around, and spices that had travelled with them on the journey south. One or other of the men would offer an opinion, or else pass on a whispered view from his wife sitting beside him, but there was no real agreement. They had asked Yasib all over again to remind them about the road ahead, and still were in no hurry to decide one way or another.

One of the handful of men guarding the line of wagons called out, and shortly afterwards a man dismounted on the edge of the firelight. He was big, and carried himself with authority. He wore a diagonal red sash with the silhouette of a wolf head embroidered in black. He walked without hesitation into the circle, where men shifted in sudden fear to the left and right to make way for him. He stood, hands on hips, head pressed forward, with the hilt of a great sword close to his hand.

"I had thought to find your clan nearer the sea, Antos."

Antos shook his head.

"This way suits us better, Periphas."

"But it does not suit the other clans so well. And looking around, it seems to me that you have stayed in this place for several days. Perhaps a week. You should keep the line and be moving on."

There was a little silence around the firelight. Periphas stared at some of the men, who avoided his gaze.

"Well? Why have you stopped here?"

The silence stretched out. Eventually Antos, in a lower voice, spoke again.

"We have suffered heavy loss, Periphas. Most of our youth were killed or badly wounded at a town towards the coast."

Periphas stared at him, and after a pause Antos continued.

"Speaking for my clan, it is time to halt the migration and settle down."

"Do you think that is your choice to make?"

There was muttering around the fire, a little protest of mingled men's and women's voices.

"I do. I am arkon here. Of course we respect the pledge between the clans, but these are my people to lead."

Periphas nodded, but there was a look of disdain on his face.

"I will see what the other clan leaders have to say about that. I think they will find your attitude disappointing. That is for another day. For now, I need you to supply a squad of men to come with me tonight and join one of the raiding groups by the coast."

There was complete silence in the group. Antos looked around.

"Periphas, look at us. We are few in number now. Our youth have just come back mauled from the last raid. Many of our families are grieving because of death; all of us are nursing the injured and praying that no more will die of their wounds. We simply have nobody who can come with you."

There were nods of agreement around the fire. As Periphas looked here and there, at men who would not meet his eyes, Nikleos suddenly spoke.

"Our lads ran into a foe who knows how to fight us. They challenged us on foot, not on their chariots. I think they have used silver to buy warriors to fight us from our own lands, our own traditions. We always knew this could happen. It is time to call a halt and settle while we can still make allies in this land."

Periphas took three steps towards Nikleos, who remained seated. Kastiandra, sitting beside him, put her hand on his arm. Dantiy and Yasib were behind him, and Periphas had not yet noticed them.

"Perhaps your young men were not properly trained? Perhaps they were cowards who ran away instead of taking the fight to the enemy." He ignored the angry look that Nikleos gave him. "But if your young men will not fight, I will take your old men instead. I need twenty to leave with me in the morning."

There was an unyielding air. Periphas continued, his voice rising.

"Do you not remember the days when we waited by Wilios? We were not afraid then to stand up against those walls, no matter how long it took. No matter what the cost. We deceived their king with our plans. We outmatched their chariots, we killed their captains, we burned their buildings, we took their women and their wealth. You were all there with me on that day, all of us following Akamunas Lykos to take that city. You can be with me again."

Antos waved a hand at him and tried to stem the flow of words.

"Things have changed, Periphas. We have lost young men and old. Our enemies have learned how to fight us. We are few and they are many. They know the land and we do not. It is time to make peace and settle here."

A ripple of agreement ran around the edge of the firelight. Periphas shook his head.

"No, Antos, nothing has changed, unless it has changed in your heart. If you came with me and talked to the other clan leaders you would hear this with your own ears. They want to persevere, they want to press on. They will not hang back in fear or with faint heart."

One or two of the men were nodding now. Antos glanced around, uncomfortable at the changing mood.

"I understand that you are weary of the journey, Antos. I hear your desire to find a home. But now is not the time to halt the journey. This is the last hour before the dawn, when we most need to stand together in one last act of courage and defiance. We have come so far together: do not falter at the last step."

Others around the circle were beginning to assent.

"I was with your lads when we took Hatsor. I was proud to fight with your people there. That was a good day. You all remember that. But you were not with me at other cities where great deeds were done. Let me tell you of Akka, let me tell you of Shuksi, let me tell you of Ikaret, where our swords ran red with blood, and our packs were piled high with gold and silver. Their men were slaughtered and their women used for our pleasure. Their..."

He stopped. Dantiy had risen to her feet. She was white with rage, and almost unable to speak. Her kef fluttered a little in a stir of night breeze.

"You boastful dog! Were you truly at Ikaret?"

"Who are you, woman?"

Periphas looked across at Antos.

"Your customs have fallen a long way. Since when have you allowed foreigners and women to speak around the fire?"

Kastiandra reached out from where she was sitting to take Dantiy's hand, but she shook the older woman away.

"My father was one of the men you slaughtered. My mother was one of the women you used for what you call pleasure. May your filthy name be cursed and your rotten seed cut short before your face."

Nikleos started to rise to his feet, but Periphas held up a hand to stop him. He took a step towards Dantiy.

"Yes, I led the attack on Ikaret; I crushed the pitiful resistance of the city guards there and took as I pleased from the ruins. Perhaps I did indeed kill your father and throw down your mother. I have no idea: there were so many. But you I missed. You escaped from the city?"

She nodded and hissed at him, wordless, her furious eyes fixed on him. He loosened the hilt of his sword.

"My humble apologies to the gods for failing to complete the task. But now I have an opportunity to redeem myself. First, woman, I shall beat you with the flat of this sword to teach you obedience and silence. Then I shall take you the same way as I took the women of Ikaret, right here beside this fire. Then I shall carry you with me to my wagon, where I can enjoy you as often as I please."

He loosed his tunic and loincloth and exposed his genitals to her, grinning. Then he dressed himself again and casually took another step towards her.

Dekseus tried to struggle to his feet, lifting himself onto one side first to avoid stretching the wounds in his chest and arms. Yasib easily pulled him down again and stood beside Dantiy.

Periphas laughed.

"Another one? You do like your headscarfs, you people. We let more of you go than I thought. Are you her husband? If you save yourself the trouble of fighting, and give her up to me now, I might forget that I ever noticed you."

"I am her brother. I am Yasib son of User-Amun and Sanay-Sura. Her father is my father and her mother is my mother. I do not think you will forget me now."

He was speaking very slowly and languidly, in a manner that Dantiy knew was calculated to irritate the bigger man.

"So much the better. Two of you together now. I can offer both of you as sacrifices side by side. Unless there are some more of your family here as well?"

He drew his sword, then paused and bared his teeth.

"You do have a weapon you can use?"

Yasib looked at the sword, head to one side.

"My, what a large sword you carry around with you. I'm sure I could not use such a thing. I'm too clumsy. I might accidentally hurt one of these good people nearby. But I do have a knife. Let me show you."

He made a show of getting his knife out from his belt. It was narrow, with decorative silver chasing around the hilt and careful lettering all along the blade. Periphas laughed.

"That's a pretty little thing. I'll add it to my collection after I cut you down like barley tonight. Have you ever done anything more than cut vegetables with it, boy?"

Yasib looked down at it and frowned, moving it uncertainly from hand to hand. "Once or twice I have skinned a rabbit with it. I think I can remember how I did that."

Periphas took another step towards him, lifting his sword. Antos called out in a warning tone. "Periphas, you cannot use that blade if all he has is a knife. The pledge certainly allows you to fight him, but not with that."

Periphas shrugged and plunged the sword into the ground. It swayed to and fro a little with the force of the thrust. To either side, men and women moved away from the two of them to make space. Kastiandra pulled at Dantiy to move back with her. Periphas crouched slightly, pulled a dagger from his own belt, and swung it in large sweeps.

Yasib smiled a little.

"Are you ready? You with the seed that is rotten and the name that is filth? You are sure you want to go on with this now?"

Periphas growled at him, an animal sound in the silent, watching ring of people. Then he closed in towards Yasib, the blade still circling in great loops. Yasib came up a little onto the front of his feet, but did not move forward. When Periphas swung the dagger towards him, he feinted one way and side-stepped the other.

Periphas paused, moved again to push Yasib back towards the fire, crackling and sparking in the evening shadows. Suddenly he jumped forward, his blade circling in a great slash from shoulder height down.

Yasib, eyes narrow, dodged again, rolled past Periphas, and slashed his knife in a deep cut across the back of the bigger man's knee as he passed. Periphas stumbled, cursing, and turned to face Yasib again. The bad leg was dragging behind him, and he no longer looked so confident. Yasib stood back again and waited for him to approach. He was expressionless, completely focused on Periphas, and was poised ready on both feet.

This time Periphas held the knife lower, swishing it from side to side to prevent Yasib trying the same move. He was keeping the injured leg back, moving forward crabwise across the ground. Suddenly he jumped forward with a great shout and a dramatic wave of his arms. He lunged at Yasib, trying to make the most of his longer reach, but the shout turned into a cry of pain as the point of Yasib's knife met the wide swing of his arm. He dropped the dagger to the ground, the fingers in one hand open and strengthless.

"Pick it up. Pick the dagger up and carry on."

Periphas picked it up in his other hand, keeping the injured one close to his body. Yasib moved across towards him, knocked the dagger away to one side and stabbed the other wrist, then took two steps back again. Periphas stared in disbelief at the blood running from both arms, looked up at Yasib, and tried to run at him, bear-like, as though he wanted to wrestle him to the ground. Yasib dodged again, ducked underneath the flailing arms, and slashed across behind the other knee. Periphas toppled to the ground.

Yasib came up to Periphas and knelt, one knee on each of his upper arms so that he could not move. He looked across at Dantiy and nodded. She stood up from her place beside Kastiandra, walked over, and bent across to look into his eyes. She wore a look of complete satisfaction.

"You pitiful little man. No more cities for you to plunder, no more men to slaughter, no more women to violate. You wanted to expose me: let this be the last thing you see in this world."

She squatted over his head, covering herself and him with her skirt, and urinated over his face. He struggled again, use-lessly. She sat back on his chest, reached out for the dagger that he had dropped nearby, and held it against his throat. She looked up briefly into Yasib's eyes.

"Here?"

He shook his head, placed his hand on hers and moved the blade around a little. He moved his legs a little, pinned Pe-riphas' head in place while still preventing him from moving his arms.

"Just here."

She nodded and leaned over to look into Periphas' eyes, staring up, wide with fear. "This is for my father and for my mother. May their living spirits rest now in peace after all their grief."

Yasib's hand tightened on hers, and together they drove the dagger through his throat and up into his skull. Periphas gave a great heave, a choked cry, and his legs thrashed once, twice before he lay still. Brother and sister stared at each other for a long moment. She pulled aside Periphas' loincloth, cut off his penis, and threw it into the fire.

"As I promised, so have I done. His seed is cut short. But I would not even let the dogs have that."

Yasib stood and helped Dantiy to her feet. He looked first at Nikleos, then at Antos. There was silence around the fire as the clan waited for Antos' judgement.

"I do not know what customs and laws you have about what we have just done. But our vengeance is now satisfied against this man for all that he did to our father and mother, and we submit to your ruling about it."

He turned his knife around and offered it hilt-forward to the clan-leader. Antos stood and shook his head.

"Keep it. Periphas was the challenger. He threatened you and your sister. He drew weapon first. You have done nothing wrong by our laws in defending your own and your family's honour. Nobody in this clan will hold a blood debt against you for this."

He looked around at the circle of faces, where little whispers were starting to spring up after the silence.

"Does anyone among us disagree with what I have said?"

There was another brief silence, as men and women looked around. Nobody spoke. Antos scratched his head and smiled a little.

"Indeed, I think that many of us will be glad that his wish to take another twenty of us away to be killed will not now be satisfied. For my part, I am content with the outcome, and you are both welcome to stay with us."

The silence gave way to noise and chatter, and suddenly there was a group of men around Yasib, of women around Dantiy.

Nikleos was gripping his arm tightly, pride in Yasib showing clearly on his features.

"That was well done, lad. I never thought I'd see the day when Periphas was felled so quickly. He has fought every step of the way since Wilios. And before that, too. I never thought anybody would be able to put him on the ground in just a few moves. So quickly! How could it happen?"

Yasib laughed, relief filling his voice. His hands were trembling slightly in the aftermath of the fight.

"You need to think like a nobleman, Nikleos. As soon as I saw him waving that dagger around I knew it would be a quick fight. He was handling it like one of your great swords. On a battlefield he would have had me dead in no time; here in a small space with knives he had no chance at all. All my life I have practiced for combat like this."

He looked around, acknowledging the words and praise of the men around him.

"By the great gods, I am hungry now. And thirsty. Is that feast ready yet?"

There was laughter all around. Men led him off to one side, sat him down with a beaker of ale and some food. Nikleos came and sat beside him.

"You know, lad, there's nothing you could have done that would win these men over faster than that. And Antos will be relieved too, now that he does not have to either lose men or speak out against Periphas. This was a good night's work. And with such wonderful trickery, to fool him into thinking he would win easily himself. The deceiver deceived. It was good: we admire such things."

Yasib leaned towards him and spoke much more quietly.

"Will any of them take the other side? Are there people here who want to go back to the raids and the fighting?"

Nikleos glanced around the firelight, measuring the mood of those nearby.

"Not any longer. Not since losing all those boys in one day, and having most of the rest brought close to death. My own Dekseus among them. If you can find us a place to settle, there's not a man here who will want any different. And look, Periphas was from the Pelestoi tribe. We are Sherden. The ties between us are weak."

Dekseus was coming slowly over to them. He nodded approvingly to Yasib. Kastiandra, with Dantiy beside her, followed him.

"Husband, I am going to take Dekseus back to the wagon to rest now."

Nikleos stood up, took her hand and kissed her. When he let her go again she laughed and straightened the clasp in her braids. He touched her cheek fondly but possessively.

"Take him back, for sure. But I want you back here straight away, you best of women. I want to dance with you here at the feast tonight until neither of us can stand up any longer. I want us to have the night for each other after all this. Dekseus will be fine on his own, won't you, lad?"

Kastiandra looked doubtful.

"Are you sure? He's only been upon his feet for a few days now. I don't think we should leave him on his own yet. What if he needed something?"

Dantiy stepped forward a little.

"I will stay with him, lady. Just now I want time away from the firelight and the noise here. I want time to remember my parents and let what has happened settle into my heart."

She hugged Yasib in a long, tight embrace.

"Thank you again, brother. Now enjoy the feast and the dance for both of us."

The two women started their slow way into the shadows, back to the wagon, with Dekseus between them. Yasib put the plate down on the ground, empty, and took another draught of ale from the beaker.

"Can I ask you a question, sir? Tonight, here around the fire, who am I allowed to dance with? I am not of your people, and I do not want a father or brother taking offence."

Nikleos laughed.

"Tonight, after what you did, you can choose anyone. There will be fathers and brothers wanting you to dance with their daughters and sisters. Why, if our Murtilis had not just moved into Kastor's wagon I would have you with her before any of the others. Enjoy the dance, Yasib."

He winked at Yasib, leaned closer, and dropped his voice to a conspiratorial whisper. "Be careful not to spend too long in the shadows, though; stay out in the firelight with them where everybody can see what is happening."

Yasib laughed, drank some more of the brew, and looked around the circle lit up by the leaping flames.

⹂⹂⹃⹃⹃⹂⹃⹃⹃

DANTIY WAITED WHILE KASTIANDRA helped Dekseus into the wagon and readied him for the night. Before long she came back down again and stood beside Dantiy, obviously eager to get back to the fire and the feast. Familiar instruments – drums and lyres, with a single high whistle – were playing unfamiliar tunes, and there was a noise of happy collective enjoyment.

Words drifted over from the fire, just about audible. Somebody had turned their exploits into song already.

> *Then youthful Yasib stood,*
> > *sole survivor of unhappy Ikaret*
> *And at his sister's side*
> > *faced down the foe.*
> *Dauntless Dantiy*
> > *taunted him with words*
> *Eager to avenge*
> > *her mother's misery.*
> *Then was the trickster tricked,*
> > *the fighter felled;*
> *Floored was Periphas the proud*
> > *by Sanay-Sura's son.*

Kastiandra's voice broke into her distraction.

"You are sure you want to stay here?"

Dantiy nodded. "Quite sure, thank you, lady. Go and enjoy the celebration with your husband."

Kastiandra took a deep breath, smiled at her, and started to go, before stopping herself again. She turned back to Dantiy and took her hands lightly.

"I am glad that you avenged all that was done to your mother. But tell me, why did you claim vengeance only in the name of your parents, and not your husband?"

Dantiy sighed. "I am sure that Halmanu was carrying out the task assigned to him by the king. There was no revenge needed for his death. It is different for my mother and father."

Quite unexpectedly, Kastiandra took her into a full embrace. "They will be proud of you as they watch from the halls of the dead. I am also proud of you for what you did for them tonight, you and Yasib both. Periphas was a brutal man, and women throughout this land will be praising your name tonight. Even some of the women amongst this clan. You will not find much grief about his passing here. If ever I had reservations about you and your brother coming into our wagon, they are gone now. Be welcome here."

She turned and was gone before Dantiy could reply, away from the wagon and back towards the fire. She watched the older woman until she was hidden in the gloom, then smiled to herself and climbed up into the wagon.

Dekseus was leaning against one end of the wagon, propped up by a bundle of cloths tied together, his body only half-covered by a blanket. He was resting on a bed made up of straw mixed with softer leaves. Some sprigs of myrtle were slipping out from behind the cloth which wrapped it all. She came over to him.

"You were magnificent, Dantiy. However did you learn such a fierce passion?"

She laughed and sat beside him.

"One day I will sing you the tale of our goddess Anath and the ways in which she exacted her own revenge. But not tonight, I think."

She leaned over him and peeled back the blanket from his bare chest to check the bandages on his arms. Parts of his body were discoloured with bruises, but he was certainly recovering. The inspection done, she stretched out her arms and laughed again.

"For the first time since leaving the city I am completely alive. Tonight I am feeling full of life."

"But you did not stay out there for the dance itself?"

She shook her head, untied the knot of her kef, folded it, and placed it nearby. He watched her, curious, but clearly with no idea what she was doing.

"It is not dancing I want." She leaned over him again, took his hand. "Thank you for trying to stand up to fight for me. It was a kind act, especially as you were not nearly healed yet."

He laughed uncertainly, started to reach out towards her with his other hand but stopped again.

"I would have tried, though it would have been a useless gesture against him. But there was no need. Your brother surprised us all. Just as you did."

He let his hand fall again by his side.

"Why didn't you want to dance tonight?"

"I have just separated a man's breath from his body. He deserved every moment of my revenge, and more, but for now I am split apart as well. Tonight I want to feel myself joined properly to another person."

He swallowed, glanced briefly away from her before his eyes were drawn back to her face.

"I am not sure you know what those words mean in our tongue."

She released his hand, reached up, and unclipped the silver clasp that Murtilis had fastened for her. She tossed her head to let the braids of hair unravel to below her shoulders. She took his hand and placed it on her leg above her knee. His fingers spread around the curve of her thigh, feeling her through the weave of her skirt.

"I know exactly what I mean."

He took a deep breath, still touching her. She leaned forward over him again, trapping his hand between her leg and her body.

"Tell me, Dekseus, have you lain with a woman before?"

He nodded, but looked troubled. He started to say something in reply, but the words would not form. She sat back again.

"What is it?"

He looked away again into the night. Before he replied, he moved his hand away from her.

"I do not think you will like the answer. I think I will offend you if I speak truth."

"Tell me anyway."

He hesitated for a long moment.

"For my first time when becoming a man, my father allowed me to use a woman a few times who we had captured in a raid and brought back to the camp. I was not the only one; others here used her too. She was with us for a while, but in the end we let her go at a village somewhere north of here. A long time ago. Then there have been women I have taken at towns we plundered."

He looked directly into her face, wanting her to understand. "We were not at Ikaret, Dantiy. We are not like Periphas. You were right to kill him. We were all afraid of him ourselves."

She looked at him for a long moment.

"So you have never known what it is to have a willing wo-man come into your bed. I think you will find the experience altogether different."

She unlaced her tunic and shrugged it from her shoulders, watching his gaze slip away from her face. Then she stood up, stripped off her skirt and girdle-cloth, and stood naked on the wooden boards of the wagon. She pulled the blanket away from him, then gently lifted his head to ease away the cloths behind his head so that he lay flat.

He reached out his hand to touch her thigh again. Almost entirely caught up in the sight and feel of her body, he never-theless held himself back.

"I don't want to have to fight your brother if he finds out about this."

She laughed a little, caressed his face and arms, took his hand and held it to her lips to kiss.

"Yasib honours all my choices."

Very hesitantly, he held out his arms to her. She straddled him, then leaned over to kiss him for a long, breathless mo-ment. His hands caressed her shoulders and back, and then he gave a little gasp as she eased down his body and took him inside herself.

Time passed with their passion. The air was warm and full of the scent of early rose petals and crushed myrtle leaves. In the distance, the feast continued.

Afterwards she lay beside him, enjoying again the sense of being full of life, full to the brim, full of his pleasure and her own. His arousal had been spent quite quickly, but with a little perseverance she had reached her own satisfaction. The response had surprised him, and had then drawn out a vein of tenderness she had not really expected to find.

After that, he had fallen asleep beside her, overcome by fatigue. It had been good; good enough for a start, at least.

But it would surely not be good if Nikleos and Kastiandra found her still naked and in their son's arms when they returned, and she had no idea how long the dance might last. In all likelihood the older couple would lose themselves in the sharing of their own pleasure later that night, but it was better all round if they did not yet think of her and Dekseus in that way.

She sighed again, took his limp hand and held it against her breast for a few heartbeats. The heat of the day was going, and she enjoyed the sensation of his warmth amidst the quickly cooling air for a while before getting up from beside him.

She grinned as she dressed again. Certainly her hair would need to be braided again to suit the customs of these people, and she knew that she would not be able to do it herself. She would go and see Murtilis tomorrow and ask for her help. Sitting beside the young man, finding to her surprise that she had become quite fond of him, she wondered who Yasib had been able to dance with.

A SON ADDRESSES HIS FATHER.

Hekanefer to his father Nesamenopeh, greetings and blessings to you. I write from just south of the city of Hatsor.

Honoured father, at the end of yesterday's journey there was a solemn reminder that although we secured a victory recently, this sorry land still suffers very many losses. We had worked our way across to Hatsor, little by little, in order that the ruler of that city could fulfil his obligations and replenish our supplies. The little towns and villages naturally supply us with the basics, but for some things we need a place which is altogether larger.

It was not to be. These wicked enemies had come to Hatsor before we did. I do not know how large a number had been sent, but they were more than enough to carry out severe damage. The first sign we got was when we came upon an open space in which many chariots had been defeated. It is by now a familiar pattern; one or both horses slain by javelins, and then the crews and their runners overpowered.

The skill and caution of our commander meant that we found this out for ourselves with only a modest loss. The king here, like so many others, seems to have committed most of the soldiers who could have defended his city in a hopeless attack, thus leaving his city defenceless. We skirted the field of battle, and very soon after saw that the buildings of the city had been set alight.

It seems that on this occasion the attackers were moving in haste. We have heard of other places where the destruction has been most thorough. Here, only the outer regions of the town had been scoured. Although the central citadel was damaged, it was still standing in reasonable order. The people of the city had fled their houses but were starting to return.

I think that this place will recover. The attack on the city was a little while ago now, and signs of life are appearing quickly.

But we could not find the king himself, or any of his senior officials. We were told several different stories, and it seems most likely that he escaped the attack through some secret way out to the north.

Those who seemed most loyal to him told us that he was doing the rounds of his territory, collecting together what forces he could in case another defence was needed. Many of our own soldiers just thought that he had run away to preserve his life. The gods alone know the truth of all this. Perhaps he will return, but we have no time to wait for him.

As for us, we were able to procure only a small part of the supplies that we wanted. It is enough to meet our needs for a while, but it means we will have to invite the occupants of other towns to help us on our way. We do not always receive the welcome that is due to soldiers of the Beloved Land when this happens, and need to take time to remind some of the people of their responsibilities.

I confess that I am bewildered by the reaction of the cities here. Of course they try to avoid paying tribute. We expect that. We also expect that every now and again some hot-tempered ruler will break the word of his oath, and that our soldiers will need to punish him and appoint a more worthy successor in his place. Such restlessness is entirely normal.

But it seems that they have no grasp of the enormity of what is happening to them. This is the worst calamity to come upon this province for a very great time, perhaps even a thousand years. It is worse than that bitter time when ruthless enemies came out of the north and east to rule here, and seize even the sedge-lands of our own sorrowful land.

Great cities are burned, well-trained soldiers are slaughtered, great numbers of people are forced from their homes to wander the lands without purpose. The order of life is turned upside-down. Nobody living can remember such a time, and even we scribes must read truly ancient texts to learn of anything so terrible. And yet these so-called kings do not realise it.

This time I believe we will hold these invaders back somewhere along the coastal plain between Amurru and the region they call the Nagb. This time, our Beloved Land will not suffer the feet of cruel invaders trampling down the reeds.

Or so I hope and believe.

I wake sometimes in a night-sweat at the thought of our own house being misused by foreigners, our courtyards and gardens soiled with their filth, my own dear family forced from the homes where generators of ancestors have been born, lived, and gone to the horizon.

May it never be.

Another thing. I am not sure that my dear mother will hear the news about Hatsor well. I remember that she had a fondness for the place after receiving gifts from there from your friend Perire, the chief priest's messenger to this province.

With that in mind, I have not told her about the destruction of this place in my letters to her.

Please also reassure her that I am well. The men are patient on this march around the province, but they are soldiers and they crave a real victory to their name. Since that great day when we first defeated a group of enemies, the gleanings on the field of battle have been slight.

When you go to my grandfather's eternal house to speak with the gods there, remind them that the Beloved Land is their land also, and press upon them the need that we all have for success.

A MAN ADDRESSES HIS BROTHER.

Hekanefer to Ramose, from somewhere in the Kinahny hill country.

Well, brother, it is some little time since I wrote to you. When I said those things we were north, somewhere between Damaseq and the Sea Road. We have moved here and there many times. At one stage we were close to Hatsor, intending to get supplies, but the local ruler had fared extremely badly against the invaders. We turned south again, and since then I have not heard a name which I know. But I am sure that we are somewhere near the town of Sychem.

Your little brother has now been in half a dozen battles. Well, skirmishes, at least. You will be surprised to hear that I have learned to overcome the trembling of hands and heart that once unmanned me. In the last fight I was close in to the hand-to-hand work, when some determined group of enemies rushed straight towards the commander himself. I have even suffered a minor wound, a scratch on my left arm which I can now boast about.

I carry no weapon except for a dagger of last resort, but as the fighting came closer I found the blade was already in my hand. I was ready for this enemy, and aimed a sharp thrust towards the nearest.

Now, it is true that my bodyguards thought me insufficiently prepared, and immediately thrust me into cover behind them. But I shall ornament the event with tales of my vast bravery when I find a willing listener, and she will think the more of me.

The new weapons and the new stratagems we are using are giving us success. But we meet only a handful of men at a time, and they have learned caution. We no longer achieve striking victories in the way we did the first once or twice. Now this wicked enemy fades away into the distance when they learn that we are more than a match for them. We kill more of them than they do of us, by a good margin, but these little successes will not win the war.

The soldiers like me now. Once they laughed behind my back, but no longer, not now that I have stood shoulder to shoulder with them and seen casts of javelins drifting through the air towards us like a swarm of hornets. I have lost count of how many amulets I have made for them, but you can see them everywhere in the camp.

These little sherds of pottery on which I trace out a few simple spells in ink are everywhere now, hanging on leather thongs around men's necks. As another skirmish draws near I see men touch them with prayers on their lips and faith in their hearts. I am doing something to help these men, brother, and it is good.

In return, they have promised me a fine time when we finally reach a city of note. These men do not know the names of any of these towns, still less how to write them down, but they are keenly aware of all the houses that a man might go to enjoy the company of friendly women. One day soon we will be in a place like that, and the hardness of the life that we all share together will be softened in the most delightful manner.

Another thing. This will interest you. Of course the priests use common words to stand for the sacred mysteries they deal with every day. That is as it should be. But I learned today that soldiers do the same. A report came to us that the king is preparing for war at sea as well as on land. When they heard this, the soldiers began talking of ships with wings, and I nearly laughed aloud to hear of such a thing. But they were most serious, and I stopped myself rather than appear a fool.

What would you make of this, brother? I think you would guess the same as me, that a ship's wings were the sails that it spreads to catch the winds of heaven. Not so. To a soldier, the wings are the oars, but as seen from the front or the back. When we scribes draw a boat or one of its signs, we draw it from the side, because that is its best and truest representation. But when a soldier thinks of a ship, they imagine it in attack, heading towards them, or in flight, heading away. And then, you see, the oars rise and fall like wings.

How splendid it is to be a scribe, and to see not only the world as it is, but also how it seems to be to others.

Pray for me every day, dear brother, especially to the gods who concern themselves with other lands. In turn I speak with them often about you and your children, and yearn for the day we can meet face to face again.

✗ ╪ ㄱ ╪ ㄱ ╪ ㄱ ╪ ✗

IN THE MIDDLE OF THE NIGHT Akiy woke Labayu.

"He's gone, chief. Shimmigar's gone. When I got up for my watch he wasn't there any more."

Labayu shook himself awake so that he could follow what Akiy was saying. He felt slow, stupid.

"Not there? Gone? What do you mean? He's just out in the bushes?"

"No, chief, no. I mean he's altogether gone. Him, his pack, everything he had. My guess is he's not coming back."

Labayu stood up and walked over to where Shimmigar had been. The place was cold, empty, abandoned.

"See now, chief, that's what I mean. He's gone."

The sky was still dark, and a waning moon had only displaced the stars in its immediate vicinity. A large part of the night remained. He sighed, angry at himself.

"I should have seen this, Akiy. Should have said more last night instead of putting it off until the morning."

They had been talking quietly, but Uriel and Ghazam had woken and were listening. Labayu looked at them.

"Well, if he doesn't want to be found we won't find him. He's at least as good a tracker as the best of us, and he has a head start. Akiy, take this watch and wake me when it's my turn. And if anyone else disagrees with my choice, kindly wake me and talk about it, rather than just slipping away."

There was a ripple of murmured assent, and the camp returned to sleep.

As the sky started to pale, when his own turn was done, Labayu woke Uriel for the final night watch. It seemed no time before he was being shaken awake again. He groaned.

"Please don't tell me somebody else has left the camp."

Uriel grinned.

"No, nothing like that. But there's a group of people on the move a little way off. Down in the valley, moving towards the coast."

Labayu sat up, his sleep dismissed.

"Another group of these newcomers?"

"I don't think so: there are men and women both, and I heard a child's voice. On the run from somewhere is my guess."

"How many?"

"A dozen or so."

"Wake the others. We'll watch them for a while. Don't strike the camp, though, we'll come back here soon enough."

Shortly afterwards the four of them were creeping through the low bushes above the track. At this point it ran half a man's depth below the ground either side. Shepherds had driven their flocks along here since the time of the ancients.

They worked their way gradually closer, but there was little need of caution. The group was trudging wearily, not caring to keep watch.

They were dressed as Kinahny, and looked to be a family group. As well as two children walking, one woman had a baby in a sling at her front. Another was pregnant. An old man with a stick was being helped by a younger one. After a time, one of the children turned to his parent.

"When are we going to stop to eat, father? Can it be soon, please?"

The woman with the baby stopped.

"I have to feed Walid here, anyway. If there's anything left in me to give him now."

They stopped, settled in a loose ring. The nursing mother untied the sling and coaxed the baby to suckle. The old man sank gratefully onto a boulder and leaned against the fig tree growing behind it.

One of the young men unravelled a cloth and looked at the contents. He glanced briefly at the pregnant woman, then gestured to one of the others to join him. From where Labayu was hiding, it was clear that each person's share would be very small. Akiy whispered to him.

"Should we help out? They're Kinahny for sure."

Labayu nodded. "Not Hatsor, but somewhere nearby, by the sound of it. One of the daughter villages, maybe."

He paused a moment longer, wondering briefly if he had any duty to these people. Then, seeing the smallness of the portions the man was giving out, and the worn out grief on the mother's face as the baby struggled to draw milk from her, he decided.

"Ghazam, go back to the camp and bring our food. We can always get more. In fact, Uriel, you go with him and just bring everything now. We'll not go back there."

As the two men set off, he stood up with Akiy and went down into the trackway. The group stiffened in surprise. One of the young men pulled out a sword, but relaxed as he saw their kefs. Labayu kept his own weapon sheathed.

"You're Kinahny? What town?"

"South, from Kephrath, near Shalem, but I have been living at Ramath-Galil. Akiy here lives in Merom just now. We answer to the Ibriym, and their warleader Abiy'el. Two of my other men are fetching you some more food from where we were camped."

The others looked at each other with mixed expressions of relief and suspicion.

"We are grateful. But why? What will we owe you?"

"Nothing. Abiy'el will make good to us for the food we share, so long as it brings gratitude to the name of the Ibriym."

The old man stirred.

"I know of the Ibriym, but mostly they live further south. Sychem and such like. Is Abiy'el wanting land up here?"

Labayu looked at him. This was hardly the place or time to discuss the long-term ambitions of the Ibriym, but the man wanted some kind of answer.

"Abiy'el will make covenant with any town that desires it. But the kings of the cities want nothing of that. I do not know where your allegiance lies, and I am not here to cut covenant with you. If you want us to leave, we will leave."

The group exchanged glances, and the old man spoke again.

"Kinahny or Ibriym, you are a more welcome sight than these bands of newcomers. I will not yet cut covenant with you, or with Abiy'el, but I am glad to meet you and share food with you. But see, though I am oldest here and have spoken first, I am weary. My daughter's husband will speak for all of us."

He gestured to the man who had brandished a sword when they had first appeared. Uriel and Ghazam came back at that point with food, and the rather stiff formality faded as they sat together and ate. The old man insisted that Labayu and his men take some of their food, so that it was a true act of sharing and not simply a gift. For all that the exchange was very one-sided.

Labayu sat back, watching the little group of wanderers. It was clear to him that they had been walking the track for a few days, and that they were unused to that way of life. But there was no sign that they had fled a battle, or seen fighting of any kind.

He listened to Akiy talking to one of the men. Of all his men, Akiy was the most likely to elicit information from the strangers; he had a comfortable way about him which put people at ease. Already, judging from what he could half-hear, Akiy had found out what town they had come from. The boy who had first asked if the group could stop for food came over to him.

"Sir, my father says that you are the leader here." Labayu nodded. "Could I know your name, sir? Then I can remember you before the gods when we are back at home and in the shrine."

"Labayu, son of Shaharti."

The lad shook his head. "That's not a proper name. Shaharti is a woman's name. Don't you know your father?"

Labayu forced a grin. It seemed the youth up here were trained early in their prejudices.

"I knew him very well, lad: Kothar was his name. But in my home town we count our descent from the mother. We do things differently where I grew up."

The boy frowned, perplexed, but rushed on after a moment. "So are you going to attack these new people now? Get us our houses back again so we can go home?"

"There are a great many of them, and only four of us just now. We will not charge straight at them. But I should like to help you to get your homes back again. My own leader would like to talk with them and find out what they want. I don't think their fight is really with us."

The boy's father joined him.

"I don't know how you will talk with them: their language is strange. I have been in the Fenku cities, and spoken with traders from the east, but these people are different again. You would need somebody to interpret. A northerner, perhaps. Maybe someone from the Khatti-lands. See, we left our homes when Hatsor was attacked, in case they did the same to us. And since then..."

"Wait. Hatsor has been attacked?"

"Oh yes. Several days ago now. The chariots were defeated somewhere outside the city, and after that, parts of the city were burned. But the citadel was not touched, and the people are returning to their homes already."

"And the king of the city?"

"I do not know, sir. I have not heard that he was killed, but when we heard the news we left our town to wander for some days in case the attackers came to us next. We had planned to go back there sooner than this, but then we decided to stay away longer. These invaders are moving south every day, and it seemed good to us to let them go past before we tried to go home. Better not to get in their way."

Labayu stood up and looked around.

"They are still heading south? Not turned east or back north?"

"Truly. They have done all they want to the cities further north, I think. Now they are here. Soon they will go south and leave us alone."

Labayu shook himself. He had been spending time up here, chasing small bands of youths and searching for Shimmigar, when all the time the invaders were pouring past him. How far would they reach? Bayth Shean? Sychem? Kephrath? Cursing himself for a dallying fool, he called his men together. In scarcely any time, they had left behind the refugee group and were heading south.

ᚷᚠᚲᚠᚲᚠᚲᚠᚷ

L ABAYU HAD LEFT the wanderers in the north several days ago. He still felt frustrated at his own ineffectiveness, meandering to and fro in the land with no real purpose. So far the only concrete achievement had been to inform Abiy'el about the new weapons. Small wonder that Shimmigar had become impatient and branched off on his own.

The four of them had worked their way generally south, trying to get a broad sense of the pattern of invasion. It seemed that the newcomers had no understanding of the natural human divisions in the land – Mitsriy, the many Kinahny groups, or the much more recent Ibriym.

Larger towns and cities were attacked, regardless of affiliation, while smaller towns and daughter villages were generally left alone. But not always: from time to time they came across quite small settlements built around a holy place which had been burned and left in ruins. Did the newcomers think they were at war with the gods of the land, or had something provocative been said?

The Ibriym had mostly abandoned their settlements in the face of all this, though Labayu suspected that their relative poverty and smallness would have shielded them. Perhaps they could have stayed and made a common peace against the kings of the land. It would have been a risk, though, and most village headmen had made the same choice as Pedayah had done at Ramath-Galil.

They saw that Magidda had been burned. They heard that Akka had been burned, and they met groups fleeing from towns down in the Valley. Inland or towards the coast, it was the same almost everywhere. The Fenku, remarkably, had been spared. Perhaps they were better able to defend themselves, but Akiy, with bitter voice, decided that they had simply paid the aggressors to pass on by.

Several times they saw Mitsriy army contingents. These had made a rapid change from idly casual clumps of men into hard, efficient playing pieces in the overall fight. From time to time, watching these organised teams training of an evening, or marching purposefully in the day, Labayu had a clear sense of the Mitsriy king leaning over one of his board games. The playing area was the Kinahny province, and the pieces were soldiers, invaders, and the refugees displaced by them.

Labayu had urged his men on day by day. They were all anxious for what they might find in the south, near Shalem. For all that they had temporary homes in the north while they helped Abiy'el defend the land, their families were in the south. Labayu often wondered what any of them would do if their own home towns had been pillaged; would they all, like Shimmigar, embark on a personal quest for revenge?

As they pushed south to Sychem, however, the pattern began to change. Mitsriy detachments became more common, and the signs of war more scarce. Sychem itself had not been abandoned by its people or its leaders, but was swollen in size with considerable numbers of Ibriym from the north.

Labayu went in to the town and spoke with the elders. They had seen Pedayah and the people of Ramath-Galil some days ago, and had sent them on south, towards Shalem. Already by then Sychem could not manage the influx of people, and nobody extra was welcome. Abiy'el had been and gone as well. He was sharing his time between as many different groups of the Ibriym as he could.

The chief elder had a dogged, strained expression as he spoke of this, and refused to meet anybody's eyes. Labayu heard, in what he left unsaid, the angry words, the fights and scuffles, the misery of those destitute who had pinned their hopes on the town.

He walked back to join his men, threading his way through areas of makeshift tents and muddy bedrolls. He had no real idea how many of the Ibriym had been forced together like this. Many hundred, certainly: perhaps a few thousand. How far could allegiance between tribes ever offset the desire to safeguard immediate family and clan relationships? The unity of the Ibriym was certainly being put to the test.

Akiy was sitting on a rock at the end of a ridge. The land started to fall away here, in its long decline to the Sea Road and the ocean beyond. The others were nearby, but Akiy called him over.

"Look, chief, I've worked out what the Mitsriy are doing."

Labayu grinned, glad to be forgetting what he had seen in and around Sychem.

"What, you're wanting now to have a new position serving the great king of the Mitsriy?"

"Perhaps. If I get weary of wandering round with you. But never mind that: look here. All these groups of Mitsriy soldiers we have seen these last few days, I've worked out what they are doing. They don't want to fight little skirmishes up here in the hill country. They've won a lot of these recently, but they won't achieve victory like that. They want to fight in the coastal plain, all together in one place with a real army."

Labayu looked out at the wooded slopes and ridges into the haze of distance. It made sense. The Mitsriy liked big battles, and they had the tradition of generalship to manage large numbers. They were gambling that the newcomers would not know how to organise themselves like that. He nodded.

"It's a good thought, Akiy. Bring them all into one place."

"Like one of those dragnets they use in the rivers for fish."

"There's risk for them, though. These newcomers travel in ships as well as ox carts. What if they circle around behind using the sea? Can the Mitsriy army survive an encirclement?"

He shrugged, and considered a little further.

"Not our problem, I suppose, but I would rather these two great powers fought one another, and that we were not caught like a nut between them and crushed. We need the Mitsriy to show their strength here, and then go back to within their own borders and leave the province alone. I don't want either of them to achieve a clear win."

Akiy nodded sombrely, and glanced away to his left. "How far south do you think they have got, chief? Do you think the Mitsriy have been successful in pushing them down to the coast?"

"That is exactly what we need to find out. We need to push on down to the Four Towns, and maybe Shalem. We need to find out what has happened to our own people, let alone the Ibriym we were supposed to protect."

Richard Abbott

Part 4 – Hill Country

A ND THEN CAME Shamgar the son of Anath, who killed six hundred Philistine men with an ox goad...

In the days of Shamgar son of Anath,
    desolate were the paths,
    and desolate the settlements in Israel.

ᐁ𒈜ᐁ𒈜ᐁ𒈜ᐁ𒈜ᐳ

NIGHT CAME. ANILAT HAD STAYED AWAY from the group
until the evening, keeping the three children near her
with the woman and her daughter. When she finally rejoined
the others, in the slightly larger house they had chosen, conversation had been brittle at first, and had only very slowly
softened. Tadugari had become increasingly withdrawn again
through the evening, but roused himself a little to offer the
evening prayers and blessings.

It was only just after the spring point where night and day
were equal. The stars came out in a cloudless sky, and the air
grew cold. Khuratsanitu built the fire up with larger pieces
of wood to keep it smouldering until the morning, while Auntie settled the three children in a side room. They had been
excited at the thought of being in a separate place.

Finally Anilat and Tadugari were left alone in what had
been the main room of the house. The door, its hinges damaged, had kept creeping open, until they leaned a stool against
it to hold it shut.

She lay beside Tadugari, not quite touching him. Neither
of them spoke. The night was very quiet. The sounds of occasional owls and night animals called from the nearby trees
and fields around the village. She supposed that the place
would previously have been more alive with noise than this.

From the next room, she heard Auntie coming up towards
her sexual climax. She lifted her head, curious: she had not
expected that Auntie would pair herself with Khuratsanitu.
She listened idly for a while, then rolled in to Tadugari and
leaned her head on his chest. Her anger with him was still
unreconciled, but desire for physical release warred against
this. He ignored her, unresponsive, making no move to hold
her. She sighed and moved away from him again, torn between frustration and grief.

After a while the house fell silent again. She knew from the sound of his breathing that Tadugari had fallen asleep, but she lay beside him in the borderland between the waking and dream worlds, unable to settle fully into either. Her heart was full of odd images.

After a time there came a soft tapping on the door. It chimed so perfectly with Anilat's own reverie that at first she ignored the sound, but it carried on.

"Lady, you have to wake up. I heard voices. I think they might be coming back."

It was the village woman, but for a while her words did not make sense. Then, shaking her head to clear it, she got up, pulled the stool away to open the door, and looked out at her. She found herself whispering, matching the other woman's low voice.

"Who's coming back? Your own people? The lot that burned your village? Who do you mean?"

"No, not them. That trader. I heard him and his men. I'm sure it was them. Over that way."

She pointed in the direction the trader had left earlier. The house they were in blocked the view. Anilat frowned.

"Are you sure? I cannot hear anything."

They both listened. There was nothing except the night noises.

"Something was there, lady. I am sure of it."

She took a step towards the corner of the house and then stopped. If there was somebody there, she did not want to meet them alone. She listened again, wondering if there really were sounds coming out of the gloom that had no innocent explanation. She was turning towards the village woman, her thoughts confused, when they both heard the sound of splintering wood from the back of the house.

The woman shook her head, whimpering, but seized Anilat's arm. "They'll be after your children. That's what they'll be coming back for. Why aren't they in the room with you?"

A great fury consumed Anilat, and she started back into the house. "You wake my husband. I will go to the children." The other woman hesitated. "Go on, he won't hurt you. We'll be lucky if he does anything at all."

She moved as quickly through the house as the shadows and scattered furniture allowed. Behind her she could hear the woman shaking Tadugari from his sleep. From the children's room she one of the twins – Rishi, she thought – was making muffled complaining noises.

She burst into the room. Two men were in there – the trader and one of his lads – and the third one was outside the open window. Rishi was struggling in the younger man's grip: Ritsani was lying bound and gagged on one of the sleeping pallets. Haleyna was nowhere in sight. She shouted and waved her arms at them, suddenly aware that she had no way to defend herself.

The younger man moved towards her, his face menacing in the shadows. She took a step backwards, frightened by his approach. Ritsani turned his head to and fro, his eyes wide, but could not free himself. Suddenly Tadugari was beside her, his short sword in his hand, cutting at the outstretched hands of the intruder. The trader pushed Rishi away from him and started scrambling out through the open window.

She ran over to Rishi, picked him up from the floor, then turned to undo Ritsani's bonds. The gag came away easily enough, but the rope around his hands was too tight for her. Behind her she could hear Tadugari swearing, and the young man stumbling, calling out for mercy.

Auntie was there with her now, wrapped in a sheet, a little knife in her hand cutting the ropes that had been so intractable. She turned to see Tadugari stab the young man in the chest and leap across the room to hack at the trader's legs as they disappeared through the window. He howled at the sword cut, but was pulled bodily out of the frame beyond Tadugari's reach.

"He's got Haleyna out there, slung over one of the donkeys."

He turned to Anilat, but she pointed at the door.

"The twins are fine. You go after those two outside."

He ran from the room, and she heard him blunder into furniture. It was all taking too long. Auntie had one arm around each of the twins. She had an untamed, protective air about her.

"See what you can see from the window, mistress. I've got these two now."

The trader was hobbling towards the donkeys, blood running down his legs. The other man was fumbling with the ropes. As Tadugari had said, Haleyna was lying over the back of one of the donkeys. Her hands were tied behind her, and she was shaking her head, worrying at the cloth gag in unsuccessful attempts to loosen it.

Khuratsanitu came running at full speed round the corner of the house. His sword was in one hand, a knife in the other, and he was entirely naked. He ran straight at the trader, who was shouting in a foreign language at his helper. With a cold efficiency Khuratsanitu knocked away the feeble defence and plunged his knife into the exposed throat.

Without waiting for the trader to fall, he turned to the younger man, who first backed away a few paces, and then turned to run away. Khuratsanitu went after him briefly, but lost him as he dodged between the houses, and turned back before he went too far. Tadugari finally appeared and crossed over to Haleyna. He started to lift her off the donkey.

"What about that one, sir? Shall I get after him? He's getting away."

Tadugari finished setting Haleyna on her feet, cut away the gag and ropes, and then shook his head.

"No point, I think. We'll never find him in the darkness. And he won't be back now we've killed the other two."

He grimaced and stretched. Then he looked at Khuratsanitu, shrugged off his tunic and handed it to the soldier.

"You didn't wait for anything before coming out, did you?"

Khuratsanitu grinned and wrapped himself in the cloth. "Best not to be late, sir."

They went back inside the house, supporting Haleyna, who was shivering and pale. When she saw Anilat, she ran to her and buried her head against her, sobbing. None of the adults said anything for a time. Finally Khuratsanitu looked at the wreckage in what had been the children's room.

"We should pick another house for the rest of the night, I think, sir. None of us will rest well here."

They moved to one of the other houses. By the time they had settled there the village woman had disappeared again. Anilat turned to Tadugari. "I'm not going anywhere away from the children tonight. Even if I can't sleep I'm not leaving them."

"No. You stay with them." He looked at the others. "I will take the watch now, out here by the door."

He waved aside Khuratsanitu's objections. "No, I will go on watch. You have done all that was needed tonight. Now it is my turn."

Inside, the group huddled together into a single room for mutual reassurance. Meanwhile, Tadugari closed the door behind him and sat with his back against it, sword open in his hand, looking out into the night.

MORNING CAME, AND ANILAT WOKE to find wet dew clinging to the grass and a light drizzle cleaning away some of the ash and dust from the houses around them. They had all slept in fits and starts. Tadugari pushed open the door and stepped inside. He looked extremely weary. Khuratsanitu stirred, then shook his head and leapt up.

"You should have woken me, sir. Shared the night watch."

"No, I decided not to." He looked around at them all. The twins were huddled in to Auntie, and Anilat had her arms around Haleyna. He took a deep breath.

"I have spent the night in prayer to every god that I know. It was difficult at first, because the gods had withdrawn from me, just as I have withdrawn from them since leaving Ikaret. But then in the middle of the night a great owl settled on the branch of the tree opposite me, as though it was a messenger sent directly from the sacred mountain. I was on the borderlands of the other world."

He paused and closed his eyes, remembering.

"Then a lioness came into the village. She sat opposite me, under the almond tree over the way, and she just looked at me for a very long time before moving on. She was utterly still as she sat there under the tree, and extremely beautiful."

"Were you not afraid, father?" Rishi's eyes were wide.

"No, child, because I knew I was in a sacred place and that the lioness would not harm me. She was sent by the gods as their holy representative, and because of the almond tree I knew I had to take note of the message."

He turned to face Anilat.

"As she sat watching me I knew in my inmost being that I have failed you all. I have not led you all as I should, nor protected you as I should. I have been consumed by my own thoughts, and not looked out for your well-being. During the night I have confessed the same to the gods, and now I confess it to you. I am full of remorse now, and from today I will be different. Please forgive me."

There was a little silence. Khuratsanitu and Auntie looked at each other and said nothing. The three children stared at him. Anilat caressed Haleyna's hair where it spilled out from under her white kef.

"What does that mean for us all?"

"It means that I shall lead and protect you all as I should have done all this time. I am ashamed that we came so close to ruin last night, and thank you all for what you each did to fight off those men."

"Should we go on to Hatsor, then, sir?"

"No. Hatsor has fallen. We heard that from the woman who lives here. If Yasib and Dantiy have not reached Hatsor, then they will avoid it; if they had already arrived there, then I trust they will have escaped its downfall as they escaped Ikaret. No. We will take a short time to gather what supplies we can, we will load them on the donkeys those men left, and we will carry on south to Shalem. Shalem is where Yasib will think to go, and that is where we shall go. I have spoken with the king of Shalem before, and he will receive us. Or his senior envoy at least, Abdi-Teshup, who I have met before both in Shalem and Ikaret."

"How much further is Shalem?"

"About a week if we went directly there. But now we know what has happened even here at Hatsor this far south, we will take longer. Shorter trips each day, and better resting places at night away from plain view. But less than two weeks, even if we take good care. First, we will swing west around Hatsor, making sure that we keep well away from the Sea Road."

He looked around to gather the mood of the others. Nobody spoke. He pulled a stool over from beside the door and sat at the focal point of the group.

"Look now, something else came to me in the night. I have been thinking of us as homeless people, fleeing like frightened birds from the destruction of our nest. But this is not so. I am an envoy of the king of Ikaret, and we are all representatives of the city. Even if the king has died, even if the city has fallen, even if we should be the very last survivors; even then it is our duty to keep the sacred flame of the city burning brightly before us. None of us are scribes, so we cannot write the tale of our land on stone or clay. But we can keep her heart alive by our deeds and by the life we make down here in the Kinahny province."

He stopped. Khuratsanitu was nodding, his face full of relief, as though a burden had been lifted away from him. Anilat wiped away a stray tear with the corner of her kef.

"Well then. Let us finish collecting what we need and then go."

"I should like to leave something else for that woman. She has helped us at every turn, especially last night by waking us up. But let me speak with her: she can only bear the presence of other women just now."

"Give her one of the donkeys, and whatever other goods you see fit. And if you think she will accept it, give her my blessing for the future."

A little later, Anilat left the others to finish the last stages of loading up, and went with Haleyna over to the woman's house. She took with her one of the donkeys, with a selection of useful items tied to the harness. Haleyna was carrying a little cloth bundle. The woman's house looked empty, but when Anilat called out, the door opened. The two went inside.

"You are going now?"

"We are. Not to Hatsor, not after what you told us. Further south."

"I don't want to know where. The less I know the better."

"See, we are leaving you one of the donkeys. And some things on it that you might find useful."

The woman looked up briefly. The bruising on her face had spread further down her neck, where they could see it, but the intensity of colour around her eyes and mouth was fading.

"Thank you for that. But it was not necessary."

"I think it is. Please accept it. And I would also like you to have these."

She nudged Haleyna, who stepped forward and held out the bundle. The woman looked at it for a long moment without moving, and finally took it.

She unwrapped the bundle, to find a pair of silver earrings. The hoops were quite large, covered with curved patterns cut into the metal. Two tiny silver bells were attached at the bottom of the curve. She stared at them, her mouth pursed shut.

"I can't take these."

"I should like you to. They have belonged to women in my family for several generations. Because of you my family is still intact, and it is right that you have these now. So you can look at them and remember what you did for me. For all of us. The value is not important."

She shook her head. "It is not the value."

She looked at the floor of her house, then rather defiantly met Anilat's eyes again.

"But these are beautiful, and look at me now. I cannot wear these."

Anilat took the woman's hands gently, with the earrings held in them as though in an empty cup.

"Put them away somewhere. Wear them another day, when your people have come back here and all this has passed us by. I shall think of you every day, and one day, perhaps you will be wearing them."

The woman shook her head, but took the earrings and put them in a round clay jar, covering them with a piece of soft cloth.

"I will accept them, with gratitude. But never think that I shall wear them."

Anilat stood to go, calling Haleyna over to her. She opened the door and then turned back. The woman was moving a piece of stone in the wall to one side and putting the clay vessel behind it.

"You could come south with us. Leave this place behind."

The woman ignored her, finished hiding the earrings, and went with her daughter into another room. The house had returned to its state of frozen organisation. Anilat sighed. At least she had made an effort.

✔ 𓏏 ✔ 𓏏 ✔ 𓏏 ✔ 𓏏 ✔

T HE DAY WAS PLEASANTLY WARM, with a light breeze coming from the coast, far out of sight to the west. Tadugari and Khuratsanitu were in the lead, with all three children between them. Anilat walked behind with Auntie, talking idly. Abruptly, Anilat put a voice to the idea that had been circling around her thoughts since the middle of the night.

"Look now, I should like to call you Damatiria instead of Auntie from this time on."

"Well, mistress, I don't know that this is the right time. I should have been in with the children last night. I was not in the place I needed to be."

"Neither was I. But they wanted to have the room all to themselves, and how were any of us to know what would happen?"

"Nevertheless, mistress, I failed both them and you. I listened to your husband speak about his time of remorse before the gods, and it seemed right that I should be remorseful towards you. You trusted me, and I failed that trust. Should we not put last night well behind us before anything else?"

"I do not think your fault was greater than mine. If indeed there was fault at all. You and Khuratsanitu came running at need, and were beside us when it mattered. Indeed, Tadugari should never have told that trader about Haleyna in the afternoon."

Damatiria was lost in her thoughts while the track went down a steeper incline.

"I don't mind, mistress. Whatever pleases you."

"It would please me. But also it seems right. We are not in Ikaret any more, nor ever likely to be there again, I think. A new journey needs a new name, or so it seems to me."

"It's all right, mistress. But it won't change anything about me, you know. I won't be calling you anything except 'mistress'. And if you were worrying that I might up and leave, there is no need. I'll not be leaving you."

Anilat nodded ruefully: she had not thought herself so transparent. They walked on together for a while, watching the children. Then she looked sideways at Damatiria.

"Anyway, I know that your heart was occupied elsewhere as night fell last night. I am happy for you. There is no shame in it."

Damatiria smiled a little and brushed a stray leaf from her smock.

"Well, mistress, we all do what we can to keep the group together. You do what you can and I do what I can. Each to her own."

Anilat laughed and linked arms with her as they walked along together.

"Easy for me, and good for you last night, I think."

Damatiria thought for a time before speaking again.

"Truly, I had not expected to find someone to kindle my heart again, mistress. Certainly not on this journey we have been forced to make. There was more to last night than just a plot or a scheme."

"Of course. I know that. See, when we find a place to live again, I want you stay with us. Both of you, if that is still your desire when the time comes."

"The children will not need me for much longer, mistress. They are growing so quickly now. And when Haleyna gets with child, if she wants a wet nurse she will need a much younger girl than I. Those years are long gone now for me. Dried up and gone once the twins let that go behind them. Perhaps I am no more use to you."

"The children may not need you. But I need you. I want us to become old women together in comfort somewhere. Look, Damatiria, I do not yet know what will become of Tadugari. Until he takes notice of me again, I do not know how to hear what he told us about his encounter with the owl and the lioness. I want to believe it, but until it moves his heart back to me, I shall continue to feel alone in my doubt."

They walked on together. Damatiria watched the children for a while, then turned to look at Anilat and nodded.

❖❖❖❖❖❖❖❖

KHURATSANITU POKED AT THE FIRE that they had used to cook a pair of rabbits and some biscuit. Little sparks crackled into the evening sky. Tadugari looked up at them sombrely, the last fires of Ikaret smouldering still in his heart. The soldier stopped when he saw his expression.

"Should I just let it die down, sir? Do we need it tonight?"

Tadugari looked around. They had settled for the night a little distance from the main Ridgeway track, among a group of boulders. Small scrubby trees were scattered all around, and the spring growth was starting to fill in between the trunks, but there was still not much cover from prying eyes. They had passed near to small settlements earlier in the day, and had taken short detours to avoid them.

"Let it go out now, I think. The night is warm. Why take the chance that somebody will see us, now we are so close?"

Together they pulled the unburned wood away, beat out the flames and scattered the ashes, covering them with earth. Tadugari smiled to himself. They had reused a firespot that somebody else had set only a few days before, and he imagined the surrounding trees and rocks watching the same act being repeated by different people many times over. They buried the rabbit carcasses a little distance from the camp. Anilat watched them while Damatiria laid out bedrolls for the three children.

"Are there any more towns on this side of Shalem? And how far is it now?"

"We could be there tomorrow, late in the afternoon, if we rushed. But why risk it now? We will take an extra night and arrive the following morning. As for what lies ahead, well, there is a town just off this Ridgeway track which we will pass tomorrow. With little villages nearby. We do not have to go into the town, but we will pass close by it."

"It's the mother town of three daughters, sir. One of the three is a fair size, nearly the same as the main one. The other two are tiny. They have an alliance among themselves. If we keep away from them, they will not trouble us."

"I did not know so much about them."

The soldier nodded.

"They say that long ago the people of these towns moved down to here. From the lands even of the King of the North, though it was long before his family took the throne. There was a man in the royal guard who had family in this land. We used to make fun at his expense, saying how he must have Kinahny blood in him."

He chuckled at the memory, then pulled a face.

"I suppose we should be more careful with our words now we are here ourselves."

"We should. The first thing we need is friendship now we have come so far. There will be no provocative talk about the Kinahny."

There were nods from around the group. The light was fading fast now, and with the fire gone they could not be seen from a distance.

"I will take the first watch tonight. From the left of that great rock there, I think."

"Let me join you for a short time, sir."

Khuratsanitu walked with him the few paces over to the lookout point. The women and children were now just darker shapes in the gloom. There was a tiny sliver of moon drifting among the wispy clouds, but it shed too little light to reveal anything.

"Sir, pardon me asking, but what if we get to Shalem and the same has happened there? These raiders are moving faster than we have been, for sure. But worse still, what if we get there safely and then are caught by them in a snare?"

Tadugari sighed, sat on the rock and placed his sword beside him within easy reach.

"I have wondered that myself, many times, in the days since we left that village near Hatsor. However, we have seen no sign of trouble on our way south since then. So I have hope about this. Perhaps the Mitsriy armies have put them to flight already. Or perhaps they have run out of strength after all this way."

Khuratsanitu was silent for a while, standing beside the boulder. Tadugari looked at him.

"You do not agree?"

"Sir, I do not want to disagree. But so many places have fallen, and their kings with them. We know of Ikaret and Hatsor, great cities both. And you yourself told me of others in the lands of the King of the North. Shalem is not a great city; its king will not have a great army. What will we find when we get there?"

"If Shalem has fallen, we will go on to the lands of the Mitsriy. In times past I would have said to go first to Gedjet, on the coast, but these invaders have been thrusting down the coast road all the way. We should not go there. We will go east across to the Kings' Road, and follow that all the way to the Mitsriy. I know the waymarks along there, and it is an altogether more important route than this Ridgeway."

He paused, scratched his head. "It will not be an easy journey. Perhaps we can join with other travellers going that same way, band into one group for protection."

"I have never gone that far south."

"The Mitsriy land is good. But the journey to reach it can be desolate and harsh, depending which way we choose. I hope it does not come to that; better by far to find that Shalem is the safe harbour that we have been looking for all this time."

"Sir, look, they still have the hunt in the Kinahny lands. You have often spoken of how you missed it: you could enjoy it again here. I do not think the Mitsriy have it, though. I hear they snare fish and birds, rather than hunt wild beasts."

"Their great kings boast of the hunt. But I have not heard that others in their land go out like that. But see, you and I could enjoy it together again: it would not be me alone."

"Then, sir, would it be so bad to stay among the Kinahny? Their ways are more like ours than those of the Mitsriy. You would find a place among the nobility here; I could serve with their guardsmen. Should we stop here rather than continue south? Surely it is a long way yet if we kept going?"

"Indeed it is. We are scarcely half way. Much further still if we travel south to their most holy places, though in that case we would go by river. But see, Khuratsanitu, when we settle again, I should like it if you stayed in my service. When I find a house again, I will need a loyal guard, and I can think of nobody better suited than you. And my wife would be glad if Damatiria stayed as well. How can I persuade you?"

"I should be honoured, lord. You have only to speak. But first you have to find a new home. Will you look for this in Shalem, or will you carry on?"

"If the king will have us, then for my part I would stay in Shalem. I think the king will look with favour on us. At least, I hope so. But my wife carries something with her that she has never shown me. We have not talked about that: she has kept it hidden. Perhaps this will drive her to keep going further still."

"Do you think we will find others there from Ikaret? Perhaps your own family who separated from us at those huts?"

Tadugari looked briefly across to where the others were lying, and lowered his voice a little.

"In truth, I fear we will never see them again. Say nothing of this to my wife or children. But my fear is that they made good speed to Hatsor and were caught up in its destruction. Surely they would have travelled faster than us. We must live here as though none of our kin escaped, I think."

Khuratsanitu leaned back against the rock.

"Perhaps they were slower than you think. Or took a different route for some reason."

Tadugari said nothing for a long time, and finally replied only, "You should get some sleep."

◊⫟⬦⫟⬦⫟⬦⫟⬦◊

THE NEXT DAY DAWNED CLEAR AND BRIGHT, and the dome of the sky stretched vast above them. The sun had not quite risen, but the eastern sky was golden in anticipation.

Anilat stretched and, for the first time for weeks, felt almost able to laugh aloud. Tadugari was still not yet awake, but he had wriggled himself against her body in his sleep, and one arm rested across her. It was a new start, and perhaps it would grow back into something better. She slipped away from him and went to kneel beside Haleyna, who already had her eyes open and was looking around.

She whispered to her daughter. "Come up on that rock with me and we'll watch Nut, Lady of the sky, give birth to the sun god. Do you remember the stories my mother used to tell?"

They scrambled up the side of the boulder, ignoring Khuratsanitu who had wandered part of the distance across to the Ridgeway track to look around. They settled on the top, arms around each other as the sun leaped into the sky like a horse released from the traces.

Anilat sighed and kissed the top of Haleyna's head. Their dark hair mingled in a slight breath of wind. Haleyna leaned in to her mother and giggled.

"Here we are both out and about in the day, and neither of us is wearing our kef. What would people say?"

"If we go all the way to the Mitsriy lands, it would not matter. Your grandmother told me that she never wore one when she was young. She put on the kef after she was married, to be modest in your grandfather's house. I suppose we would just go bare headed every day if ever we went there."

"I will never stop wearing the kef. You chose this for me in the great market in Ikaret, as well as the patterned kef for festivals, and they will forever remind me of our old home."

Anilat nodded, but felt a sudden pang all through her body. Haleyna continued before she could speak.

"Anyway, I don't want to just keep going on and on. I want to live in a house again. Can we find somewhere in this Shalem place?"

Anilat felt under her smock for the little closed box her mother had trusted to her. If they settled here in the Kinahny province, how could she fulfil her promise about this? But she knew that, like her daughter, her soul longed to be rooted again in a place she could make her own.

"Let us wait and see what Shalem is like. I have never seen it, but your father says it is small. Nothing like the city that we have known. Perhaps we will not like it, or not be able to find a home there. But at least we can rest somewhere better than the wilderness, or in one of these little sheep huts for a few days."

The two watched the sun a little longer. In the still air to the south, a little haze of smoke drifted upwards. Anilat caught her breath for a moment, but then realised that it was the sign of village life, not of plunder and the burning of cities. Somewhere close at hand, families like her own were getting ready for the day.

"Haleyna, your grandmother trusted me with something on that last evening. She knew before the rest of us that she would not live through the attack on the city, so she gave me something precious."

Haleyna looked curiously at her.

"What is it, mother? Do you have it still?"

"Of course. I have carried it against my body all through the journey."

She paused.

"But it is a secret thing still, and I cannot show it to you just yet. She made me promise to take it to a Mitsriy priest who would know how to look after it properly. If we do not carry on, I do not know if I will be able to keep that promise."

"Perhaps there is a priest like that in Shalem?"

Anilat nodded.

"That is a good prayer. I want to keep the promise I made, but I do not want to keep wandering onwards without an end. When the time comes, if those were the only two choices ahead of me, I do not know which I would pick. Surely my own mother would not want me to keep my children homeless? If I make the choice to settle, surely she will see from the other side and understand? But see: the others are waking up, and we should go to them. Say nothing to your brothers about this."

Anilat climbed down the short distance to the ground. Haleyna was still sitting there. She turned to look at Anilat with sudden resolve.

"Mother, back at that little village with the woman you gave earrings to."

"Bayth Ma'acath?"

Haleyna nodded and rushed on.

"When we heard the trader talking, and the woman thought it was those others had come back."

She stopped, swallowed, and looked away. Anilat reached out impulsively to touch her, but stopped herself before finishing the movement.

"I know you had your knife with you. What would you have done if it had been an army? Would you have done what our guardsman told you?"

Anilat shivered a little, telling herself that it was simply the morning air.

"There was no need to do anything then."

"No, not then, but I need to know. Would you have done it?"

They looked at each other finally, eyes flinching away and then returning.

"Haleyna, I do not know if I could. When I asked Khuratsanitu how to do this, back in the valley, I thought it would be better for you and the twins to die by my hand, by me who loves you. Better that, I thought, than for you three to be mistreated by strangers. But would I be able to, if it ever came to that moment? Who can say? Every evening and every morning I thank the gods that they have spared us that moment."

Haleyna looked at her for a long moment, then clambered down without accepting her mother's offered hand and started to walk off on her own. Anilat watched her go a few paces before the anger she felt pushed some words out.

"Haleyna, don't just walk away from me."

Her daughter stopped, but turned only her head to look back at her.

"Back at Bayth Ma'acath, that trader took you from the room, and gagged you, and tied you across his donkey. What if we had not been able to rescue you and your brothers? What if you were me, seeing your children carried away to some dreadful fate? What if it was you that Khuratsanitu had given instruction to about the knife? What then?"

Haleyna turned then to look at her properly. Her face was still stubborn, but she made no reply, and waited for Anilat to come over to her. Together, then went back to the others, where Rishi was nudging Ritsani into wakefulness.

A SON ADDRESSES HIS FATHER.

Hekanefer to his father Nesamenopeh, greetings and blessings to you. I write from the Kinahny hill country.

Once again, father, I have good news to impart to you, though perhaps you have already heard it from the priests nearby. It lifted up the hearts of the men here to a quite extraordinary degree. This is good, since our own duties have been repetitious, and we long to find a way to enjoy victory. We move rapidly from place to place still, seeking to engage the enemy when we can.

It is a strange war, this one, and the soldiers tell me that it is unlike anything they have known before. They want the enemy to gather into one place so that two armies may fight in a proper way. The enemy avoid this, preferring to keep in separate bands.

Our commander is under orders to harry them on every side; he tells me that his goal is to drive them all into a single place. For the time being we break camp every morning, pursue them in the day, and settle again every night.

This good news was brought to us by a scout on horseback, riding hard up from Gedjet with messages from the Beloved Land. The great king User-ma'at-Re Mery-Imun, who lives in prosperity and health, has achieved a remarkable victory at sea, on the very fringes of the sedge lands. All of us, up and down the land in our camps and tents, all of us are being told so that our hearts might be stirred up.

It is like this. We knew from spies that the enemy use ships to transport their men from place to place, and so can arrive rapidly in unexpected places. So the great king who lives in prosperity and health collected his fleet into one flock, and filled his ships with the best of our bowmen.

Then he waited, patiently watching his prey draw near. A lesser general would have declared his intention sooner, and most likely the enemy would have scattered like frightened birds who hear the noise of the fowler's snare.

But the great king, magnificent in splendour and trained in every art of war, waited for them all to come into his trap. Then he stretched out his powerful hand. His ships suddenly closed in on them, the bowmen rained arrows down from the skies, and there was no escape. It was like the day of Sekhmet when she raged rampant through the land, slaughtering men on every side, intoxicated by her own ruthlessness.

Few indeed of that wicked enemy reached the land that they craved, and more of our men were waiting for those who finally waded ashore. It was a glorious victory, and one which will be proclaimed in word and song forever. Our king is a heroic lord. Fear goes ahead of him, and scatters the ranks of those who stand against him.

But, great as that victory was, the war is not over.

There are still a great many enemy soldiers on land, moving here and there in groups through the Kinahny province. They still ravage the people here like wild beasts. We still come across destitute families who are fleeing the swords of the enemy. We still march through towns which have been burned and looted.

At least when we enter an intact town or village now, the occupants cheer our arrival, since we represent peace and security for them.

And so our own resolve is daily put to the test. My commander means to herd these rebels into a single place so that a final battle can be fought. Other commanders have the same orders. No longer will they be allowed to move here and there in small bands, doing as they please. Together we will drive them towards the coastal plain and the Sea Road, and there we will make a day of fighting and a day of victory.

Honoured father, remember me before all the gods that when that day comes, I shall cover myself with honour, so that the name of our family will increase in the land. In the morning, and when the sun goes down, stand with my dear mother, the lady Hemesherit, and offer incense and beautiful gifts in my name at the household shrine.

When I first came out to this land I was anxious, and feared for every moment of my life: now I am proud to stand along-side these mighty warriors as they strive to defend the Beloved Land itself. I shall not turn away from the battle, but will keep my face towards the enemy. Think of me every day, fa-ther, for I do not know when this battle will take place.

A MAN ADDRESSES HIS BROTHER.

Hekanefer to Ramose, on the Ridgeway track some small distance from Shalem.

Brother, all of a sudden I am separated from the men whose camp and whose tents I have shared these many days. Orders came out from Gedjet, and as you know orders must be obeyed. So I find myself, quite suddenly, almost alone on the road. I quite miss my former companions. This little band consists of five of us: myself, the second officer, and the three unwounded members of my bodyguard. And we are heading for Shalem. More of that later.

Another thing before that, though. Our mother has noticed how rarely I talk about that girl Nodjmet these days. She is concerned in case my heart has grown cold. Of course I replied that it had not, but in truth I cannot think of her with much interest any longer. What I remember of her is a whining voice and an ungenerous spirit, and these things do not invite me to return to her.

I suppose that family duty will prevail, and when I go back to the Beloved Land the marriage that our father has planned will take place. Remember me to every god in this, brother, that I shall not disappoint him. And pray for me, that when she becomes my wife she will not disappoint me. I now have a greater fear of this than I do of the war around me. I suppose once duty has been done with her, I shall be able to find pleasure in other ways.

Another thing. I have been enjoying the wine of this land. It is rich and dark, better than we can make at home, and quite unlike our own beer. It is very good for reviving the spirit inside a man. The area we are moving towards is said to have a long tradition of producing good wine, and I intend to find out if this is true. If so, then I will purchase a skin or two with a little of the silver I have accumulated. Shall I acquire some for you as well?

Beyond that lies Shalem, a town name that you and I both learned in our apprenticeship. I am sure you can still recite every way station home to the Beloved Land from there. But my friends the soldiers tell me that it is a small place. There is not likely to be much by way of amusement there. We will go, conduct our business, and leave again. Perhaps for Gedjet, though this is not certain.

I have kept you waiting long enough. You keep asking why I should be going to Shalem, and with such a small group.

Well, the orders came very abruptly. One morning we fully expected to be marching in our haphazard route around the hill country in search of another band of raiders, when a rider approached from the direction of the King's Road. He went straight to the commander, and before any time had passed I was called in to his tent along with the second officer.

The commander was more excited than I have ever seen him. It was like seeing the dawn on the first day of the Festival of the Beautiful Valley.

"Two things," he said. "The first is that the plan of the great king has succeeded. The enemy is gathering all of his strength into one place. The fight that we have been preparing for will be fought on the coastal plain, somewhere between Gedjet and the land of the Fenku."

The second officer was delighted, and congratulated him. I myself found a wave of fierce exultation rising up from my innards. I was going to be a soldier, participating in the battle of battles, fighting in defence of the Beloved Land against this enemy. The flame of our wrath would be going before us, cleansing this unhappy land of these vile enemies.

"Secondly, the two of you are to be sent elsewhere. I require you both to go to Shalem. I can spare three men to protect you, but no more."

I confess, brother, that the junior officer grasped the consequences faster than I did. We were not to be anywhere near the battle after all. He protested that his place was beside his commander's side, but no to avail. The chief officer was kind to us, but implacable.

"I need you both in Shalem to enforce oaths and treaties. You because you speak their language, and you because I need to send the most senior available officer to represent the land. You will hear the oaths of the king reconfirmed. Or his most senior official, a man called Abdi-Teshup, if the king is not there."

He was patient with us for a short time, but would not change his orders. So, brother, I am no longer a soldier, but a translator now. Here in this province there can be so many changes of occupation for a man who thought he was there simply to make an official record.

Laugh at me if you will, but my heart felt a pang of regret as we set off away from the rest of the camp. The bodyguard do not share these feelings, but are happy to be out of danger's path.

So here we are, working our way east up to the Ridgeway track where, as you know very well, we shall turn south. It is quiet here, with only four companions to share a camp instead of a whole gaggle of soldiers and camp followers. I miss the noise, and the sense of being at the centre of everything.

DEKSEUS FOLLOWED HIS FATHER'S WAGON as it lumbered through the stands of trees. They were now on the east side of the River, heading south again. It had taken a day or so to get to a shallow place where they could cross the River, and another few days to work a very slow way down the eastern side of the Valley.

They had been in no hurry, and had given the animals more rest time from hauling the wagons than they had ever known before. It also meant that the outriding scouts could set snares of a morning and still circle back to collect the catch the same evening.

Yasib had suggested the ford they had used, well upstream from the nearest Mitsriy town. While it still looked as though the clan was coming down from the north, he had suggested, it was better to avoid contact. Across the River things would be different; for one thing the Mitsriy cared less about events on that side, and for another they could present themselves as though migrating from the east, following after others who had done this before. Antos and the other clan leaders accepted his word.

The day after they had crossed the River they had stopped for an afternoon of games. Back at their former home across the sea, games had been a regular pleasure, but there had been little opportunity on the long journey. Now that it seemed likely that they would be settling soon again, it had seemed good to them all to revisit the old traditions.

The atmosphere had been subdued by the loss of so many of their youth, and the injuries that slowed so many of the living. Older men joined in to make up numbers, and they had all tried to make the mood festive rather than competitive. Javelins were thrown, and the bronze disc. There was archery, and wrestling, riddle games and the singing of songs.

Yasib had joined in with the bow, and proved himself good enough to compete against the hunters, though he was far from the best among them. After the feast, prizes had been given out by Antos in the circle of firelight. Two of the best storytellers challenged one another to a duel of words, each trying to make the most far-fetched tale from one of the traditional starting rhymes.

Then Dantiy sang a song of Ikaret in her own language. Dekseus understood none of it, but it sounded to him full of the plaint of the sea and the cry of the flocks of wading birds that she spoke of. The patterns of sound were not like the patterns of his own people, but there was a rhythm about it, an ebb and flow which he could recognise. Yasib was in tears by the end.

Since then, they had kept away from paths and small towns and, with the help of Arkelawos and the other scouts, met nobody. Instead, they picked a careful way through glade and meadow, alive with spring and the promise of fertility. It was a good land, much richer than the narrow valleys and thin soil of their homeland, far away to the north. Eastward, the ground rose up quite steeply in the distance, and the sense of living in a protective hollow in the land grew with each passing day.

The air was full with the scent of blossom, the sky with birds, and the woods with game. In a few months, fruit of all kinds would ripen across the land. If they found a village somewhere which would receive them before the autumn, they would harvest crops in abundance the following year. Dekseus could remember something of the rhythm of farming from the days of his youth across the sea, and the older men were becoming enthusiastic about the promise of settled life ahead.

He was acutely aware that he had had no opportunity to lie with Dantiy again. With Murtilis gone, the three young people set their bedding together at the opposite end of the wagon from Nikleos and Kastiandra. He longed even to touch her hand, but Kastiandra had placed Yasib between him and Dantiy. He understood that this was needed for the sake of appearance, but he found it particularly frustrating.

Then in the late afternoon, after another short day's journey, he was away from the camp hunting small game. He heard footsteps behind him, and after listening for a short time knew that it was her. He waited so that she could find him beside a pool in the woodlands, and there they made space for their passion under the singing canopy of the trees.

He had recovered a great deal of his strength in the days since the festival for the coming of spring, and this time could be active with her. But remembering all that had happened on the night of the dance, he tempered his haste, and was sensitive to her own desire.

As they relaxed, he looked down into her eyes. They were darker than the women of his own clan, and shaped like almonds. He laughed. Her face was flushed, she was still breathing hard, and he could feel her rapid heartbeat through the flesh of their joined bodies. He stroked her hair.

"I thought you had forgotten all about me after that night."

She shook her head, looked curiously at him.

"Today is the last day that it is prudent for us to be together for a while."

He assumed that she meant that they needed to avoid drawing attention to themselves. He sat up so that he could enjoy the sight of her, stretched full length beside him.

"Dantiy, you are right, someone could find out about us if we are not careful. My parents, your brother, anybody. We should think how best to protect you here in the clan."

"Protect me?"

"At this moment you have no assured place here. Everybody knows that my father has accepted you and Yasib into his wagon. But if he should die, your place has gone. You would be a fugitive again, or perhaps a captive. I do not want that to happen to you."

She sighed, rolled onto her side to face him.

"What can we do according to your customs?"

"If we were married, you would have a place that would be promised, even if father died. Even if I myself died."

She nodded. "Well, it is not what I imagined when I had to leave Ikaret, but it would be a new start."

She sat up, looked away towards the north as though trying to see what her own people might think. Then she reached out for her skirt.

"So how do I marry you?"

"It is nothing to do with us. Your brother has to approach my father. My father has to view you and find you acceptable as my wife. Your brother has to provide a dowry for you to bring in to the household."

She laughed, tried to retrieve her smock from where it was lying on the other side of him.

"All very organised, I'm sure. Very tidy. And after that we get to lie together in the wagon as your own parents do up at their end? Enjoy one another as much as they do?"

He frowned.

"These are our ways. This is how it has to happen. And look, it is a sign of other things. When we settle in this land, it will be like a marriage of one land and another. How better to show that than for you and I to join?"

He held the smock away from her, teasing her briefly before passing it over and gathering his own clothes together.

She nodded and looked north again as she tied her kef back into place.

"I agree. It will be a good thing."

She paused, frowned, then suddenly spoke again in a rush.

"But look, Dekseus, you should know that over half of the silver we brought with us has gone. Our guard Tarmanni stole all that was in Yasib's bag when he left that day."

"Why did you not tell us? We could have pursued him that day itself, forced him to give back what he had taken. Thieving from your neighbour is the worst of crimes. Why did you not want revenge?"

"It did not matter up until now. We had ample for our needs. But now, who knows? I understand dowry, and I understand how families are involved. I can fit myself around your customs. How much silver would my brother need, to secure your father's favour for this marriage?"

He shook his head.

"Your brother should not speak about silver. Instead, he should present as dowry the fact that I am alive thanks to your healing efforts."

"Your mother did as much as I."

She saw the protest in his face.

"But we understand negotiation too, and Yasib is good at it."

She looked around to make sure nothing had been forgotten, then suddenly laughed as she hugged him.

"Dekseus, you shall see me sitting there all quiet and obedient as your sister did when Kastor came across. That will be worth more dowry than all the silver my family have ever owned. Now, you finish with your hunting and I will collect some herbs, so that we go back to the wagons separately."

≒⊫⼍⼍⼍⼍⼍⼍≒

THAT EVENING, DANTIY TOOK YASIB outside the camp so that they could speak privately. She told him what Dekseus had said. He thought about it for a while, pacing silently among the stumpy trees. She sat on a convenient stone and waited.

"Are you sure this is best for you? Is this what father and mother would want?"

"I think we have to choose that for ourselves now. But surely the choice is clear. You yourself said that these people will control the future of the land."

He stopped to think about that, nodded.

"Very well. So why then would they accept this match? With all that they have suffered, they are short of men rather than women."

"If I stay here, you will stay here. If I leave, you have no reason to stay. They want you for your knowledge. I am their means to hold you."

"So is Dekseus the right choice? He is only the son of Nikleos."

"Of course he is not the son of their leader; Antos has lost all his sons on the journey. But the voice of Nikleos carries weight when they meet in the circle around the fire. Antos will choose a successor before the next new moon. Nikleos is the most likely to be chosen. You know this."

He nodded.

"So Nikleos will be named, and Dekseus after him? And you will be married to a clan head in time?"

"I think so. Your words and your knowledge have given Nikleos very good standing among them. They are quiet when he speaks, and follow what he suggests. And look, they are in great need now of us joining them. Both of us. It is a matter of great concern to their elders. If we had come to them half a year ago they would have sent us away. Today, they will welcome us in."

He laughed, a short, nervous sound in the gloaming.

"So Ikaret will join itself to this clan of migrants."

She looked at him quizzically but said nothing. He nodded at her silence, at the expression on her face.

"But yes, a clan of migrants who will be a force to reckon with in this land. It could be a good union."

She stood up.

"Ikaret will not just join itself to these people; Ikaret will rule these people. I do not know if our city will rise again in the manner that we knew, but you and I must ensure that our way of life does not die. I am content with this."

He paced up and down for a while, thinking, and in the end was standing in front of her. He took her hands.

"He will expect you to have children. Soon, as well. He will not be patient about that."

"I know. But they will not just be his children. They will be Ikaret's children, and that is something I desire as well. The sooner I have a child, the sooner something new of Ikaret will spring up again. I would get a child by him tomorrow if I could. And give birth next week to keep Ikaret alive if my body would let me. For sure I will be pregnant by him just as soon as I can, without being killed off as a wicked woman. You should be thinking of this as well. For all we know, the others are dead and we are all that is left of the city."

He was silent, and looked very sombre.

"Well, it has to be like this, I think. I will approach Nikleos in the way you have told me. He will agree; you and Dekseus will marry according to their customs. But I would like to hear that he will not humiliate you in any way."

She shook her head.

"In truth, Dekseus is not a bad choice. His past experience of women has taught him very little, and he is quite unimaginative. But he is learning to be kind to me. He is easily pleased; he is easily led. He wants me, and his desires leave him open. I can lead him in the way that I want. I know exactly what I am doing here. And he is not a harsh man. I would endure a great deal for the sake of Ikaret and for the survival of our family, but where he is concerned there is no great hardship."

He nodded. "Very well. You must teach me all that I have to say to Nikleos about this."

"For sure I will. It must be said correctly."

"So then I must find another place to live. I think it will be altogether too frustrating to share a wagon with two married couples."

"Antos will take you into his household, I think. I hear that his life became empty after the last of his sons was killed at Hatsor. He might not formally adopt you, being a foreigner, but he would have you sit beside him readily enough. It would shield him from other parents who think that their own sons should be there. And think how useful it would be to us if you were right at his side."

His face lit up with interest.

"You think this is possible?"

"I do. And Kastiandra has said much the same herself. She schemes with the rest of the women about this. Antos will not marry again – he has said this openly to all – and so it is needful to seek his favour in other ways. If I marry Dekseus, Kastiandra will plot on your behalf."

"But this is perfect. We could hardly have found a better outcome anywhere in the province. If we have to live this far away from the land we love, let us at least show that our people can still rule."

He turned as if to go, but she stopped him.

"If we are to rule, then we need to decide how we can use your own marriage to advance this. I used to think that it would be better for you to marry a Kinahny girl of rank."

He pulled a face.

"That is not very appealing. All my life I have grown up with stories about how unsuitable a Kinahny girl would be."

"We are in no longer in a position where our choices should be ruled by old opinions. If being joined to a Kinahny girl is best for Ikaret, then you will join with a Kinahny girl. But I was saying that that was my previous opinion. I do not think that would be acceptable to our new hosts. I think they will expect you to marry within the clan. They want men, they want your abilities, and there are available girls here who have lost the men they were intended to marry. It will be better for us to find you a suitable match here. I will find someone for you."

He was silent for a while, his face speckled in the moonlight. Eventually he nodded, and she took his hand.

"First, however, you need to persuade Nikleos that I am worth viewing. Before we go back, I need to school you in what to say."

YASIB WAS PLEASED WITH THEIR PROGRESS. Towards the end of the afternoon they reached the small town that he had been aiming for. It was called Yabesh, and held allegiance only to a local king. Here on this side of the River, the Mitsriy exerted no authority other than occasional punitive raids, and Yabesh was not large enough to have become an object of desire to the larger regional groups. The clan camped well outside of the outermost ring of buildings. They were seeking contact, and did not want to appear a threat.

Yasib had made time the previous day to walk alongside Nikleos as he led the oxen. Dekseus was walking beside a different wagon, helping out where the eldest son had been killed. It was a slow, mindless process as they threaded their way south without becoming mired in softer ground. The oxen were growing idle and stubborn. Frequent rest days, in a land full of verdant spring vegetation unscorched by the summer's heat, had spoiled them from their former lean enthusiasm, and they needed constant persuasion to stay on course.

As they chafed and chivvied the beasts, Yasib had opened the conversation.

"Nikleos, as head of your household I would like you to consider my sister as a fit wife for your son."

Nikleos had grunted, but with an air of acceptance around him. They had walked on for a while together as the older man thought. Finally he looked across at Yasib.

"Why should I accept this offer?"

"She is skilled in the art of making a home for a man. She can be hospitable to his neighbours and welcoming to his guests. She has been trained by our mother in all the things a woman needs to know, in order to be a good wife."

"The girl is not intact. There is a previous marriage. There could be dispute over offspring."

"Sir, her previous union was brief and did not result in children. Enough time has passed that this is certain, and the man in question is dead. Offspring of a marriage to Dekseus would belong to your household. There is no other family who would seek to lay claim to them."

"There is proof that she is not with child now?"

"She will provide the proof of this month to your own wife."

"What of her family line?"

"Her own mother bore three living children, though one has been lost, and her grandmother gave birth to five. Her lineage is fruitful."

Nikleos paused to tug at the head of the ox on his side. Yasib turned his head to wink at Dantiy, who was sitting beside Kastiandra. Both women were pretending not to listen.

"What wealth would this woman bring into my household? You have no livestock, and little enough by way of possessions."

"It is true, sir, and I would not insult you by offering silver in its place. Our family was great in Ikaret, even though presently we wander the lands just as you do. My sister's union with your son will restore strength and stability to both our houses. But my sister has already given you the best of all gifts; the life of your own son when he was close to death. You know this; you know how close the breath of the destroyer came to him. My sister sat there at his side and brought him back to health, even though she had no duty to do so. How much more will she do the same when the two are joined?"

Nikleos walked on in silence for a while, and finally said only, "I will view the girl. But I make no promises."

For the rest of that day's journey and the first half of the next they avoided the subject completely, and Nikleos talked with Dantiy as much and as little as he always had. Yasib, for his own part, spent time with Antos, explaining what he needed to know of the customs of the land.

In the afternoon Nikleos viewed Dantiy.

They settled the oxen and made camp, which as usual took some time. Finally Nikleos was satisfied that everything was in its place, and looked across at Kastiandra.

"I am going to view a girl shortly. She might be suitable for Dekseus."

She nodded, ignoring Dantiy who was standing quite close to her. "Where will you go to view this girl?"

"In fact, I will be viewing her right here, in our own wagon itself. Her brother will be presenting her in the absence of her father, who was killed in battle. I have to see Antos with Dekseus and Yasib just now, but I expect she will be sitting here ready when I get back."

He set off with Yasib across the open space between the wagons without looking back. Kastiandra turned to Dantiy. "We have to prepare you for this. Borrow a smock and dress from me. I will braid your hair again. You know that Nikleos will be talking with Yasib and will expect you to be silent?"

"I watched your Murtilis prepare for this. I appreciate the offer of clothing. In truth, I have nothing of my own that would be suitable for this occasion."

She paused briefly, then rushed on. "But lady, I will still wear my kef itself. It is all I have left which keeps the memory of my mother alive. She gave me this; she first showed me how to tie it. I will not give it up, and I think that your son will not ask me to."

"It is not Dekseus you must persuade, but Nikleos. Dekseus will not be here, and in any case he will do as he is instructed. But the kef will be acceptable, I think. You can keep that."

They moved swiftly through the changes of clothing, and then Kastiandra worked on Dantiy's hair. As they finished, the older woman's face, with its sharp nose and clearly defined cheek bones, was just in front of Dantiy's softer, rounder one.

Dantiy held Kastiandra's hands to pause the brushing briefly, and looked directly into her eyes.

"Thank you, lady. This is a gift I cannot repay."

Kastiandra shook her head.

"Giving me Dekseus back is what cannot be repaid. But see, the men are returning now and we both have to look quiet and obedient for them. Remember: say nothing at all. If Nikleos seems to be asking you a question, it is actually directed at your brother."

The experience was one which Yasib was unlikely to forget. Nikleos had talked with Antos for a while, then the two of them had come back together leaving Dekseus at the other wagon.

Dantiy was sitting with a demure expression he hardly recognised, eyes carefully cast down. She was wearing a broad striped skirt, together with a yellow smock which left her shoulders bare. A pattern of black embroidery decorated the shoulders and ran down the chest. Her kef was in place, but arranged so that her braided hair still showed on either side. He felt immensely proud to be her brother.

Nikleos offered him a beaker of wine, and sat opposite him, Kastiandra at his side. He proceeded to ask Yasib a series of questions about Dantiy and her family, her lineage, the fertility of her female relatives.

Yasib, forewarned, carefully avoided looking at Dantiy as he answered. It was as though neither of the women was even present. The process continued for what seemed to him a very long time.

Eventually there was silence. Yasib wondered briefly what Dantiy had thought of his handling of the process, but dared not look at her. Nikleos was carefully studying his face. Finally the older man stood.

"The girl is acceptable. I will inform my son of the match."

Then he laughed and gave Yasib a great hug.

"Your family and mine will be joined through these two. You will be thirsty after all that. But you did well, for a foreigner. Have more to drink, then my wife will help your sister to prepare a place for her new husband. You and I can go to the wagon of Antos, and tell Dekseus the news of his marriage together. There will be a ceremony in due course, but I see no value in making them wait for each other. Let him unbraid his new wife and enjoy her tonight."

Yasib, holding back his own opinion of Nikleos' words, nodded. He turned to Dantiy as Nikleos jumped down from the wagon, kissed on both cheeks, and whispered in her ear, in their own language, "I hope you appreciate this new marriage as much as Nikleos seems to."

He felt her lips smile against his own cheek.

"More than you will appreciate the celibacy you have to face just now. Do not offend these people by rushing into anything."

He laughed with her, then followed Nikleos across the thick grass to where Antos and Dekseus were waiting. Antos called out as they drew near.

"There has been a messenger come out from this village. Their head man wants to know what we intend. Yasib, will you come with me to speak peace with them?"

"Of course. But this is sooner than I expected. I thought they would wait for the new day and see if we moved on with the sunrise."

"Apparently not. Shall we go now?"

They set off towards the houses, clearly visible at the crown of the low hill just to the east of them. Nikleos and Dekseus followed along, talking, and Yasib caught a few words.

"Son, I have found a wife for you. I have viewed her and found her acceptable. Your mother is preparing a place for her in the wagon, and she will be waiting for you to unbraid when we get back there."

At that point Antos touched his arm and pointed a little to the right, where a rough track curved up the slope to a stone gate.

"Why do they have a gate when there is no wall?"

"The Mitsriy did not allow new defences to be built anywhere except for a few towns here and there, mostly older ones. Although this was never really their land, they imposed the ban by force of arms anyway. Now, you must remember that the gate is the heart of the life of the town. It is where all the important decisions are made public – judgements, punishments, marriages, covenants. We ourselves will meet with their headman there. It would be improper for us as strangers to enter by any other way."

Antos nodded.

"How do we approach these people? I do not really want to threaten them, but we do not have much to offer by way of a bribe, except for precious things which are too obviously the rewards of battle. I will deceive them if need be, but what is your advice?"

Yasib had been trying to catch the exchange of words between father and son behind him as Antos spoke, but all he heard was Dantiy's name being tossed between them.

"First we need to find out if the chief here can decide his own terms, or if he needs to call on an overlord. But either way, we are offering fair partnership. Our labour, our talent, shared with the village in exchange for land nearby to make homes and raise crops."

Antos looked at him with amusement.

"You are speaking like one of my own people."

"Do you mind?"

"Not at all, so long as your actions match your words, and you continue to show that the well-being of my people is in your heart. But what about deception?"

"No deception if we can avoid it. Not if we want to settle nearby. These people have long memories, and will continue a feud through generations if they feel they have been wronged."

They walked on for another few paces. They were drawing quite near to the ring of houses, near enough to see a group of three men waiting for them under the shadow of the gate, when Antos suddenly spoke again.

"Nikleos' wagon will be very full after today. Mine, on the other hand, is mostly empty now. And I will need to speak with you often about these people. It would be a favour to me if you were to rest in my wagon for a time."

Yasib looked at him gratefully.

"It is a great kindness you offer, sir, and one which I accept with gratitude. But I know that some of your people may resent that. Eumedes, for one. He will counsel you not to trust a man who is not from the clan."

Antos nodded. "You are right. You must be able to master their resentment, if you want honour here in the clan. I am not asking you to rest in my wagon because it is easy, but because it will be difficult. These men will not fight you, not now you have proved yourself. But they will challenge what you say or the ideas you bring."

"I am used to that. But see, these men are close at hand; let us talk to one another later."

The three men were dressed in quite ordinary fashion, and Yasib suspected even before he greeted them that they held no special place of rank. Their introduction confirmed that they were simply the three men of the town who farmed most land or had the largest flocks. Yasib passed the words on to Antos as they spoke. Their dialect was heavier than he was used to, but could be followed. After the formalities, the oldest of the men pointed across at the camp.

"It is not often that we see such a large group of travellers. Not here, not this far away from the Kings' Road."

"We do not intend you harm. We are here seeking pasture for our beasts and land for our fields."

The three conferred, too quietly and quickly for Yasib to follow.

"News has reached us that towns have been burned further north. Even great cities like Ikaret and Akka. Do you know who has done this? Are you fleeing from them?"

It was a delicate moment. Antos thought how to answer for a while. The other men waited with wary expressions.

"We have heard of this. We have not been near Ikaret, nor Akka. There was a man from another tribe who came to our camp once, who had been at the assaults of Akka, Shuksi and Ikaret, but he made threats and was killed in fair combat. We had a dispute with the King of the North which was settled, and now we are looking for a new home. If you do not want us, we have no quarrel with your people and will move on peacefully. But others may come behind us with different plans. If we stay, if we swear oaths with one another, we will help you defend yourselves. We will do all that we can to make Yabesh thrive."

The oldest man glanced at the other two.

"For our own part, of course we will accept your words. We will trust a binding promise of your honourable intentions for the next few days. But you will need to swear your proper oaths to our headman, or to the king of Shalem. Or to the chief of the Ibriym who also claims this land."

"We would be happy to do so, good sir. Where should we go to do this?"

"Go up first to Shalem. The headman is there."

Antos looked at Yasib. "Is it far to Shalem?"

Yasib shook his head, and pointed south and a little west, back across the River again.

"Not far, no. At least, not far for a group on foot. We cannot take the oxen up that way; the path is quite steep in places. We should make whatever promise these people want, so that we can leave the wagons here with most of the clan. Then just a few of us will go on up on foot. If we leave with the light tomorrow, we will be there on the third day."

"And these Ibriym? Who are they?"

"They are a new group. They first came across the River from the south and east somewhere, and into the hills up there to our west perhaps twenty years ago. They have been trying to claim territory on both sides of the River, with some success and some failure. Their power does not extend to the lands close to Shalem, nor over as far as the Great Sea, and stops short of Hatsor in the north."

"Very well. Then tell these three men this. Most of us will remain here, bound by promises to help and not harm, while some of us go to see their headman and his chief at Shalem. And tell them that we would like to trade with them, and that we will deal with them honestly, as a people who desire to become their neighbours."

The three men accepted the offer, though Yasib suspected that they were not convinced of what had been said. But once words of promise had been spoken one to another, a few men from the town went out to the circle of wagons to find out what could be exchanged. Meetings began: integration was, perhaps, just starting.

While that was happening, Antos chose the group that he would take up to Shalem. Nikleos was his first choice, together with Yasib as advisor and translator. Yasib refused to go without Dantiy at his side, as a second person who knew something of the province. Dekseus would not let her go without him. Eumedes and Towanos were added to the group because of their own talents.

As the sun set, they separated, agreeing to leave with the first light. He watched Dantiy as she went back with Dekseus to the wagon, still dressed as a new wife in Kastiandra's borrowed clothing. Then he turned and followed Antos in another direction.

╪ ᛉ ᚴ ᛉ ᚴ ᛉ ᚴ ᛉ ╪

YASIB AND THE OTHERS CAMPED for the last night before reaching Shalem at the top of a long uphill track. They had followed the flat ground at the base of the Valley at first, and then branched up the western side in order to reach the higher ground there. Their camp was close to the Ridgeway track, and Yasib intended to follow that for the last stage of the journey.

Their present position was not very far south of where he had persuaded the clan to turn back northward in order to cross the River and avoid getting too far into Mitsriy territory. However, by choosing the other route they had successfully moved the ox carts across to the east. These would not have been able to go down the track they had just climbed, and so far as he knew there was no suitable route further south for a very long way.

Antos sat down beside him. They watched Nikleos and Eumedes turning a rabbit they had snared, on an improvised spit over the fire. Antos was restless, he felt, perhaps because he was still quite ignorant of how matters were conducted in the land. As they came together as a group to eat, Yasib explained all over again about Shalem and its place in the southern hill country.

The town was quite small, but the local line of kings had for many years enjoyed close relations with the Mitsriy, giving them a regional voice and influence considerably larger than the size of the kingdom warranted.

So far as Yasib knew, that was still the case even now that the Mitsriy had withdrawn many of their people from the area. It made sense that the headman of Yabesh would have travelled here, and also that the Ibriym, newcomers to the area, would have come to Shalem to negotiate with them both.

He had never personally travelled this far south, but his uncle had once come through the town when travelling to Gedjet by way of Hatsor.

It was a place, he explained, that Ikaret did not consider significant enough to warrant a permanent spy in the palace. Instead, they relied on information from traders, and the occasional report from a paid informer. It was not ideal, but it had never been necessary to have more.

Nikleos and Eumedes were amused by the casual way in which Yasib talked about spies and informers, since it came closer to some of their own deceptions in the past than anything else Yasib had talked about. Antos took the matter very seriously and continued his questioning. Yasib and Dantiy both dredged their memory for anything that might be helpful over the coming days.

Finally Antos was satisfied. He leaned back against the boulder behind him and poured each of them some of the local wine they had bartered for at Yabesh.

"So we shall meet with the king of Shalem?"

"Or perhaps his most senior envoy. My uncle has spoken about him. He is of northern ancestry but his family have served the kings of Shalem for many years. Abdi-Teshup is his name. The king trusts him with most of his dealings, and only sometimes intervenes in person. But it makes no difference to the negotiation."

"In all of my days, I have never met a king. I have seen them on the fields of battle, as ally or enemy both. But I have never spoken with a king, nor needed to exchange oaths and promises with one."

Yasib grinned. "But I have, and the king of Shalem is by no means the greatest of them. We have nothing to fear from him, so long as there is something that he needs from us. With the Mitsriy withdrawing from their province year by year, and with your distant cousins working their way along the Sea Road, this king will need new allies at his back. He will talk with us; all being well he will give us exactly what we want."

The moon rose over the hill country, bright, and close to the full. The group began to settle for the night, separating here and there around the firelight. Antos put another piece of wood on the fire and stirred it, so that the flames leaped up. Then he turned back to Yasib.

"I am glad you came to be with us. Your advice has given purpose to our movement south, and to our rest. I should like to settle at Yabesh, so pray to your gods that the headman and these others look favourably on us." He laughed. "It is as though my people were being viewed for a marriage. I shall need your help to know how to answer their questions."

"You have it. One thing I will say just now, though. When you speak at Shalem, we will announce you as an important leader among the Sherden. We will use your title of arkon, which they do not know, and in every way we will speak of you as though you were a king yourself. It will be better that way."

Antos laughed again.

"Very well, I shall be the equal of a king. Yasib, you should know that I appreciate all your help. Of all the places you and your sister might have gone, I am happy that you stumbled upon Nikleos' wagon. You have both given a great deal to my people, and I am grateful."

He paused, looking hard at the fire as it gradually subsided again into a quieter glow.

"What will you do when we have seen all these people at Shalem? Suppose they agree that we can live on their land. What will you do?"

"I would like to come back with you. Settle at Yabesh, and make a home among your clan."

"You would? But why? Yabesh is a little village, and you have known great cities. I am leader of only a small clan, for all that we may magnify it in Shalem. You are accustomed to speaking with kings and noblemen. How will it be for you to live with us in a place like that?"

His shrewd eyes were searching the younger man's face. Yasib stopped to think for a while. He had the sense that Nikleos was also listening, but his head was covered in shadows and Yasib could not be sure.

"Your people have shown us kindness since we first came, and have given both of us a home. You spoke of purpose: look now, with you we have found our own sense of purpose again. How could I consider going anywhere else?"

"But what if you hear that the city of Ikaret is springing to life again?"

He shook his head, definitely.

"Even then I will never go back. My life has changed. I lost everything that I knew at Ikaret, or along the road since then. Every friend, every family member except for Dantiy. Going back would be unbearable."

"Or perhaps at Shalem there will be others who have come down from Ikaret like you. Would you not rather share their company? Have you thought what you might do if you were to meet them?"

Yasib stared at him, not sure what to say. Antos shrugged.

"Well, it is possible. Your own family, even, who you last saw just outside your city. I have wondered several times since we left Yabesh what you would do then."

"It will not change my intention. I am sure of that. I would like to stay with your people. But it is not likely to happen. My uncle and aunt: yes, indeed, they might come to Shalem. They were certainly heading south. But for the rest, why should they arrive at Shalem? But in any case, be they many or none, my future is with you and your people now."

Antos was silent for a while, and then drained his beaker and grinned.

"Good. I am glad to hear it. Truly, I was expecting this answer from you. So I have arranged to view three girls on your behalf after we get back to the camp."

He smiled a little at the surprise on Yasib's face.

"I turned away two others who were not really suitable. Almost all the fathers in the camp who have unmarried daughters have hinted to me that their girl was the best, but only these five were worth taking further."

Yasib shook his head again, this time not in rejection but caught by surprise.

"Who are they? Do I know them?"

Antos shrugged.

"Perhaps, but that is not important. Better that you do not know at this stage. Whoever I choose, you will come to know them in time."

He considered the stubbornness on Yasib's face.

"Look, Yasib, this must be done correctly. The loss of so many of our young men is hard for us. Some of my people resent the fact that Dekseus took your sister Dantiy, who was a foreigner, at a time when so many girls within the camp had lost the men they were promised to. Your own marriage must be arranged in such a way that nobody can fault it. I will choose: that is my burden to carry. Get to know the woman after you unbraid her."

Yasib looked away into the night, remembering the customs of Ikaret for a long moment and confronting the protest curdling in his heart, before recalling what Dantiy had said and nodding curtly. Antos studied him for a moment longer and then banked up the fire a little for the night.

"But see, I have the first watch tonight and you should sleep."

A SON ADDRESSES HIS FATHER.

Hekanefer to his father Nesamenopeh, greetings and blessings to you. I write beside the road near Shalem.

Father, I am writing this in the early morning, while the small band of soldiers are going through their training exercises. Soon we will strike down the tents and make the last stage of the journey along the ridge to Shalem.

A little to the south of us is a group of four towns – two are of respectable size, but the other two are very small. But we will take no notice of them and press on.

Your son is now a trusted envoy of the great king who lives in prosperity and health. You see, we suspect that the king of Shalem will think to meet with representatives of these invaders. An alliance between these two groups is exactly what we cannot allow. The commander chose me, in the company of his second officer and a trusted group of skilled soldiers, to visit this king and remind him of his obligations.

In this province, while this war continues, a capable man can rise rapidly in responsibility. I am sure that you are proud that your son has been able to do this. Tomorrow I shall be speaking in the name of the Beloved Land, and the vassals of this province must listen to what I say.

But at the same time, I regret not being with the commander I have served until now, and with the men he will lead into battle. When they arise against this enemy somewhere along the Sea Road, it will be the deciding conflict of our days. I should have liked to say to my children, whenever they might be born, that I was there on that day.

Perhaps indeed that battle has already taken place. Up here, we may not hear the outcome for some time, but I trust in the strength and courage of our men, the skill and experience of their officers, and the fierce wrath of our magnificent king who lives in prosperity and health. Surely the Beloved Land will prevail over this vile enemy.

I will be obedient, and go where I am sent. But a part of my soul longs to be at the central place of all these things, not out in some little town on the periphery. When I arose this morning, I could look out over the wooded slopes which fall away westwards, and imagine the scene down there towards the coast. A light haze has come up now, so the view is veiled to the eye, though clear and sharp to the imagination.

The soldiers are finishing their morning exercises now, so I must stop writing. Remember me before all the gods, and speak of me often with my dear mother, the lady Hemesherit, whenever you stand together at the household shrine. Today we travel to Shalem: tomorrow I will speak with a king.

ᚷ ᚦ ᚾ ᚦ ᚾ ᚦ ᚾ ᚦ ᚷ

LABAYU WALKED OVER to the fire that Akiy was building in the lee of a boulder. They were less than a day from Shalem now, and had simply been following the Ridgeway track for speed. Soon after Sychem they had stopped seeing any signs that the newcomers were ahead of them. A holy place near the older settlement of Luz had been despoiled, but that would only have taken a handful of attackers to drive away the occupants and burn the buildings.

All of them were relieved. Akiy and Labayu had grown up in the Four Towns, while Ghazam came from Bayth Horon, a small village down the track towards the town of Laksh. Uriel's family lived just south of Shalem: his father had served as a guard for a Mitsriy shrine there. So for each of them, the absence of the enemy was a sign of hope.

Labayu clambered on top of a boulder a little to one side of the camp, and looked towards the west. The sky was fiery with the day's end, and the contours of the land were flattened into dark outlines. But just over there, as he knew very well, was his family home. His mother would be there, enjoying the bustle around her as her daughter ran the household.

Perhaps his nephew and niece would, just now as the sun set, be taking gifts of respect to the tombs of the ancestors, in memory of his father. It seemed only yesterday that he had been laid to rest in the caves in the bluff ridge behind the high place and the sacred stones.

That was in Kephrath. A little further away from tonight's camp, Ashtartiy would be settling the children in the little covered space on the roof of her mother's house in Giybon. After all the rushing to and fro of the last few weeks, he found himself missing her. He hoped she was also missing him, and that they could celebrate coming together again with real passion before long.

He had been very tempted to make the detour off the Ridge-way track, but duty had prevailed. He could have gone home to rest with family, or to Giybon to test how far separation could rekindle attraction. He had done neither. There would be time enough for rest and for pleasure when the present crisis was over, and he could not justify the delay to himself.

He started walking back towards the others. Uriel turned as he called out, then stiffened and looked beyond him, south along the ridge. Ghazam dropped the pack he had been emptying of the last of their bread, a stricken look on his face. Akiy pulled the pan of food away from the flame.

Labayu turned, hand dropping to the dagger at his belt, expecting to see someone close at hand rushing towards them. In all their travelling, they had never yet been caught unawares, and it would be particularly foolish if it happened so close to Shalem. But there was nobody, and Labayu was perplexed for a moment until he looked up at the horizon.

To the south a bank of low clouds hung over the uplands, and a flicker of flames was bright against them. Labayu swallowed. There was fire at Shalem. In the gloom they could just make out a plume of smoke drifting into the sky, barely dispersed in the gentle breeze.

The others came over to stand with him. Ghazam groaned.

"I suppose we are too late, chief."

Uriel shook his head, slowly.

"I don't think so, Ghazam. Those flames aren't coming from Shalem. Too far east for the town. It's one of the villages, I think. Memmaset, perhaps? No. Ayn Shamsh. It must be Ayn Shamsh."

The others all looked at him. "You are sure?"

"Oh yes. Too far east for Shalem, I think..." He hesitated, rubbed his head, then nodded confidently. "Yes, I am sure. No doubt about it. That's not in the town at all. The fire's at Ayn

Shamsh. But I can't think why anybody would want to burn that village. It makes no sense for a group of invaders."

Together they went back to the camp fire. Akiy, shrugging, reheated the food. They sat in a loose circle, glancing all the while at the smoke plume as they ate. Whoever had caused this, it proved to be a small thing. Before too long, the smoke started to thin and dissipate, and the red glow against the low clouds faded into the night.

"So you don't think this is the act of these northern invaders?"

"There would be no purpose. They would not waste time out there. The village has no wealth to take; it does not straddle an important route, nor control anything of value. Everything we have seen tells me that if they came this far south, they would go directly to Shalem and attack there. They would not waste their time anywhere else."

Labayu wanted to believe Uriel's judgement, to trust his knowledge of the land immediately around Shalem. But the feeling of anxiety, and the possibility of complete failure, continued to nag at him as they settled for the night.

It was only just past the time of year when night and day were equal, poised like a balance to swing one way or the other. He was filled with an acute sense of the hazards of life, and felt almost entirely out of control of the events rushing around him in the hill country.

The next morning they were on the move early. None of them had slept well. The last stretch along the Ridgeway track seemed long beneath them, but the morning had only half gone when they started to meet groups of Ibriym who had moved here from further north.

Then the trackway started to have stones laid here and there in the rougher parts. They had reached the territory that the king of Shalem considered it his duty to maintain.

There was an air of tension among the people. Everybody had seen the signs of fire in the sky, but nobody knew what had happened. Some wanted to abandon the land altogether and move back to the other side of the Valley. Old memories from across the River turned it into a place of victory and security, in contrast to the uncertainty on this side.

They all agreed that Abiy'el was somewhere over in that direction, towards the flames and smoke of last night. The four of them turned that way and continued.

Before long they started meeting groups of people going the opposite way, aimless except to get away from more destruction. Gradually, as the afternoon crept on, a consistent story began to emerge. Only Ayn Shamsh had been touched. It was not an attack, but an act of frustration. It had been carried out not by some new invading army, but by a small band of Ibriym. Abiy'el was there now, speaking with the soldiers of the king of Shalem.

Labayu's sense of urgency increased. He needed to get to Abiy'el; he needed to support his warleader's choices. He urged his men onto a greater speed.

ＸＦ¬ＦＦ¬Ｆ¬ＦＸ

A T LAST, LABAYU AND HIS MEN crested the last low ridge and looked down on Ayn Shamsh. It was a small place, meagre, and its only noteworthy feature was the spring which gave the village its name. To Labayu's eyes it was considerably smaller than any of the Four Towns, even Meyim.

A handful of houses had been damaged by last night's fire, but only one was completely ruined. From their vantage, they could see that the starting point had been a storage hut near the village cistern. There was a large angry group of people in a huddle to one side. The village gate was a token affair of two tall cairns with a wooden cross piece, but today it was serving its purpose as a place of meeting.

They went towards it. About half a dozen soldiers were there, stern and competent. They were led by a man who looked far too high ranking to be simply in charge of a squad of troops. His kef was elaborately embroidered, he was wearing the tokens of the king of Shalem, and he had a firm, authoritative air about him. The soldiers were keeping a clear space around him from the press of the crowd, and the village elders were treating him with extreme respect.

Abiy'el was talking with the man, agreeing with him, and seemed to be making profuse apologies. Around the two, the people of Ayn Shamsh formed a seething swarm. Labayu turned to the nearest of the villagers.

"What happened here? This was the fire last night, yes?"

The man turned outraged eyes on him, then saw his Kinahny kef and softened a little.

"Some of the Ibriym burned our town last night. We told them we couldn't take them in, not with all else around, but they wouldn't hear it and turned on us. They burned our food and our homes. But the food was for us, and for tribute to Shalem, and what will we do now?"

Labayu was going to ask more, but the man had already turned back to watch the central drama. There was no way to push closer. Labayu nudged Ghazam.

"Who is the man in charge there?"

"They call him Abdi-Teshup. He's the chief envoy for the king of Shalem, does all his talking with other rulers, or the Mitsriy, whoever. He hardly ever leaves the royal citadel; they must think this is important for him to be here. Those soldiers are part of the king's own guard."

The buzz of the crowd had hushed, and they could hear what was being said between the envoy and Abiy'el.

"You agree that this act was done by men under your authority, Abiy'el chief of the Ibriym?"

"So your people have said, great lord, but I deny any responsibility for their wicked actions."

The tall man looked consideringly at him.

"Continue."

"I have given my people – all my people – strict instructions that the land and people lawfully belonging to your honoured master, the king of Shalem, should be respected as if they belonged to their own kin."

"Apparently this group of evil doers did not hear your word. Perhaps it was not spread about in the way you wanted? Will there be other times like this, when my lord's natural compassion for his people is stirred into anger and a determination for vengeance?"

Labayu grimaced. His father had often said that the former chief of the Ibriym, Yahusharar, was a hugely capable man with words as well as weapons. Not so Abiy'el, who was being easily outmanoeuvred by the envoy, and just now was shaking his head, face full of anxiety.

"May it never be so, great lord. My words concerning your king's city and people have been said many times in many places. Surely all of my people who have listening ears have heard them. This is the solitary act of a group of lawless men who have rejected the word of their elders."

"So this will not happen again? My lord is a patient man whose heart recoils in horror from the very thought of breaking a covenant. Such as the covenant we have with you, now. Yet the wellbeing of his people weighs most heavily on him, and he will not shrink back from exacting justice. Wealth for wealth, home for home, life for life."

Abiy'el was still shaking his head. Labayu could see in him the burden of the scattered tribes and clans of his people, camped out on the periphery of Shalem's land, exposed and vulnerable.

"I pray that you will calm your honoured lord's outraged heart. He need not feel protective of his boundaries, for we will care for them as if they were our own. All of my people who obey my words know this."

"He will be glad to hear this, for he is a peaceful man who delights in justice. But see now."

He gestured around at the silent throng of villagers.

"What of their loss, which is my lord's loss as well? What of their need to see justice done, and know that they can rest in their homes without fear? You have said that it was some of your own people who did this; how will you show us all that you honour your covenant and the way of law?"

"You and I will assess the loss here, in food, and in the means of livelihood such as tools. I will ensure that my people make good the loss either in weight of silver or days of labour."

"And houses, store rooms, livestock, and the like."

Abiy'el looked across at the hut where the fire had started, and the ruined houses near it. The faces of the villagers were starting to fill with anticipation as well as anger. The soldiers nearby were grinning. Labayu shook his head: this was going to become costly for the Ibriym.

The envoy waited as Abiy'el hesitated. Little murmurs came from the crowd. Finally Abiy'el nodded. "Indeed. All those things."

There was a ripple of satisfaction around the gate, but the envoy was not finished.

"Excellent. But what about the punishment of the criminals who did this?"

Abiy'el looked across at them.

"I will find out who it was, and submit them to the judgment of their elders. Your lord's people will not be troubled again."

The envoy put on a face of regret.

"How then will these honest servants of my lord the king know that justice has been served? They have heard that in other lands the ways of law are not respected. How shall they know that these men will not simply be set free again?"

"What are you suggesting, my lord?"

Labayu grimaced. With every word that he spoke, the Ibriym warleader was yielding ground to the envoy from Shalem. However this turned out, Abiy'el was being diminished.

"When you find who did this, do not allow your own elders to decide what is just. Instead, bring them to Shalem for my lord the king to exact punishment as he sees fit."

The noise of the crowd rose up and drowned his voice, triumphant. The envoy said nothing to quieten them, but simply waited at the centre of the hubbub. Abiy'el started to speak twice, but could not be heard. The envoy raised a hand, and silence fell again.

"My lord, I was saying that we do not exact punishment on a man without the sworn word of two witnesses."

The envoy nodded, looked around, and pointed at a man in the mob.

"You are the chief elder here. Tell me what happened."

He nodded, tongue-tied at first but then gaining courage.

"They were here in the night, burning and stealing. We saw their kefs: they were Ibriym, not Kinahny. There were six of them came yesterday, making threats against us. We would not agree to their demands, so they came back..."

"Enough." He turned to the chief soldier. "Officer, give me your report."

The soldier stepped forward and stood at the ready.

"We were patrolling the land, great lord, when we saw some men running from this town. We went in pursuit, but they had too great an advantage of distance, and we could not catch them. They were running towards the Ibriym camps and were dressed like some of the ones who live north of here, between Giybon and Sychem. In their flight they abandoned a sack of food they were carrying, as well as some small silver items and the means to set a fire."

The envoy nodded and turned back to Abiy'el. "Two witnesses."

Abiy'el was silent. He looked around, saw Labayu and his men, and shook his head. Labayu was not sure what he meant, but he had no intention of intervening in the situation even if the warleader had asked it of him. This was hardly the time or place for a dramatic stand, and it could only worsen the situation with the king of Shalem.

The pause stretched out, and the crowd started to mutter again. Abiy'el lifted his head briefly to the sky in the patchy sunlight before replying.

"My lord, in your name, and in the name of the king your lord, I will find out the truth and bring the men to Shalem for justice."

The crowd cheered wildly and pressed in closer. The envoy nodded.

"In that case, Abiy'el, my lord's justice will be satisfied and the covenant maintained. My lord will be pleased to hear that you have been obedient in this way. Go now to fulfil your word, and present yourself to me in Shalem within ten days. We will discuss the recompense in silver at that time."

Abiy'el came over to Labayu and his men, and they set off together. He said nothing, but was clearly furious. They hurried back up the little ridge away from the town. From behind, the voices rose to a roar of triumph. Abiy'el remained silent until they were over the crest and out of sight of all the houses.

Then he stopped and pounded his fist against one of the trees.

"It was men from Gera's tribe, I am sure of it. They have no respect for the people of the land, and little enough for me. I shall be telling their elders, and all the clans, that their wicked folly nearly cost all the Ibriym their homes, as well as any possibility of food and shelter – all of us, every man, woman and child among us. One of you must go with the news while I go to Shalem and meet the king himself. Or more likely that envoy again. I have heard that these invaders from the north, the ones moving along the Sea Road, are likely to come up into the hill country soon. We need to be standing with Shalem for that, not fighting each other."

There was a pause. Labayu and his men looked at each other. Finally Labayu spoke.

"Abiy'el, how can we go to Gera's tribe with this news? We will not be heard. It has to be you who goes there. For the sake of your own position as warleader, you must go, or they will choose another to replace you. They will not listen to us, and they will certainly not let us take some of their men away to face the king's judgement in Shalem."

Abiy'el stared at them all, pursed his lips, and scowled.

"You are right. It has to be me. But take note of this, all of you."

He took out his dagger, nicked his arm and marked the trunk of the tree with his blood.

"On this tree and by my blood I swear. One day we will make a reckoning for every word we have swallowed today, and every life that has been diminished by Shalem. That day will not come yet a while: perhaps not in my lifetime or my leadership. But it will come."

He started walking again, quite suddenly, and the others hurried to catch up.

"I will come with you part of the way. Then you go into Shalem and speak for me, and I will turn north and find out who did this."

𐤗 𐤅 𐤓 𐤅 𐤓 𐤅 𐤓 𐤅 𐤗

L ABAYU OPENED THE DOOR of the shepherd's hut and put the armful of wood he had collected onto the pile. Akiy handed him some bread pulled off one of the flat rounds they had been given yesterday, together with a portion of the meat he had been roasting over the fire on the end of his knife.

"Sit down now, chief, we've more than enough for tonight."

"It's just habit, Akiy. Whenever I've used huts like this I've tried to leave more than I took."

Uriel laughed.

"And I wonder what you'd be using a hut like this for?"

Ghazam reached over and took Uriel's hand, gazing into his eyes.

"Oh, Ashtartiy, won't you come with me to my hut in the woods? I can make you so happy there."

Uriel made a valiant attempt to look modest and demure.

"Oh, Labayu, I've never been to a hut in the woods. How will I know what to do? Will I really be happy?"

They all laughed together. Labayu waved a hand at them both and sat down to eat. Uriel pushed Ghazam away, and he made a show of sprawling on the floor with his legs in the air. Abiy'el looked up from the corner where he had perched, a little isolated from the others.

"That's always supposing he could remember the name of the girl he was with."

"I never forget a name. Not even in the wildest moments." They laughed again, and Labayu looked at Abiy'el.

"Look now, Abiy'el, why don't you come over and join us properly. You've cut yourself off ever since that runner lad brought a word to you in the afternoon."

Abiy'el got up and joined them. He looked at each in turn.

"We have to go in separate directions now. You to Shalem, me up towards Sychem to try to find the group that attacked Ayn Shamsh. Tomorrow, as early in the day as we can."

"No more running around the different groups of Ibriym nearby, then?"

"No."

They had spent about a week since Ayn Shamsh moving from one encamped group of Ibriym to the next, speaking re-assurance to them. At the same time, Abiy'el had been trying to find out who had been at Ayn Shamsh. The response had been mixed. Some supported Abiy'el's intention, but others were offended at what they believed was a casual subordination of their own people.

Abiy'el described all this as a way to check that his people were managing in their enforced spring camps. Labayu, how-ever, could only see it as an attempt to ensure that he still had broad support as warleader.

As such, it was a qualified success. Some of the more fiery individuals thought that he should have refused the envoy's demands then and there. Failing that, he should at very least have gone straight back with a band of men to make a stand. Most accepted the necessity of what he had done. But Labayu could see that accepting necessity was a far cry from enthu-siasm for his leadership. Unless something happened soon to enhance his reputation, Abiy'el's days as leader were num-bered.

"No," he repeated. "We will visit the last of the clans later on. We cannot spend the extra time to go around to them now. Especially, we cannot put off the journey to Shalem. Or rather, you cannot. Since we have not found the culprits, you have to hold back any action by the king. You must tell him that I am hot in pursuit of them, and will bring them to his justice very soon."

"Has the king there changed his mind about recompense for Ayn Shamsh?"

"Not that he has told me. It is not that that I fear most, but something much worse. I fear that the king's envoy is about to meet a delegation of these newcomers."

He looked around the group again.

"You see, we cannot let such an alliance happen. If Shalem joins with these new northern clans, we are caught between two millstones. None of my people in the whole stretch between Shalem and Hatsor will have any safety in their homes any more. We might have to abandon all the new settlements up that way. Retreat across the River again. Or maybe live just in this southern part. With your people, Labayu, at our northern boundary."

They digested the news in silence. Finally Uriel spoke. "I suppose this would not be a popular answer for the Ibriym tribes?"

Abiy'el laughed, a short dismissive bark.

"It will be unacceptable. The tribes would want to go to war over this, but it is a war that just now we could not win."

He looked at Labayu. "You know Pedayah: how do you think he would hear such a piece of news? Then sum up that self-same reaction across a hundred village leaders like him. My position is so precarious just now that someone more war-like would push me aside tomorrow."

Labayu frowned, then realised something about the war-leader's words.

"Pedayah does not know yet?"

"No, nor anyone else that I can avoid. The lad came to me from somebody in my own town, somebody who I know is loyal. I have perhaps a couple of days before this news becomes widely known: a couple of days only. A couple of days to decide whether I will be pushed aside and the tribes call each other out for a war we cannot win, or whether I can find a better answer in Shalem."

"Are you sure this is a true word? Perhaps you are anxious over nothing?"

He shook his head.

"My cousin saw a group camping out near the Ridgeway track last night. A couple of Kinahny, but mostly these new-comers. They had come up from the Valley in the day, heading towards Shalem for sure. They will not be very far from us, off west a little perhaps. If I thought that we could find them, I would be inclined to kill them as they sleep to prevent an alliance."

"What will the Mitsriy do? They will not abandon their land so easily. And we have seen they are seeking to drive these northerners down towards the coastal plain."

"If I knew what they would do, my choices would be eas-ier. But I cannot be sure. We have never yet made covenant with the Mitsriy, but these are strange times and we may not be able to pick and choose our allies as we would like. But my favoured choice would be to persuade Shalem that his lands are under threat from these newcomers, and that his best choice is to side with us."

Ghazam had been listening without comment.

"I think these newcomers are weary of war, Abiy'el. Some of them at least. Look now, they were burning and plunder-ing everywhere in the north. Hatsor, Akka, Magidda. Other places further away, even Ikaret. But no more of this in the hill country. If any of them still want war, they are the ones who will face the Mitsriy down at the coast. Let Laksh look out for itself, or even Gedjet. But up here in the hill country, I think they may be looking for peace and alliance ."

"My heart wants to believe that you are right, Ghazam, but it also fears that you are wrong."

A profound unease stirred Labayu.

"What about Shimmigar? When we left him in the north, he had gone out to exact retribution on every one of them. How will things turn out if he still seeks that? Your attempts to find peace may yet be spoiled by one of our own."

They were all silent for a while.

"I suppose you will find out tomorrow at Shalem. Look now, I am asking you to represent me there. You are not Ibriym, but you are all in covenant with us. And because of that I can trust you not to favour any one of the tribes over another. Your loyalty is to me, or to the Ibriym as a whole, not to any one tribe. And it seems to me that the king of Shalem will hear a word more readily from a Kinahny mouth than an Ibriym one just now."

Ghazam leaned forward,

"I do not think you should go alone, Abiy'el. That makes it far too easy for anybody who takes a dislike to you to find a quick answer."

Labayu nodded. "I will take Akiy only; let Ghazam and Uriel go with you."

"I would feel much happier with that." Abiy'el paused and looked at each in turn. "Thank you. All of you. Whatever else happens, whatever other demands Shalem makes, do not let peace be made with these northerners."

ᚷ ᚨ ᚲ ᚨ ᚲ ᚨ ᚲ ᚨ ᚷ

Part 5 – Shalem

I EXTENDED ALL the borders of Kemet.

I slew Danuna from their isles,
reduced Tjekker and Peleset to ashes,
Sherden and the Sea-Weshwesh too –
all as though they had never been.

I settled them in forts.

𒀭𒈗𒀭𒈗𒀭𒈗𒀭𒈗

A NILAT AND HER FAMILY walked in file into the main audience chamber of the royal palace at Shalem. Silent slaves
had opened double doors, and after a quick glance around,
Tadugari had started to walk down the aisle between the double line of columns. The others followed, their footsteps loud
on the stone flags. Haleyna was behind her, then the twins
side by side, looking about with undisguised curiosity. Damatiria and Khuratsanitu had wanted to stay back in one of the
anterooms, but Tadugari had insisted on their presence as
personal guard and attendant. They brought up the rear.

Behind the pillars to either side, scattered here and there
according to a pattern she could not decipher, a few noble men
and women stood watching, some with their own guards and
attendants. But at this time of day the hall was largely empty.

The royal chair sat empty at the far end of the room. A tall
man with a complex design embroidered on his kef stood to
the right of the chair. Wooden and stone figurines alternated
in alcoves on the wall ahead of them. Among them was a
matched pair of carved lion heads. Their eyes were wide, dark,
and Anilat was sure that they masked a spy chamber like the
one she had hidden in before leaving Ikaret.

She looked down at her own clothes, feeling shabby beside
this man's obvious rank. They had stopped at the house of a
man Tadugari knew, and borrowed something appropriate as
over-garments, but beneath the surface finery she knew that
the traces of their wanderings were all too apparent.

They approached the front portion of the room, a dais raised
about a hand width above the rest of the floor. Tadugari halted
before stepping up, bowed with a flourish, and announced
himself in a voice which filled the room.

"I am Tadugari son of Anziniy, envoy of Ikaret. I bring
brotherly greetings and honour to the king of Shalem, mighty

in word and deed, from his friend the king of Ikaret, great in renown in all the lands. But also I bring news of calamity, for my lord and master, the king of Ikaret, has been killed in battle, and the great city of Ikaret herself has been cast down and cruelly treated. I have brought my family and personal retinue here to Shalem to request the indulgence of your lord the king, and his permission to stay a while within your protecting walls."

Anilat had been looking round covertly as he spoke at the reaction around them. It was clear that this was not news to them. However, she had been thrilled to hear the way in which Tadugari had announced himself. It was what she had wanted and expected all through the journey. Now, at last, the envoy had returned.

The man in the kef was coming forward, his arms outstretched in greeting.

"Tadugari, be welcome in this house. In the king's name I welcome you."

The two men embraced.

"Abdi-Teshup, how good it is to see you again. The journey has not been easy, but seeing you at its end refreshes my heart."

Abdi-Teshup looked at Anilat, then more briefly at the rest of the party. His glance took in the state of their dress, their footwear, their fatigue.

"The sorry news concerning Ikaret has already reached us. My lord the king was most profoundly grieved to hear of it. And other great cities too: Akka, Hatsor, Qatna, all fallen as this scourge has come upon the land. The hearts of so many have melted. How happy I am that you have survived all this, and that you have even travelled safely all this long way."

He led Tadugari up onto the raised part of the floor, and gestured across to one side.

"Your children and their attendants may wait in comfort in the adjacent hall." He gestured off to one side of the chamber. "And let your wife stand close by, over there."

He waited while a slave took the others from the room.

"We have several petitioners to hear today, Tadugari. Indulge me by standing at my side while I hear them. Then eat at my house tonight. You and your lady wife together, I mean. We shall talk of Ikaret, or other things as you please. Come now, we have a short time. While we wait, tell me again what you need."

"My friend, your invitation is a shower of rain in the heat of summer. Most of all we shall need a place to live."

"Consider it done. I will order a house for you all. Somewhere not too far from my own, so that we can talk whenever we please."

The two men walked to the place beside the king's chair, and turned to face out into the room. Anilat, watching Tadugari, knew that there was more that he wanted to say. Abdi-Teshup glanced sideways at him.

"We do not have long before the first person arrives. If there is something else to say, say it now."

"I want to command an army of revenge. I want to go back to Ikaret and avenge the blood of my city."

Abdi-Teshup's face was without expression, but his voice was full of regret.

"You are not a renowned commander of armies, my friend. The soldiers of this city do not know you, and they would not follow you. I will give you a house among the nobles here, I will give you a voice in the king's hall, I will give you whatever you need so that your family has a place of honour in the city. But not an army. You must not ask this of me."

Tadugari began to speak again, but Abdi-Teshup lifted a hand and shook his head. Abruptly, he was cold, implacable.

"Listen to me, my friend. You must not in any way ask this of me. Shall I give you an army to go all that long way north to Ikaret, and leave Shalem unguarded? It cannot be done. Never. Do not ask it of me again."

Tadugari looked down, struggling to keep disappointment from showing. Abdi-Teshup nodded, affable again.

"But, see, these foreigners are no longer at Ikaret. They are all along the coastal plain now, at the gates of Gedjet. We must look to our own lands first, for if the Mitsriy cannot defeat them, whatever shall we do here?"

Tadugari swallowed, and after a long pause nodded once.

"How can I help? I am your servant, and the servant of the lord your king."

"For today, you can help by standing with me to receive the various petitioners this morning. I doubt that you will find many of them of interest. And later we will talk about other ways for you to show your value to the city. But before that I will take you myself to the house I have in mind for you."

Anilat, deciding that Tadugari did not need her listening ears for this part of the conversation, looked around again. The room showed every sign that a former grandeur had declined somewhat.

Parts of the woodwork – originally of fine quality and good craftsmanship – had been patched clumsily. A stone statue in an alcove had toppled recently, and repaired insensitively. Flowers and animals painted onto the stone walls were fading where the sun fell directly against them.

Tadugari had spoken rapidly, efficiently, about the town, on the last stages of their approach. It seemed that the withdrawal of the Mitsriy, and the arrival of new groups from across the River, had all taken a toll. The indifferent upkeep of the king's audience chamber told the same story of diminishment.

Shalem was, of course, a much smaller place than Ikaret, and lacked the immediate access to the sea routes that her city had enjoyed. But she was a little disappointed by what she saw, and consoled herself with the thought that the king might simply be spending his wealth in other ways. At least they had been promised a home, and she would ensure that that was kept properly.

The first few petitioners came and went, alternately halting and eloquent with their grievance. Tadugari and Abdi-Teshup dealt with them swiftly. They were all minor ranking nobles, their cases dull. She amused herself by watching the elite of Shalem standing and shifting so they would be noticed, making exaggerated noises of approval or dismissal. It was all very provincial.

Finally, after a short break for sweet bread and thin wine, something interesting happened. The doors swung open and two Mitsriy stood there. One was a military officer of some intermediate rank, the other a scribe. They both looked weathered, toughened by recent life in the field, and the scribe's customary baldness was hidden beneath a fuzz of short hair. Behind them was a row of three ordinary soldiers.

The scribe stepped forward and, in a voice familiar with oratory, announced their presence.

"Receive now the officer Bakaa Sa-Nehesy, here in the name of his commander Penre Sa-Bunakhtef, sent here according to the will of the great king User-ma'at-Re Mery-Imun, who lives in prosperity and health and is the great sun shedding light on all the lands, before whom all people everywhere fall down in obedience seven times and seven times again. And I am the scribe Hekanefer who will mediate your words, for the officer Bakaa Sa-Nehesy is not fluent in your tongue."

Anilat watched eagerly as the scribe and the officer moved forward, towards the dais, leaving the common soldiers near the door. She had often seen Mitsriy scribes and negotiators at

Ikaret, mostly of much higher rank than the two men here in Shalem. Despite Ikaret's abandonment of the covenant with the Mitsriy in favour of the king of the North, such visitors were comparatively common. Her parents had, from time to time, received Mitsriy guests within their own house, as the king had instructed.

She saw the scribe's gaze flick around the room as he came up, stop briefly on Tadugari and then again on her. He nodded to himself, obviously seeing past the borrowed outer clothes to the fact of their foreignness. Then he leaned in to the officer and whispered to him. The two conferred briefly.

Abdi-Teshup bowed with full formality.

"I am Abdi-Teshup, who speaks in the name of the king of Shalem, leader of the rulers of the hill country and devoted servant of our great master, who lives in prosperity and health, whose keen eyes and strong arms protect us all. My lord the king honours the presence of our great suzerain, who we recognise here today in your two persons. Shalem is, as ever, at the service of your lord the king: how may we serve you today?"

"The heart of my lord the king who lives in prosperity and health is happy when he hears the loyal profession of his devoted servants. Today we are here to renew our oaths and promises, each to the other, and to consider what actions you will take against these northerners who have come into the land. They have respect for neither Mitsriy nor Kinahny, and only by standing together according to the treaties established by our ancestors will we turn away this threat."

"Shalem will hear your words and honour all of our agreements."

The scribe nodded, his serious expression unchanging. He turned to Tadugari.

"My lord the king who lives in prosperity and health was grieved to hear of the calamity which befell his former friends, that great city of Ikaret. How happy is my heart that I see that not all of the people of Ikaret were caught in its downfall."

Tadugari blinked and bowed to him, then gestured to Anilat and the others.

"Your lord's words are like water on a dry day, and my wife and I thank you for your kindness. As we have travelled south we have heard that the powerful arm and outstretched hand of the great king who lives in prosperity and health has been fierce against these invaders, and that he intends to bring them to ruin in the climactic battle of our age. May he triumph in victory on that day."

ᐊ᠊᠊ᐅ

HEKANEFER LOOKED AROUND AGAIN. He was surprised only by the presence of the couple from Ikaret, and the rest of the assorted nobility of Shalem in the room was of no interest to him.

The Shalemite envoy was speaking again.

"Everyone has heard of the deeds of your troops, how these invaders have been forced together into one place close to the Sea Road. Perhaps today we will hear news of your victory?"

"The commander Penre Sa-Bunakhtef has laboured night and day to fulfil my lord the king's oath to protect his cities. This far south you have seen none of the wicked enemy, I think?"

"We have seen none of them. But our friend Tadugari here can tell you more."

Hekanefer looked at Tadugari and nodded permission to speak again.

"We have evaded groups of them at every step, my lord scribe. Once we hid from a group, led by one who seemed to be feared among them, wearing tokens of rank. We have also seen, very often, the scars of their passage as we have come down. I believe they are of the same stock as the pirates and raiders who have harried the coasts of Alashiya and the King of the North these many years. But we have never known them move in such numbers before. They are filth. They cannot be reasoned with."

Hekanefer frowned.

"You are correct about their origins. But we have learned how to defeat them from mercenary teachers drawn from their own lands. Some of these people fight with us: they are not all alike. I have walked alongside some of them and count those men as faithful allies."

He held up a hand as Tadugari started to protest.

"I assure you this is true. Although, no doubt, you yourself are a person of sound morals, your city has no great history of loyalty. Perhaps it is difficult to recognise it in others?"

With some satisfaction he saw Tadugari swallow his words. Turning back to Abdi-Teshup he continued.

"The armies of the great king who lives in prosperity and health will draw in as many of the invaders as they can. But we cannot be certain to catch all of them in the same snare. The officer Bakaa Sa-Nehesy is here to instruct Shalem what to do if one such group should come up into the hill country."

"This is a military matter. I will arrange for your officer to meet with the commander of my lord's army."

"But not a military matter only. Oaths must be renewed."

Abdi-Teshup's voice dripped with regret.

"My lord the king is unable to speak with you at this time. He is away from the city, vigilant on his borders against this enemy."

"I am instructed to accept these oaths if you make them on behalf of Shalem, and your king will be bound by them as if he spoke them himself."

The envoy paused, clearly trying to think of a way to avoid the oath. Hekanefer felt abruptly weary, depressed. Here he was, playing verbal sparring games with the Kinahny, while the men with whom he had shared the deprivations of the open field were engaging in real battle. Yet again, these petty rulers showed no gratitude for all that was done for them.

"My lord scribe, the oath that we swore in the past we will honour. I will renew it if that seems good to you. But before that is done, I need to listen on my lord the king's behalf to your intentions towards these newcomers."

Hekanefer frowned, and to conceal his puzzlement spoke briefly to the officer Bakaa about what had been said.

"My officer wishes to understand your meaning. Are our deeds until now not eloquent enough?"

"These people are a new force in the Kinahny lands, my lord. To be sure we have seen them before in small numbers, but never like this. And never before have we seen them bring women and children in ox carts. They mean to settle here, I believe. How will your lord the great king deal with them? Will our title to the cities and lands that we rule on behalf of the Mitsriy be guaranteed?"

"The great king who lives in prosperity and health is vigorous as a raging bull towards all his enemies, but his heart desires peace among the nations when all is done. If these newcomers throw down their weapons, if they cool their fierce temper, if they agree to live in obedience, then there will be peace. But prior agreements such as with your lord the king will remain in effect, so long as the trust we place in him is met with loyalty and not with double-dealing."

"His lands are safe, then?"

"His lands are safe. He and his descendants after him will enjoy this place for as many generations as they remain true in their faithfulness."

He stepped a little closer to the envoy, stopping right at the edge of the dais.

"As you recall, your lord's two eldest sons live even now in the land of my lord the great king, the great sun who rises over every land. They are learning all that they must do in years to come. They are witness to all that happens to those whose hearts are unswerving in their obedience, and all that happens to those who turn away in disobedience. I am sure that both the father and the children will choose wisdom."

The envoy inclined his head: it could not really be called a bow, but at least it marked acquiescence.

"If my lord the king's title to these lands is secure, then I will speak the words of the oath with you today."

Hekanefer was relieved. He had half-expected that the negotiations would take longer, but it seemed that the envoy was willing to be reasonable. He was part-way through repeating the details to Bakaa when the double doors opened behind him, and a young voice was announcing somebody new.

"Receive now Antos, arkon of the Sherden people, who has travelled from afar to make peace and cut covenant with the leading men and the chief city of this land."

Hekanefer turned, curious. He had not heard the title arkon before, but it sounded like the kind of invented rank that a migrant group would fashion to suit their own sense of aggrandisement. The new party was mixed. There was a Kinahny youth in the lead with an older man, presumably the arkon Antos, and behind them a group of men together with a Kinahny girl.

The men were clearly of similar stock to the groups of invaders they had been pursuing, but also similar to the mercenaries who had helped the commander Penre to defeat them. Possibly allies, then, but more likely enemies just now.

He exchanged glances with Bakaa, who had been watching them with the same ambivalence that he felt. But this was not their city or their audience chamber, and it was not their place to speak first. But before Abdi-Teshup could say anything, the woman from Ikaret, over to his left, gave a little gasp, then a cry of delight.

"Dantiy! Yasib! You both live! But why are you with these people? Do you not know who they are?"

She took two involuntary steps towards the group. From the dais, Tadugari made a warning sound.

"Anilat, my wife, it is not our place here to speak without invitation."

Abdi-Teshup stepped towards the newcomers.

"I have never met representatives of the Sherden people before, but my lord the king of Shalem welcomes all who come in peace into his city. And you are doubly welcome if you are friends of my own friend Tadugari son of Anziniy. We will hear all your words."

Hekanefer nodded to himself. Both the youth and the girl were looking with undisguised relief at Tadugari and Anilat. Now that he looked more closely at them, they were obviously from Ikaret rather than somewhere in the Kinahny province. That added a complication, but was explicable. What was more concerning was Abdi-Teshup's reaction. Penre had made it quite clear that alliance between Shalem and the newcomers was not to be allowed.

Bakaa was tugging at his sleeve, and he hastily repeated all that had been said, noticing with some amusement that the same kind of exchange was happening in the Sherden group. Beside him, Anilat and Tadugari were deep in whispered conversation. Abdi-Teshup glanced at them all, a look of amusement on his face, then spoke up in a loud voice for the benefit of the nobility of Shalem.

"The daily audience is at an end. The great ones of Shalem may withdraw and go about their own business. I will receive my friend Tadugari and his wife, the Mitsriy officials, and the arkon of the Sherden people with his retinue in private."

There was a buzz of speculation in the room, and then slaves led the nobles in one direction while Abdi-Teshup ushered the others through a side door into a smaller chamber. There was a long table in it, along the central axis of the room. Hekanefer, seeing a chance to regain something of the initiative, walked firmly forward and was first into the room. He sat down with Bakaa at one end of the table.

D ANTIY FILED INTO THE ROOM just behind Eumedes and Towanos, just ahead of the Shalemite envoy. As she went through the door, Anilat took her arm. The two women kissed each other.

"Aunt, I am very happy that you are here with my uncle. And the children are here too? When we saw what had happened to Hatsor we feared for you."

"And us for you, Dantiy. But why are you with this, this..."

Words failed her, and she gestured at the Sherden in a kind of stabbing movement. Dantiy shook her head, took Dekseus by the arm, and presented him to Anilat.

"Please meet my husband, aunt. His name is Dekseus."

Dekseus, understanding his own name but hardly anything else, bobbed his head and looked slightly confused. Towanos looked back, said a few words to Dekseus in their own language. Dekseus beamed, bowed more properly to Anilat, and said, haltingly, "It is happiness to meet my wife's female relative."

Anilat forced a smile and, as Dekseus moved towards the table to sit with the others, pulled Dantiy close so she could speak privately to her.

"Do you not know what he is, Dantiy? Have you no feelings for our city? And what have they done to your hair?" She stopped, as though appalled by a sudden thought. "Surely he is not truly your husband yet? Surely it is in name only? Only betrothal at this time?"

Dantiy drew away a little.

"Aunt, you do not know these people as I do. Or as Yasib does. We have both come to honour them, and we are both of one heart in this. Dekseus truly is my husband in every way: I very much hope I already carry his child. When I am sure of it, you will be among the first to know. This my child, and all those other children that Dekseus will give me in time: these children are the future of Ikaret. You would do well to prepare Haleyna for the same. There is more future in my husband's clan than there is for all the Kinahny cities put together."

Leaving her aunt standing, hand to mouth, she stepped proudly away and sat beside Dekseus. After a moment, Anilat went to be with Tadugari. Dantiy watched as she whispered urgently in his ear. Tadugari frowned, shook his head, and glanced briefly at Dantiy where she sat amongst the Sherden.

Dantiy looked curiously at the Mitsriy scribe. He was, perhaps, the least predictable person in the room. She had a good idea how the envoy Abdi-Teshup might think, and there would be time in the future to persuade her aunt and uncle concerning her marriage. But it would be important that the Mitsriy gained the right impression of her new people. Abdi-Teshup stood to speak.

"Antos, arkon of the Sherden, I will hear what it is you seek of the lord my king."

Dantiy continued to watch the Mitsriy scribe. It was becoming clear to her that he was not likely to look on the Sherden with sympathy. Seeing that Yasib was about to speak for Antos, she leaned past Dekseus to speak quietly with Towanos.

"The Shalemite will agree to what we want. But that Mitsriy scribe there – he is the one we must persuade."

Towanos nodded slowly, then looked across at Yasib as he began.

"The clan of the arkon Antos is camped across the River, north of here and east. We seek peace. We seek land to tend as our own, a place to graze animals, and fruit trees to care for in their season. The leading men of the town of Yabesh told us that in order to remain, we must swear oaths of allegiance to the headman and to the king of Shalem both, and that we would find these men here in the city. The arkon Antos is ready to take these oaths and covenants on behalf of his people, that we might lend our strength to yours and, together, flourish in the land."

"I will receive your promises in the name of my lord the king of Shalem. The headman of Yabesh left this city earlier today, but your oath to my lord the king surpasses any words you might speak with the headman."

At the head of the table, the scribe was shaking his head.

"As the loyal vassal of the great king User-ma'at-Re Mery-Imun, who lives in prosperity and health, you must refer all such commitments to me. Perhaps he who is the sun over all the lands will not accept this promise as valid."

Yasib looked mildly at the scribe, and then turned back to Abdi-Teshup.

"In times past the Mitsriy had no interest in the lands across the River. Perhaps your lord the king of Shalem – who

will become our lord the king also, once the oath is taken –
perhaps he does not need the approval of the Mitsriy in this
case. Tell me, does the arm of the king of the Mitsriy stretch
now to the other side of the River?"

Abdi-Teshup shrugged. "The arm of the Mitsriy is no longer
than it has ever been. But my lord the king would be reluctant
to make a new alliance which would offend those who are his
friends today."

"The great king who lives in prosperity and health has no
love for those who go up against cities with fire, who act as
rebels in the land, and who refuse to submit to his authority
and wisdom."

Tadugari leaned forward.

"Yasib, these people burned Ikaret, killed our king, and left
our people unburied in the streets. How is it that you take
their part in this?"

"Uncle, these are not of the same tribe. The Sherden had no
part in the downfall of our city. Other tribes did that: Peleset,
Lukka, Tursha and so on. Do you think that Dantiy and I
would forget the city of our birth so quickly?"

"Are you so sure? Perhaps these people have not told you
all the truth?"

Yasib took a deep breath. Dantiy was sure he was on the
verge of an angry retort when Antos touched his arm, pulled
him close so that the two could converse quietly. The scribe
and Tadugari exchanged knowing glances. Antos gestured to
Yasib to continue, but he looked embarrassed, shook his head.
In the pause Towanos stood up.

"Our friend Yasib will not say this in case it sounds a boast.
But I say for him. Your man Yasib has been the avenger of
Ikaret. He and the sister both. He fought the man who led
the attack at Ikaret and defeated him. He and the sister both
took their revenge." He nodded to Tadugari. "Your revenge

also. The man is dead: they killed him. And also, we Sherden were never at Ikaret. Not anywhere nearby."

He sat again. Tadugari gripped Anilat's hand, staring all the while at Yasib. Anilat looked a question at Dantiy, who nodded with pride.

"It is truth, aunt. Yasib and I together held the knife that killed that foul man, after Yasib had defeated him. Before that, Nikleos here took us in as guests, and gave us a home when we had none. These people are not our enemy."

She watched Anilat take a long breath, watched her aunt's gaze flicker between her and Dekseus, knew exactly what was filling her heart. She leaned forward before the older woman could speak.

"This is a good union, aunt. Dekseus and myself: Ikaret and the Sherden. Our children will be new life arising from the ashes."

Abdi-Teshup nodded affably, and turned to the scribe.

"So there is no difficulty. My lord the king's interests align with your own. Here we have the enemy of our mutual enemy; can there be any reason not to swear oaths of allegiance? I feel sure that your lord the great king would be pleased to see all his loyal friends join together."

Dantiy watched the scribe's face. He was evidently uncomfortable at the turn of events. The two Mitsriy spoke together, too quickly and quietly for her to follow. Antos rested his hand on Yasib's shoulder as he looked round the table, the table, slightly flushed but quite satisfied at the reaction.

Finally the scribe looked across at Antos, gesturing after each phrase for Yasib to translate.

"I suppose that as arkon of your clan, your oath will bind each and every one of your people?"

"It will."

"And it is true that the place where you are living is on the far side of the River?"

"It is true."

Antos had answered only briefly, but Yasib continued the thought.

"The Sherden will make no claim and have no aspiration on this side of the River. We want only to live in peace near to Yabesh. To build houses, to farm, to trade with our neighbours. To take our place amongst the great of this land."

Antos had been listening closely to Yasib, and when he finished he stood up and looked around the room.

"Our journey has been long. Now we will live in peace at Yabesh itself. Swear peace to the Mitsriy and Shalem both." He nodded to Tadugari. "Yasib has been good for us. And Dantiy also. I would be pleased to know their family."

The scribe was still hesitating. Dantiy felt some compassion for him. He had clearly not expected to have to deal with anything more than a renewal of Shalem's oath, and the burden of this new responsibility was heavy. What would his superiors think if he committed the Mitsriy to a new alliance?

He spoke one more brief time with the military officer, and had seemingly just reached a decision, when the door opened. A slave came over to Abdi-Teshup and whispered to him. He laughed shortly and stood up while the slave went back out again. They could hear talking from the audience chamber.

"It seems that one more voice must be heard in this room before we are done. One of the Ibriym is here, speaking today for their warleader Abiy'el."

Dantiy and Yasib exchanged glances. They had not expected to have to deal with the Ibriym at this early stage, nor in a situation where everyone was in the same room to hear all that was said. The scribe was once again conversing with his officer.

A man came in, thin and rugged, wearing a Kinahny kef in a casual way. He also had an outdoor air, as though more used to the wilderness than the court. He looked carefully round the room, taking in the diversity of people. Abdi-Teshup gestured to an empty place at the long table, but the man paused to speak before sitting.

"I am Labayu son of Shaharti, of the town of Kephrath." He looked around again to find out if the listeners recognised the name. "A short distance north of here. My people are in covenant with the Ibriym. The warleader Abiy'el is still fulfilling a promise he made to Shalem concerning some criminals, and so I am here to represent him."

He sat down. As he had said the word 'criminals', he had stared pointedly at Antos. Abdi-Teshup, meanwhile, had been watching the scribe closely, observing his reaction.

"Labayu son of Shaharti, you are welcome here. I look forward to Abiy'el's return with these criminals, but for today we are here to speak of this man Antos. His Sherden clan wish to settle on the far side of the River, near Yabesh. This concerns the Ibriym as well as Shalem."

Dantiy and Yasib looked at each other again. Labayu's hostility towards the Sherden was obvious, and it was not yet clear how to deflect it. Yasib leaned in to Antos to speak quietly with him.

LABAYU HAD REALISED on first coming into the room that he had only just arrived in time to intervene. It sounded as though the various groups were all too close to agreement. He thought rapidly as Abdi-Teshup continued.

"See now, Labayu son of Shaharti, this is the scribe Hekanefer and a military officer, Bakaa by name, sent up to Shalem from the Mitsriy armies. And also the lord Tadugari, son of Anziniy, envoy of Ikaret, who escaped the destruction of that city and has a new home here. And Antos, arkon of the Sherden, and his advisers, particularly Yasib, who translates for him. The Sherden have petitioned for a place to live on the far side of the River. Since Abiy'el has not yet apprehended the criminals who attacked my lord's people, nor delivered the agreed sum of restitution, I must ask what message you have come to deliver?"

"Abiy'el sends once again his blessing, and his pledge of continued obedience to his lord the king of Shalem. And recognises the rule over every land of the great king of the Mitsriy, who lives in prosperity and health. I have come in haste from the north of the country, beyond Hatsor, to warn our allies and suzerains against any alliance whatsoever with these newcomers in the land. They are lawless and brutal, caring for neither the people of the land nor their rulers. They are locusts and rabid wolves: they cannot be trusted."

Hekanefer looked at him for a long moment, sizing up his appearance as well as his message. Antos was deep in conversation with the Kinahny lad Yasib, sitting beside him. Nobody spoke for a short time. Outside the room they could hear soldiers being drilled, as though Shalem was advertising her ability to defend herself.

"Tell me, Labayu, why should my lord the king fear these Sherden? They are few in number, and peaceable, and seek only land beside Yabesh. They have spoken only courtesy in this room, and have neither made demands nor breathed threats. They strike me as neither locusts nor wolves."

Labayu paused to think. His opening words had, perhaps, been too direct, and had certainly not had the effect he had wanted.

"My lord envoy, my lord scribe, I have seen first hand what these people have done. Though they come down from the north, they do not recognise the King of the North. They do not acknowledge any of the rulers here in the land. They do not submit to the words of the great king of the Mitsriy. They have burned great cities that have stood for generations – Hatsor, Akka, Magidda and others. I have seen even farms and villages made into ruins, their families slaughtered like beasts and left unburied like carrion. I have seen all this, and more besides. These are not the deeds of a people seeking peace. Look now, we have people from Ikaret here who witnessed the downfall of their city and their king; ask them how their life has been since these people came to their gates."

He sat back again. The woman from Ikaret was reliving in her heart the destruction of her home, and sat with tears trickling down her cheeks below her neatly tied kef. Her husband, Tadugari, placed a hand on her arm.

"Labayu of Kephrath, until today I would have agreed with every word of that. After fleeing Ikaret in flames, I wanted nothing more than revenge, and to see every last one of these invaders executed. But I have learned that they are not all the same. Look now, my wife and I are not the only people from Ikaret here: ask my nephew and niece how their life has been since joining with the Sherden."

Labayu blinked in surprise. The man from Ikaret was the last one he had expected to oppose him. For a disorienting moment he wondered if he had muddled the identities of everybody present. Yasib was nodding.

"Not all the clans who have come here are alike, sir. The Sherden took us in when we were homeless. They have been kind and open-handed. Your enemies are those who rage along the Sea Road. The Ibriym and the Sherden can live in peace with each other, and with Shalem. My sister has joined with Dekseus here in marriage. Would she have done that if these people had been at Ikaret?"

The room was silent, and Labayu felt that all eyes were on him. He had no idea how he could explain any of this to Abiy'el, but every plan that he had made before entering the room had to be discarded. If the Ibriym were not to appear as misguided and obstructive, he needed to recover ground very quickly. The girl beside Yasib – his sister – was speaking.

"Sir, it is as my brother says. The sea clans are not all alike. See, you yourself are Kinahny, but you are in covenant with the Ibriym. Are you content with every deed of every tribesman of the Ibriym? Do all their words please you? Do you not find yourself sometimes ashamed – not of the covenant itself, but of some of those with whom you are joined?"

Labayu looked at them both, then at Antos, whose shrewd eyes were fixed on him. Although the arkon was relying on Yasib to translate, Labayu had a strong sense that he actually understood a great deal of what he heard.

He felt that Abiy'el's position had been entirely undermined by the group from Ikaret. Thinking back, Ghazam had said something very similar, but he had ignored it at the time. The girl's comments about his own relationship with the Ibriym had cut very deep. Perhaps it would be best for Abiy'el to switch allegiance away from the Mitsriy now, and find common cause with these newcomers. Abiy'el was not here, and he had to make the best decisions that he could.

"I hear your words, and withdraw what I said at first. I spoke without understanding the differences between the sea clans, and I have no reason to doubt the good faith of the Sherden."

He looked directly at Antos as he said this, and saw the light of understanding dawning in the older man's expression even before Yasib finished translating. He nodded to the arkon, feeling an unexpected sense of kinship with him. Here was another man whose life was outdoors, in the wilderness. His people could easily end up as cousins in covenant with the Sherden as a result of today. It would be good to have such cousins: it would counterbalance the coldness he had encountered in the north. Whatever else this Antos might be, he was not cold.

Abdi-Teshup looked around and nodded, pleased.

"So we are all in agreement, then. I shall call for one of the priests to bring the necessary items, and..."

He stopped. The scribe Hekanefer's chair had scraped emphatically across the floor as he had risen to his feet.

"The great king who rules in prosperity and health appreciates the zeal of his vassal Shalem. However, I am here as the representative of the Beloved Land, and so it will be me who first hears the pledges of obedience from those present. Once that is done, you are free to speak secondary promises one to another as you see fit, so long as they in no way subvert your first loyalty to the great king."

Labayu was not very surprised, and judging by the expression on the envoy's face, neither was he. The attempt to claim the centre ground by being the first to hear promises had failed, owing to the scribe's attentiveness. Still standing, Hekanefer was looking with a sardonic expression at Abdi-Teshup, who smiled and shrugged.

"Quite so, lord scribe. But see, the morning has now passed, and we ought to satisfy the needs of the body before we turn to ceremony. I invite you all to enjoy the generosity of my lord the king. Food and wine will be served to you in the adjoining room."

Labayu rose along with the others and went through a side door. Several tables round the edges of the room had been loaded with bread, fruit, cold meat, and basins of the region's wine. He stood back, curious to see how the group would form into knots and clumps once free of the table that had separated them.

The Mitsriy scribe and officer kept apart from the rest, but took wine into a corner and buried themselves in intense conversation. The two women, aunt and niece, also separated from the rest. Abdi-Teshup moved from person to person, acting as the generous host, ensuring that plates and juglets were kept full.

But the others, of the Sherden and Ikaret alike, mingled together with no reservation. Labayu, feeling rather alone, picked up some flat bread and a fig to keep himself busy. One of the Sherden came across to him, and Labayu struggled for a moment with a mixture of feelings.

"Labayu son of Shaharti?" The man's accent was thick, but comprehensible. "I am Towanos. It is good to meet. Did I hear right, that you are with the Ibriym, but not one of them?"

"That is correct, Towanos. My people are Kinahny, not Ibriym. But we have been in covenant with the Ibriym for most of my life. My people were the first to welcome them, and stand with them, when they arrived here from over the River."

"You have seen some of the other sea clans? Yes? You have angry feelings about them?"

Labayu hesitated, and the other man laughed cheerfully and waved a hand.

"Labayu, please, I do not speak to trick you. I am not an envoy. I have been a farmer, and a traveller, and a fighter, and now if your land will have us I will be a farmer again. You and I, we are more at home away from the city, I think. In time, I should like for you to visit our new homes, when we have unharnessed the oxen for the last time and built new houses of wood and stone."

Labayu grinned. Once again, he found himself liking the bluntness of these Sherden. He started to reply, but Towanos took his arm and led him across to the large window. As they moved, Towanos was speaking loudly.

"Show me the lie of the land, Labayu."

The window faced north, and Labayu looked at once in the direction of the Four Towns. Towanos continued more quietly.

"Yasib himself, he warned us that statues on the walls often have people hidden behind them. No need for Shalem to hear everything we say. But perhaps together we should speak about the anger that has separated us. Even if it was not our doing in the first place."

Labayu glanced around the room, realising suddenly that the tables with food and drink were laid out so that the gaps between them each had its own ornate carving. He snorted.

"The deceit of the city."

Towanos nodded.

"Well, I do enjoy trickery. But I enjoy it more if I have tricked the trickster. Let us point from the window from time to time as we speak. At least we are sure nobody listens from out there."

There was a narrow ledge, but below that the wall was sheer down to the courtyard below, where soldiers were practicing with the bow against man-sized wooden targets.

"That was how Yasib secured a place amongst us, by outwitting Periphas in a fight with knives."

"Good for him. But who was Periphas?"

"A man of the Pelestoi. A skilled fighter, but brutal. He was among the first into the city of Wilios when we finally captured it. He killed a great many there, and for no purpose except the pleasure of it. We were afraid of him, especially the women. Yasib did us all good by killing him."

Labayu looked at him.

"Was he a big man? Wore a red sash?"

"Truly, yes. The sash had a wolf's head on it, but you would only see that if you were close by. Why? Have you seen him?"

"Not I, but one of my men, Shimmigar. North of here, close to Hatsor, nearly a month ago now. Shimmigar said that the youths were all afraid of him. So this Yasib killed him?"

He turned to look at Yasib, who was standing between Antos and Tadugari helping them talk to each other.

"He did. And he avenged the death of his family in Ikaret with the same act. His father and mother will be proud of him as they watch from the other side. I hope to meet others in this land that share his courage and skill."

Labayu nodded slowly, then turned to look out of the window again.

"See, Towanos, where the track heading north curls around that ridge over there? My wife's house is in Giybon, a short distance along that road and off to the left. Less than half a day. You would have passed near it when you came up from Yabesh. When we are all in covenant, you and I will break bread together there."

And then, all unbidden, the thought of Shimmigar rose up in his mind, intent on vengeance. Would Shimmigar see the differences between one of the sea clans and another?

𐤗 𐤟 𐤚 𐤟 𐤚 𐤟 𐤚 𐤟 𐤗

𐤟𐤼𐤶𐤼𐤶𐤼𐤶𐤼𐤟

D ANTIY WAS STILL CONVINCED that her aunt did not approve of her marriage, but the two women had managed to talk together without discussing the subject openly. Anilat had only very obliquely touched on the idea of family duty, and had easily allowed herself to be steered away from that in order to listen to Dantiy's experience of traveller life.

She looked around the room with satisfaction. Yasib's idea of getting Towanos to talk with Labayu was clearly a good one. The two men were now talking and laughing together, gesticulating out of the window from time to time as though it was a great joke.

Only the two Mitsriy stood alone, keeping their own company, separate from the others. She decided to take the initiative and, leaving Dekseus with the group around her uncle, walked over to them.

They stopped talking as she approached. The officer nodded and said something which she vaguely recognised as a standard Mitsriy greeting. The scribe, however, gave her an unnecessarily formal bow and used her own language.

"Dantiy, daughter of Ikaret. How happy am I to meet you, who have survived the downfall of your city, and have made for yourself a new life here in the Kinahny province."

"Lord scribe, I am happier today that you are willing to speak words of peace with my husband's people. Your great king who lives in prosperity and health will not regret welcoming the Sherden alongside his friends."

"I hope that the Sherden will enjoy the benefits of living in obedience. And Ikaret too. Surely many of your people will have survived – and I pray to all your gods that they have – and perhaps they will find a new future living under the protection of my country once again."

"Lord scribe, my new people hope to settle by Yabesh, which is outside the traditional borders of your province. The Sherden intend to live in friendship and for mutual benefit, rather than in strict obedience as vassals."

The scribe nodded, with a weary expression. Dantiy suddenly, uncharacteristically, felt another rush of compassion for him. She frowned inwardly at herself, while keeping her features calm. All through the day she had been feeling unexpected surges of emotion like this, and she needed to be careful what she ended up saying.

"We must seem very difficult to you, my lord scribe. Quite unappreciative of all that your land offers."

Surprised, caught unguarded, he nodded, and then rubbed his head. He started to say something else, when the door opened in a rush. The entire room turned. Abdi-Teshup lifted his hands and stepped forward. Dekseus was already half way across to Dantiy before she could see who was there.

Two men burst in. The first was one of the Mitsriy soldiers. His face was twisted with emotion, and he came towards the scribe at a run. Behind him, a Shalemite guardsman was going to Abdi-Teshup.

The scribe turned politely to Dantiy.

"Lady, I must attend to this news."

He nodded briefly to Dekseus, who reached Dantiy just as the soldier halted, and the three Mitsriy withdrew into one of the window alcoves to talk rapidly with each other.

She let Dekseus take her back over to Nikleos and the others.

"Can you tell what they are saying?"

She shook her head. The soldier was facing away from her, and her knowledge of the Mitsriy tongue was too weak to follow their talk.

"But husband, it is clearly bad news."

The officer was shaking his head in disbelief, and the scribe looked distraught.

"The battle down at the Sea Road?"

Abdi-Teshup had gone over to the door with his own guardsman, and, having now dismissed him, turned to the others. It was as though he had discovered some new puzzle or wonder, and his whole being was questing forward to explore it.

"My lords, would you like to tell the others what we have just heard?"

But the officer ignored him, turning away from the group to look blindly out of the window. The scribe, leaning on the table, buckled at the waist. Dantiy thought for a moment that he was going to vomit, but he stayed silent, bent over with his arms draped along the grain of the wood, sprawled amongst the bowls of uneaten food and undrunk wine. Head on knee, she realised, remembering her grandmother's Mitsriy expression.

The soldier looked from one to the other helplessly, then took up an alert position beside his officer, looking at nobody. Abdi-Teshup, a slightly cruel smile on his features, repeated his question. Again there was no reply.

"My honoured guests, then it falls to me to inform you. The armies of the newcomers from the north, and of the Mitsriy, have fought their great battle together, along the Sea Road north of Gedjet."

The room was absolutely silent as he continued, relishing his role.

"The battle was costly to both sides, but inconclusive. Both armies claim to have won, but the truth of the matter is that neither has. They have bled the strength out of each other and are exhausted."

Dantiy was fixed to the spot, her gaze unswerving from the envoy. Nearby she heard the faint whisper of her brother, once again faithfully translating the words for the Sherden.

"There is more. The Mitsriy general, acting with the full knowledge and approval of his great king, has offered peace to the sea clans. He has granted them lands and towns along the Sea Road, to govern and order themselves as they see fit. The great city of Gedjet is one, which for a time will be jointly ruled by the Mitsriy and the Peleset. There are four other cities granted, two along the coast and two a little way inland."

He paused. At his words a buzz of anxiety had flared up around the room, hushed again as he looked at the Mitsriy.

"Correct me if I am wrong, lord scribe, but I believe that this is the first time in – let me think – in at least twenty-five generations that the Mitsriy have willingly given away land and towns in this province, which at one time belonged entirely to them."

The scribe ignored him, lost in his own world of disorientation. The envoy's face wore a rather malevolent look; observing the scribe's misery was a delight to him. Tadugari stepped forward and cleared his throat.

"Abdi-Teshup, my old friend, calm yourself. Let our words and the inclinations of all our hearts be peaceable now. This news could signal calamity for all of us. I believe we all hoped the Mitsriy would exact our revenge for us – against those who plundered Ikaret, against those who compelled the peaceable to make war, against those who slaughtered the innocent living in farms and scattered villages. This is not a time for being triumphant. This is a time for standing together, all of us here in this room and the peoples we represent. This is a time for making alliance and promising faithfulness and unity."

Abdi-Teshup stopped himself on the verge of another torrent of words. He turned to Tadugari.

"You think so?"

"I do, old friend. Show the leadership of Shalem by breaking the bread of peace and sharing the wine of friendship with us all. It is your city's time to draw the land together, not to mock those who suffer."

The envoy looked at the Mitsriy, his eyes brimming with the years of service, and with a great effort forced their memory back below the surface. He took a deep breath and nodded.

"Well. Let us allow our Mitsriy guests time to adjust to this disaster. I would like to invite the rest of you back into the main room, where a priest is waiting with sacred tokens to witness our oaths, each to the other."

Without waiting, he swept back into the other room, and, in pairs and little groups, the rest came after. Dantiy looked around as she followed Shalem's lead. On each face, to greater or lesser degree, was the same concern; would the more vigorous and warlike sea clans be satisfied with five towns, or would they be seeking expansion into the hill country?

⊨⊨𐤀𐤀𐤀𐤀𐤀⊨⊨

𐤁𐤁𐤁𐤁𐤁𐤁𐤁𐤁𐤁

A NILAT TOOK COMFORT from the confident grip that Tadugari kept on her arm. She had been profoundly moved by his intervention in the face of Abdi-Teshup's cruelty. It had been necessary, and she was relieved at the new direction that had been set. More than that, though, hope continued to stir in her for their own future together.

That was, however, a personal matter, and for the time being she should concentrate on the whole land. In so many ways this stalemate was a bad outcome for them all. The undefeated aggression of the raiders was scant days from their new home, and it would not take long for the sea clans, once settled in their new cities, to look at the lands around them.

The memory of Ikaret was both too fresh and too deeply scored into her for anything but grief and fear.

To be sure, it was worse for the Mitsriy, and the scribe Hekanefer had clearly been profoundly crushed. He trailed along as an afterthought to the others, avoiding any contact with anybody. The officer and soldier had remained where they stood in the other room, a picture of denial. That offered her very little consolation.

They arranged themselves around the long table in much the same order as before. She looked carefully at Abdi-Teshup.

For all his air of command, under a thin surface she could see the anxiety that had displaced his mockery. Indeed, he should be anxious on behalf of his king – Shalem was not a big city, but it was influential and wealthy beyond the expectation of mere size. It might well seem a fine prize for a restless war-leader to pluck.

Perhaps the Sherden were in the best position, she mused. Their new home was furthest of all of them from the coast, and their temporary estrangement from their distant relatives might easily be forgotten in an hour of need.

She half listened as Abdi-Teshup spoke at length about the value and dignity of covenant life. Small wonder: he would be wanting secure borders at his back with the newly arrived Sherden, and to each side with the Ibriym and their handful of Kinahny allies. It seemed altogether likely that the business of compensation that had been demanded would be quietly forgotten by Shalem in the need for security.

Tadugari had clearly succeeded in affecting Abdi-Teshup exactly as he had wanted. Now that the words had taken root, Ikaret was content for the time being to settle into the background, letting Shalem take up the lead. What now remained was to see how the patterns of alliance and enmity would shape themselves in the years to come.

The priest of Shalem slaughtered a pigeon, draining the blood into a pan and sending an acolyte away with the carcass. She supposed it would be used for divination later.

Then he spent a considerable time in prayer, watched with varying degrees of interest, understanding, and faith by the people around. She liked the elaboration of the ritual, and allowed her thoughts to drift away in quiet contemplation of her own losses. Perhaps a settlement of the heart would be possible, in time.

Finally a single loaf was broken into many pieces, and a full silver cup of the region's wine was set beside it. Abdi-Teshup,

Tadugari, Labayu, and Antos stood together. Yasib attended immediately behind Antos to guide his hand and his words. His parents would be proud of what he was becoming, and grief flooded into her again as she remembered her brother and his wife.

While the priest was supervising the lengthy promises the various parties made each to the other, she used the time and the holy space to commune with her own absent family. Hekanefer, conspicuously, took no part in the ceremony.

Then, after a final blessing, they exchanged the tokens with one another. She sighed. Covenant had been spoken, food shared, sacrificial blood spilled. Memory of the past had been put into use. Nothing now remained except to live on in the light, and under the shadow, of the promises. It was a good outcome.

The men remained standing together, united now in a silence that stretched out much longer than she expected. Her heart wandered away from the room, to muse to itself about the house she had been promised. What would she put in it, she wondered, that would recall the greatness of Ikaret?

A MAN ADDRESSES HIS BROTHER.

Hekanefer to his older brother Ramose, from Shalem.

My dear brother, this is my first letter from Shalem, and it will be my last as an army scribe. Until this afternoon, I had supposed without thinking that one day, when the campaign was over, I would be returning to Gedjet. This is no longer certain. Nothing is certain, after today's news.

I have already written to my officer by way of formal report, and one of the soldiers has left the city with the document. That missive was almost entirely official. Shortly I must write to our parents: that will not be easy. For now I am writing to you. In truth, it might be said that I am simply hiding in the room made available by Shalem's envoy. I am stealing a short time for myself before duty calls again, writing to you in these precious signs that nobody else here can read.

How will the mighty ones of the past look at us? Those great kings who have gone now to the horizon and put on godly flesh, those soldiers who pressed forward to claim the territory for us, those scribes and officials who managed the land in an efficient and honourable manner. What will they be saying on the other side of the Sea of Reeds about all that has happened?

We have been defeated, Ramose. Not just in battle, but in heart. When I heard the news of the battle's outcome, I was overcome with grief – not just my own, I believe, but that of our Beloved Land herself.

I have no heart just yet to go back to the others and wear a cheerful mask. So here I am writing to you, staying hidden away in this shabby place like a frog in its muddy home. This is partly, of course, because sharing these things with you is like finding the fragrant lotus in the shallow pools beside that best of all rivers. It is life to my heart. The mud that is home to the frog is also root for the lily.

But as well as that, I am writing simply to avoid the unpleasant duty of going back among those people and being courteous. Being, so to speak, the dignified embodiment of our Beloved Land.

Ah, Ramose, what is happening to us? Yesterday we made peace with these newcomers – these Peleset, Tursha and so on. We gave them land along the coastal plain. We gave them what they wanted. We gave them Gedjet, and a handful of other cities. Tomorrow perhaps we will give them the whole of this province.

I can understand negotiating with the Sherden, for they seem inclined to peace. In any case they are only looking for land across the River here, outside of our traditional borders. But to grant land which was our own, in regions that we have administered all these years? To these fierce tribes with whom we were locked in combat all this time? It defies belief. Our days here seem to be drawing to an end.

So what will I do now? The officer has invited me to rejoin his men, but I have declined. That would mean going back to Gedjet, to help keep the peace in that city. Do I have the heart for that? To spend my days recording minor infractions of the rule of law? And then at some time soon, all too soon, to make careful notes about our abandonment of that place? I do not think so.

But my heart recoils too from the thought of simply returning to the Beloved Land and trying to settle back there. Would I join one of the temples and record daily devotions, births and deaths? Or work on a farm keeping track of grain and olives, pottery and slaves? And along with that, try to be comfortable with Nodjmet? I think not.

No, brother, my desire is to remain here in this province – even if it is destined to go its own way and cease to be our vassal. This is what I have told the officer. There is vitality out here which our Beloved Land is losing. In a few lives of men I am convinced we will regain it, and my descendants will once again enjoy the company and the conversation of true culture.

But I have only a single life before I cross the Reeds, and I have chosen to spend it out here. Here, where there is ample opportunity for both work and pleasure. It is a better choice than to simply trudge home, or shrink away from what I can only see as defeat. Yes, defeat, no matter how much the scribes of the king will dress it as victory. Out here, one can still be bold.

I shall be writing to Nodjmet and her mother, and to our parents, to explain that I shall not be returning home to complete the betrothal. I do not expect them to understand.

They tell me there is a man in this city, a scribe and artist who came out from Waset. He has organised other craftsmen into a kind of team. They work together to provide the things that the king of this place and his nobles want. I have seen some of their work, and it is good. I think I will join them, for a while, since there is nobody among them who has my particular talents.

Then I will find a woman companion, both for my own satisfaction and also, in time, to turn aside the wrath of my father by providing him a grandchild. I am expecting fierce words from him, but they will evaporate like the dew on a summer morning once he hears that his seed is flourishing.

I hear your familiar voice: who might this most fortunate of women be? I do not yet know. But I saw today before entering the audience chamber that a refugee man and wife from Ikaret have a daughter, who is not unattractive. How would it be for the Beloved Land to join together with Ikaret?

Until today I never even considered such a possibility, but being out here stimulates ideas in a most invigorating manner. Would she be a faithful companion, or would that dismal trait of Ikaret towards inconstancy always lie between us? I shall at least find out her name, and look again at her face.

So there we have it, Ramose. I shall not be returning to the Beloved Land. I shall remain here and share the life of the province. What a strange path I have taken since leaving Gedjet, less than three months ago. Just like the marching route I took with the soldiers as we sought our prize, it has twisted and turned all around the land. It has strayed away from the familiar places that you and I both learned.

At first, all my heart craved was to return to the peace and security of the family home. Now, a new home and a new future calls to me.

Receive my love, brother, and wish me yours in return. It will be a while, I think, before we meet again. Perhaps I shall never return to the land of my birth.

Richard Abbott

Epilogue

PEACE UPON HER

    Peace upon her family
    Peace upon her kindred
    Peace upon her house.

Peace upon Ikaret
    Peace upon her gates.

〈✦📬✦📬✦📬✦📬〉

D AMATIRIA'S SHADOW FELL across Anilat's hands, as she sat holding the little box with the leather thong, in the courtyard beside the almond tree.

"You should come and see this priest, mistress."

She looked up at Damatiria and blinked back some unshed tears.

"Come with me, mistress, and we'll see him together. Give your mother the peace she deserves."

"I thought there was no Mitsriy temple here."

"There's not: they have all long gone. But this man has at least seen the Mitsriy lands, and the great river that your mother of blessed memory used to talk about. You should speak with him. Perhaps he can help."

Anilat stood. Tadugari was away at the king's palace, as he was most days now. The twins were learning about Shalem city life – words and weapons – from a senior officer in the royal guard who Tadugari had appointed as tutor. Haleyna was busy somewhere in the house. Only Damatiria was with her. There was no reason not to visit this priest.

An ache clutched at her heart: never in all the wanderings had she found herself as purposeless as the last few days settling here in Shalem. For all the difficulty and danger of the journey, for all those days when Tadugari had been withdrawn and unreachable, they had achieved something united as a family.

Now it seemed that every day they scattered to different places, each focused on different tasks. Shalem had welcomed them in, but it had also swallowed them up.

She had yet to find resolution in her soul.

"Do you think that I should bring Haleyna?"

"You should, mistress. Your mother's rest concerns all the women of the family."

She grimaced. Death still lay between her and Haleyna, and they were not yet fully reconciled. Damatiria was right, though, and Haleyna should be there. She stood up, feeling weak, and they went into the house to find her.

"Come with me, Damatiria. We shall all go together."

Before long they were leaving the comfort of their house, close up against the royal citadel. The ground was damp and the air fresh with the spring rain which had fallen overnight. They passed near a market, rich with the odour of spices, food, and animals, and went towards a middle-ranking enclave of housing in a pocket of the city wall.

"How did you even hear of such a place?"

Damatiria smiled and threaded through some alleyways to a door. As they approached in the sunshine, it opened from inside. To her surprise, the Mitsriy scribe Hekanefer emerged. He bowed briefly to her in acknowledgement, smiled with excessive warmth at Haleyna, and was gone. The door had remained open, and children's voices came from inside.

Anilat looked around at the nearby houses, perplexed as to what should happen next, but Damatiria called out. After a short pause a woman of about Anilat's own age came to the door and looked out at them. Anilat could not place her origins; she was neither Mitsriy nor Kinahny, but she wore a Kinahny kef. She looked enquiringly at them.

"A bright morning to you all."

"And to you and yours, lady. Forgive this unexpected visit. This is my mistress Anilat, wife of the lord Tadugari, son of Anziniy of Ikaret. And her daughter Haleyna. I have served them both for many years. We have come because we heard there was a priest here who knew a little of the Mitsriy customs of death."

The woman nodded, curious.

"My husband's mother's husband. He knows a little about that. He does not live with us, but by good chance he is here today. My husband is not at home to welcome you himself, but he will be here later."

She led them into the house. There was a small hallway, with several doors leading off it in different directions. Mitsriy paintings and writing decorated some of the walls, and there was a board game in progress on a wooden table: Senet, she thought, but could not be sure.

They followed the woman straight ahead into a larger room. An elderly couple were sitting there on wooden stools, and a girl who was a little older than Haleyna was bringing in some mint tea. They had clearly heard the explanation at the door.

Anilat went and knelt at the feet of the priest. He rested a hand on her forehead lightly for a moment's blessing – she felt the tremor of age in his touch – and then leaned back against the wall to look at her more easily. She kept her eyes down at the ground.

"My name is Damariel, son of Yeresheth. This is my wife Nepheret. We formerly served as chief seers and priests in the Four Towns, a short distance north of here, though that task has now fallen to others. Do I know you, daughter? You have travelled a very long way from Ikaret to meet me. I have never been so far north. I am sorry for the loss that has come upon you."

"Lord priest, I fled from Ikaret with my family when the city fell. My mother gave her own life to protect us. But before she died she gave me something of herself to be laid in the earth in the Mitsriy way. She was born in the Beloved Land, although she moved from place to place in her life. Here..."

She fumbled with the knot that held the little box around her neck, but it had tightened in the damp air and in the end she lifted it over her head and passed it to him. She had never given it to anybody before. He held it lightly on the palm of his hand, making no effort to open it. Haleyna took hesitant steps towards her, drawn across the room by the box. Aware of the priest's eyes on her, Anilat rushed on.

"There is something of her in there that she wanted kept for burial. And of my father too. She wanted them to rest together. In truth she wanted the place to be down beside the great river in the Mitsriy lands, but I am very weary, and I do not think I will ever travel that far. But they say you have been there."

"I have been there. I have stood on the banks of the River just after the time of its inundation, and marvelled at the gods' abundant richness left on its banks."

He stopped to think, then looked at the woman of the house.

"Milashuniyet, could you bring a stool for this lady. I am old, and I shall get stiff looking down to where she is kneeling."

There was a flurry of activity. The priest continued.

"You should know that I am not Mitsriy myself. I can give your mother rest according to our Kinahny traditions, but not those of the Mitsriy. Would this be important to her?"

Anilat shivered a little.

"Lord priest, her body is lost, everything about her is lost except for what is here. And I have not even the slightest idea where my father fell. Far north of here, north of Ikaret somewhere, perhaps not even in any of the lands I know. Is it important, do you think, that their bodies are scattered here and there? And see, I only have a single amulet to leave with her. Does it matter?"

"In the Mitsriy traditions, perhaps it would matter. Who can say? My traditions are more flexible about this."

He frowned, and turned to the old woman who was sitting at his side.

"Nepheret, I suppose Mitsriy priests still live in Gedjet?"

"Yes, indeed. They have just completed a holy place there in the centre of the city with a sacred stone for the Lady Anath alongside the Mitsriy shrines. We could travel there and ask, perhaps."

The woman's intonation caught at Anilat and she glanced up, briefly, into the woman's face.

"Oh! You are Mitsriy yourself. But you live somewhere here, near to Shalem?"

"Yes, daughter, in the town of Kephrath. Since these many years now. But I remember living in Gedjet as though it was yesterday, and before that in the sedge lands."

"My mother lived in Gedjet once. Before she was married. She was daughter to the high priest there, and left his house to join with her husband. And so in time she came to Ikaret and met her end there."

The priest was silent, puzzled, looking at her. In the pause Anilat spoke again, a decision crystallising in her heart.

"I would be happy for her to be buried according to your traditions, lord priest. Not Gedjet, which she left years ago: she never once spoke to me about returning there. Better to be buried with honour here than never committed into the earth at all. I think she would say this."

She glanced up at Haleyna, fearful of her reaction, but finding approval in her daughter's eyes.

"Would you do this for us, lord priest?"

"I will, if this is indeed your wish. But would you have her rest here in Shalem, where she never lived? It would be better outside the town: there used to be a shrine to the Lady of Turquoise nearby."

Anilat leaned back and took Haleyna's hand, enjoying some measure of reconciliation while they met around her mother.

"What do you think, Haleyna?"

Haleyna reached out and, very carefully, touched the little wooden box.

"Would grandmother like to be in the city or outside the town altogether?"

"Not the city, I think. She lived in cities with your grandfather almost all my life, but she always yearned to see the sown land and the wilderness. She once told me that when she first moved to Gedjet with her own father, it seemed a huge place, where a person could get lost. Her own mother had died by then, back in the Beloved Land, and the household was still in mourning."

She glanced up at the priest quickly, but he was still looking directly at her and she dropped her eyes again. He cleared his throat as though to speak, but his wife intervened.

"How long has it been since your mother was in Gedjet?"

Anilat shook her head.

"Before I was born. Years and years. I do not know exactly. I was their firstborn, and I was born about a year after they moved to Djedenen."

"She was not married when she left Gedjet?"

Anilat was puzzled at the questions. "No, lady, she lived there alone with my grandfather. Pardon me for repeating myself, but she left to go north to Djedenen when the offer of marriage from my father was accepted."

The old couple looked at each other. The priest scratched his head before speaking.

"Can I ask if your grandfather left Gedjet for Waset, to serve in the great holy place there, shortly after your mother left for Djedenen?"

She looked directly at him, forgetting propriety in her surprise at the question.

"Yes. Yes, truly he did. But how could you know such a thing?"

"I once met your grandfather, there in Gedjet."

"You did?"

He smiled a little and took his wife's hand. He looked down at the little box.

"Indeed I did. I met the lord priest Senenptah once, shortly before he returned to the Beloved Land."

His eyes went distant with memory for a few heartbeats, and then sharpened on hers.

"I even met your mother, briefly. His daughter, Duat. Let me think now: Sheded-em-duat-Iset, that was her name in full, was it not?"

She stood in consternation. The stool spilled over behind her. Haleyna, still beside her, held on to her arm.

"How can this be?"

She stared at him, mouth open. Then suddenly she shivered at the realisation.

"Oh, lord priest, I think you are the wild man."

She clutched at Haleyna for support.

"I never heard of you until right at the end. Then she spoke of you, in her room when she gave me this box."

His mouth twitched a little, and then he suddenly laughed aloud.

"I have never thought of myself like that."

He paused to reflect, and looked at his wife, who was vastly entertained at the thought.

"To the lord priest you would have been a wild man. And to his daughter. Especially back then. Fortunate for both of us he let you buy a slave from his household."

Anilat was looking from one to the other, not quite comprehending. He sighed.

"As a young man I visited Senenptah at his house in Gedjet, imagining that I would go back up to Kephrath with his daughter – your mother – as wife. That did not happen. But things turned out so much better than that. Instead, Nepheret came back with me, and has walked alongside me ever since. I never thought to hear anything of Duat again in this life. On this side of the Reeds, as she might have said."

He looked at the box again where it rested still on his open hand, and placed it very carefully on the nearby table.

Damatiria had straightened the stool, and helped Anilat to sit down again. She was speechless. She realised that she was still staring directly at the priest, and looked around the room in consternation. She was suddenly overwhelmed by a flood of tears, and yielded to them, holding on to Haleyna as though to the bow rope of a ship.

"So lord priest, my grandmother might have lived somewhere up here instead of Ikaret? I might have been your granddaughter?"

Anilat looked at her daughter through wet eyes, shocked at her presumption. "Haleyna!"

But the priest was not offended, and took the question seriously.

"Well, if the gods had caused all our lives to go differently, then perhaps. You might have grown up as a village girl in Kephrath. But in fact this did not happen. Your grandmother chose otherwise: I chose otherwise. I think that both of us were happy with our choices. I certainly have no regrets."

He paused, looking at mother and daughter. Anilat had steadied herself again.

"Look now, you must make a choice together. I would be honoured to commit these last remains of the lady Duat into the ground, to give her rest and dignity in death. But you must help me choose where. Haleyna, sit with your mother now and help me."

Haleyna nodded, and sat on another stool to listen.

"Now, I do not think she should rest in Kephrath. She has no kin there, and she chose to walk another path through life. But here at Shalem, just outside the city, there is the place I spoke of, where Mitsriy and Kinahny women together used to tend a shrine to the Lady of Turquoise. They have gone now, but the fragrance of worship still hangs there in the air and the soil. Do you think that we should finish Duat's story there? Or would you rather I came with you down to Gedjet? What do you think?"

Anilat knew what her own heart was saying, but with an effort she stopped herself and waited for Haleyna.

"What is the place called, lord priest?"

"It is called Ramoth Hurriy. My wife Nepheret here visited it several times while it was a living place. I have been inside only after it was abandoned, since men were not permitted beforehand. Holiness still rests there, and the memory of the Mitsriy gods."

"I think she would like that. Don't you think so, mother?"

Anilat nodded and squeezed Haleyna's arm.

"I do. She kept the memories of her own Mitsriy youth alive until the end, and worked out how to blend them with the Kinahny ways of my father. It will be perfect for them to rest there together. When can we go there with you?"

"If we leave now, we will be there before noon. Would you like to do this today, or would you prefer more time to make your farewells?"

"I will wait no longer for this. If you are willing, could we go now?"

𐎀𐎊𐎀𐎊𐎀𐎊𐎀𐎊

A LITTLE LATER, THEY STOOD at what had been the gateway of a walled area. Wild grasses and bright flowers straggled between the buildings. It had indeed been a short distance, but the old couple moved only at a slow pace. They had headed south from the city, away from the house near the city wall, away from the area containing Anilat's new home, past the scattering of dwellings starting to spill outside the old boundary.

The spring sun shone on the holy place. It was deserted now, the buildings of the interior lying empty. Anilat recognised the design from places that her mother had spoken of. Beside her, just outside the walls, was a guardhouse. Ahead of her was the main shrine, stripped now of everything valuable. Over to one side were halls where the women would have eaten, sung, and slept. On the other side was a low stone enclosure wall. The priest, Damariel, led them towards it.

The track they walked on curved around behind the wall, and then stopped at a flight of steps going down. Anilat realised that they led underground, under the walled area. The stone flags of the steps were still neat, but trailing thorns and briars were starting to encroach. The bottom of the stairs lay in a pool of shadow. Nepheret struck fire from a stone and lit a small clay lamp.

They went down the stairs in a group. The two priests were first, with Anilat following closely. Haleyna was on her right, and Damatiria on her left, and all three women had linked arms. As they descended the steps into the shadows, the flame in Nepheret's hand cast ever darker shadows behind them. Little rustling sounds came from crevices in the rocks.

At the bottom of the stairs they stood on a bare earth floor. Rock pillars, decorated with twisting painted vines and lotus flowers, supported the vaulted ceiling. The air was a little damp, and the patterns on the pillars were already starting to fade. The lamplight was lost in the curves of the roof, but Anilat could see that the dark expanse above them was sprinkled with stars. Damariel took Anilat by the hand and stepped confidently across the floor away from the daylight, then turned to his right through a narrow arch into a second room.

Pillars leaned out of the gloom like tree trunks. Here, the darkness was thick, silent. The little flame cast only a small puddle of light. They approached the end wall.

A great figure of the Lady Nut stretched from side to side. Her feet were arched, with her toes on the ground to their left, her body stretched over their heads, and her fingertips touched the earth again on their right. Her naked body was speckled with the stars of the heavens, and her eye gazed at them without blinking. She was glorious, magnificent, life-affirming.

The wall itself was pierced with little alcoves and pockets. Small jars and pots rested in some of them, but most were empty. Damariel gestured towards them, the shadow of his hand ranging across the wall as the flame bowed and danced. His voice sounded hollow in the chamber.

"You should choose one of these little alcoves in the wall for your mother's resting place. It is not the same as having an eternal house in the Beloved Land, and everything that comes with that, but perhaps it will satisfy you."

Anilat stepped forward, reached out to touch Nut's body. Below the curve of her belly was an emptiness where the figure of her father, Shu, would normally stand. Most of the crevices there were already occupied. She looked around at the many gaps and niches, thinking. She turned her head to see Haleyna standing back, holding on to Damatiria's arm.

"Haleyna, come and help me choose, will you?"

She pointed to the wall.

"I will not have a place beside the Lady's mouth, for that is where she swallows the sun and takes it into darkness inside herself. And the places beside her breasts are already taken by others. We should choose a place under the Lady's thighs, where she gives birth to the new day again. Where life first springs into the world. Then when we think of my mother it will be with the hope of her walking in the Light-land, on the other side of the Reeds."

Haleyna started to speak, but her voice squeaked in the solemn air. She took a deep breath, clutched her mother's arm, and tried again.

"You pick one, mother. I do not know how to do this."

Anilat shook her head.

"I want you to decide where your grandfather and grand-mother will rest. And remember the place, so that in years to come, your father and I can rest here as well."

Haleyna looked startled, then held even more tightly to her. Then she too reached out to the wall, not quite touching the odd assortment of vessels, each of which held the remains of a human story. Her fingers moved uncertainly from place to place, as though trying to feel some minute difference.

Finally her hand stopped over a particular empty space. It was on the edge of an irregular group of other niches, mostly unoccupied, just below the angle of the Lady's hips. She looked enquiringly back at Anilat.

"Do you think here, mother?"

"Why there?"

"There is empty space here for them to rest. It is an easy place for their roaming spirits to find when they have been out and want to come back again. And for others to join them when the time comes."

She hesitated, looked around, and then rushed on.

"Also the pattern of the spaces here looks like the city of Ikaret and the land beside it. And here, where they have drawn the Lady's thighs and where she gives birth, this is the great bay of Ikaret and the open sea beyond."

Anilat nodded and hugged her, feeling her grief fill her own body and then run out in tears, like the tide running out of the bay, leaving exposed the rock pools and the shoreline life they held.

"It is a good choice, Haleyna. We will put her on the edge of the sea, where she and my father will go further than we ever have. May the Lady always give them new life."

She felt in the little cloth bag she had kept hidden under her clothes for so long and pulled out an amulet. It had been made by a craftsman in Ikaret in happier days, in copy of a Mitsriy design. It had a few Mitsriy signs which her mother had said were imperfect, but adequate, and a lovingly shaped figure of Iset between two trees.

She turned her head, but Damariel was already coming forward.

He gave her the box, and she very carefully placed it together with the amulet in the little alcove. She released it reluctantly, and then she stood back, head high.

The two priests knelt in front of the wall, below the arch of the Lady Nut's body, and Anilat joined them, the bare soil damp against her knees and shins.

They prayed together for a long time.

The prayers were not quite like the ones she knew from the temples at Ikaret, and still less like those the Mitsriy said in the great temples. They satisfied her, however, and she could say the words of assent after each one, in the waiting pause that followed the spoken words.

Finally a silence fell and stretched out for a long time. It was the end. Damariel held out a hand to Haleyna.

"Help me up again, young lady, if you will, and we four will go outside and wait for your mother to say what she will in private."

After he was standing again, he placed the little pottery lamp beside Anilat and, without saying anything else, led the others away. Anilat sat back on her heels, looking up at the wall and the Lady's unblinking eye, and finally stood up. She had nothing more to say, really, having carried the box against her heart all the days since leaving the city, having whispered to it sometimes in the nights in the wilderness. Her sorrow had ebbed with the water in the great bay of Ikaret.

She touched the box one last time, picked up the lamp with its olive oil flame, and took three steps backward, as though from a king and queen. Then she turned to go back into the first chamber. She looked back one last time, past the columns to where the stars adorning the Lady's body still showed dimly in the lamplight. Then she snuffed out the flame, restoring darkness to the inner chamber, and went up the steps, blinking as she came out again into the sunshine.

Damariel and Damatiria were sitting on the low wall close by, while Haleyna walked with Nepheret over beside the holy place. She watched them, the old woman and the girl together, as Haleyna followed where Nepheret was pointing out to the wooded ridges of the hill country, out across the open grass and the spring flowers, bright amongst the abandoned ruins.

The eyes of her own heart were far away to the north.

There, where the tide was turning towards the flood again, two wading birds slipped away from the flock dabbling in the shallows. Their legs dipping in the water with ever longer strides, they spread their wings, caught the offshore wind and took flight out towards the horizon and the open sea.

◁◈◁◈◁◈◁◈◁

Notes

About the author

Richard Abbott has visited some of the places that feature in this story and others set in broadly the same region. As well as writing fictional accounts of the period, he has also participated in the lively academic debate surrounding it.

Richard now lives in London, England. When not writing he works on the development and testing of computer and internet applications, and also creates mobile and tablet apps with a focus on the ancient world. He enjoys spending time with family, walking and wildlife – ideally combining all three of those pursuits at the same time.

Follow the author on:

- Web site – www.kephrath.com

- Blog – richardabbott.authorsxpress.com/

- Google+ – google.com/+Kephrath

- Facebook – www.facebook.com/pages/
  In-a-Milk-and-Honeyed-Land/156263524498129

- Twitter – @MilkHoneyedLand

Look out for his other works, which include the following.

Fiction – full-length novels

- *In a Milk and Honeyed Land*, available from most online retailers, and general booksellers in

  - soft-cover – ISBN 978-1-4669-2166-5

  - hard-cover – ISBN 978-1-4669-2167-2

  - ebook format – ISBN 978-1-4669-2165-8

In case of difficulty please check the website http://www.kephrath.com for purchasing options.

Feedback for this novel includes:
"the author is an authority on the subject, and it shows through the captivating descriptions of the ancient rituals, songs, village life, and even a battle scene... the story grabs hold of the imagination... satisfies as a love story, coming-of-age tale, and historical narrative..."

Blue Ink Review

"...The lives of these ordinary people are brought to life on the page in a way that's absorbing and credible. The changes that are going to take place in this area are quite incredible... a wonderous land that seems both alien and yet somehow familiar..."

Historical Novel Society UK Review

- *Scenes from a Life*, available from most online retailers, and general booksellers in

  - soft-cover – ISBN 978-0-9545535-9-3

  - hard-cover – ISBN 978-0-9545535-7-9

  - ebook format – ISBN 978-0-9545535-8-6

In case of difficulty please check the website http://www.kephrath.com for purchasing options.
Feedback for this novel includes:

"The author is extremely knowledgeable of his subject and the minute detail brings the story vividly to life, to the point where you can almost feel the sand and the heat..."

Historical Novel Society UK Review

"...lovely description – evocative sentences or phrases that add so much to the atmosphere of the book"

The Review Group

"The striking thing about 'Scenes' is... its sensitivity: its assured, mature observation of people"

Breakfast with Pandora

Fiction – short stories

- *The Man in the Cistern*, a short story of Kephrath, published in ebook format by Matteh Publications and available at online retailers, ISBN 978-0-9545-5351-7 (kindle) or 978-0-9545-5354-8 (epub).

- *The Lady of the Lions*, a short story of Kephrath, published in ebook format by Matteh Publications and available at online retailers, ISBN 978-0-9545-5353-1 (kindle) or 978-0-9545-5355-5 (epub).

Non-fiction

- *Triumphal Accounts in Hebrew and Egyptian*, published in ebook format by Matteh Publications and available at online retailers, ISBN 978-0-9545-5352-4 (kindle) or 978-0-9545-5356-2 (epub).

About Matteh Publications

Matteh Publications is a small publisher based in north London offering a small range of specialised books, mostly in ebook form only. For information concerning current or forthcoming titles please see
http://mattehpublications.datascenesdev.com/.

Background and Glossary

Historical notes

This book is the third in the series of novels featuring the Canaanite town of Kephrath, known as Kephirah in the Hebrew Bible. The first book, *In a Milk and Honeyed Land*, introduced the town, some of its inhabitants, and the reasons why they broke off their former alliances and sided with new arrivals in the hill country. Set about twenty years later, *Scenes from a Life* describes a man's journey from Egypt in search of his missing past. *The Flame Before Us* moves on another ten years, when the land is under threat from new tribes arriving from the north. The stories can be read separately without confusion, but the connections between them, in terms of events and people, will be more evident if you have read them in order.

The historical events on which this book is based are a small part of one of the biggest calamities ever faced by the ancient Near East. Comparative stability and international discourse had lasted for centuries until this point. The status quo had been maintained by a small group of powerful "great kings", each controlling a considerable number of vassal states on their borders. Within a few decades the region fragmented into many tiny nations, each struggling fiercely to maintain its own borders. Prosperous cities all round the eastern Mediterranean were captured and plundered, starting in modern Turkey and including Cyprus and Crete, Syria, Lebanon, Israel, and Jordan. Many of them – like Aleppo or Megiddo – recovered in time and flourished again. Others were abandoned and never occupied on a large scale again.

Ugarit, on the Syrian coast, where this story opens, is one of these. Ugarit had been wealthy and influential throughout the Bronze Age, juggling alliances with the great kings through the years to its advantage. Its rulers made good use of its natural harbour to trade across the Mediterranean. Once on land, the goods could be moved north and south along the coast road, or inland towards Mesopotamia. The city supported a flourishing religious and literary life, and judging by the diversity of written languages found there, was multicultural and cosmopolitan.

A few years after 1200BC all this came to an end. The city walls were breached, the palaces, temples and houses burned, and the population scattered. We have no real understanding of where the people who had lived in Ugarit went. Many no doubt died during or soon after the assault, and a few tried to continue an impoverished life in their old homes. For a few years small groups squatted in the ruins, but the task of rebuilding was beyond them, and before long the site was abandoned. Others managed to escape and make their way elsewhere. Then, as now, groups of refugees would be seeking to find, or make, a new home for themselves.

Ugarit was lost to knowledge, except for references in the texts of other nations, until it was rediscovered by chance in 1929. Since then, a series of archaeological digs has brought the rich life of this city back into the light, and given fascinating insights into the Levant of the second millennium BC.

It is generally agreed that the destroyers of Ugarit were migrating groups who the Egyptians called the Sea Peoples. Egypt had fought small contingents of them before, and had also employed others as mercenaries. This time they appeared in larger numbers, with family groups travelling in ox carts along with the warriors. Something different was happening; this was a determined migration, not a simple raid in search of loot. There has been considerable debate as to whether their preferred transport was by land or sea, but it seems certain that in practice, both means were used.

Beyond Ugarit, the Hittite empire never recovered from the shock. Hittite culture survived for a while only in isolated regions outside the former heartland. Egypt lasted better, having fought the newcomers to a weary standstill just outside her borders, but was unable to hold on to the province of Canaan for much longer. Eventually, a few vigorous pharaohs were able to campaign through the region again, but the magnificence of the New Kingdom would never return.

Scholars differ as to the root cause of this pattern of destruction. The Sea Peoples had been known as raiders for several centuries, and their impact had been quite limited. It is not clear why this incursion should have been so much more destructive than previous occasions, and the effects so much longer lasting. Suggestions have included rebellion of the workforce, social collapse, or natural disasters such as earthquakes or famine, as alternatives to external conquest. Basically the choice is whether the Sea Peoples' migration was the cause or the consequence of the problem.

The view taken in this book, following the scholar Robert Drews, is that they were a primary cause. In his reconstruction, the rapid adoption of new weapons, coupled with new battlefield tactics, brought to an end the previous dominance of the chariot. Military organisation was intimately tied in to the social order, and chariot commanders were the nobility of the age. Thus their defeat had a much more severe effect than the simple loss of a battle. Just as the adoption of longbows and gunpowder signalled the end of the mounted knight in Medieval Europe, these innovations meant that the age of the charioteer's supremacy was over. After the crisis had passed, chariots became a vehicle for transport only, and could no longer rule the fields of battle as they had done.

Where there is clear artistic licence in *The Flame Before Us* is in the speed of events. While the incursion of the Sea Peoples was rapid in historical terms, it did take longer than the short time covered by this story. The process, and the domino-like fall of the cities, was certainly slower than this. That said, the basic pattern of defences failing and traditional methods of warfare proving ineffective is rooted in history.

Different perspectives

The last couple of centuries of the second millennium, known as the Iron I period, used to be viewed as a confusing "dark age", but slowly more details have emerged about the period. Ambitious leaders, free of the yoke of the former great kings, set up small kingdoms and fought each other for territory. Archaeology shows that there was widespread experimentation with town layout, defensive structures, and social organisation, but all on a small scale. The long distance commercial and cultural links of the Bronze Age disappeared rapidly, and did not return for many centuries.

We still have only a few written records of this time. The Hittites left no accounts of their defeat. From Ugarit we read about the build up towards disaster in a letter from the city's king – *"...the enemy ships came... they did evil things to my country... all my troops and chariots are in the Hittite country... seven ships of the enemy that came here inflicted much damage..."* – but the city's actual downfall can be read only in ruins, not texts.

Egypt presented the engagements as a series of victories, but since these ended with them giving away land and cities, it seems unlikely that the outcome was as favourable as the scribes of Ramesses III presented it. However, the Egyptian records help by showing that these newcomers consisted of many tribes, which sometimes cooperated and were sometimes in conflict.

From Greece, memories of this time are preserved in the Iliad and other smaller writings. These were committed to writing after a lengthy period of oral transmission, and include some features typical of later times. However, it is broadly agreed that the core of these great classics dates from the era in question. The Iliad focuses on the capture of the city of Troy, called *Ilios* or *Troas* in classical Greek. However, the earlier form is *Wilios*, and the Hittites knew the city and area around it as *Wilusa* or *Taruwisa*. The Greek tales focus on those soldiers who returned home, like Odysseus, rather than those who carried on wandering.

The Hebrew Bible also retains some scattered references of this time. In the biblical view, all of the Sea Peoples were combined into one group, the Philistines, regarded as a dangerous and powerful enemy. Philistines appeared in small numbers from the north early in the book of Judges, challenged by an Israelite leader called Shamgar. They steadily increased in power and threat when they settled along the coastal plain, until finally defeated a couple of centuries later. The patchwork nature of Sea Peoples' identity, quite similar to the Israelites' own tribal groupings, is not mentioned. However, the general trend of infiltration from the north, followed by permanent militaristic settlement along the coastal plain, is clear.

The origin of the Sea Peoples

The historical homeland of the Sea Peoples remains a mystery. We know the names of many of these groups, though not their inter-relationships – as well as Sherden, we have Lukka, Tursha, Peleset, Danuna, Peleset, Tjekker, Weshwesh, Shekelesh and so on. However, the various ancient literary sources do not give enough information about these people to be sure where they came from.

The Egyptians recorded where they met the various groups, but not their ultimate point of origin. One word used of them is, unfortunately, ambiguous: it can be applied to either islands or coastal regions. The Hebrew Bible notes in passing that the Philistines arrived from *Caphtor* (Crete), but this is generally viewed in the same way as the Egyptian references – it tells us an immediate embarkation point rather than an original homeland.

So, research has largely focused around other areas to give indirect information. The most popular one has been to look at place names around the Mediterranean, and decide if these give clues. Other people have looked at language relics, or archaeological links from their later settlement in the five cities in Canaan given by Egypt to different possible starting points.

Four major theories have emerged:

Various Mediterranean islands, with the links supplied by name – *Sherden* from *Sardinia*, *Shekelesh* from *Sicily*, and so on. This theory arose in the 19th century, and is probably the idea most commonly encountered.

Various places in Asia Minor, or more specifically southern Turkey, with name links such as *Sherden* from *Sardes*, *Shekelesh* from *Sagalassos*, etc. This theory has never really gained a great following, perhaps because it does not tackle the question of their relationships with the Hittites.

Various locations in the Balkan peninsula, along either the Aegean or Adriatic coasts. For example, Pliny lists *Sardeates* and *Siculi* as people-groups in this area, which recent scholars have linked to *Sherden* and *Shekelesh* respectively.

Various Mycenaean Greek locations. Although various name correspondences with the writings of Homer have been suggested, such as *Peleset* from *Pylos*, the main argument here is in fact archaeological. The twelfth century BC bichrome pottery from south-west Palestine known as Philistine Ware is considered similar to Aegean Late Helladic IIIC, suggesting that a travelling people brought their pottery techniques and designs with them. This is the theory followed in the novel.

The destructive pattern attributed to the Sea Peoples is, perhaps, best seen as an extension of the Trojan War recounted in the Iliad and elsewhere. That war, stripped to a basic historical core, tells how Mycenaean Greeks travelled in ships to plunder a city on the western edge of the Hittite world. Seen in this way, the fall of Troy is simply the first episode in a chain of events that rippled around the eastern Mediterranean, encompassing Ugarit and Hatsor among many other cities.

Names

Inevitably when dealing with multiple cultures and perspectives, we meet different names in the historical record. In earlier books in this series, the city Ugarit (the name used in records from the city itself) was called *Ikaret*, the name found in Egypt. For consistency that name is still used here, even by those characters who were resident in the city.

The various Sea Peoples' groups are called by the names used in Egyptian texts, except that Periphas' tribe is variously called *Pelestoi* or *Peleset*, depending on the speaker. Periphas appears in Virgil's *Aeneid* as one of the Greeks who is prominent in the sack of Troy. As briefly mentioned above, this book assumes that the Sea Peoples were drawn from a variety of coastal tribes, led by those from Greek islands and the Balkans. Therefore, the personal names used in the novel are taken from early Greek material such as Linear B inscriptions. The leader at the sack of Troy, known in the Greek classical period as *Agamemnon*, is called *Akamunas* here, based on a name found in Hittite texts.

Ugaritic names are drawn from a wide cross-section of the cultures of the ancient near east. Some are barely different from those found throughout the province of Canaan, some distance to the south from the perspective of Ugarit. Others share the same Semitic language root, but are found only rarely to the south – *Dantiy* or *Yasib* would be examples of these. But as well as these, other names are drawn from the Indo-European language group, including some that are remarkably similar to names from northern India – like Anilat's sister-in-law *Sanay-Sura*. Other northern influences include Hurrian, Hittite and Luwian. Add to that the continuing use of Egyptian names and name-elements, and the diversity of Ugarit is brought to life.

Biblical *Shamgar* has turned into *Shimmigar* here. The name *Shamgar* is not a typical Hebrew or general Semitic name, and scholars have suggested that in origin it comes from a northern group of people called Hurrians. There was a scattering of Hurrians throughout the Levant at this time, often rising into positions of leadership. For such a person, *Shimmigar* would be a culturally suitable name. The group which Labayu leads, and Shimmigar is part of, uses the title "Sons of Anath" for themselves. This name is found both in biblical texts and also etched into weapon blades such as arrowheads. We do not know the origin of the title, but I have assumed it was a recognised nickname taken on to signal military skill.

Archaeology

A number of archaeological finds from the last few years have made their way into these pages. The fact that in some places, Sea Peoples and Israelites were not at war but coexisted peacefully, had been suspected for some time. It was positively confirmed by Swedish archaeologists when they published the results of a 2010 dig at Tell Abu al-Kharaz.

Here, a large building from about a century later than this story shows traces of Sea Peoples and Canaanites living together in peace – pottery, loom weights, and so forth. The site, in modern Jordan, is usually identified with biblical Jabesh Gilead – Yabesh of this story. The Hebrew Bible speaks positively of the city on several occasions. Although some of the occupants may have been distant relatives of the Philistines, these were friends of the Israelites rather than enemies.

When Labayu inscribes the letters of his name on arrowheads while waiting for Shimmigar to arrive, he was joining in a fairly common habit of this age. Arrowheads, and slightly larger javelin heads, have been a useful source of early alphabetic writing, helping to give understanding of the way letter shapes evolved through time. Dozens have been found and the details published. The fact that they were produced informally, rather than as official tomb inscriptions or the like, reveals something about the use of alphabetic writing in different parts of society.

These short messages – typically a handful of letters long – follow a few characteristic patterns. The introductory phrase "Arrow of" is common, followed by a name. Some examples are *'d' bn 'ky*, "Addo, son of Akiy" and *'bdlb't*, "Abdi-Labiyt". The second name means "Servant of the Lion-Lady" and is similar in linguistic origins to Labayu of this story. The same name – perhaps even the same person – appears on another arrowhead with *bn 'nt*, "Son of Anath" on the other side. The relatively common appearance of this phrase on these weapons has led numerous scholars to suggest that it was a military title rather than family identity, though opinions vary whether the group were mercenaries, a hereditary clan, a specific elite group, or simply individuals aiming to identify themselves with the warlike traits of the goddess.

The earrings that Anilat gives to the woman shrine tender in Bayth Ma'acath were again inspired by a real find, at the site of this very town. Called Abel Beth Maacah in the Hebrew Bible, it is at the extreme northern edge of tribal territory at its full extent, some two hundred years later.

During the dig season of summer 2014, an American team excavating a building found a pottery jug leaning against one of the walls. It contained several pairs of silver earrings, crushed together into a ball when the wall collapsed, together with some pieces of "hacksilver". This term refers to pieces of the metal cut from larger objects and used for gifts or trade.

The abandoned items date from exactly the period of this story. The motives for hiding them, and the reasons why they were never recovered, remain unknown. Similar small hoards have been found in many countries, and often signal an abrupt departure in the face of an immediate threat. The earrings that Anilat gave to the shrine tender were more ornate, and more valuable, than those which have so far been recovered from the town.

Unlike Jabesh Gilead, there is no evidence that the Sea Peoples settled near this town. Elsewhere in the north of modern Israel such evidence can be found, typically showing cooperation rather than aggression. The general picture is that only the sea clans which settled along the coastal plain continued the violence for any length of time. In terms of the story, I have assumed that the warlike first wave of attackers was followed by other groups who, like the Sherden here, were more interested in settlement than battle.

People and relationships

The following gives a list of the various people and groups involved in this story. Names in **bold text** are major characters.

Ikaret
Sheded-em-duat-Iset, daughter of the Mitsriy priest Senenptah, married to Kikirriyani
- User-Amun, married to Sanay-Sura
    - **Dantiy**, marries Dekseus during this story
    - **Yasib**
- **Anilat**, married to **Tadugari**
    - **Haleyna**
    - Twins **Rishi** and **Ritsani**
    - Also in household
        - **Damatiria**, also called "Auntie", wet-nurse
        - **Khuratsanitu**, a soldier
- Djoseret-Ibeti, presumed killed in the attack

The Sherden
Nikleos, married to **Kastiandra**
- Moqsos, already dead
- **Dekseus**, marries Dantiy during this story
- **Murtilis**, marries Arkelawos during this story

Kastor, married to Aigla
- Otus, dies during this story
- Arkelawos, marries Murtilis during this story

Antos, clan leader or arkon
Eumedes, trains youth in javelin throwing
Towanos, one of the few Sherden who speaks Kinahny

The Mitsriy
Nesamenopeh, married to Hemesherit
- Ramose
- **Hekanefer**, scribe, marriage arranged to Nodjmet
- Mereriyt

Penre Sa-Bunakhtef, a senior officer
Bakaa Sa-Nehesy, a junior officer

The Ibriym
Abiy'el, warleader
Pedayah, headman of Ramath-Galil

From the Four Towns
Damariel, married to **Nepheret**, former priests at Kephrath
Kothar, deceased, formerly married to Shaharti
- **Labayu**, married to Ashtartiy

Other "Sons of Anath"
- Shimmigar
- Akiy
- Uriel
- Ghazam

In a Milk and Honeyed Land

An extract:

THERE WERE FOUR CHILDREN of the god that year. I remember hearing that, many times over, through all my growing years, though it was a long time before I understood what it meant. That year was a unique year, a unique time to be alive. There were more of us then than any other year, before or since.

Perhaps such a year will never come again, not now the hill country is changing and the new houses are leaping up in little clearings everywhere. Indeed the whole land is changing. Had I wanted, they would have built for me one of these houses in whatever village I chose, as a reward for all my efforts. Some would once have said that this would have been the reward for betrayal rather than the wages of labour.

But even these newcomers could see that my place was in the great house beside the high place of Kephrath, among the families of my birth. The place where I lived and laboured, loved and learned loss. So, whether through gratitude or pity, here I live still. I am at home among my people to be sure, but I am also a stranger in the eyes of these strangers. They even tie their kefs differently to us, bundled oddly around their head. I have not troubled to learn their style. I am strange here to them, though I have lived here my whole life, and the land is becoming strange to me, though I know every hill and valley in it. They still need us to uphold the new alliances, but the need sits uncomfortably with some of them.

I feel, however, some kinship with them. They have had something of an uncertain, shifting childhood, and have chosen to be here, to live here in this place that is beautiful but not overflowing with wealth. They have been brought up singing one song, and then have tried to learn another. They have found themselves willing to unite with people who they had not planned to meet, and who they came upon by chance. Though their customs are odd, their yearning is not. They feel, like me and like my own people, the hunger that comes with displacement, and the thirst that impels one to find a home.

This story tells of we three who lived past infancy, and the things that we did and said in those days. Although there were four of us born, Mahur was a sickly boy who died before the year of his birth had turned. Then there were three, for a little while. Then there were only two. We were the linen sashes that tied up all the leather-bundled tales of our village life.

I remember those bundles that were carried on the backs of the Mitsriy scribes. They still travel the roads down near the coast, still with their escort of bowmen, but they have not come up this way now for many years. The traders who brought little caravans of donkeys up and down the great ridgeway road, or across the rough hillside tracks, still come to us, but less often now, and at erratic intervals instead of every season.

I have been seer to my people, and sung the songs of the great cycle around the stones of the high place. Now I tell tales. I have watched over the threshold that divides the living and the dead, and although I am still doorkeeper in my own house, it is becoming a different house, a different life.

There were four children of the god that year. We were reckoned as once-orphaned, living each in the house of our mothers, brought up as foster child by their husbands, with half-brothers and half-sisters according to the overflow of life in that family. We did not understand what it was to be a child of the god for many years – the words that had meant so much to empty wombs passed us by in the silent air.

The words meant nothing, but some of us grew familiar with estrangement as we grew up, looks of darkness and rejection from unwilling surrogate fathers, a sense of displacement amongst our peers, mixed pride and disdain. Others found happy acceptance. We still clung to each other. This is our story.

Scenes From a Life

SCENES
FROM A
LIFE

RICHARD ABBOTT

An extract:

H OW SHOULD THE PATTERN BE FINISHED? Makty-Rasut leaned back against the tomb wall, rough and unsmoothed as yet, and nowhere near the full length it would extend out to. The courtyard designs were all complete, but the details for the transverse corridor had only been recently agreed with the senior priest whose eternal home it would be. Only a few of the key highlights of the main approach had been roughed out. In any case, these were just designs at this stage. They had not been called out of their potential to be created in sculpture and paint.

The man had insisted on one of the less common variations of the scene where his heart was being weighed. He had good reasons from his own religious experience, and Makty-Rasut had readily agreed once the request had been made. But in other things the old man was willing to be flexible. They had sat together while the priest told him something of his life's endeavours, and they worked together on the ideas that emerged.

Makty-Rasut marked two deep parallel lines on the pottery sherd he had brought, to represent the walls of the corridor. He had sent the rest of the team home early. It was a festival day tomorrow anyway, and he wanted the time to himself to think, alone in the tomb. It was easier. He wanted to have some ideas to show the priest when they next met, and he could not think clearly when the area was full of his team working and jibing.

Dreams had steered much of the old man's life. A dream had first sent him out, years ago now, into the provinces. Gedjet mainly, with a short spell up in Beth Shean at one point, and other brief sojourns elsewhere. Another dream had called him back to Waset. Other dreams, too, at different times, held less profound significance but were still vivid in the priest's memory. So dreams should figure prominently on the chamber walls. The journey out to Gedjet was a focal point. It could blend several traditional elements with some unique ones. That should please the old man, whose words often betrayed the same mix of past and future, convention and innovation.

He sat there for a while looking at the space available, working out in his mind where the main pictures and writing should go. Finally, happy that he had something definite to present to the priest at their next meeting, he added the ideas as rough notes scratched onto the sherd. He packed everything away. He would do a neat copy tonight, back at home with better tools and more light. For the time being he was content, and sat back again against the end wall.

He was very tired. There had been a series of long days. He had never worked with some of this team before, and he had wanted to be first in the workings every day and last out. It set a good example, and also gave him a good sense of the new men's attitudes. It was as usual: some good and some poor.

His second man, Sanedjem-Keni, was an old colleague, and Makty-Rasut had had no hesitation in choosing him. He had worked with him before, both recently here and also longer ago elsewhere in the land. For the first few weeks Sanedjem would lead the left side while he led the right himself. Then when the team came up to full strength he would move Sanedjem onto the right so as to be able to concentrate on the overall design and finishing.

He had no idea yet who would lead the team on the left. He was short of good draftsmen, who could take a plan and a blank wall and rough out the designs well enough to be ready for the painting. Several of the workers he had wanted on his team had moved up from working in the tombs of nobles to those of royalty.

Let them, he thought. The nobles' tombs were more interesting, and more diverse, than the eternal homes of those who were of higher rank. In them, the same religious motifs had to be portrayed in very much the same way, with very much the same words, over and over again. And they took so much longer. Years even. His work for the nobility suited him perfectly – a few weeks, or a few months, maybe a season or two, then the job was done and he could move on to the next one.

In fact, he thought as his eyes blinked shut, perhaps it was time to think about moving on from Waset altogether. It was considerably more than two years since he had come here, bored with the trips out into the eastern desert overseeing the gold mining. It had been a good couple of years, but perhaps it was getting to be time to move on again.

South to where the River turned turbulent, perhaps? That sounded very promising. He had no particular desire to head downstream again, back towards former homes, but there were enough places to ply his trade further up the River to keep him in work for a long time to come.

He caught himself falling asleep and sat up straight again. He would just wait a little longer in case some further inspiration came to him about the patterns. He really was extremely weary, though. His thoughts were flitting about like dragonflies, hovering here and there over the stream with constantly moving wings, unable to settle. For a little while he daydreamed about a woman he had seen briefly in the marketplace over at Waset last week, a junior singer at one of the temples from her dress. But she seemed very remote, separated from him by the width of the River as well as profession.

He sighed. He could not even remember her appearance well enough to conjure it in his mind's eye, and the daydream kept slipping back into an everyday fantasy, with nothing to distinguish her imagined body from that of any other woman.

It was hardly different from reflecting on occasional nights spent at the houses of pleasure over on the east side of the River, although some part of his soul wanted the experience to have more meaning. The brief glimpse had not been enough to feed him with anything substantial.

He bundled the headscarf that he had needed in the cool of the morning behind his head, closed his eyes and leaned back against the wall, rough but solid and secure behind him. Perhaps he would think better like that. But in fact he must have fallen asleep, because all at once the dream came to him.

It was a familiar dream. He had had similar ones several times before, each time with minor variations.

He was inside a darkened boat, somewhere below decks where the light of moon and stars would not reach. He was rocking in little waves, as though the boat was crossing gentle ripples as it drifted downstream. It was warm, and his body was cradled in a nest of soft fabric, dark and red all around him. The boat had eyes on the prow that watched out ahead, he knew, though he could not see them just now. The boat contained ample nourishment to satisfy him, though just now he did not need it. The boat had a wide beam that made her stable in the water. It was all deeply pleasant.

He looked down, still in the dream. He was wearing a pair of startlingly white sandals. The sandals were of a style and an extravagance that he would never think to wear in waking life, but here it was fine. More than fine: just right, in fact.

But then all at once the boat and the warmth, the eyes and the provisions were gone, and he was plunged in the cold water, tumbling in one of the River's turbulent places. The current pushed him away. He could not reach the banks of the River, could not see them in the windy mist that clung to him. He felt coldness everywhere, coldness throughout his body, clinging at him, and his mouth was filling up with water. He was still wearing the sandals, and they made it just about possible to remain at the surface.

He woke all in a rush, pushing away the scarf that had now tangled itself around him. He sat there for a while to allow his racing heart to return to a normal beat, trying to root himself back in this world. His oil lamp had long since gone out. Finally he got up, felt for his bag of tools, and walked slowly along the corridor from memory with his left hand trailing along the wall to guide him. Looking out from the courtyard, east towards the River, he found that the sky was starting to fill with stars, like jewels adorning the clothing of night. There was a sharp scent of a nearby herb, clinging to a crevice in the rock. No-one else was anywhere near him.

How long had he been asleep? The air breathing down the hillside from his right, down from Meretseger's peak, was cool against his skin. He held on to the upright timber of the doorframe and steadied himself. Eventually he walked home, offered a pinch of incense and a brief prayer at the little shrine to Seshat that he kept, pulled at some bread and dried fish without really tasting either, and finally settled himself on top of his bedroll, tossing his unwanted clothes into a corner. He lay there for a while alone in the dark, feeling dislocated, and finally fell asleep again.

Richard Abbott

The Man in the Cistern

The Man in
the Cistern

A Short Story of Kephrath
~ Richard Abbott ~

A short story of Kephrath

Set in the years between *In a Milk and Honeyed Land* and *Scenes from a Life*, this short story follows Damariel and Nepheret as they tackle a new challenge to the four towns. A group of migrants has set up an encampment just down the trackway towards Shalem. What are their intentions? Do they come in peace or war?

The Lady of the Lions

A short story of Kephrath

Set about one hundred and fifty years before the *In a Milk and Honeyed Land*, this short story is based on two historical letters written by a Canaanite woman to the great king in

The Lady of the Lions

A Short Story of Kephrath
~ Richard Abbott ~

Egypt. The people of the four towns are being threatened by a band of rebels disdainful of the provincial ruler. Kephrath and her sister towns are outmatched by the raiders – can they secure help before their deadline runs out?

Richard Abbott

Triumphal Accounts in Hebrew and Egyptian

Triumphal Accounts in
Hebrew and Egyptian

~ Richard Abbott ~

An academic thesis

This ebook contains the text approved by the external and internal PhD examiners for a thesis carried out under the supervision of Dr John Bimson at Trinity College, Bristol, England. It will be of interest to those who wish to explore cross-cultural connections between early Israel and New Kingdom Egypt, as expressed in triumphal literature. The thesis looks at issues to do with the creation of poetry in each of those cultures, and the links between them, as well as investigating when appropriate cross-cultural contacts might have happened to forge common links between them.